RICHARD ROACH

NEVER A WOMAN

NEVER A WOMAN

iUniverse books may be ordered through booksellers or by contacting:

iUniverse
1663 Liberty Drive
Bloomington, IN 47403
www.iuniverse.com
1-800-Authors (1-800-288-4677)

ISBN: 978-1-4917-8504-1 (sc)
ISBN: 978-1-4917-8506-5 (hc)
ISBN: 978-1-4917-8505-8 (e)

Library of Congress Control Number: 2016900439

Print information available on the last page.

iUniverse rev. date: 01/22/2016

To the healing of the millions of women suffering from female genital mutilation and the courageous women who have refused.

To Ken and Connie Shingledecker, who provided a home for me whenever I was in Kenya and healed my wife when she was so ill.

To Marceline, who showed great love to our family, killed the first day of the Rwandan holocaust.

Acknowledgments

I WOULD LIKE TO THANK the many women for whom I cared during the time I served as a physician in Kenya and Rwanda and the experiences they were willing to share with me. I listened to their stories as they described their pain related to complications of female genital mutilation. I have shared their joy after successful surgery to restore them to health, no longer incontinent of urine and with their genital tears healed. I have listened to the tragedy of ostracism forced some on women who refused. This is Kwamboka's story.

I want to acknowledge the Kisii online news. After reading more than five hundred articles, I had a much better understanding of their rich cultural values but was also shocked to realize that the witch burnings still occur. I am deeply indebted to Ken and Connie Schingledecker, who consistently provided hospitality for me and my wife whenever we were in Nairobi and nursed my wife back to health when she was so sick. I will never take for granted the safe, potable water that they taught me was so precious. As I rested in their living room, I read in the Nairobi newspaper and watched on their television similar events to those in this novel.

A special thanks to the staff at Kibagora Hospital in Rwanda. The patients were so open in their conversations, and the staff was so helpful in explaining the cultural background and lifestyle of those for whom I cared deeply. I still feel the tragic loss of Bizimanna, our cook, and Marceline, our housekeeper, who were murdered in the first days of the ethnic cleansing.

Another special thanks to the staff at Kijabe Hospital in Kenya for the opportunity to work there and consult on their patients. I will never forget the evenings looking out over the Rift Valley at sunset, tired from seeing so many patients with HIV and tuberculosis but rejoicing that these patients had caring staff willing to treat them when other hospitals refused to admit them.

My wife, Priscilla, has always been an encouragement and strongly suggested that this third novel should be about our experience in Africa. She has suffered months away from home living in difficult situations to provide me with the opportunity and experience to share this novel. Our children, Temujin and Tirzah, were both forever changed by their experience in Rwanda and Kenya. Yet their friends in Michigan often teased them about their perspective of care and compassion for African people. A special thanks to my brother, William Roach, and his wife, Deborah, who have read every one of my novels and been a consistent encouragement.

My hope is that in some small way this story will stimulate the abandonment of female genital mutilation and provide awareness of the struggles of those caught in the human trafficking and sex trade.

Exiled

A SMALL VILLAGE IN WESTERN Kenya, 2002

"I want that maize all harvested before you even think about resting. Get up, Kwamboka, you lazy good-for-nothing." He shook his stick and shouted at me from the edge of the field. "That sun is getting low on the horizon. Are you planning on working in the dark?"

Even a healthy teenage girl gets tired, but I jumped up at my uncle's command. My dark skin glistened as the sweat rolled down my forehead and dripped from my chin. My slender, muscular body cried out in exhaustion. "I'm almost done, Uncle Osiemo."

"You better be. And don't you drop a single piece of my maize."

I wanted to shout back, "It's not yours. This is my father's field." But I knew that would entitle me to welts across my back with his stick. Besides, Kisii girls are required to show respect to their elders.

The last of the maize harvested, my long legs buckled under me. I collapsed in the rich, fertile Kenyan soil. I took a deep breath and got up, prodding my poor legs to get me home. My home was built of dried mud bricks and had a tin roof. Not everyone in our village had a tin roof, but since my mother had been a schoolteacher, we had one. When my parents were still alive, our home had been cozy and warm, full of joy.

Too tired to eat, I collapsed onto my straw mattress as the sun set. I fell asleep as I thought the day through. *I've harvested enough maize to live on for many months. Maybe I even have enough to exchange for some meat and new clothes.*

It was still dark when my sneezing startled me awake. Acrid smoke burned my eyes and choked my lungs. I gasped to breathe. *What's happening?*

With a crack, one of the house beams over my head burst into flames. I jumped up, wide awake. Toxic smoke scorched my throat and burned my eyes as they blurred with tears. I dropped to the floor, coughing. Flames jumped across the rafters. The house was on fire. *How did this happen? How can I escape?* I wrapped my *kitamba* around me and crawled to the door. But where was my leather pouch? That was my life. I could hear Mother's voice warning me, "If you are ever in danger, take your pouch."

I coughed incessantly. My throat was raw. I coughed up blood. The smoke obscured the early-dawn light coming through the window like a black sheet.

I crawled back to my sleeping mat and reached under and around it. Where was my pouch? Disoriented and frantic, I searched for the feel of leather.

The house was about to collapse. My tears stung my eyes in a vain attempt to wash away the burning smoke. With one more desperate thrust, my hand felt the smooth leather of the pouch. I grabbed it, hung the leather thong around my neck, and crawled to the doorway. Startled by a blast, I turned to see the ceiling of the bedroom crash to the floor. My straw mat burst into flames. Tin from the roof collapsed into the room. I reached up to unlatch the door and pushed. It wouldn't open. I was trapped.

I coughed so hard my vision turned red. Smoke thickened in my throat. I put my face close to the ground to suck the cooler air from under the door. After taking a deep breath, I stood and rammed the door with my shoulder. It barely moved. I again collapsed to the floor. Was something braced against it? Frantic, I slammed my full body weight against it.

I fell to the floor, gasping for a few more cool night breaths of air from under the door. *I have to get out.* The room was now ablaze around me. *I just need to push the door a bit more, and then I should be able to squirm through the crack.* After taking another deep breath, I stood back and rammed the door, smashing it with all my weight. It opened just a bit more, but it was enough. As I angled through the crack, the rough wood of the door frame tore at my chest, back, and belly, leaving scrapes and splinters in its wake. I was stuck. I ignored the excruciating pain. Out of desperation, I kicked with all the strength I could muster and freed myself from the door frame.

I stumbled away from the burning house, gasped for breath, and fell to the ground coughing. Crouched on all fours in the wet grass, I coughed until I vomited. Nothing came up from my empty stomach. I dry heaved again.

The early-morning dew felt like soothing salve on my abrasions. I turned to see my home blaze to rubble. I pulled my kitamba around me to protect my back from the blistering heat and my front from the morning chill. Goose bumps formed across my bare chest. The only place I had ever called home was now a black, sunken mass of smoldering embers.

I glanced up to see Uncle Osiemo strutting in the shadows. *He'll help me,* I thought. *He is obligated to help me. It's Kisii law that he is my guardian and protector.* Light from the smoldering remains danced across his sardonic face. I reached out to him.

He only laughed. "Nice escape, Kwamboka. I think I will give you a special present for your eighteenth birthday," he said. He poked my bruised ribs with his walking stick. "Your life."

"Uncle Osiemo," I pleaded, "you are my closest relative. You are supposed to care for me. It is Kisii law. I am not lazy. I worked all day harvesting maize. I am a good Kisii woman."

"You're no woman," he snarled. "You will never be a woman. You refused your circumcision, so you are still a little girl. You will always be nothing but a worthless little girl. Now you are too old to go through puberty rites. The women are not willing to circumcise you now. You're worth nothing. I can't even get a single cow for you. None of the men want to marry you."

"Please be kind to me, Uncle. Mother did not want me to be like the other girls. You know she went to the university to be a schoolteacher. She learned that Kisii girls don't have to be mutilated." I lowered my head. "Besides, it is against Kenyan law."

"Kisii law is older than Kenyan law. We follow the old ways. Besides, your mother was a witch." He grabbed his belly as it shook from laughter. "But we got rid of her witchcraft."

"Mother was not a witch." My knees trembled as I tried to stand. I coughed black mucus into my hand and wiped it on the dew-laden grass. "People thought she was a witch only because you told everyone she was." I straightened up on my knees.

Rancor deformed his face. "She killed your father, my brother. She probably poisoned him."

"That's not true. He died of HIV-AIDS, and you know it."

"See," he seethed, "your mother gave him that horrible virus. She was a witch. We kill witches. That is why we burned her in the ditch. She did not follow Kisii ways. She got so much education she became a witch."

He spat at me. The glob dribbled down my chest. He whipped his stick across my back. The pain made me jump to my feet. I stumbled away from him and fell back on the ground. He limped forward to land another blow across my back.

"If she had just married me when the year of mourning was complete, none of this would have happened."

"To be your fourth wife?" I said. I regained my footing and jumped backward toward the trees, out of range of his stick. I screamed at him. "You just wanted my father's property. You didn't care about my mother. You don't even know how to drive Father's truck. You're just going to let it rust, you wretched old man." I moved back out of his reach until I felt the tall grass against my legs.

I was ready to run. The arthritis in his knees would not let him catch me. *I'll run all the way to Nairobi and never come back. I love my people.* I was a good Kisii, but I decided that as long as my uncle lived, I could never come back to my village.

"You slimy cockroach," he seethed and swung his stick at me. "How dare you talk to me like that! You are not giving me proper respect."

"Give me wages for harvesting the maize yesterday, and I'll leave. You owe me that," I said.

"I owe you nothing. I'm letting you live. That's enough." He grabbed his knee and dug his stick into the ground for support. "That land was your father's, my brother's. Now it belongs to me. Everything you harvested is mine. Mine—do you hear me?" He raised his stick and lunged for me.

I ran.

"Run for the river. It fits your name—Kwamboka, the one who crosses the river," he said, laughing at his joke. I could hear his heavy breathing, which started one of his coughing fits, as I ran.

I followed the trail through the brush down to the river. Even in the dark shadows of early morning I knew the path well. Thorns scratched my legs and tugged at my kitamba. When I reached the river, it reminded me of a black snake slithering through the grass in the early-morning light. It had swelled from rain that must have fallen in the mountains the previous night. The turbulence raised haystacks of foam

5

around the rocks. Mother had taught me to swim even when the other village girls were afraid. The seething river before me made me doubt that I could make it across, but what did it matter if the river swallowed me? I had no home. If I swam to the other side, what then?

I edged into the stream. The strong current swirled around my ankles. My legs shook with terror. I tied my kitamba tight around my waist, clenched my leather pouch in my teeth, and jumped in the waves. The current seized me. I had no control as it flailed my body among the rocks. I gasped to catch my breath, not wanting to lose my grip on my pouch. Sharp rocks struck at my legs, bouncing my hips and chest against boulders. It took all my strength and the skills my mother had taught me just to keep my head above the water. Where would the river deposit me?

Maasai Mara

HOURS LATER AND FAR DOWNSTREAM, the river current tossed me among the rocks on the opposite side. I crawled out of the river, bruised but safe from my uncle. I looked around and didn't recognize anything. I had never been this far from home. I stumbled along the boulders on the shore, gasping for breath. Seeking a refuge, I curled under a large rock shelf to dry. *This must be Maasai territory*, I reasoned, the land of our Kisii enemies, the home of the people my uncle had hired to murder my mother. Even the bushes and trees appeared unfamiliar. Were there wild animals hiding there to attack me?

I didn't belong there. My stomach screamed with hunger; I had not eaten anything in almost a day. Where could I find food? I felt like I should just hide under that rock and die. At least my body would be food for the vultures, and Uncle Osiemo couldn't get me. I curled up with my head between my knees, and, even though Kisii girls are taught never to show emotion, I cried.

Then I heard something different: bells tinkling. I wiped the tears from my eyes and peeked out from behind my sanctuary. A tall, stately Maasai woman was walking down to the river with her water jug. She was elderly, judging by her wrinkled face. Wrapped in traditional red fabric that flowed over her thin, bony frame, she strode with such a confident gait. Her long neck was encircled with metal rings; the bells around her ankles made the tinkling sound I had heard. *Maasai are so arrogant*, I thought. I tried to stay hidden.

She squatted to fill her water jug and then turned. I knew she had seen me because she glanced at my hiding place. I must have seemed like a goat caught in a thicket. I slid back into the brush beside the rock shelf as she approached. She kneeled and extended her dry, withered hand to me. The gray arches around her eyes and the deep weathering of her face told of years of living in the bush, exposed to the elements of the Rift Valley. Cowering before her, I grabbed the few coins in my pouch, bowed my head, and offered them with both hands. "For my life," I said in Swahili.

"Blessings on you, my daughter," she responded in Swahili. "Put your money away. I have no use for it." She touched my forehead. Her touch was soft despite her weather-ravaged hands. "You are lost now, but you will find your way. God has blessed you."

"Thank you, Mother," I said, maintaining a posture of submission.

She rubbed her spindly fingers through my wet hair. I felt disgraced by my spiteful attitude. Tears welled in my eyes as words spilled out of my mouth. "I don't know which way to go. I have no family."

"Can you see the morning sun, my child?" she asked. Her tone was serene.

I looked up. The sun was now bright over the horizon. "Yes." I sobbed.

"Follow it, my little gazelle, and don't give up. You will reach your goal, but you have much to suffer before you return home. I sense that your spirit is very strong." She took her hand off my head, took my hands in hers, and lifted me to my feet. "Run now, and don't turn back."

Following the same road that she had walked to the river, I ran until I was breathless. When I turned back, she had disappeared. I kept running, only pausing to catch my breath.

By midmorning my stomach roared for food. There were no markets in the area, and I had only a few shillings in my pouch. There was no one in sight. I just kept running toward the morning sun. I was not sure what was ahead, but I decided to go to Nairobi. I had never been there, but I knew it was toward the east. Besides, that was where Nairobi University was.

My father drove his Tusker truck to Nairobi every week to purchase beer for the Kisii kiosks. I would sit on his knee when he came home and ask him to tell me about the road. He had told me about driving to Nairobi in his big truck, but now the details escaped me.

I pictured the map of Kenya on the wall in the geography classroom. Walking to Nairobi must take several days. The Maasai woman had sent me in the right direction, but I did not like the part of her prophecy about suffering before I returned. I didn't want to return. I didn't want to ever see my uncle again. I continued to run, but the running made me hungry.

I loosened my kitamba from my shoulders and retied it just around my waist so that I could run uninhibited. I had to get to Nairobi as fast as I could. I had always been athletic. In secondary school, I played soccer with the boys and won the track and field award for running the mile. I even beat most of the boys.

The sun edged higher in the sky. It seared my face, reminding me of the heat of my burning house. I needed water even more than food.

A bus came down the road. I was startled and choked on the dust that flew into the air as it passed. It was painted with zebra stripes. My cough changed to laughter as I thought about a bus disguised as a zebra.

The bus squeaked to a stop. Tourists jumped out to take

my picture. I was stunned. The flash of their cameras blinded me. I shook my head to get my vision back. Maybe they would like to see the full Kisii pattern of my kitamba. I untied it from around my waist and rewrapped it over my shoulder to show the pattern in their pictures.

They stopped taking pictures and jumped back in the bus. Why did they want pictures of a Kisii girl?

"This is Maasai Mara," said the guide in English.

"I am not Maasai," I explained in Swahili. "I am Kisii."

The guide yelled at his crowd, "You must pay her for taking her picture." The tourists threw Kenyan shillings out of the bus windows. They scattered across the red packed clay.

As I stooped to pick up the money, an older gentleman stood at the bus door to help a woman with a cane up the step. Dressed in striped shorts and a floral shirt, he turned and looked at me with an expressive smile. His hair was black, but unlike my kinky hair, it stuck straight out in all directions. His squinty eyes curled upward as he asked, "May I take more photos?"

I answered in English, "Yes, certainly, but the background is all wrong. I am from the Kisii tribe, and this background is Maasai territory. Do you understand?"

"You speak English better than I do," he said as his camera flashed. He handed me an unopened bottle of water with a ten-shilling note and a bow. A white flag with a red circle fell out of his shirt pocket. He picked it up with a chuckle and stuck it back into his pocket. He seemed embarrassed. I thanked him for the water and the money.

"Honorable girl, you are most welcome," he said.

I coughed again from the exhaust of the bus as it sped down the dirt road. *How strange*, I thought. *Why would they want to take my picture?*

I gathered the last of the shillings from the dirt and deposited them in my pouch. The bottle of water was a treasure. I had never had bottled water. They sold water in bottles at the kiosks in our village with soda and beer, but mother always laughed at me when I asked to try it.

"It's just water," she would say. "Why pay for something you can get for free?"

I marveled at the unique label. I opened it and drank. It was cold, so I only took a sip. Kisii know that drinking cold water will make you sick. But the refreshment soothed my smoke-raw throat like a healing potion. I held it up to the light. Its clearness was not like the water in the river but more like the water from Lake Victoria.

Refreshed, I walked farther, but the scorching sun drove me to the shade in a grove of trees. I resolved to sleep until it was cooler and then run the rest of the way to Nairobi. Nestled in the grass and leaves, I rubbed my stomach as it growled with hunger. More tired than hungry, I fell asleep cradled in the sun's warmth.

The cool evening air awakened me. I sensed an urgency to walk—or maybe I should run. I would never get to Nairobi by sleeping under a tree. As the sun at my back dropped below the horizon, a myriad of stars sparkled in the clear sky illuminating the road. When the moon rose, I had no trouble seeing where I was going.

Then I recalled a biology class lesson that greatly troubled me. Lions hunt at night, and I was a thin, muscular Kisii girl who would be a delicious treat for the pride. I realized that I would be safer hidden in a cave with a fire to ward off the lions, but that would not get me to Nairobi. Besides, walking in the cool of the night was so pleasant.

Several hyenas roused me with their sinister barks, but their sound was off in the distance. I wrapped my kitamba high over my shoulders and around my neck. No one could see my thighs at night anyway. A Kisii girl always keeps her thighs covered, even when she is working in the fields. I quickened my pace, scanning the darkness for movement.

I heard the bark again. Hyenas attack people sometimes, and when lions take down their prey, they force the lions to abandon their kill. The lions would still be very hungry. I was very hungry. *Maybe they wouldn't eat me since I am not well-fed*, I tried to convince myself. I kept walking. How far was it to Nairobi? My fear of what might be stalking me in the dark encouraged me to run.

Water

HALF AWAKE, I TRIED TO remember where I was and how I got there. Sometime during the night I had fallen, too exhausted to get up. I tried to get to my feet, but they throbbed, and my leg muscles cramped. Collapsed near an acacia bush at the base of a baobab tree, I fell into unconsciousness. I was half-awakened by the cooing of the mourning doves. The music they sang was glorious.

Ping, ping. Something hit my arm, but I ignored it. *Ping, ping.* Something hit me again. Was it a stone or something from the baobab tree? Closing my eyes tighter, I was determined to sleep. *Ping.* A pebble hit my face. Were they falling out of the tree? Pebbles don't fall out of trees. I opened one eye. A gecko stared back at me, twisting his eye to focus on my face. *Ping, ping.* Geckos do not throw pebbles. This time I saw the pebble hit my arm.

Startled, I sat up and grabbed my kitamba. A small boy, dressed only in shredded shorts, squatted a few feet away. His dyed red hair was greased and stood straight up on his head. His thin body was scarred with crusted sores. He smiled as he sorted through the pebbles in his hand.

"So you are alive," he said in stiff Swahili. "I thought I discovered a dead body." I heard the scuffling of goats and saw the herd assemble behind him at the sound of his voice. Hundreds of elliptical goat eyes focused on me.

"I am thirsty and hungry. Is there water near here?" I said.

"Follow me," he replied.

I picked myself out of the brush, pulled out the thorns stuck in my kitamba, and brushed off the pebbles and dust. I followed the goatherd as he led his flock along a ridge and then down a worn path into a small valley. In the shade at the far end was a pool. He dipped a gourd into the water just before his goats surrounded the pond. I drank, unsure if I would get sick. But I had to have water. He dipped the gourd again, careful to avoid the water his herd had disturbed, and drank from it himself. Refreshed, I sat on a rock and pulled out my empty water bottle. He filled and capped it before tossing it back to me. Red dirt settled to the bottom.

Sitting on a rotted tree trunk, he asked, "What is a pretty girl doing here? Why are you not home helping your mother?"

"I'm going to the university in Nairobi."

He broke off a piece of crusty bread and tossed it to me. Then he pulled some dried meat and cheese from his pack and gave them to me. They would have been disgusting if I had not been so hungry. It took a long time to chew before I could swallow.

"It is very far to Nairobi," he said and whistled to emphasize the distance. "I have never been there, but my father has. He talks about it when we sit by the fire at night. There is a government there. Father says that governments are dangerous. You should not go to Nairobi."

"I am going to school there. I have a scholarship," I said.

He twisted his face, not recognizing the word. Scratching the rotted wood with his shepherd staff, he uncovered a termite, grabbed it, and offered it to me. I refused, and he popped it in his mouth.

"Father says that if I take good care of the goats and they have lots of kids, he will let me go to school. Did you work very hard for your father to send you to school?" he said.

"No, my father died … of HIV-AIDS," I said quietly.

"I have heard of that disease. Is your mother sick?" he asked.

"My mother was a schoolteacher," I said.

"Why are you saying 'was?'" he asked with a puzzled look.

"She died too," I said. My voice was almost inaudible.

"Why is your uncle not taking care of you?" he asked.

"He wanted my father's possessions," I explained, "but he didn't want me."

"Your father must have had many cows that he would get rid of a pretty girl like you," he said. He whistled at me.

"I guess he wants my father's land too," I said.

"How can a person own land? All land belongs to god."

I was unable to answer his question. I was not sure I could explain it to him even if he understood Ekegusii or English, which was unlikely. I couldn't think of an explanation in Swahili, so we sat in silence. The morning mist rose over the Rift Valley, and the doves finished their morning songs. The goats, refreshed from drinking from the pool, crowded around the goatherd. He pointed his staff. "That is the direction to Nairobi."

"Thank you." I offered him a few shillings for his kindness, but he refused.

"What would I do with money? Do you see a store around here?" he said, laughing.

I bowed my head and said, "Then I have nothing to give you."

"I have everything I need. I am Maasai. I need nothing but what god gives me. You go to school in Nairobi," he said, gathering his goats around him, "and then come back and teach me how to read words. That will be your gift to me."

His smile made the dangling loops of his ears wiggle. He waved as he led his herd up over the rise and disappeared to the south.

I sat and looked at the muddy water. Had I really drunk that? Would I get sick? But the goatherd had drunk it too. Would he get sick?

Hungry

THE SUN MOVED TO FOUR fingers from the horizon before I discovered the paved highway. I rejoiced to see a sign pointing to Nairobi. I was on the right road. There was a chill in the air, so I wrapped my kitamba tight around me to stop the goose bumps. I quickened my pace. Trucks sped past as I searched the horizon for evidence of a city. Nothing but scattered trees and brush met my tired eyes, except for a giant dish in the distance. I had seen small dishes in the Kisii towns. My father said that rich people used them to watch television, but this dish was huge. Then I recalled Father talking about the giant dish on the way to Nairobi. He said it was for communication with satellites, I think.

I picked up a stick someone had tossed beside the road. It gave me confidence that I was walking toward my goal. Other people were walking along the road. A young couple walking in the other direction greeted me with a warm "Jambo." Following in their wake was an entourage carrying a bed, a mattress, and a small dresser. I congratulated the newlyweds. Tears blurred my vision as I turned away. If my uncle was correct, I would never marry. I would never have a husband to care for me, and I would never have children. I wiped the tears from my face with the corner of my kitamba. My conscience chided me, *You should be happy for the young couple, not thinking about yourself.*

All night I walked. The pavement and the trucks made me feel secure; lions avoid the noise of traffic, or so I chose to believe. The clear sky danced with bright stars since there was no artificial light to dim them. By morning the traffic had increased. I covered my face and held my breath as the passing trucks spat debris and dust at me. The acrid smell of exhaust and the noise of acceleration polluted the air. Some of the trucks plumed red dust when they hit bumps in the road, shedding the accumulated dirt from the miles of unpaved roads they had traveled before turning onto the highway. Every vehicle seemed frantic to reach its goal. My pace was so slow in comparison. I ran at times, but compared to the trucks, my effort felt futile. Besides, I was so hungry. Each time a truck passed, I paused to focus on the giant dish on the horizon. It seemed like I would never get there.

The heat of the sun boiled off the pavement, blurring my vision. I had to walk in the dirt. The pavement was too hot for my bare feet. As I searched the horizon, a building sprouted from the brush. Was it a mirage? I sprinted toward it, but when I stopped, winded and coughing from inhaled dust, it seemed no closer. I knew I could run almost an hour without stopping. I had done so in many track and field races. How come I could see the building, but it was still so far away? Squatting beside the road, I sweated with exhaustion. I slowed my pace to save energy.

It was well after noon before I collapsed in the shade under the awning of a petrol station. Tired, dirty, and exhausted, I was ready to give up. *If I die here, at least the lions won't get me*, I reasoned.

"Jambo," an elderly woman greeted me. She sat beside a charcoal brazier, scorching maize. She wore a colorful print and a straw hat. Her large breasts filled her dress and collapsed on her well-fed belly. I had seldom seen a woman so large.

"Jambo," I squeaked out from my parched throat and

buried my head between my knees. I remembered the hungry days, when the schoolmaster refused to pay Mother for teaching and there was nothing to harvest from our garden. But this hunger was worse because I was discouraged. *I will never reach Nairobi.*

"Come here, child," the woman said. "You look hungry."

She was not Kisii or Maasai, but I did not recognize her tribe. "Why would you help me?" I asked.

"Come," she insisted.

My legs rebelled as I tried to stand, so I crawled next to her. "I have a few shillings to offer you." My voice was so weak I was not sure the sound came out of my mouth.

"What would I do with your few shillings?" She gave me a cob of broiled maize and a cup of weak tea. "Here is some sugar. Do you usually drink your tea with sugar? I'm sorry that I have no milk," she said.

I bit into the maize, reminding myself to chew well and eat slowly. I was too ashamed to let her know how hungry I was. She put two tablespoons of sugar in my tea and stirred it for me. "Thank you, Grandmother," I said in my most polite Swahili.

She pinched my belly. "You need to eat better, child. You're wasting away. Did your mother forget to feed you?"

"My mother is dead." I grimaced, covering my face in shame. "I didn't mean to tell you. I'm sorry. That was impolite. It just popped out of my mouth."

"Eat up, child. Don't let my questions stop you," she said.

I ate every kernel on my cob. Then I chewed on the cob, hoping it would quell the gnawing in my stomach. I drank the tea and then licked the grains of undissolved sugar from the edge of the cup. My eyes focused on the woman.

She poked at her charcoal and turned her maize until it was scorched golden brown on all sides. Then she set it on clean brown paper beside her. She stood as a tourist bus stopped for petrol. She sauntered over to the bus, offering her maize cobs to the tourists. They bought most of what she had roasted. Satisfied with her sales, she flashed a jubilant smile. I was shocked at the number of shillings she showed me as she sat back down beside her brazier. She waved at the tourists as the bus left. She turned to me. "Do you see, child, why I refused your pathetic few shillings?"

"But you could have sold what you gave me," I said, bewildered.

"No. No one would buy that small cob." She jiggled her belly. "And you need it a lot more than those tourists. Did you see them? They are all well fed, fat, and happy." Her laughter shocked the doves on the roof. They flew off but soon returned.

"So where is my poor orphan child going?"

I leaned back against the cement blocks of the petrol station. They felt cool on my sweaty back. I closed my eyes. I started to answer, but the smell of the petrol irritated my nose, and I sneezed. "I'm sorry," I said. She handed me a white cloth to wipe my nose.

"I have a scholarship for Nairobi University." I opened my eyes to see her expression. "Am I going the right way? Is this the road to Nairobi? How long will it take me?"

She reached over and touched my cheek. Shaking her head, she said, "Oh, child, you have many days to go yet."

I cradled my face between my knees and cried, but there were no tears. She picked me up and held me as I trembled against her corpulent body. She wiped my face, and I saw days of dust curdled on the cloth.

I searched her kind face. "Why would you help me? You are not even from my tribe."

"Master Jesus does not care about tribes. He commands me to help the orphans along my path," she explained as she spat on the cloth and wiped my face again. She turned me to face the ribbon of pavement going east. "Nairobi is down that road, but you still need to climb the escarpment, honey."

Escarpment, escarpment … My mind scrolled through my vocabulary. "Like a big cliff, Mother?" I asked.

"Yes, child, there is a plenty big cliff you must climb. Oh, Lordy, it's thousands of feet high," she said.

"How will I climb it? Isn't there a road?" A barrage of questions filled my mind.

"You will know where to climb because you will see a small, small church at the base of the cliff. Climb the road there. A very gentle road switches back and forth," she said, waving her corpulent arm to show me. "At the top of the cliff, you will find the widest road you have ever seen in your life. It goes to Nairobi. But be careful. The trucks drive very fast on that road, so fast that they cannot stop if you are in the road. They will kill you."

She turned me around for a hug. "Rest here a while till the sun is behind you, then travel again. Do you have a water bottle?"

I pulled my water bottle out of my leather pouch. "A kind man with a flag in his pocket gave this to me, but I drank it all. I filled it from a pond and drank that too. I am so thirsty."

She rinsed out the red dirt out of the bottom with her water bottle. Then she poured two tablespoons of sugar into the bottle and filled it with tea. "That should help you."

I sat in the shade beside the petrol station and closed my eyes. Visions of scrub brush, dusty roads, and lots of trucks dissipated into sleep. My aching muscles melted and fasciculated as I fell into exhausted repose.

When I awoke, the sun colored the dust in the western sky with vibrant red streaks. The woman was gone. I stretched my stiff legs and stumbled to my feet. A kind of bread, wrapped in clear paper, sat in my lap. The word "cellophane" came to my lips as the package fell to the ground. The shopkeepers sold such things in the kiosk back home, but Mother always said that the little things were too expensive. *Where did this come from? Did that kind grandmother give it to me?* I deposited it in my pouch for later. I left the petrol station, running with new energy down the road.

"Many days," the woman had told me. *Should I give up? What should I do?* My eyes throbbed from lack of sleep and the constant dust in the air. I cleaned them with the white cloth the kind woman had left. As the sun set behind me, light glanced off the giant dish. I still wondered about that dish. Someday I would understand. Maybe at Nairobi University they would explain it to me. More important was the appearance of the massive cliff above the dust on the horizon. Now I just had to find that small church.

Collapsed

THE CELLOPHANE-WRAPPED PASTRY AND THE tea in my water bottle were long gone by the time I saw the morning sun peak over the cliff and glance off the cross on top of the small church. My feet were numb from walking, but when I saw the cross, I felt renewed. Just as the kind woman had told me, a switch backed road led up the cliff through the trees. The cliff scared me. I had never seen such a cliff. There was nothing like it in Kisii country. I could just see the rooftops of houses on the peak of the cliff. How could people live on top of such a cliff?

It seemed as if I could reach out and touch the church, but I knew it was many miles away. The Rift Valley plays tricks on your vision. I left the highway and trekked cross-country toward the church, thinking it would be shorter than following the paved road. All day I evaded thorn bushes and cattle droppings. Darkness fell over the Rift Valley as clouds obscured the sun. *Will it rain? I have no protection.* I quickened my pace in the direction of the church, but I could no longer see it. Afraid I might walk in circles without my focus for direction, I rejoiced when a streak of light glinted through the clouds and fell on the church's steeple.

I froze at the roar of a lion. Was it stalking me? Was it near? I crouched beneath a thorn bush, but that was no protection from a predator who hunted by scent. Something squirmed in the dead leaves. Was it a snake? "We have many poisonous snakes in Kenya," I remembered my biology teacher saying. He had tried to teach us which snakes were poisonous and which were not. I wished that I had listened more carefully that day. The snake was gone before I got a good look at it.

I shivered as a chilly wind began to blow, and I heard voices from some young men nearby. I hid and listened, but they must have been Maasai because I couldn't understand their language. I grabbed the stout stem of the thorn bush to keep from shaking. I didn't move until silence returned to the valley.

When I quit shaking and stood, I could see the church. Even as night blanketed the valley, the moon lit up the small cross. My stomach cramped. At first I assumed it was just hunger, but a moment later as I pulled my kitamba aside and pulled down my panties, diarrhea erupted from my bowels. How could I have diarrhea when I hadn't eaten much in— how many days? I couldn't count the days. I buried my face in the dirt as the tears dripped from my eyes and the stool poured out my bottom. Something sprung at my face. A scorpion's carapace glinted in the moonlight.

"Please, master scorpion, do not sting me. I am just a poor, lost orphan girl. I am not worthy of your venom." I watched him raise his tail. He moved one way and then the other. I was too sick to get out of his path, but soon he lost interest in me and wandered into the brush.

I covered my feces by pushing dirt over it with a stick. I felt so weak, I just wanted to lay my head on a rock and die. I argued with my feelings. Wouldn't it be better to die walking? Would it be more peaceful to die here? I had to reach Nairobi. Half-convinced, I used a thorn bush stem to balance on my feet. The moon came out from behind the clouds, and once more I caught a glimpse of the church steeple. How could it be so far away?

I stumbled forward until the cramps hit me again. All my bowels poured out with watery stool. I clung to a tree, too weak to keep from falling into my own feces. Was this where I would die? I was still clinging to the tree when I felt myself losing consciousness.

A cold wind revived me. I pulled up my panties and tucked my kitamba around my waist. I was still weak, but the cramps had stopped. I was surprised that I could still walk. I tried to run but fell. Rocks and gravel abraded my hands. I grabbed one of the stones and threw it in anger. *Just walk, silly girl.*

It was still dark, but the morning sun promised dawn just over the top of the cliff. Then I saw the church again. As sunlight peeked over the cliff, the cross shone in the brilliant light.

Was it tenacity or stubbornness that allowed me to reach the church? I will never know. "Help," I cried, but my voice made no sound. With my last strength, I grabbed the plaque beside the road. "This memorial chapel," it read, "is dedicated to the Italian workmen who built the road up the escarpment."

It's just a memorial. I wanted to scream in anguish. A huge padlock hung from a chain on the door. It didn't even provide shelter. I collapsed to my knees. My grimy hands covered my face. I had no strength to climb the escarpment. I decided to die. I had failed. I would never reach Nairobi.

Voices startled me. Through the brush, I saw a gang of young men coming down the road. I tried to crawl off the steps into the shadows. Although I could not understand their speech, I recognized Kikuyu. I peeked through a thorn bush. Kikuyu were not friendly to Kisii. They were the dominant tribe in the government, and they thought that they were better than everyone else in Kenya. These men were well fed and muscular. I could never fight them off. Would they rape me? Would they kill me?

I panicked and tried to get up to run. My legs collapsed like broken reeds. Gravel from the roadbed abraded my face as I fell. I had no voice and no tears left.

Casualty

"Where am I?" No one responded to my wispy voice. Attempting to speak hurt my throat. My body was covered with the whitest sheet I have ever seen. I was on a bed that had metal rails on each side. I wiggled my toes. They felt numb, but I could make them move. *Is this heaven? Am I wrapped in a shroud? Am I dead?*

No, maybe this is purgatory. Mother told me stories about purgatory, where the dead go until someone prays for them to go to heaven. But there was no one to pray for me. I looked around. There were people scattered on beds: men, women, and even children. Some had blood on their faces. I wiped my hand across my face. There was no blood, but I felt crusted scabs. The massive room smelled like the iodine mother put on my cuts. Sparkling clean blue and white cement walls surrounded me.

Then I noticed spiders forming webs on the ceiling above me. *Are there spiders in purgatory? What would they eat?* Since I was a little girl I have always been fascinated with spiders. They were my friends. If there were spiders here I must still be alive.

Once I was sick with malaria; I felt hot, but I shook the bed from cold. "Am I going to die?" I asked mother.

"No, child, you have malaria. You will survive," she said in her comforting voice.

"Who gave me malaria, mother?"

"Mosquitoes," she said.

"Who are the mosquitoes' worst enemies?" I asked in my delirium.

"Spiders and bats eat them," mother said.

That was when I decided that spiders and bats would forever be my special friends. I seldom saw bats, except in the evening just as the sun set, but there were lots of spiders in Kisii country. Mother questioned me when I captured spiders from our garden and brought them into my bedroom. "What are you doing, Kwamboka?"

"Making the mosquitoes afraid," I said. Mother laughed at me but let me keep the spiders in my room. They made me feel safe. I never got malaria again.

One of the spiders in the corner of the ceiling caught a fly in its web. I watched as the spider sucked it dry. I hate flies. They carry disease like their friends the mosquitoes. Now there was one less fly. I tried to laugh, but the scabs on my cheeks cracked and hurt. I took a deep breath. A sharp pain in my ribs was so intense, it grabbed my breath. *You don't hurt when you're dead*, I reasoned, *so I must be alive. But what is this place?*

Scanning the room, I saw a word over the doorway in large black letters: "Casualty." *Am I a casualty?* I forced my mind to recall what the word meant. I was not a soldier in a war, but maybe I had been injured in an accident. *That's it. I was in an accident. This is a hospital.*

What was the last thing I could remember? Some men were coming down the road. Then what happened? I tried to piece my memories together, but they blurred. *Was I attacked? Those men must have raped me and left me to die alongside the road. Is that why I am a casualty? But then who brought me here?*

I ran my hands over my chest, across my belly, and down my legs. Everything seemed to be working, even though I hurt all over. I felt my groin. There was no pain. I pulled my hands out from under the clean white sheet and checked for blood. There was none. Then maybe I wasn't raped.

Then I panicked. Where was my leather pouch? Everything that was valuable to me was in that pouch. *Did those nasty Kikuyu boys steal it?* There was a lump under my back and an itch that needed scratching. I reached back to scratch it and sighed. My leather pouch was tucked under me. I pulled it out and checked the contents. Everything was there, even the few shillings the tourists had thrown to me. *The Kikuyu boys didn't rob me. Why didn't they? Kikuyu boys hate Kisii girls.*

Then I saw nurses and doctors scurry around the other patients in the room. The thin white curtains didn't conceal much. A small boy was covered with blood, crying in pain; a woman wailed at his side. No one paid any attention to me. I tried to sit up. The room was full of people and beds, and the blue walls spun around. The room went black as I collapsed back on to the bed.

When my vision cleared, a nurse was standing over my gurney. "They found you on the road," she said in Swahili. "You were dehydrated. I am going to start IV fluids in your arm as soon as we get these people from the matatu accident stabilized. You must stay down. Do not move or try to get up. You are not ready."

"Where am I? Who found me?" I asked in English, forcing my weak voice. It didn't sound like me. "I remember some men coming down the road. Were they were drunk?" I whispered, "Did they rape me? Why am I in Casualty?"

She didn't answer but returned to the victims of the bus accident. I closed my eyes and rested. A few minutes later, she returned. "You are at Kijabe Hospital." She pulled my arm down to my side and wiped it with alcohol-soaked gauze. She looked at the dirt on it and wiped my arm with a clean one. "Some of our male nurses who had just finished their shift were walking home. They saw you stumble on the road. They carried you up the escarpment to the hospital. We are taking good care of you. This is not a place to be afraid." She placed a gentle hand across my forehead. "What's your name, child?"

"Kwamboka. I crossed the river." She did not understand the joke of my name but focused on my arm. "So, those Kikuyu men were nurses?"

"Yes, Kwamboka. They saved your life," she said.

I thought back to the lady at the petrol station. What would she say if I told her that strong Kikuyu men carried me up the escarpment? I didn't even have to walk up that snaky road. She would laugh. But I couldn't understand why Kikuyu men would want to help a Kisii girl.

The nurse placed a bottle of water upside down on a stand attached to my gurney. My eye followed the clear tubing from the bottle to a huge needle she held, poised above the soft part of my arm. "Kwamboka, now I am going to start this IV. You need the fluids. It will hurt, but just for a moment. Hold still."

A tall, muscular man in a white gown interrupted. His skin was black as mine. He had sweat dripping from his forehead and looked tired. He stuck a needle into my arm. I jumped, but I did not scream. From the time we are little, Kisii girls are taught not to scream. It is a disgrace to show any emotion from pain.

"This is the laboratory technician. He needs a blood sample," the nurse explained. The needle was so sharp that it was like being stuck by a thorn bush. I watched the blood squirt out of my arm into a glass tube.

"Thank you," he said in Swahili. "I apologize for not introducing myself. Forgive me. I am Jonathan. I work in the laboratory." He rushed off with his supplies and my blood.

The nurse braced my forearm as her gloved finger explored my arm. "You have beautiful veins. You must have done hard physical labor for such a young, beautiful girl." I tried to turn my head to see what she was admiring as she stuck a needle through my skin and up into the vein in my arm. I didn't move. She taped the needle onto my skin.

"Take it out, kind nurse. Please, take it out. That man already took my blood," I pleaded, trying to keep the emotion out of my voice.

"I am not taking it out. The doctor commands that it be there. See?" She pointed to the big glass bottle with a tube that went down to the needle. "That is the fluid that is giving you your life back. You must not move your arm or I will have to stick the needle somewhere else. That will be more painful so that you will remember not to move. It is easier if you learn the lesson the first time."

I decided that I didn't like her. She seemed to be a nice person at first. *How could she say such nice things to me and then be so mean? Does she do mean things to everybody? Does the hospital know she is putting needles in people and leaving them there?*

After a while, a young man dressed in blue wheeled my gurney out of Casualty. "I am Nathan. I am bringing you to the women's ward," he said. I hadn't realized that my bed had wheels. Clean and bright light radiated through the large windows, illuminating the gauze curtains like spiderwebs between the beds. The magic of the ward calmed my fear.

But many of the women in the beds groaned in pain. Most of them were attached to bottles hanging beside their beds and had needles taped to their arms. That nurse must have put needles in all these women.

"Here is your bed," Nathan said as he scooted me onto clean white sheets. He was careful to avoid moving the needle in my arm that was attached to the bottle. The nurse must have warned him.

The bed was soft. Nathan fluffed a pillow under my head. "Comfortable?" he asked. I nodded as I searched the surrounding beds for a friendly face.

"I am wishing you a good morning," said a kind-looking woman in the next bed. "You are alive today."

"Thank you for telling me," I said. "But I am very angry with that the nurse who put this needle in my arm. She commanded me not to move. I pleaded with her to take it out, but she got very nasty."

I noticed that the woman had a bottle hanging with a tube down to her arm as well. "That nasty nurse put a needle in your arm too. Did she command you not to move?"

She laughed. "That's an IV, an intravenous, child. It will not be in there long. When you start to piss a lot, they will take it out. You may not move your arm, but you may move anything else."

"Oh, good," I said, shaking my other arm in defiance.

She giggled at my antics as she introduced herself. "I am Joyce Nwamende. What's your name?"

"I am named Kwamboka Muwami, Mother Joyce." I shifted my hips. I was so sore everywhere in my body. "Your last name is like mine. I am sorry to be impatient, but how will I get up and piss, I mean urinate, if I am not allowed to move my arm?"

"Oh, you poor child," Joyce said, "I am not able to say your name properly. You must be Kisii. I can tell by your accent. Have you ever been in the hospital before?"

"I am Kisii, but I must tell you that I do not have an accent. This is the way to speak English properly. And no, I have never been in a hospital before," I said.

"See that button?" said Joyce, pointing at the object hanging on the bed rail.

I looked at the contraption beside me. "Yes," I said.

"Push that button when you need to piss, and the nurse will come to help you, Kwab …" She stuttered. "See, I am not able to say your name properly. May I call you Kitzi?"

"I like the sound of that name. Yes, Mother Joyce, you may call me Kitzi." I nodded in approval.

"Your speech is excellent, Kitzi. Where did you learn to speak the Queen's English so well?" asked Joyce.

"The queen did not teach me to speak properly. My mother was a schoolteacher and made me use correct pronunciation."

Joyce nodded.

"But I have only read about hospitals. I have never even seen one. I don't remember coming here. I was climbing the road up the escarpment by the Italian workers' chapel on my way to Nairobi. That was my last memory." I pulled a small stick out of my hair. "Do you know that chapel?"

"Yes. Everyone knows that chapel, but it's just a memorial. There is never any priest there," she said.

"Why are you in this hospital, Mother Joyce?" I covered my face with my free hand. "I am sorry. It is rude for me to ask a mother so many questions."

"It's all right. We're going to be roommates for a couple days. We might as well get to know each other," Joyce said.

"You are so gracious to me," I said.

Joyce rolled onto her side to tell me her story. "My womb was always bleeding. I was so weak I could hardly walk. I came here, and the kind surgeon removed it so I would not bleed any more. Now I feel much better."

"They cut into you and took out your womb?" My stomach cramped.

"Yes. See the scar?" She lifted up her hospital gown to show me.

"Oh, Mother," I said, "how many women held you down? That must have been very painful. When my friend had her circumcision, two women held her down while the circumcision woman cut her." I turned my head as tears burst from my eyes.

"They have medicine here that puts you to sleep. I didn't feel a thing. But you said your friend was circumcised. Were you circumcised too?"

"My mother wouldn't let me. At first, I was very angry with

her. All my friends went through the ceremony to become women but me." I wiped the tears off my face with the corner of the bed sheet. "But then my best friend died of infection. It was horrible. The pus was coming out of her vagina. Her female lips were all red and swollen, and then she died."

"I am so sorry, Kitzi," Joyce said.

"The old woman who cut her said that she was not worthy to be a woman. I guess I am not either. My uncle said that no one will ever want to marry me because I will never be a woman, so I am on my way to Nairobi to go to school. I can still be a teacher. Then I will have lots of children since men will not marry me," I said.

I wiped my tears and turned toward my roommate, making sure that I did not disturb the IV in my arm, "Do you have children, Mother Joyce?"

Joyce turned her head toward the window. Her voice quivered. "They all died."

"Oh, Mother Joyce, I am so sorry that I asked you," I said. "Your husband must have been very sad."

"He was so sad that he left me and married another woman," she said.

A tall, muscular man with very dark skin appeared like a phantom at my bedside. I gasped. He yanked the curtain around my bed as the nurse who put the needle into me joined him. "This is your doctor, Doctor Charles," the nurse said.

I suspected that she was pretending to be gentle. "I hope that you notice that I haven't moved my arm."

She said nothing but picked up a chart at the end of the bed and handed it to the doctor. "Kwamboka Muwami," he said and then spoke in Swahili. "Glad to meet you."

The nurse said, "She speaks excellent English."

The doctor pulled down my kitamba so that he could put an instrument on my chest. "This is a stethoscope," he said, switching to English. "It allows me to listen to your heart."

He sat me up. I felt dizzy, and there was a sharp pain in my chest when he asked me to take a deep breath. I almost moved my arm. My kitamba fell in my lap. "Can you take another deep breath? I'm listening to your lungs." He moved the stethoscope across my back. "Again, please?"

He let me lie back down and pulled my kitamba up to my shoulders. Then he poked my exposed belly. Frightening thoughts marched through my mind. Could he see my thighs? Was he allowed to look at my female parts? The nurse was standing next to my bed watching him.

He pulled the sheet over me. "Your blood tests show that you were very dehydrated, young lady. Your stool exam showed infectious diarrhea and several parasites." He paused to let me comprehend the words.

How did he check my stool? I wondered.

"You could have died along the road. Are you feeling better with IV fluids?" I nodded as he showed me the chart and explained my blood tests. "It is important to take the medicine the nurse gives you to get rid of the giardia and ascaris we discovered in your stool."

"I am amazed that those numbers from my blood tell you so much about my body. And I thank you for telling me, but I am very troubled by this needle in my arm. That nurse," I turned my face away from her as I pointed, "told me that I am not allowed to move. I need to urinate very badly, and I might still have diarrhea."

He laughed and turned to the nurse. "Could you assist her to the water closet? I don't think she is completely oriented."

"I am oriented. I am ashamed to contradict you, Grandfather Doctor. I know that I am Kwamboka Muwami, a Kisii girl, that I am in a hospital, and that I am on my way to Nairobi. I just don't remember coming here. I have never been in a hospital before. And how did you know my name?"

He laughed at my tirade. "Call me Doctor Charles. I am not old enough to be your grandfather. As to your name,

34

you had your identification card in your leather pouch. The nurses found it when they picked you up from the road. You were not oriented then, young lady." He put his strong, gentle hand on my shoulder. "I can see that you are oriented now. I did not mean to insult you. Please forgive me."

I had never heard someone older than me ask for forgiveness. I decided that Doctor Charles was a very great man. He looked at the nurse. "Could you please help our very intelligent, English-speaking patient to the water closet? She has to urinate."

I looked the nurse in the eye, "Yes, I have to urinate and maybe defecate as well." The nurse smiled at my words as she inspected the IV in my arm. She helped me out of bed and down the hall. *Maybe she isn't mean all the time,* I thought.

I looked around the ward as we moved together. There was a myriad of sick women in the ward. Many had tubes like mine in their arms, and some even had wires attached to them. Tubes were coming out from under their sheets and flowing into bags hanging beside their beds.

"Is that urine?" I said as my weak legs shuffled along the corridor.

"Yes, Kwamboka. They are too sick to walk to the water closet. The tube goes into their bladder to drain their urine."

I decided that I did not want to be so sick that this nurse would have to put a tube into my bladder. *Maybe this nurse helped save my life.* When she came with pills, she was very insistent. "You have no choice, Kwamboka. Take your medicine."

Later a hospital worker in a blue uniform brought me food to eat. It tasted very good. There was even fresh fruit. After so many days walking across the Rift Valley, I was very hungry.

Mother Joyce and I became friends. We laughed and talked at mealtime and at teatime. My strength came back, and I no longer needed help to go to the WC. Joyce taught me that I could walk with the metal stand my bottle hung on because it had steel legs and little wheels.

Several days later, my muscles felt firm and strong. The diarrhea was gone, and I ate everything they brought me. I decided that I was ready to walk the rest of the way to Nairobi. But there was a gnawing in my mind. How would I pay these kind people? They had searched my leather pouch to know my name, so they must know that I had very few shillings.

On to Nairobi

"YOU ARE WELL ENOUGH TO take a shower now, Kwamboka," the nurse said. She taped plastic over the needle in my skin, which she still refused to take out. "Don't get it wet."

I understood that she cared about me, but I was sure that her nasty side would come out if my needle got wet. A hospital matron gave me soap and a towel, and then she guided me down the hall to the showers.

"Make sure you tell the nurse how careful I am with her needle," I said as I dropped my kitamba and slipped off my panties to step into the shower.

"I most certainly will," she said. She had a cute smile and a twist in her voice.

"I am sorry to inform you that I have never taken a shower before. Please show me how it works."

She showed me how the controls worked, how to adjust the temperature, and how to turn it off when I was done. It was like bathing under a waterfall, but with hot water. I washed the snags out of my hair. I giggled as the soapy bubbles tickled my skin. Never had I felt so clean. When I stepped out of the shower, the matron reappeared and handed me a comb, a towel, and a clean hospital gown. But where was my kitamba? Had she stolen it?

When I returned to my bed from the glorious shower, there was an older man waiting for me. I adjusted my hospital gown to cover my thighs for modesty and sat on the bed. "I'm Kwamboka. Were you searching for me?"

"I am Joseph, the chaplain here at Kijabe Hospital. I understand that you are feeling much better."

He was a slight, clean-shaven man with his hair cut very short. He was dressed in a blue suit, white shirt, and tie, but his clothes didn't fit him well because he was so thin. He carried a worn-out Bible with him.

"You don't look Kikuyu," I said.

"No, I'm not. I am Kipsigis, but to Jesus it makes no difference. Here at Kijabe Hospital it makes no difference. We are here to help anyone who needs healing."

I thought, *He will be kind to me, since Kipsigis are friends of Kisii.* "My physician said that since my blood tests have improved, I may have this intravenous removed soon. Then I will be discharged. I'm on my way to Nairobi." I was excited to tell him but tried to speak slowly and properly.

He giggled. "I am very impressed with your English. I seldom speak with someone so articulate."

I knew he was testing my vocabulary. "I am articulate because I focused on my studies. I'm now prepared for university matriculation."

"I have never met a teenager like you, Kwamboka." He laughed so hard his tie slipped out from his suit. He put it back in place. "You were very sick when you came. I saw you in Casualty, but you did not respond then."

Pastor Joseph stroked my head and became serious. "This is a Christian hospital, Kwamboka. It is our mission to take care of anyone who comes here. As you have seen, you do not have to bribe the nurses or the doctors to care for you."

"My mother was a Christian," I said, "but not my father. He worshiped Engoro, the god of the Kisii ancestors." Pastor Joseph's face showed no criticism, so I continued. "He was a truck driver. He drove a Tusker truck to Nairobi to supply beer to the resorts along Lake Victoria and the bars and kiosks in Kisii town."

Joseph's voice was gentle. "Was a truck driver? Is your father deceased?"

Tears welled in my eyes, but I didn't cry. "Yes, that is true. My father died of HIV-AIDS about a year ago. Mother said that his sexual urges required that he seek the services of prostitutes when he was away. One of them infected him with HIV. He became so thin and weak that he couldn't drive his truck. Then he died."

I took a deep breath. Pastor Joseph didn't interrupt, so I continued, "We got along for a while. Mother was a schoolteacher, so we still had an income. She taught me vocabulary and how to speak English properly. I was required to learn a new word every day and use it correctly five times before I could go to bed." I smiled. "It was silly and I resented it, but it helped when I took the exams."

"Did she die of HIV-AIDS too?" inquired the chaplain.

The words I wanted to say choked my throat. Pastor Joseph pulled up a chair beside my bed and closed the curtains around us. He held my trembling hand and waited for me to answer. I looked at the ceiling. A spider was organizing a new web. She would protect me from any malaria-infected mosquitoes tonight.

"I might as well tell you." The words come out as I wiped my eyes with the handkerchief he handed me. "When one's husband dies, it is Kisii custom to marry one of your husband's brothers after a year of mourning. But mother refused to become my Uncle Osiemo's fourth wife. He did not love her. He wanted my father's land and possessions. He waited over a year, and when she refused to marry him, he spread rumors that she was a witch. He hired Mr. Osebe, an Abaragori ..."

Joseph nodded. *He must understand that an Abaragori is*

a mage who determines who is a witch. I continued, "And had my mother declared a witch."

My head throbbed. An abscess of fear and resentment was about to burst open. "My uncle is a clan elder, so everyone believed him. But it wasn't true."

Pastor Joseph touched my cheek. "I understand what you're telling me. Continue, even if it hurts."

I squeezed the side rail and scrunched my eyes. *Should I tell him everything?* In my mind I remembered again the raucous cries of the men as they raped my mother and cut her; I saw the flames burning her body. The image scared me. My heart raced. I snapped open my eyes, ready to scream. Pastor Joseph squeezed my hand. It calmed me.

"I am calm again," I said. "I will tell you the story. Soon the parents of my mother's students refused to let their children come to class because they heard that she was a witch. They were afraid that a witch would ruin their children's chances on the national exam. Then the principal refused to pay Mother because she was not teaching anyone. We became very poor and hungry." I rubbed my stomach.

"What happened then? I see that you are very thin. Did she starve to death?"

"I wish she had starved. No, Uncle Osiemo arranged for the Chinkororo …" The expression on his face showed that he did not understand. "It's a Maasai gang. They kill people for hire."

He sighed and rubbed his wrinkled forehead. He took the handkerchief from his pocket, wiped his brow, and said, "I am trying to understand." I could see in his face that his compassion for patients had worn deep scars in his soul.

"They surrounded our house and broke down the door," I said, taking a deep breath that still hurt my chest. "I hid, but I saw the whole thing. They jerked her onto the table, tied her arms to the table legs, pulled her legs apart, and took turns raping her, laughing as she screamed. Then when they were done, one pretended his knife was a penis and thrust it back and forth in her vagina. I almost screamed, but I put my fist in my mouth so they wouldn't discover me. Then they dragged her outside, the blood pouring from between her legs.

"I followed in the shadows. I am good at hiding. Many men with pangas surrounded her and slashed her as she tried to escape their circle. I saw deep cuts across her back, and her intestines were coming out of the slashes across her belly. They cut off her breasts and sucked on the nipples in her face. When she fell down and couldn't get up, they tied her to a tree so they could keep cutting her.

"When she didn't cry any more, they asked the village people to gather around. 'What should we do with this witch?' they asked. 'Burn her,' the village people screamed. 'That's what we do to witches.' I hid in the bushes beside the road as they built a fire of sticks in the ditch. When it blazed hot, they untied her from the tree and threw her in the fire. She didn't even move. I think she was already dead."

Pastor Joseph sobbed as he squeezed my hand and stroked my arm. "Child, I am so sorry. I am heartbroken." His tears dripped onto my arm. I had never seen a man cry, nor had I ever met a man so kind. No man in my life had ever been this sensitive, not even my father.

He wiped his eyes with his handkerchief. "Is that when you ran away?"

I explained how I hid in the bushes expecting to be killed if they found me, but eventually my hunger drove me back to the village. To be killed seemed better than starving to death. Besides, the Chinkororo had not burned our house. Pastor Joseph was familiar with our customs and knew that my uncle was responsible for me.

"Did he treat you well?" Pastor Joseph moved his chair closer.

"Let me tell you the story about how he treated me. It was a warm, sultry evening. I remember that the air felt heavy. I had worked all day in my father's fields. It was almost time to harvest the maize. When I approached my Uncle Osiemo's, compound I waited outside. It is polite." Pastor Joseph nodded. "Abigail, his youngest wife, came to me and invited me to supper. Uncle Osiemo ate most of the food and then invited his wives to eat. He said that I had to wait."

"I was very hungry but very polite as I waited for his wives to finish. His second wife is very fat and ate more than her portion and all the rest of the meat. All that remained was some maize porridge. Uncle Osiemo took the bowl of porridge and threw it in the dirt. He laughed and said, 'Eat it quick, Kwamboka, before the dogs get it.' He grabbed my hair and forced my face into the porridge and the dirt. He yelled, 'Swallow, girl, or you will starve.' When he let go of my hair, I ran home."

"How did you survive?" he asked as he blew his nose.

"Everybody left me alone. I ate some early maize and other vegetables from our garden. Several days later I harvested all the maize. I worked from sunrise until I couldn't see in the dark. After I carried the harvest to the granary, I fell asleep, too tired to eat." I rubbed my stomach.

"Uncle Osiemo started my house on fire the next morning. He blocked the door so I would burn inside, but as you can see, I am skinny and agile. I escaped. He beat me with a stick but said that he would give me my life for a gift."

"My dearest child," Pastor Joseph said. "What are you going to do with no parents and no relatives to care for you? You are a long way from Kisii land."

"I have walked from my village to that small Italian chapel. I can't remember how many days it took. Some people threw me some money for taking my picture. I hope I have enough to pay for this hospital's kindness."

"You walked all the way from Kisii land?" asked Pastor Joseph.

"Yes." I opened my pouch to show him my schillings.

"And here is my Kenya Certificate of Secondary Education. I got an A-level. Then I received this acceptance letter to Nairobi University, so I'm on my way to Nairobi to learn to be a teacher. Maybe when my uncle dies, I can teach Kisii children not to believe in witches."

He looked at my papers. "Amazing," he said. "I have never seen such high scores on this exam."

"So, Pastor Joseph, do I have enough money to pay the hospital?" I asked as I cleared my throat and adjusted the hospital gown over my knees. "Or do I have to work to pay for the nurses, physician, and medicine? And they have given me good food. I should pay for that as well. I'm sorry that I do not know about such things. Then I will continue walking to Nairobi."

"You have enough," he said. "May I read a psalm from the Holy Bible to you?"

His voice was mellow as an angel's. I had never seen an angel, but my mother told me when I was afraid that angels would protect me. Maybe Pastor Joseph was an angel. When he finished reading about a shepherd caring for sheep, he got up from his seat. "And I will pray for you." His hands were sweating as he placed them on my damp hair. He prayed for me to get better so that I would be able to do well in school. He prayed that I would learn about Jesus who loved me.

"Thank you, Pastor Joseph." I felt a sense of peace that I had not known since my mother hugged me the night before she was murdered.

He pulled back the curtain and took his Bible to pray with a family who gathered around an elderly woman. She looked pale and ready to die. He pulled the curtain around the bed for privacy.

"Kitzi, is all that really true? The way your father died of AIDS and your mother was burned?" Joyce asked.

I heaved a sigh. "The story is completely true. I should not have told Pastor Joseph if I knew you were listening. I hope it did not upset you. I am sorry, Mother Joyce."

"It did upset me, Kitzi, but I am honored that you let me hear your story. We are both being discharged tomorrow. I live in Nairobi, not far from that university. Why don't you come live with me?"

"Do you really mean it?"

"Yes. I own a tailoring shop, and you can help me sell dresses and suits when you are not going to classes," Joyce said. "We will take the bus to my house. Then you will not have to walk all the rest of the way to Nairobi."

"How many schillings is the bus, Mother Joyce?"

She told me. I counted out what I had. "I have enough for the bus, but then I will have nothing for the hospital. Will they release me or make me work here?"

"Don't worry, Kitzi. You are in the arms of Christ Jesus. He will care for you," she said.

I fell asleep wondering about Christ Jesus. I didn't know who he was. I did remember that mother used to end her prayers "in Jesus's name, amen." Then I dreamt about the university. My tuition was free because of my test scores and my letter, and now I had a place to live, but would Joyce feed me?

Hospitality

AFTER A TASTY BREAKFAST OF fruit and cereal, Joyce and I were discharged. I was so excited when the nurse pulled the needle out of my arm that I jumped out of bed and twisted in the air.

Joyce laughed. "You are acting like a gazelle who just escaped from the lion's jaws, Kitzi. What did they put in your IV to make you like this?"

"I am just so happy to be alive," I said.

The matron brought me donated clothes and returned my kitamba and panties, all washed and folded. I hardly recognized them. "I thought you stole them."

"I would never do such a thing, honey," she said.

The clothes she gave me felt odd. They were tight and constricting. But Joyce said that my kitamba was not modest enough for Nairobi. I would have to wear the donated clothes until she made me new ones.

Pastor Joseph came to wish me good-bye. "Your hospital stay has been paid for by an anonymous donor." He paused. "Not me. Don't look at me like that."

He laughed and held my hand. "But when God has blessed you with riches, do not forget Kijabe Hospital."

"I will never forget the kindness I experienced here, but I hope I can forget about that nurse putting the needle in my arm and commanding me not to move."

"It saved your life, Kwamboka," he said.

"Then I will choose to be grateful for the needle, Pastor Joseph, but it is still hard for me to accept."

"True kindness is not always pleasant," Pastor Joseph said as he put both hands on my head and prayed for me. It was a long prayer about a lost sheep found in the wilderness. He ended with, "In Christ Jesus's name, amen."

"Christ Jesus is the Christian god?"

"Yes, Kwamboka. He made all things, and he loves you. Don't ever forget that," said Pastor Joseph.

"Did Christ Jesus make spiders?"

Pastor Joseph laughed. "Yes, he made spiders."

"Then I choose to love him too," I said. "I love spiders … and bats too."

"Jesus made bats too," he said and then nodded at Joyce. "Can you teach her about Jesus?"

"I will," Joyce said.

We climbed the hill east of the hospital to the highway. I could not wait to see the city where my father used to drive his truck. Joyce had spent hours while we were in the hospital trying to explain to me what the city was like. But I could not visualize the tall buildings, the crowds of people, and the myriad of vehicles she described. It all seemed imaginary.

When we reached the highway, I felt invigorated and raced ahead. "Careful," she yelled. I ran back and tried to increase Joyce's pace. Joyce showed me where to stand so that the matatu bus would stop for us and not run over us. We stood between the kiosks selling tea, pastries and Tusker's beer. I recognized the Tusker's Beer logo on the side of the building from Father's truck.

The smell was wonderful. I could smell the pastries and tea from the kiosk. The smell of the exhaust from the trucks and cars seemed so exotic, but it made me sneeze. I wondered if my father had enjoyed the smell. "Father drove all the way to Nairobi and back to pick up loads of beer," I told

Joyce. "It took him two or three days when the roads were good but sometimes almost a week. He would never tell me what Nairobi was like. He would just say, 'Too many people, Kwamboka, too many people.'"

"I do not approve of beer," Joyce said. "It makes people mad."

I looked down the road searching for the matatu. My mind was racing. *I'd better not talk about beer again*, I thought. But I was so excited. Tonight I was going to be in Nairobi. "Father got HIV in Nairobi," I told Joyce. "I sure don't want to get it."

"If you stay away from men, you won't get it," she said. "Lots of men in Nairobi have HIV-AIDS from crawling in bed with prostitutes who have the virus. And then they bring it home to their wives and kill them."

"Do not explain any more, Joyce. Now I understand things about my father that I did not want to know." I covered my face in shame. But I wondered, *Why did mother not get the virus?*

The matatu arrived. It was crowded, but a friendly gentleman gave Joyce his seat. I stood beside her. At first, I almost fell over every time the bus stopped and started, but after a while I adjusted to the motion.

"Kijabe is in a rural area, but you will see not far down the road businesses have sprung up like mushrooms after a rain," Joyce explained.

"Why did you come to Kijabe to have your surgery? Aren't there hospitals in Nairobi?" I asked.

"There are plenty of hospitals in Nairobi. But Kijabe is a Christian hospital, and they take better care of you there. Nairobi hospitals are crowded. I would probably have had to share a bed with another patient."

"My father always said, 'too many people.' Right, Joyce?"

When I saw the Welcome to Nairobi sign, I was so excited that I stood on my tiptoes to take it all in. There was plenty of time to see everything because there were so many vehicles that the matatu moved in short bursts amid raucous honking and smelly traffic.

Joyce explained the lights to me. "When the cars are stopped for a red light, then you can walk across the street right in front of them and they will not run you over."

"Oh, thank you for explaining that, Mother Joyce. When will we be at your stop? And how does the driver know we want to get off? And—"

"You're sure full of questions today." Joyce laughed as she pulled the cord to the bell that told the driver that we wanted to get off at the next stop. "Let's get off here so I can show you Nairobi University." We paid our shillings to the young man holding the door as we climbed out the back of the matatu. On the street I looked around. Everything was so amazing. I took in the smells of flowers, food cooking on braziers, and a rich caramel scent. "What is that smell, Joyce?"

"Coffee. They roast coffee here in Nairobi. But I prefer tea."

My eyes caught the way people were dressed and the multitude of flashing lights. I couldn't take it all in. We walked past building after building that reached up into the sky. "This is all part of the university," Joyce said, waving her hand at the buildings.

I patted my leather pouch. "Soon, very soon, Nairobi University, you will meet Kwamboka," I whispered. "We will be great friends."

I grabbed Joyce's hand. "I hope I get to go to every building."

We turned and walked past several businesses and then stopped in front of a picture window. There was a mannequin in the window wearing a wedding dress. We paused by a green painted door. "This is my tailor shop," Joyce said. There was a sign in the window of the door that read, "Closed due to illness."

"That will change tomorrow, won't it?" I asked.

"Tomorrow is Sunday. We will go to church and praise

Christ Jesus that we are healed. Then Monday I will open my shop," said Joyce.

Down a dirt road behind the business street, we came to Joyce's house. It was a small, square concrete structure with a tin roof. She unlocked the door to show me three rooms: a small kitchen, a nice sitting room, and her bedroom. It smelled sweet, like baked bread. "There is a toilet out back," she said.

"This is wonderful," I said, spinning around, "and so close to Nairobi University."

I turned to Joyce. "May I sleep on this soft couch?" I said as I sat down. Then I looked at her and jumped up from the couch. "Or should I sleep on the floor? Was I being rude?"

"Of course you can sleep on the couch, Kitzi," she said.

I smiled and lay down on the couch. "This is so comfortable. I have never slept on something so soft. You are so gracious to me, Mother."

The weeks before classes were very busy. I went to Nairobi University to register. When the woman at the registration desk looked at my test scores and invitation letter, she smiled and welcomed me. She found my registration and another copy of my invitation in her file. I signed the necessary papers. I was overwhelmed when she showed me the class options. "I'd better bring this home and discuss it with my mother," I said to her.

"Understandable, but bring it back first thing in the morning," the secretary said. "Some of those classes fill up very fast. A smart girl like you should be able to take whatever classes she wants."

I took the papers home to get Mother Joyce's advice.

"I have no idea. I never went to a university," Joyce said.

She seemed indignant that I was asking her. "My father thought that education was a waste of time and money for girls."

"Then I will have to sit and study this, Mother Joyce. I am sorry that your father said that about your education. I can tell that you are a very intelligent woman by the way you make dresses."

I decided to focus on the sociology department. I thought it out. *I can be a teacher if I take those classes.* An anthropology class coincided with the required classes, and I found some others in the sociology department that interested me. I filled out the papers and set them aside to take back to the registration office in the morning.

The next day we marched to Joyce's tailor shop. She was so fast with her sewing machine and her sharp scissors. All the fabrics she had stored fascinated me. She knew all of them by touch. I made her tell me what each fabric was with her eyes closed. She described every one accurately.

"You are amazing, Mother Joyce."

After the tour of her shop she took my measurements. "Stand still," she said as I wiggled in the fitting room. "I have to know your shape to make a dress for you to go to the university." She put the tape measure around my chest.

"But it tickles." I giggled and did not hold perfectly still. I could tell that she was upset with me, so I tried harder.

"If you move I will stick you with a pin," she said. She put the tape measure around my chest and waist. Then she measured my thighs. She wrote numbers on a tablet.

I covered my face in horror. "I have never had anyone measure me. Do not even tell me the numbers you are writing down."

"You have a nice form," she said. "My dresses will look beautiful on you. That will be good advertising for me, and you will look nice when you go to Nairobi University."

After the measurements I excused myself and ran to the

registration office to turn in my class requests. I paid close attention to what the students roaming the campus were wearing. Some had dresses like Joyce was making for me, but others, even women, were wearing slacks. I wondered what was the proper custom.

That night at supper I was careful not to eat too much. In Kisii culture, adults eat first and then children. Since I was not a woman, I sat on the couch while Joyce ate.

"This is how a proper Kisii girl behaves," I said. "I will come to the table when you are done eating and see what you have left for me." In the days that followed she always left more than I could eat.

But one night several days later, as she put the food on the table, she said, "This is ridiculous. Come eat with me." Then she shook her finger at me and laughed. "But don't eat so much that you change dress sizes."

A week later she invited me to the shop for a fitting. We were in the back room. Three beautiful dresses were laid out ready for me to try on. I stripped to my panties. "You should wear a bra with these dresses," she said.

"I don't like to wear them. They feel constricting," I said, thinking, *I don't even know how to wear a bra.*

"Here, I bought you a new bra that should feel nice," she insisted as she handed the garment to me. I held it like a foreign artifact, unsure what to do with it.

Joyce helped me put it on. I didn't like the way it felt, but when I put on the dresses, they fit so well over the bra that I hardly realized I was wearing it. I ran outside the shop and told some women passing by, "If you want a beautiful dress like the one I am wearing, Joyce can make it for you."

Several women did come in later that morning and showed an interest. I posed so the ladies could examine the seams. One at a time she took them into the fitting room to measure them. After the third woman left, Joyce took me aside and said to me, "You have increased my sales enough today to pay for the food you eat for a month." We danced around the shop together.

The night after my three dresses were finished, I wore one of them to supper. When it started feeling tight, I put down my spoon and felt my belly. "My stomach is full now, and my dress still fits just fine. I will not eat any more." She just smiled and shook her head.

In the evening I wrapped my kitamba around my waist and curled up on the couch. I felt so content. Then I saw a strange look on Joyce's face. "What's wrong?" I said. She seemed to be staring at me. "This is the way Kisii girls relax in their home."

Joyce explained to me that a Christian woman should keep her breasts covered. But I felt odd. It wasn't relaxing. And besides, I was just in the house with a woman. But Joyce seemed bothered, so I readjusted my kitamba.

"Do you have any books to read? At home I always read books in the evening," I said, searching the room.

"Only this one." She handed me her Bible. "Start reading with Matthew."

I thought it odd to start reading a book in the middle, but I was soon interested in the wonderful stories about Jesus. I was fascinated that he knew his relatives for so many generations. This is a sign of a great man in Kisii culture. I laughed when I read about the trouble he got into but was impressed that he did not scream when the men did horrible things to him. I sat up shocked when he climbed out of his grave. "He would have been a very great Kisii man," I told Joyce. She looked pleased.

When the sun set, Joyce locked the door. Iron grates on the windows made the house secure. She had no electricity, but light from an oil lantern filled the room with a warm glow in the evening. When I was not reading, we had wonderful chats. She knew so many things about Nairobi: how to get what you needed, how to negotiate for good prices on material, and most important, how to stay safe in the city.

"Do not wear jewelry into town. It sets you up as a mark for thieves," she warned. I tried to remember everything she told me. I decided that she must be a very wise woman.

"I will have to study very hard to maintain my government scholarship, and I do not want to burn all of your oil," I said one evening. "I will need to study at the university library and come home when I am done. Then we can sit and talk until bedtime."

"I do not think you should come home after dark. It is too dangerous," she said, frowning at me in disapproval and concern. "I only have one key. You know that I lock the door at dark, and then I bolt the top and bottom. If I am asleep when you come home, I may not hear you."

She wrinkled her brow. "You would be out all night. It is too dangerous. You must come home before dark."

I glared at her, pleading, "You do not understand the demands of the university. I have to study. The library is where the books are. I cannot afford all the books the professors expect us to read. I must read them in the library after my classes."

She stomped to her room and slammed the door. Was she angry because she thought I was disobedient, or was she afraid for me? I had grown so independent, unaccustomed to having someone to care for me as my mother had. But I did not want to seem ungrateful or hurt her.

Bookstores

Joyce ate breakfast alone the next morning. She said nothing. I put on the dress she had made me that was her favorite, but it did not melt her heart. When it was time to leave, she pushed me out the door as she turned to lock it. I focused on the key as she put it in her apron pocket. What if she would not let me back into her house? What would I do? She quickened her pace as we walked to her shop in silence. When we arrived, she entered and slammed the door behind her, leaving me standing on the street. I stared through the picture window, unsure what to do.

I started walking toward the university and glanced in the store windows along the way. I stopped at a bookstore. I couldn't recall any bookstores in Kisii town. Maybe there were some, but I never got to go to them.

My mother taught me to love books. We had many in our house, but they were all burned up now. She would order them, and then Father would pick them up at some bookstore when he drove his truck to Nairobi. Standing in front of this bookstore, gazing at the huge number of books in the window, I wondered, *Was this one of the stores from which she ordered? But there must be many bookstores in Nairobi.*

I was excited about the classes for which I had registered and anticipated the professors opening the knowledge of the books to me. Would I have to buy books? I had no money for such things. I just hoped that what I had told Joyce about the books I needed for my classes was true and they would all be in the library.

A display of photographic books in the window caught my eye. I couldn't buy anything, but I was driven by curiosity. I wanted to see what was inside each one. Would the owner chase me out of the store when he realized that I couldn't buy anything?

As I walked in, I smelled curry. The Indian book shop owner looked up from his newspaper. I felt trapped. He scanned me head to toe. I froze. Then he took a sip of tea, adjusted his glasses, and nodded at a worker.

"Can I help you find something?" said a handsome young fellow. He was just a bit shorter than I, dressed in a pressed and starched white shirt tucked into black pants sporting sharp creases down each leg. His pocket held a pen and pad of paper for writing orders.

I abandoned hope of looking at the photography books and decided to change tactics. "I start at Nairobi University next week. I'm registered in the sociology department. Do you know what books they require?"

"I am also a student," he said, smiling as if we were friends. "I've been studying there for three years now." He took the pen out of his pocket and twirled it in his fingers. "I do not know what books they require in the sociology department because I'm attending classes in the business administration department. Wait for the first day of class. The professors will tell you what to buy." With a wide grin he added, "Then come back, and I will be very glad to serve you."

I'm free, I thought. *He doesn't expect me to buy anything now.* "I am wondering what the classes will be like. I am just beginning," I said.

"I will buy you a cup of tea and tell you. Is that all right?" He looked around the store. There were no customers. He asked the owner, "May I take my morning tea now?"

I smiled as I watched the young clerk stand straight as if he were addressing a military officer. The owner folded his paper, took off his glasses, and put them in his pocket. "Sure, fine. But be back by eleven o'clock. Some professors are expected to come to buy books, and I will need your help."

"Most certainly, sir," the young man said as he grabbed my hand and escorted me out of the shop. "My name is Caleb. The best tea shop near the university is just around the corner. What is your name?"

"I am called Kitzi."

Over tea and biscuits, Caleb explained how the professors taught their classes, how the exams were administered, and how the students competed for grades. "Some of them cheat on exams."

"I don't want to know that part," I said.

He changed the subject to sporting events. "I play forward on the football team," he said.

"I played with the boys in my school in the village, but I was the only girl who was interested. I ran track and field events too," I said.

He touched my hand. "You are a most beautiful woman. I would like to get to know you better."

I pulled my hand away and covered my face. "You are embarrassing me, Caleb." I peeked through my fingers. "But thank you for noticing that I am beautiful."

I folded my hands in my lap. "And thank you for the tea. You are not allowed to know where I live, but I know where your bookstore is. I can find you again." *He doesn't know that I am not a woman.*

Caleb glanced at his wristwatch. "Time to go." He paid for our tea and biscuits.

I clasped my hands as we walked back. At the bookstore, he opened the door for me. I smiled but avoided his gaze. "I want to see you again," he said.

"Oh, you will," I said. The light-headed feeling dissipated as I walked away. *Next time I will look at those photography books. I'm sure Caleb will let me.*

A jewelry store caught my eye. In Kisii country I am sure that we did not have such stores. The glittering gems, gold filigree necklaces, and bracelets fascinated me. I couldn't even conceive of owning such things. I looked at the price on the small white tags. The necklaces cost more money than my mother made in a year of teaching.

"These necklaces are certainly a work of art," a woman said from behind me.

I turned. She was Caucasian and small-boned but tall, and she was dressed in a pantsuit.

"Yes, they are very nice," I answered, puzzled. She spoke English with an accent that I knew was not British.

"I'd love to buy that necklace, but I doubt my husband would approve. What I came to town for was to buy some dresses. Where did you get the nice dress you are wearing? That is exactly what I am looking for, something Kenyan but formal."

"You are interested in this dress?" I asked.

"Yes, where did you get it?" She blushed. "I'm sorry for being so forward. That's not like me. I'm usually quite shy."

"Feel the fabric," I said. She touched my lapel.

"Very nice. The pattern matches perfectly at the seams, and it's so well sewn. But I suppose you want to keep it a secret … where you got it."

"No, I am delighted to show you where I got it," I said.

"Is it far from here? My car is parked over there." She pointed at a shiny black Land Rover. Two boys waved back. "Those are the guards I hired. I don't quite trust them."

I pointed toward Joyce's shop. "It is not very far, just down that street and beyond those stores. It is a tailor shop. All the dresses are custom made."

"They must be very expensive," she said as we walked toward her car.

"I do not think so," I replied.

"I'm sorry. I didn't introduce myself. I'm Clara Boersma. My husband works for the Netherlands embassy."

"It is a pleasure to meet you, Clara Boersma. I am called Kitzi."

She switched to Swahili to discuss her plans with the guards. "See these schillings? They are yours … when I come back … to my car."

I smiled at her lack of command of Swahili. Her two guards didn't seem to understand. I thought they were pretending, so I reiterated where we are going, and I threatened them. "Clara Boersma better find her car in good shape when she returns, or I will help her find you. And I live in this neighborhood." They bowed.

"Thank you. I am struggling to learn Swahili," she admitted. "I just can't seem to get my tongue around it. I speak English well, don't you think?"

I nodded.

"Dutch is my native tongue, and I had no trouble learning French, but Swahili is difficult for me."

"Do not worry, Clara Boersma. You are learning well. I think they understood you."

"Thank you, Kitzi. Did I say your name correctly?"

She chatted as we walked down the avenue and turned onto the back street. She was so friendly, and she told funny stories about her struggles adjusting to Kenyan life all the way to Joyce's shop.

When I walked into the shop, Joyce gave me a disgruntled look. But when she saw that I was accompanied by a customer, her frown turned to a smile. I could see that she was still struggling over our unresolved argument. I introduced her to the customer. "This is Clara Boersma from the Netherlands embassy. She would like to order some dresses." I stepped aside. Joyce exuded charm.

As she explained the tailoring process, I displayed the fit of my dress. Clara checked my seams and how the sleeves were attached. I felt embarrassed by the way she scrutinized my every stitch. I was glad there were no men in the store because she lifted my skirt to examine the hem. I was also glad I had bathed that morning.

For over an hour, the two of them discussed fabric and style. Joyce took out her tape to measure Clara's waist, bust, leg length, and arm size, all the measurements necessary to make the dress fit properly.

Then they negotiated price. "That is a little more than I wanted to pay," said Clara. I stood still at the counter as the negotiations proceeded. Ten minutes later, Clara trumped Joyce with, "If you will agree to my price, I will order five dresses, one of each of the fabrics you showed me. But make them each a different style. Can you do that?"

"Five dresses?" Joyce clasped both hands to her heart.

I was enjoying the negotiations.

"Exactly. Here, I will give you …" She pulled out more schillings than I had never seen before and put them in Joyce's hand. "This should be about a third of the total. I will give you another third at my fitting and the rest when I pick up the dresses. How soon can you have them ready? There is an embassy reception next month."

Joyce's hand was trembling as she put the Shillings on the counter, but her voice was strong as she gave Clara a date.

"Excellent. Thank you. That will be just in time." Clara looked at me. "You are a wonderful advertisement for your mother," she said as she put her purse into her bag and walked out the door.

Joyce hid the fistful of money in her lock box and then returned to the counter. She stood silent, staring out the door. I stood like the mannequin in the window and waited.

Kisii girls are very good at waiting in silence. We are taught this when we are very young.

She stuttered when she finally spoke. "That is more than I usually make in six months."

I said nothing. I didn't even flinch.

She wiped her nose with the handkerchief she kept in her pocket. "You are like the daughter I never had."

I stared out the window. A bicycle loaded with wrapped parcels splashed mud on the curb as the cyclist rode through a puddle. The sunshine glinted through the clouds that brought the early-morning rain.

"I never finished secondary school. I am not understanding why education is so important to you. My father said education was wasted on girls. I am slowly, slowly learning that it means a lot for you to do well at the university."

I tilted my head. "Are you speaking to me?"

"Yes, Kitzi, I am speaking to you." She sounded frustrated.

"Education means everything to me," I said, pretending to pay attention to the people passing by the window.

Joyce shook her head and said, "I was not acting as a Christian woman this morning. I am learning how to have a daughter that is an adult." She took a deep sigh. "I am sorry."

I was stunned by her apology but remained silent as stone.

"We will work out a system so that you can study at the university library and get home safely. I will teach you a special knock so that I know it is you. But I will not go to bed until you are home and safe." She paused to think of a signal. "Two hard knocks, a soft one, and then four more."

I smiled. "Thank you, Mother Joyce."

"And I will ask my nephew, Reuben, to walk you to and from the university," she said.

Who is this nephew? I wondered. But she interrupted my thoughts with a hug. "You are one clever saleswoman," she said. "I will make you a very fine supper tonight. You deserve it. Let's close the shop early so that I can take this money to the bank. I do not want this much money in my shop. Then we will go to the butcher and get a nice, fat piece of goat meat to celebrate."

She rifled through her pockets and gave me a wad of shillings. "Here is your commission for the sale today. When we go to the bank, you can start your own account. There is a Barclays on Loita Street not far from the university."

"I don't deserve anything, Joyce. You feed me and clothe me and give me a couch to sleep on," I said. Hesitant to consider the money mine, I handed it back to her. She folded my fingers around the money and searched my eyes. "That is your money. I promise never, before Jesus my savior, to ask what you spend it on."

"Maybe I will buy some books so that I can study at home." She smiled. I was grateful for the money and tucked it into my dress pocket. But I wondered about Reuben.

Nairobi University

"HOLD STILL, KITZI," JOYCE SAID as she snipped my hair preparing me for my first day at the university. My laugh interrupted her concentration. "What's so funny?"

"My mother cut my hair when I got head lice from the other children at school. I associate haircuts with head lice," I said.

"You have no lice, so quit laughing and let me finish," she quipped. After cutting my hair, she braided beads into it. It was my first day at the university, and she got me up before sunrise to make sure I was prepared. "I just want you to look nice," she said, handing me a small mirror.

"I'm well coiffed." I saw a questioning look on her face. "It means you did a nice job of fixing my hair," I explained to her.

"I wish you wouldn't use those university words. They make me feel dumb," said Joyce.

"I'm sorry, Joyce. It just came out of my mouth. My mother made me study vocabulary …"

"And made you use it every day," she finished my sentence. She relaxed the scissors.

"I could teach you a new word every day, and then when those ambassador women come to your shop, you could impress them." Her head gesture indicated that she was not accepting the offer.

"Thank you, Mother Joyce, for fixing my hair. I feel very pretty now," I said.

"You are most welcome, Kitzi, my dearest daughter."

"You didn't just do it to sell more dresses, did you?" I asked.

She picked up a wooden spoon. "I should beat you for that."

"That would not be very Christian," I yelled as I ran out the door. Reuben stood at attention in the yard waiting for me. I didn't understand how Joyce arranged things, but my escort was ready.

"I am Joyce's nephew. I am bringing you to your classes," he said. His demeanor was stiff, but the top of his head just cleared my chin. I felt as if I were walking him to primary school. He was dressed in a white shirt with a blue pinstriped suit, both of which were too big for him.

Joyce hid the wooden spoon behind her back. "Thank you, Reuben," she said. "Make sure she stays safe."

"I will, Aunt Joyce." We walked out of the alley and onto the boulevard that led to Nairobi University. He insisted on walking ahead of me and on the street side of the walkway, even when pedestrians going the other way impaired his progress.

As we passed the bookstore, I saw Caleb arranging a new display in the window and waved. He grimaced, apparently unsure what to make of my escort. I smiled and nodded at Reuben, who was marching two steps ahead, oblivious to our communication.

When we approached the College of Humanities, Reuben paused. "When am I to be here to walk you home?" We set a time that gave me ample opportunity to explore the campus. "I will be right here," he said, "under this tree."

The lectures exhilarated me. I learned new things all day. I could not believe that my dream had come true. Having earned free tuition because of my test scores provoked me to study harder. The government of Kenya had invested in me. I thought of all the nights that Mother made me study when I wanted to go out and play with the boys. I could hear her voice. "You must study hard. Your life depends on it, Kwamboka. There will be plenty of time to play with boys later."

But I felt sad that many of my friends from high school would never get a chance to study at a university, especially the teenagers whose mothers did not allow them to attend my mother's class. They did poorly on their exams, and now it was impossible for them to go to any university. Someday I wanted to start a school free of false accusations interfering with education.

At noon I sneaked over to the bookstore. "Caleb, have you had lunch yet?"

He looked at the shop owner, who nodded. Then he escorted me out of the shop. Down the street to the tea shop, we walked in silence. As the waiter seated us at a sidewalk table he asked, "So, who is the guy you were with this morning?"

"I thought you would be curious about that," I said with a winsome smile.

When the waiter came to our table, Caleb ordered tea and sandwiches. He rearranged his silverware and then looked at me to continue.

"That's Mother Joyce's nephew."

"Your cousin, then." He relaxed.

"I guess so." *It's too difficult to explain otherwise*, I thought.

"Anyway, Mother feels that it is important that I have an escort. That's Reuben. Do you think he could protect me?"

"That little guy?" The waiter set down our orders, and Caleb took a bite of his sandwich. "No."

"How is the bookstore doing?" I asked.

"Very well. The Indian merchant I work for is kind and honest. But someday I want to have a bookstore of my own," he said.

"I plan to be a schoolteacher," I said. "When you own your own bookstore, Caleb, I will order the books for my students exclusively from you."

He took my hand in his. "That would be excellent."

After a few weeks, I fell into a routine. Reuben walked me to the campus. I attended lectures, took notes, returned to the library to review my notes, and then met Reuben under the tree to be escorted home. Once a week I ran to the bookstore to have lunch with Caleb. He told me about the books he had read. Sometimes he brought samples of new photography books for me to peruse. Those books were very expensive, so I made sure my hands were clean before I touched them.

There were some very handsome men in my classes. They were all nice and willing to talk to me, but I think it was because of how Joyce's dresses flattered my figure and drew their attention. Most of them had girlfriends, whom I avoided.

"I would like to study with you," said a kind voice behind me as I gathered my books to head for the library. The young fellow who spoke was tall and muscular. He looked as if he were from a costal tribe. Wearing a pressed floral shirt, sleek black pants, and a gold necklace, he was so well groomed that his black skin shined. His arms bulged in his sleeves.

He opened the door for me and slung his suit jacket over his shoulder. Despite his cosmopolitan look, he wore sandals. "My name is Mokoli."

I redistributed my books to my other arm and shook his hand. "I am called Kitzi. I was planning on studying in the library, Mokoli. Would you care to join me?"

"I do not recognize your tribe from the name Kitzi," he said.

"It's a nickname my mother gave me. I am Kisii. You do not hate Kisii, do you?"

He laughed at my question. "I do not think I have ever met a Kisii woman. It is a pleasure to meet you, Kitzi."

"My Kisii name is Kwamboka, but please just keep calling me Kitzi."

He looked at his feet and scuffed his heel. "I am in the same anthropology class as you. I did not understand the professor's comments today. He was explaining the difference between ethnicity and cultural identity. Did you understand the difference?" he said as we stroll toward the library.

"I think he was trying to say that if you divorce yourself from the culture in which you were raised you still retain your ethnicity, but you may lose your cultural identity."

"How could that happen?" Mokoli asks. "I am Achonyi and will always be."

"So, if you lived here in Nairobi and became a rich merchant," I said.

He smiled, contemplating the possibility.

"And then you moved to London to expand your business," I continued, "and you married a wealthy British woman and all your friends were British, would you still consider yourself culturally Achonyi? Would your children be culturally Achonyi, or would they consider themselves part of British culture?"

"But my children would still be part Achonyi. They would be from my loins."

And you do have nice loins, I thought but caught myself. "They would have your ethnicity, but would they retain your culture while living in London? Would you have your daughters circumcised?"

"We Achonyi do not mutilate our women. But I think that I understand the principle," he asserted.

"Turn it around," I said. "Imagine if an American came and lived with the Kisii."

"You're from around Lake Victoria area, aren't you? That is why you are so beautiful." He beamed.

Was it admiration? I wasn't sure. "I am trying to explain something to you," I said, scolding him to focus on the lesson.

"But your beauty is making it difficult for me to concentrate," he said, grinning and showing his beautiful teeth.

"I see that your tribe did not eat sugar cane either," I added.

"It is taboo," he quipped.

I laughed as I set my books on the opposite side of the study table. "I think you'd better concentrate on your study notes for a while."

He blushed. "I apologize for my lack of focus, Kitzi," he said, still smiling as he went to the library stacks and returned with one of the books on the professor's reading list.

I took out my notes from the lecture to avoid his glance. We studied in silence. I glanced up from my book, but he was concentrating on class material.

After about an hour, he said, "That example really clarifies what the professor was saying. After looking at these references, I think I understand the difference in terms. Thanks, Kitzi."

A young woman appeared, dressed in a large floral print. She was well nourished, with a large bosom and strong hands that startled Mokoli when as she started massaging his shoulders. "You sure make yourself hard to find," she said.

"I am studying the books that our professor told us to study," he explained.

"And who are you?" She glared at me.

I stood to greet her. "I am called Kitzi. It is nice to meet you. What is your name?"

"What bush did you crawl out from?" she scoffed.

Mokoli stood and hugged his girlfriend. "She is a Kisii woman who is in my anthropology class. Be nice to her. She was just helping me study."

She grabbed his arm, ignoring me, and said to Mokoli, "You promised to take me to that new Indian pizza palace. It's getting late. I am very hungry."

"Yes, the time escaped me," he said as he looked at his wristwatch. "Excuse us, Kitzi. Thank you for explaining the professor's …"

She dragged him from the table and pushed him toward the door. I heard her tell him, "Kisii girls are rural trash. They don't know anything. Why are you associating with her?"

"Because she is very intelligent," he replied.

Thereafter, she was at the door to meet him when class was completed, so he sat in back of me and asked me to clarify the professor's lectures before we left class. I tried to greet her, but she shunned me. She grabbed his arm as soon as he was outside the classroom. She always seemed hungry.

Most of the women in my classes were friendly. When they asked about my clothes, I gave them the address of the tailor shop. "Just tell Joyce that Kitzi sent you. You will get a good discount." Several accepted my offer. When they wore their new dresses, I told them, "You look so nice today."

They thanked me for the recommendation and said that the prices were good, but a few of them avoided me afterward. I did not understand why.

There were a few Kisii women at Nairobi University but none from my village. I invited them out for tea. Several became friends. I made friends easily with women from other rural tribes as well. One day I invited a group out for lunch at a restaurant across from the campus. We laughed about the environment back home.

"Electricity is sure magical, isn't it?" said Beatrice. She was a Kipsigis girl who came from a village just northeast of Kisii. She belonged to the same tribe as Pastor Joseph. We laughed together as we sipped our tea.

Lucy, a Turkana, woman flipped a peanut up in the air and caught it in her mouth. "Have you noticed that tall guy in our economics class?" We all smiled because we knew to whom she was referring. "I like my men tall and muscular."

"I would like to have a boyfriend like him someday," I said.

"You have a boyfriend," said Lucy. "I see him walk you home every day from the university.

"Oh, he is not my boyfriend," I said. "He's not tall or muscular. Besides, he's my escort."

"Escort?" A puzzled expression scrolled across each face. The girls leaned over their tea and stared as Lucy whispered, "Like a sex slave?"

"No, no, no," I said as my face got hot. "Wrong definition of 'escort.' He's my mother's nephew. She makes him walk me home for safety."

"Then you're *available*?" Lucy curled her tongue around the word.

"Yes, I'm available." My friends giggled, but I wondered how they would respond if they knew that I was not circumcised. Maybe university women didn't care about such things. My classmates back home didn't think I was available.

"Then you are part of the competition," Beatrice said, leaning back in her chair. "That's why you dress so nicely. Don't you ever wear old clothes?"

Tears popped into my eyes, and I choked on my words. "I have no old clothes. My uncle burned all my clothes when he tried to kill me."

The girls gasped. "I'm sorry," Beatrice said.

"I'm embarrassed. I didn't mean to tell you that."

"Oh, Kitzi, I'm sorry," Lucy said as she got up and hugged me. "But tell us the story."

I told the story of my last days in the village and my escape from my uncle. "Someday I would like to see an end to such horrible things. I would like to set up a school where children don't believe in witchcraft and—" I paused to search each girl's face. "And do not have to go through genital mutilation." They all agreed. I sighed.

"It is just horrible," said Beatrice.

"Maybe education will change that," said Lucy.

We finished our tea in silence.

I experienced the most prejudice from Kikuyu women. Several whom I met didn't think girls from the rural areas deserved an education. They would say, "You're not the ones who are going to run this country. Why is education important to you?" These women were well fed. Most had very wealthy parents, fathers who were politicians, or both.

One woman, Martha, from my economics class was particularly nasty. I noticed that she did well on a quiz, so I asked, "Would you like to study together?" She was the same height as I but weighed many stones more.

"How did a Kisii girl get into Nairobi University?" she sneered. "Your father must have sold a whole herd of cattle to bribe the administration to admit you."

She grabbed my dress and twisted it in her fist. "And you're so scrawny the wind should blow you away."

"I am sorry that I am offensive to you. I am here on scholarship. My father did not sell any cows. I noticed that you did well on the quiz and only wished to congratulate you," I said, maintaining my composure.

"If you scored well, you must have cheated," she continued, adding demeaning insults that I didn't even understand.

"I did not cheat," I said, backing away.

After that day, I stayed away from Martha. She seemed indignant when we received our midterm exam scores. Although the grades were posted only by student number, somehow she found out my grade.

"There was no way an insect from the shit pile could score so high on that exam. Where did you get the answers from, you cockroach?" she demanded.

I turned and ran to the library, but I could not concentrate. I decided to go for a walk around campus to clear my head. I smelled the blossoms on the trees and relished the rows of flowers. I felt uplifted as I overheard clustered students discussing intellectual subjects. Several of the men waved at me. I just kept walking around campus until it was time for Reuben to walk me home.

As he walked ahead of me, he divulged how much Joyce paid him to escort me and then continued, "My father owns a shop in Nairobi that sells carvings to tourists. When he goes on treks across Kenya to buy carvings from suppliers, I'm in charge." I was curious as to why he was telling me about his business until he stopped and grabbed my hand. "I am very interested in you," he said, stroking my hand, "as a lady."

It was late. I had an exam the next day for which I needed to study. I was tired from walking off my anger at Martha, and I didn't want to have this conversation. Reuben frequently quizzed me on what I had learned. Usually I didn't mind telling him, but tonight his tone was domineering.

"To me, you are very beautiful," he said waiting for my response.

"Thank you, Reuben." I shook him off and walked faster. He picked up his pace.

"I want to know you as a man knows a woman," he persisted, panting beside me, trying to keep up. He pulled a condom out of his pocket.

I stopped at the corner of the street and glared at him. "You have been very kind to me, Reuben. I can depend on your punctuality."

I took a deep breath. From the look on his face he did not know what "punctuality" meant.

"You are always on time."

He nodded. I grabbed his shoulders, keeping him at arm's length. "But I need to study very hard to continue my scholarship, and I have no interest in men right now. Think of me as still a girl, not a woman ready to be married."

He wrinkled his face as I released my grip. I started walking. He followed silently until we turned down the alley. He waved a condom in my face. "My house is very near here, and I am prepared to treat you as a nice woman."

"I am not ready. Besides, it would cost you six cows to marry me, since I am a university student."

He put his condom back in his pocket. "You are too expensive."

"And when I graduate, it will cost you ten cows." We marched to Joyce's door, and I knocked.

As she let me in, he stood dejected in the shadows. Joyce thanked him and gave him some shillings. After bolting the door, she asked, "What's wrong with Reuben?"

"He wants to marry me, and I turned him down," I said.

"Will you consider him later?" asked Joyce.

"No," I replied emphatically.

"You need to marry someone soon, Kitzi. It's only natural."

Infatuated

I CHOSE A SEAT IN the front of my sociology class. We were supposed to have a guest speaker, so I wanted to be able to see whoever it was. Besides, I didn't want to sit with anyone. I was upset. Since Joyce paid Reuben to walk me to class and pick me up each afternoon, I expected our relationship to remain formal. But this morning he had put his hand on my shoulder and told me that I should be his "girlfriend." "Come to my house on the way home this afternoon," he said. I pushed him off, thinking, *you short little weasel.*

My negative thoughts were interrupted as Professor Naiguta addressed the class. "Today we have a visiting professor from Boston College in the United States of America. He has been doing research for his PhD in western Kenya on the support systems of women in Kisii culture. Please welcome Phillip Schoenberg to Nairobi University."

There was a rousing applause. I sat straight up in my chair. The words "Kisii culture" caught my attention. Phillip Schoenberg was muscular and tan from long periods in the bush. He dressed in a tan short-sleeved shirt. His pants were cinched with a belt that had lost a few notches. *He probably didn't eat well in Kisii country,* I reasoned.

"We are very interested in your research. Thank you for sharing with us today," Professor Naiguta continued and then sat down. Phillip took the podium.

"I've been working with the Kisii tribe near Lake Victoria. I'm collecting data on extended family impact on postpartum depression. Compared to people in the United States, the Kisii have an impressive support system in their community." He shuffled his notes. "Are any of you Kisii?"

I raised my hand. I was the only one in the class. I quickly dropped it as Martha in the front row turned to sneer at me. *What is she doing here?* I wondered. *She was not registered for this class.*

I didn't learn much from the lecture because it was like hearing about my own family. Besides, I was distracted by how Phillip moved and gestured. He was so attractive. He spoke with authority and respect for Kisii culture, but what he said was not entirely accurate. As the class progressed I felt light-headed, so I pushed my fists into my belly. *Kwamboka, stop. Your hormones are running away with you.*

After class, I chided myself on my lack of attention and girlish infatuation. I gathered my books and avoided looking toward the front of the room. There was a tap on my shoulder. When I turned, Phillip Schoenberg was standing there. "Imbuya ore?"

"Buya," I respond in Ekegusii.

"I would like to meet with you and review my research. I am concerned about the accuracy of my assessments. You were the only Kisii in class." He extended his hand. "It is an honor to meet a Kisii at the university level. I have not found much interest in higher education among the women I've interviewed."

My heart jumped in my chest. I wanted to tell him that he had a skewed subject set, but I held my tongue. I focused on the books in my arm, feeling like a silly goat. When I found my voice, I looked up at him. "I have another lecture to attend right now."

"Could we meet for lunch? I'll pay," he said.

We arranged to meet at an Italian restaurant near

campus, and I scurried off to economics class. The lecture was boring; the professor reviewed the questions on our recent examination. I tried to sit up straight and listen, but my mind kept drifting to lunch with Phillip Schoenberg.

As class ended, I grabbed my books and headed for the door.

"Miss Muwami, I need to see you," a voice behind me said.

Not now. I panicked, but I turned respectfully to Professor Omboga. "Yes, sir."

"Come with me to my office," he said.

I followed him down the hall, hoping this would not take too long. He offered me a chair in his office and shut the door. The wood paneling was made of rosewood, as was his desk. His diplomas and citations as teacher of the year were displayed across the walls. His office smelled of lemon oil.

Shuffling some papers, he handed me my exam. "You were the only one in any of my classes who scored 100 percent on this exam."

"Thank you." I grabbed my test and stood up. He motioned for me to sit.

"I received an anonymous note claiming that you cheated. This is a serious accusation, Miss Muwami. You could be suspended and lose credit for the entire year."

My face felt hot. I panicked. I wanted to get up and run. My belly cramped. *Why would anyone accuse me of cheating?* I waved the still air in the office to fan my face. "I did not cheat, Professor Omboga. I have great respect for you. I would do no such thing."

"And the note was anonymous, which means that I have no way of verifying the accusation. It said that you got copies of the questions in advance. I don't see how that is possible, since they were never out of my possession. So I have decided to give you a chance to prove you know the material." He handed me a paper with a list of questions. "I've prepared this test with different questions. Answer these four questions in front of me, and I will believe you and ignore this complaint."

His stern gaze paralyzed me. I scanned the questions on the sheet. The words blurred. I could not read them. He offered me a drink of water. I was a field mouse trapped by a hawk. I took a sip of water. *Kwamboka, just focus on the questions*, I told myself. *You know the material.* I scrunched my eyes closed and then opened them. My vision cleared, and my voice returned. I started to answer the first question.

He was intent on detail and asked me to clarify several answers. He showed no change in his demeanor. I felt the sweat trickle down my back.

"Go on to the next question," he said after a few minutes.

I sensed his satisfaction with my initial answer. On the next question I felt more confident. My heart was pounding against my ribs, but the words weren't dancing on the page anymore.

When I completed the fourth question, he sighed, took the exam paper from me, put it in his folder, and closed it. "You know the material well. Now I understand that this was a false accusation. Do you have any idea why someone would accuse you of such a thing?"

"I do not wish to speculate. It would be too painful for me." I covered my eyes and put my head between my knees. The blood flowed like fire through my face. As I read the questions and answered, I had not blinked once, concerned that he would doubt my credibility. Now my eyes burned.

"You are wise as well as intelligent. I am deeply sorry to have put you through this. You will be excused from the next quiz. I will give you an automatic A."

I opened my eyes, stood, and grabbed the desk to keep from fainting. "May I be excused?"

"Yes," said Professor Omboga.

I ran out the door, through campus, and down the street toward the restaurant. I was still a half block away when I saw

Phillip standing beside an umbrella table, sipping his tea. He paid the waitress and started to leave.

"I'm here," I yelled. He glanced in my direction down the block.

"I thought you stood me up," he said when I finally reached the restaurant and grabbed the table for support.

"Never," I said.

Country Culture

I SAT DOWN AND TRIED to regain my composure as I related the experience in Professor Omboga's office.

"I am fascinated with how tribalism is so destructive in this country," he said after I told him of the morning's events.

"Do you think what happened to me was tribalism? I think someone was jealous of my test score," I replied.

"Kitzi, you are from a minor tribe in this country. No one expects you to do well. When you do, students from the major tribes—the Kikuyu, for example—are embarrassed and attack you," he surmised.

"Most of the students are Kikuyu. So who would do such a thing?" I thought about the concept as the waitress brought our order. It was a pasta dish, but not spaghetti. I was not sure what it was called. I rolled the spices around in my mouth. It was so different from any food I had ever eaten. I looked at him and smiled. "I like Italian food."

"I'm glad," he said. "What I wanted to talk to you about is my research. I am heading out to the field next week. Can you give me some recommendations on how to get more valid data? Who should I talk to? It's hard to get data from women as a man, even when I use a female translator."

I twirled the pasta in the sauce on my plate. The spices titillated my tongue. "How old was your translator?" I asked.

"About twenty, I think," he said.

"Did you discuss what you were doing with the clan elders?" I asked.

"No. Mostly, I worked in the urban areas. It was easier to get an audience, but I fear that urbanization has mutated the cultural values I'm studying."

"Your data are skewed," I said as I wiped the last of the sauce off my plate with a piece of bread, pushed it onto my fork, and plopped the tasty morsel into my mouth. "From the perspective of aboriginal culture."

He took my hand as I laid my fork down. I was not prepared for his touch. I pulled away. My hands were sweaty.

"Can you help me get better data? From what you're saying, I need to interview the rural women, women who are the heart and soul of the culture."

He ordered tea as I gave him the names of the clan elders in several of the rural villages. He took out a notebook and jotted down the names. I was impressed that he spelled them correctly. "You've studied my language, I see."

"I enrolled a language teacher, a young woman who was willing to talk to me." He rattled off some Kisii phrases.

I laughed so hard I had to hold my full stomach.

"What's so funny?" he asked.

"You speak Ekegusii like a teenage girl. Men say things differently," I said.

He wrung his serviette.

When I stopped laughing, I tried to explain, "If I learned English from a pubescent male, the slang phrases I would use would sound like a teenage boy."

I tried to be serious, but I could not stop giggling. "You sounded so comical. I'm sorry to laugh at you, but I needed some comic relief after what I experienced this morning. You've made this a wonderful day for me."

His face flushed. "And you speak English like a British matron."

I laughed again. "I'll accept that as a compliment."

"Where did you learn your vocabulary? No one I interviewed here in Kenya speaks English so correctly and with such vocabulary," he said.

"My mother was an English teacher. She graduated from Oxford University in England. She came back to Kenya to teach children and see them succeed in the school system." Tears formed in my eyes, and I brushed them away with my serviette. I didn't intend to say anything more.

"What happened?" he asked, wanting to know more.

I took a deep breath. "When my father died—" I sighed. "You know from studying our culture that my mother was supposed to remarry within a year … one of my father's clan, my uncle, for example."

"She didn't want to, did she?" he asked.

"My uncle was a very hateful man and already had three wives. My mother was not willing to be number four."

"Did she marry someone else?" he continued to get all the details.

"No. So my uncle initiated a rumor that she was a witch. The students in her class were frightened and refused to come to class, so naturally they performed poorly on the national exam. He told the parents that my mother had bewitched them to fail and arranged for a gang to beat and rape her."

I started crying, and Phillip moved his chair next to me and put his arm over my shoulder. "Then they burned her to death—or she was dead already. I don't know."

"Oh, Kitzi, I'm so sorry," he said.

I saw the compassion in his face through my tears. I wiped my face with my serviette and regained my composure. "That is why you must never mention my name when you are doing your field work. If my uncle finds out that I am still alive, he will send someone to kill me or sell me into slavery." I grabbed his hand and dug my nails into his palm. "Do you promise?"

"I promise." he said, pulling his hand away. He shook it. "Gosh, you're strong."

After I calmed down, we returned to discussing his research and how he could survey the women in the rural areas. His folder was jammed with notes by the time we finished our pudding—"tiramisu," it was called. The creamy filling smelled so fragrant. *What a pudding*, I thought.

"This is so helpful. I am very grateful." He packed his notebook into his folder and put everything into his briefcase. "Would it be all right if we met again? I am leaving for Kisii Town, but I may have a few more questions when I return."

"Anytime. You know where I attend class." I stood and extended my hand, but he hugged me. We held hands as we walked back toward the campus. Never had I felt so giddy.

At the intersection, I let go of his hand and turned toward Joyce's shop. "Do you live down this street?" he asked.

"See that tailor shop at the end of the block? That's where I work for room and board," I said.

"Can I find you there?" he asked.

"Only as a backup. I'd prefer you find me at school," I said.

As I walked into the tailor shop, Joyce looked up. "It is only three o'clock. Where is Reuben?"

"I finished early, and one of the visiting professors escorted me here. I have no tests, and I am all caught up on my studies."

Joyce rushed out the door and handed a shilling to a passing street boy. When she came back into the shop she said, "I sent a message to Reuben that he does not need to meet you tonight."

"I'm sure he'll be disappointed," I said, grabbing a piece of material and wrapping it around my waist. "This would make a nice skirt, don't you think?"

"You have enough skirts," Joyce said.

That night I had trouble sleeping. I kept thinking about Phillip's strong, tan arms around my shoulder. In my village I was shielded from such feelings because I hadn't gone through the puberty ritual. Not only were the boys in my school not desirable but they shunned me. Yet it was ridiculous to fall in love with an American visiting professor, and a Caucasian one at that. What did we have in common? Why would he be interested in a black girl like me?

Two weeks later I got a letter from Kisii Town addressed to my student mailbox at Nairobi University. Phillip wrote that he was doing much better obtaining the data he needed. He met with the clan elders, and they provided an older woman to translate so that he could conduct interviews with pregnant women. With their approval, he conducted interviews in the open and didn't struggle with jealous husbands and women who wouldn't talk. He ended the letter, "with deepest appreciation, Phillip. PS: I found a male language teacher, so I don't sound like a teenage girl anymore."

Pizza

"I'M FINDING THE SAME INCIDENCE of postpartum depression among the Kisii women as is reported in the United States. But Kisii women have a more elaborate support system," Phillip said as he laid out his papers on the Formica tabletop. He had a diagram showing who was related to whom and who helped the woman after delivery.

We were eating pizza at the Nairobi Pizza Palace, owned by an Indian merchant. I wondered how someone from India had decided to make pizza, but that was what one found in Nairobi. The pizza had pepperoni and onions with lots of cheese. It was cut into little squares. I licked the melted cheese off my lips. "There are advantages to polygamy if the wives help each other," I said.

He wiped the dripping sauce off his mouth. "I found that many women in the village helped someone who was struggling. Some took care of her children, and others cooked and helped with the chores. It was quite impressive. But I was uncertain of the relationships these women had with the one who was struggling."

"If the wives and the women in the village work together, it is very positive." I stopped Phillip from writing. "But if they decide someone is a witch, then that same village attitude becomes destructive." I let go of his hand to take another piece of pizza.

"Maybe I should study functional versus nonfunctional polygamous families. How could I write a survey to distinguish?" he said, apparently pondering the possibilities.

By the time we finished talking, the last piece of pizza lay cold, dried, and curled on the aluminum serving plate. Time stopped as we discussed positive and negative aspects of Kisii culture in comparison to other cultures.

"So," I asked him, "If your mother was depressed after you were born, who would have helped her?"

"I suppose she would have asked her sister or mother to help her." He thought through his response. "But probably not. My aunt lived in Seattle, and my grandmother lived in Minneapolis when I was born. My parents lived in Boston."

"Those cities are quite distant, if I remember my US geography," I said.

"Yes, I suppose she would have gone to her doctor and would have been given medication," he said. "An antidepressant or something."

"So if your father had other wives, could they have helped her when you were born?" I asked.

"My mother has always been very jealous of my father's attention. She probably would have killed the other wives." He chuckled at his response.

We left the Pizza Palace laughing. As I headed back to the library to study I requested, "Tell me more about your mother."

"She is fastidious, an immaculate housekeeper." He turned to see if I understood.

I twisted a grin and answered with a Swahili accent. "What? You not thinking a Kisii girl knows those words like that?"

He hugged me. I put my arm around him. It was so comfortable to be with Phillip. I had never felt this way about a man. But in the recesses of my mind, I was thinking: *He is white, and I am black. Are we allowed to love each other?*

I tried to study that afternoon. I opened several books. I was supposed to write a paper comparing different economic theories and how each attempted to explain the economic problems in Kenya. I was deep in thought when I felt something hit the back of my head. Startled, I turned to see Martha.

"I am surprised that you are still attending the university," she blurted out so that other students turned to the commotion. "Next time you cheat, I will make sure that you get caught."

"I never cheat, Martha. Why are you so angry with me?"

"I don't have to answer a Kisii cockroach that has infiltrated this university." She walked away, her ample buttocks gyrating in her tight pants.

After I left the library, I found Reuben under the jacaranda tree waiting to walk me home. He gave no greeting but turned and walked ahead of me as we headed down the street. The silence was stifling.

I spoke in Swahili, "What's the problem, Reuben? I know something is bothering you."

"I saw you walk past my shop this afternoon with your arm around a white man." His face twisted. He looked angry.

"So?" I responded.

"White men are imperialists. They are the ones who have caused all the trouble in Kenya. They are just here to take advantage of us." He turned on me. "You should not be flirting with white men."

"Even if all the black men reject me?" I retorted.

"I have not rejected you," he said.

"You would really marry an uncircumcised Kisii girl who never went through puberty rites as your first wife? That would give you no status," I said, daring to reveal my secret.

He scrunched up his face. "You're not circumcised? You didn't complete puberty? Did your mother raise you to be a whore?" he said, raising his voice.

I saw my value plummet in his eyes. "See, you are rejecting me." I walked faster, and his short legs struggled to keep his proper place. I switched from Swahili to English. "For your information, Reuben, I was with a visiting professor helping him with his anthropological research."

He sneered in Swahili, "You had to have your arm around him to help him with his research?" He shook his fist in my face. "Was his white ass firm enough for you?"

When Phillip returned to Kisii country to do his field work, Reuben was more willing to talk to me. I think he decided that I had lost interest in Phillip, since he didn't see us together any more, but I soon learned that he had spoken to Joyce about us.

"Kitzi, I don't know if you should be with that white man. It is not proper," Joyce said in a motherly, reprimanding tone.

"He is kind and smart, and we talk about everything. I am comfortable with him, and he has never tried to take advantage of me," I replied.

"Yes, but when he returns to England …" started Joyce.

I interrupted, "He's American, from Boston, not British. And he is working on his PhD studying Kisii culture."

"All right, so when he returns to Boston, America, he will break your heart," argued Joyce.

"What if I marry him and go to Boston with him? Is he taking advantage of me then? Will that break my heart?"

"That's foolish talk. He will never do that," she fumed.

"You always tell me that you want me to marry a Christian man. Phillip is a Christian. He goes to the Lutheran church. Isn't that a Christian church?"

"Why can't you marry one of the nice young men at the African Inland Mission church?" she asked.

I glared at her. I paused to choose my words with great care. "When I accompanied you to your church, I met some young men. Some of them are quite handsome and nice gentlemen. I've talked to them. Do you call that flirting? I know that you have noticed. But they want me to forget about going to Nairobi University. They want me to have lots of babies and to cook their meals for them every day. That is not what Kwamboka is going to do."

Months later, when Phillip returned from the field, he greeted me outside my anthropology class. "Naki ogendererete."

"You sound like a man now. That is much better," I said.

"I hired a clan elder as a language instructor."

"That's great," I said.

"I met Uncle Osiemo," he said with caution in his voice.

"Yes." I waited for the rest.

"Now I understand why you do not want me to mention your name. He thinks himself a very powerful man. He's head of his clan now," he informed me.

"So what is my dear uncle doing?" I asked.

"He owns some land up against the forest. He's turned it into a tea plantation and is making a lot of money."

"He loves money." I turned to wipe my eyes.

"What's wrong?" he asked.

I swallowed. "That is my father's land. I have the deed. It belongs to me, but it is very hard for a woman to own land in Kisii country, even though legally the Kenyan government acknowledges a woman's right to own land. If I had a brother or were married, the land would be mine." I sighed. "My mother's dream was to build a private school at the base of the forest. Now that will never happen."

Phillip rubbed my back. "Don't give up on your dreams, Kitzi. You are a year from graduation, and maybe you will be able to have a school there someday."

"Someday." I patted my face to make the blotches go away. "I'm sorry, Phillip. A Kisii girl is not supposed to show emotion. I meant to ask about your research. How much information did you accumulate?"

"Come, I'll show you." We headed to a café for tea. He pulled reams of papers out of his briefcase. "There is quite a network for women in need, but I'm surprised that it is usually a sister or an aunt that helps a woman in distress, not the other wives of their husband. Last time we talked about the advantages of polygamy."

I interrupted. "But as I told you, that depends upon the husband. Some encourage their wives to work together; many don't bother."

"You're right, of course. My research demonstrated that some wives do cooperate, but others don't. For example, one woman I interviewed, with her husband's permission—you were right about getting the husband's approval. Anyway, this woman had a miscarriage and was quite anemic. She was too sick to tend her garden. She was married to a man who had two other wives. The other wives did not help her at all while she was sick. Her sisters, her mother, and even her grandmother helped her, but the other wives ignored her. Is that customary?" I nodded.

He went on, "The other wives were in competition. When she was sick, her husband didn't command them to help her. They were busy trying to benefit their own children and captivate the husband's attention. I even observed a woman who had not borne a son when her husband died. She became destitute. No one wanted to marry her. She had no rights to any land. It was divided among the sons of the other wives. She had no way to provide for herself. She died, Kitzi, I think of starvation, and no one seemed to care."

Graduation

"Aren't you coming to my graduation, Mother Joyce?"

"I have clients scheduled to come to the tailor shop today. Besides, I told you that I don't understand why a girl needs an education," she answered with indifference.

"But Joyce, you have supported me through these four years, and I want you to celebrate with me. You are the reason I was able to go to Nairobi University," I asserted.

"Is Phillip going to be there?" she asked.

"Yes, of course," I said.

"You know I don't approve of him. If he is going to be there, I'm not going," she announced.

"Why? Because he is Caucasian or because he's American?" I asked, trying to understand her reasoning.

Joyce slammed the teakettle on the table. "No. Because I think he is taking advantage of you. I think that he is just trying to get you in bed with him."

"That's not true. Now, Reuben, he's been trying to have sex with me for years. He has propositioned me so many times, I've lost count. But you still pay him to walk me back and forth to the university. Maybe you should pay him to quit propositioning me."

She turned in anger and shoved me away.

"Reuben thinks that because I'm not circumcised—*mutilated*—my mother raised me to be a whore. He dangled his condom in front of me and told me that I should have sex with him. Phillip doesn't do that."

I sat on the wooden stool and waited for my heart rate to slow. The silence was painful. I scrunched my face, swallowed my anger, and decided to be gentle. "Listen, you are just like a mother to me. This graduation is very important. It is what I have dreamed about my whole life. I want you to come. I want to honor you for everything you have done for me."

She stormed toward her room. "I'm not going to your graduation, and that's final. I need help in the shop. That's what you should be doing today." She slammed her bedroom door.

I yelled back, "You do not need my help in the shop." I wiped the dishes and put them away to calm down, picked up my things, and put everything away. When it was time to go, I knocked on her door. "I love you, Mother Joyce. I am sorry that I yelled. Please forgive me. You have been a wonderful mother to me. When I graduate today it will be because you helped me. I would have died along the road without you."

There was no answer.

Phillip met me just off campus and walked me to the outdoor auditorium. It was crowded with graduates and their parents. Everyone was celebrating. "This is so exciting, Kitzi," Phillip said as he rubbed the small of my back, "and you look so beautiful."

The waiting area was hot and stuffy. There was no breeze, and I sweated beneath my formal gown. But I was excited. "This is what my mother always wanted for me," I said, almost in tears. Why couldn't Joyce have come? I felt devastated.

"I'm so proud of you," said Phillip as he found a place in the first rows for guests. Joyce should have been sitting in the empty seat next to him. Ever since he had taken Joyce and me out for dinner, she had been angry with him. Joyce said that he "took liberties" with me, by which she meant holding my hand and hugging and kissing me after dinner. I thought it was sweet, but not Joyce. She snarled when we got home, "That is an inappropriate public display of affection."

I changed my thoughts. I had to think about something pleasant. This day was too important to spoil. A soft breeze flowed through the flowering trees, giving a sweet scent to the air. I tried to remain calm to avoid perspiring, but it was impossible. It didn't matter. I was graduating. Yet a disturbing feeling came over me as I waited for my name to be called. *What will I do now?*

"Kwamboka Muwami" came over the loudspeaker. I stood, stabilized my shaking knees, and headed for the platform. "Ms. Muwami has exceeded all the expectations of her department. She is the top student graduating today in the social science department and receives this award for excellence."

He held up a certificate. I flushed with embarrassment. "We wish her well in her future academic career. We expect her to apply to graduate school. I know she will make Kenya and Nairobi University proud of her achievements." The crowd cheered.

I was shocked. The provost and the social science department director led me to the microphone as they gave me the achievement award. "Give a little speech," they whispered in my ear.

"I woke up this morning and found myself alive, but now I think I am dreaming." Applause reverberated through the crowd. "My mother back in Kisii encouraged me and gave me the dream to come to Nairobi University. As a poor country girl I never thought such a dream could come true. I want to thank all of you students who helped me with my studies and the many things that I did not understand when I came to Nairobi. Without the support of my fellow students, I would have floundered. But I want to especially honor Joyce Nwamende. She is my Nairobi mother. She has taken me into her home, fed me, and clothed me even though I am not related to her in any way. Without her, I would never have experienced this graduation day." The stadium stood to applaud as I shook hands again with the director.

"I'm so impressed," said Phillip as students collected on the lawn with their families. "Why didn't you tell me that you were the smartest one in your class?"

"I didn't know it," I said.

"Right," he said in a tone of disbelief.

We strolled off campus to his car and drove toward the hotels on the boulevard. Phillip greeted the doorman at the New Stanley Hotel and tipped the person parking the vehicles.

"This is a nice place. Let's eat here," he offered. I felt like I was in a cloud as the maitre d' escorted us to a waiting table.

The table set for three had a white linen tablecloth with a brilliant display of red flowers. There were more forks and spoons than I was sure I could ever need. I was still counting them when Phillip pulled out the chair for me. The chair was padded and very comfortable. The rich smell of roasted meat and vegetables permeated the air.

Phillip asked me what I wanted to eat, not letting me even glimpse at the menu. "I'm paying for it. Just tell me what you want."

"I am so glad to be done with classes." I took a deep sigh. "Do they have goat on the menu? Kisii always celebrate with goat meat."

"There's no goat, but I'll order something similar." When the waiter came to our table. I was so distracted that I didn't even listen to what Phillip ordered. I took out my award and read it. *How did I get this?* I wondered.

"What are you going to do now?" Phillip asked. "Are you going to graduate school like the department head said at commencement? You're smart enough."

"I never told him to say that. Besides, where would I go?"

"The United States or England, perhaps. You said that your mother went to Oxford. I'm sure you could get in there. How about Boston College? You could get your master's or doctorate in public health and then work for a NGO here in Kenya. Maybe you could start a private school. That's what you've always dreamed of doing, isn't it?"

I chattered all through the meal. I was so euphoric that I didn't even know what I was talking about most of the time. Twice I looked at my food to see what I was eating. My head was so full of dreams, I couldn't remember what I had eaten.

"I wouldn't even know how to start," I said, taking a bite of the pudding Phillip ordered. I was so full, but the fresh fruit was fragrant.

As I nibbled some sliced mango, he explained, "First you need to take the TOFEL test. That's to make sure you speak English well enough." He laughed. "Even though you speak better than me."

"I. Better than I. The verb is understood; the pronoun is in the nominative case," I said.

"I stand corrected," he said. "Then you take the GRE, the Graduate Record Exam, and you're all set to apply for a position. With your grades, it will be no problem."

The problem was not the exams. Over the next few weeks Phillip helped me register and fill out the applications. The TOFEL test was easy. The GRE had difficult questions, but I felt confident that I had done well. The problem was Joyce. She was delighted when she read my speech in the Nairobi newspaper and saw her name, but she was irritated that I was interested in graduate school.

"Phillip put you up to this, didn't he? He's just trying to take you away from me."

"No, Joyce, he's not. He is trying to help me achieve my potential. If I can get a master's or doctorate in public health, I can work for the government or even a nongovernment organization and make a difference in this country." I felt like stamping my foot.

She wouldn't listen. We argued several nights in a row, and her solution was to shut herself in her room. After that, we had many silent meals, even though Phillip returned to Kisii country to gather more data. His "taking advantage of me," as she said, was not up for discussion. I couldn't convince her otherwise.

But in the tailor shop, I helped Joyce arrange an accounting system on the computer. She surprised me by how easily she adjusted her accounting to the computer, considering her initial resistance. She learned fast, even seeming to have knack for it. Discussing her finances was an area of healthy communication between us.

When Phillip returned from his field research, he came to the tailor shop to see my GRE score. "That's higher than mine. Kitzi, that means you're smarter than me." He gave me a hug. "You are one amazing woman."

No one had ever told me that I was amazing or a woman. Even my mother had never said that. It was gratifying to think that this man considered me a woman and thought that I was amazing. I was sure he loved me. Was this real, or was I dreaming?

"Joyce, you have turned this caterpillar of a Kisii girl into a giant butterfly. I heard at graduation that she gave you all the credit," Phillip said.

"I fed her and put a roof over her head," she said. I sensed that she did not want to even answer him.

"She credits you with her very survival," Phillip added. "She has never said a single unkind word about you."

"I am glad that she has done well. She has an education. Now she needs to do some work," Joyce replied.

"I put all the receivables into the computer this morning, Joyce. Phillip and I would like to spend some time together. Is that all right?" I asked.

"Go," she said as she scrambled into the back room.

"I'll be back soon." There was no response. Phillip took my hand, and we walked out the door. I waved good-bye, but Joyce wasn't there.

"The last step is to apply to Boston College," he said, putting his arm around my waist. "I know they will accept you. I'll send for an application. You might even be able to do it online. Hey, let's go to my place. I have an Internet hookup. Let's see if we can do it that way."

His place was a suite at the top of the New Stanley Hotel. He used a pass key on the elevator. Three large rooms opened to a skyline view of Nairobi. "This is where you live?" I was amazed.

"When I'm not in the bush," he said.

"Isn't it expensive?" I took in the view through the picture window out over the city.

"Not really. I need a pleasant, safe place to work through my data." He took my hand and toured me through the kitchenette, the bright living room, and the spacious bedroom. We stopped at the desk. He opened his computer, which lit up at a touch. "Pull up a chair."

In no time the Boston College website flashed onto the screen. He clicked on the application and typed as I dictated. He claimed that the connection was slow, but it only took a few minutes for the website to acknowledge receiving my application.

"Let's take a break," he said with a flourish.

"What kind of a break?" *Was Joyce right? Is he going to take advantage of me now, rape me? Will he want to have sex because he helped me?* I suddenly realized that nobody knew I was in this big suite at the top of the hotel. My heart raced like a Thompson gazelle cornered by a lion. Was I the carrion for this vulture? I searched Phillip's face.

"I pretty much finished my data collection for my project. I was thinking of going down to Mombasa to get some sunshine before heading back to Boston. Sun and sand—what do you say? You want to go?"

"Sounds like fun." I relaxed. "I've dreamed of seeing the ocean. I used to swim in the river by our village all the time." I covered my face. "But I'm ashamed."

"Why are you ashamed?" he asked.

"I don't have a swimsuit. When I swam in the river back home, I didn't wear one." I blushed despite my black skin.

"Wish I could have seen that," he said.

I slapped his shoulder. "Phillip, I'm embarrassed."

"Don't worry. I'll buy you a swimsuit," he said.

We made plans. He showed me the Internet sites of several resorts on the coast north of Mombasa.

"I'll rent a car. We can leave on Wednesday when there is less traffic," said Phillip.

I wiggled my toes in my shoes. "I'm excited. I've always wanted to smell the brine and feel the sand between my toes." I shook my head. "But I'll have to talk to Joyce."

"I know."

Mombasa

"ABSOLUTELY NOT," JOYCE SHOUTED. SHE was so angry she could hardly talk. She stopped planting her flowers and slammed her garden trowel on a rock. "You can't go. I forbid it." She spat the words at me.

"Joyce, I am a grown woman. I like Phillip. I might even love him. He's a Christian man." She cringed at the word. "If he planned to take advantage of me, wouldn't he have already done so? We were alone in his apartment for hours and nothing happened. He didn't even kiss me."

"You should have never been alone with him in his apartment. That's sinful and disgraceful." She stood to face me. "I'm surprised you even told me."

"I'm sorry. Nothing happened." I lowered my voice to a whisper. "Besides, I want to see the ocean."

"No," she said as she picked up her walking stick and swung it at me. "It is too dangerous."

The swinging stick brought back memories of my uncle. I suddenly felt defiant. "You can't stop me."

She shook her stick at my face. "If he has sex with you, young lady, you are no longer welcome in this house."

"What if I marry him? Then are we allowed to have sex? Isn't that what Christians do, Joyce, get married and have sex?" I stormed into the house to pick up the bag I had packed.

"I love you, Joyce, more than anyone in the world, but I have to do this."

I stormed down the alley to where Phillip was waiting in the rental vehicle.

It was a long drive. I was so upset I couldn't even talk for the first hour. Then I noticed the changing topography. I had studied the land formations and the various ecosystems of Kenya in geography class, but to see the terrain change as we traveled was so different from reading about it in a book. As I observed the people along the road, I could tell that they were from different tribes. It seemed strange to have lived in Kenya all my life and not realized its diversity.

We stopped overnight at Tsavo Park. Phillip hired a guide who took us out to see the herds. I was impressed as a herd of zebra engulfed the vehicle. When I had walked across the Rift Valley, I had been frightened. But from the safety of an automobile, it was a pleasure.

"Look at the elephants," he shouted, pointing out his window.

I stared at the massive creatures and slid down in my seat. "They're huge."

Phillip teased, "Of course—what did you expect?"

"I'm glad that I didn't see elephants when I was traversing the Rift Valley. I probably would have died of fright." After a while, I sat up in the seat, curiosity overcoming my fear.

"Aren't they beautiful?" Phillip said. I nodded.

We drove over a small hill, and in the shade of a large tree was a pride of lions. I almost screamed when the guide pointed them out because I hadn't seen them as we rolled to a stop in front of the tree. We sat for an hour watching the male pace around the tree. The female nurtured her cubs. *I am glad I didn't fall asleep under that tree*, I thought.

That night we stayed in tent lodging, had supper around a campfire, and heard stories that the Maasai told to tourists. I didn't mind. It was comical, and I was exhausted by the time we headed for our cots.

After an early breakfast, cooked just outside our tent, we drove southeast toward Mombasa. When the ocean came into view, my heart jumped in my chest. I strained my eyes to the horizon, perceiving water and more water, as far as I could see.

"What is on the other side?" I asked.

"India," Phillip replied.

"Of course. I knew that," I said, recalling the world map.

"You asked," he said.

"It was a rhetorical question," I snipped.

"I knew that." His tone was sarcastic, and I swatted him.

As we drove along the oceanfront, I watched the waves lick the sand. It was such a gentle sound. It was midday, and the sun was warm. I opened my window, even though the air conditioner was on, to feel the sun on my arms and to catch the smell of salt water and the fragrance of the tropical flowers blooming along the grassy hills. I stuck my tongue in the air and tasted a hint of fish. I noticed the trails leading to the beach through the haze of hot, humid air. "Look, Phillip, a camel."

He slowed and pulled to the side of the road so that we could watch the camel and driver walk down the beach. "I can arrange a camel ride if you would like."

"I would love it."

We turned off the road where a sign pointed to the Serena Beach Hotel and Spa. The lobby featured white stucco, with wall tapestries and pictures of Kenya. As I wandered through the lobby, I got the sense that I would be content to stay here the rest of my life. Oil paintings and watercolors of elephants, hippopotamuses, and lions hung next to photographs of tribal people in ritual dress. I wandered while Phillip checked in, but I kept my eye on him for fear that I would get lost. The lobby was a massive museum of my country's cultural diversity, from Maasai and Kisii to Arab and even Portuguese.

"This is so beautiful. I have never been in such a palace. Are you sure this is where we're staying?" I caught his eye. "Or are you teasing me?"

Phillip hugged me. "Here's the room key. The next stop on the tour is our room."

I cringed. *Our room? Are we staying in the same room? Sleeping in the same bed? Was Joyce right? Now he is going to take advantage of me. Now I am defenseless.* Phillip opened the door. I gasped. The room was bigger than our house in Kisii and Joyce's house combined.

"This is our room?" I trembled. Was it from dread or excitement? I didn't know which.

"Just for the two of us," he said.

I wandered through the sitting room like a lost goat. In the bedroom, there was only one bed, but it was huge. A whole family of Kisii could sleep in it. I touched the bedspread, red in Maasai print. There was a fruit bowl and bouquet of flowers.

Phillip smiled. "They knew we were coming."

A terrace off the bedroom featured a panorama of the Indian Ocean. I opened the sliding doors to a breeze blowing the smells of the sea to my nostrils. Phillip hugged me.

"This is more beautiful than a Kisii girl deserves," I said. He kissed me. He had never kissed me like that before.

"The tide is in. Do you want to go for a swim?" he asked.

There was a knock on the door. Phillip let in the bellhop, who placed his suitcase and my bag in the closet. Phillip gave him some shillings, and he backed out the door, looking quite pleased.

He grabbed his suitcase and produced a package wrapped in golden paper with a white bow. "Here's your swimsuit."

I opened it to find small pieces of fabric tied together with strings. "This is a swimsuit?"

"It is more than you said you wore when you went swimming in the river back home." He took the top and placed it over my dress. "It ties in the back. And this is your bikini bottom. It ties on the sides."

Unsure how this miniscule fabric was supposed to cover my thighs, I took it from him and headed into the bathroom. "I'm taking a shower," I yelled through the door. "We have a very nice shower."

As the hot water washed the travel sweat off me, I wondered, *There is only one bed. We're not married. Am I supposed to sleep on the couch?* I washed with the scented soap. There was even shampoo for my hair and oil to rub on my skin when I finished. The bikini sat on the counter by the sink. *Phillip calls this a swimsuit?* I put on the bottom and fumbled with the strings. It barely covered my groin. I looked at myself in the mirror. *This bikini thing does not cover my thighs.* I had never let a man see my thighs. I have worked in the maize fields topless but always had my kitamba. I wrapped a towel around my waist.

"Are you almost done in there?" he yelled through the door.

"Come on in. I can't figure out how to tie all these strings on the top," I said.

He came into the bathroom wearing a swimsuit and showed me how to tie the top. There were two terrycloth bathrobes hanging by the door. He took the larger one and handed me the other. "Put on this bathrobe, and we'll head to the beach."

"I prefer my kitamba." I pulled out my bag, dropped the towel, and wrapped up in my kitamba. "Ready?"

He put the room key in his bathrobe pocket, and we headed toward the beach. "First I want to show you the garden," he said. We walked through a tropical paradise full of fragrant plants. Palm trees on each side of the path led to two observation stations, each vista more exotic than the previous. At the end of the garden, we found ourselves at a crossroad. "Beach or pool?"

"Beach. I want to swim in the ocean." We turned toward the beach, and I pulled him back. "Am I allowed on the beach in this swimsuit?"

"Certainly," he said. "There will probably be women there in even less."

"You're sure?" I said doubtfully.

"Come on—I'll show you," Phillip said.

The ocean was immense. I ran just to feel the surf tickle my toes. I had never experienced such a smell. It contained a whole world: sharp but gentle, fragrant yet poignant. I loved the continuous roar of the surf beyond the reef and the lapping of the waves at my feet. It was surreal.

Phillip took off his robe, folded it, and placed it on a table under an umbrella. He took my kitamba and laid it beside his robe. I felt naked as we jumped into the waves, but no one seemed to notice. Phillip's tug on my arm changed my focus. We swirled and twisted in the surf, pulled by the undertow and splashed by each successive wave. Exhilarated, I stood to catch my breath. Phillip, heading for shore, turned and laughed at my antics. I dived again and surfaced. My top came askew, and I twisted it back in place as I walked toward him.

"You're like a dolphin in the water," he said as he gave me a towel so I could dry off. Then I quickly wrapped in my kitamba. I was breathless. We rested on deck chairs in the shade of an umbrella. A waiter appeared to offer us drinks. Phillip ordered something for me.

"Is this my graduation present?" I asked.

"And more," he said.

I couldn't fathom anything more. He closed his eyes, but I was too excited. When the waiter came, he set a large glass with a big straw on the small table beside me. I sipped it. "Oh, guava juice—this is my favorite." I relaxed in my chair and scanned the infinity of the ocean. The blue-green waves splashed foam on the crystal-white shore; the movement was repetitive yet exhilarating.

I turned to observe what the other women on the beach were wearing. I saw that they were wearing bikinis similar to mine. Even mothers with children were wearing bikinis. Weren't they self-conscious that the men could see their thighs? Some of them had flabby thighs and stretch marks from pregnancy, yet they did not seem embarrassed. I watched as a waiter served lunch to a family. They did not even wait for their men before they started eating. After much deliberation, I untied my kitamba and let it slip onto the deck chair. No one paid any attention.

Phillip turned in his deck chair and sighed. He opened one eye. "Ready for another swim?"

He grabbed my hand and, before I could answer, lifted me off my chair. We ran into the ocean. The salt water stung my eyes. I jumped up and rubbed them.

"I'm sorry. Did the salt water get in your eyes?"

"I wanted to see what was in the water. I forgot."

"I'll get you some goggles. I'm sure they have some, maybe even snorkels," he said.

"What are snorkels?" I asked.

"You can breathe through them while watching what's under the water," he explained.

"Oh, so we can see the fish?"

In no time, a man called the water-sports director had supplied us with gear. My eyes felt better, and we swam together along the breakwater. I was enchanted by the ebb and flow of the waves and the crystal-clear water dappled with sunshine. But most enchanting were the multicolored fish. The snorkeling took some practice. At first I tried to breathe at the wrong time, but I finally relaxed enough to breathe correctly with my face in the water. Soon I was exhausted from fighting the current. I stood to catch my breath.

Phillip put his arm around my waist. "Isn't this great?"

His hand was touching bare skin. No one had ever held me like this. My heart pounded my ribs. "It's great. I'm so happy."

"Race you back to shore." I was winning until he turned toward a shower on the beach. "To wash off the salt," he explained.

We showered together. Phillip put on his robe, and I wrapped up in my kitamba. My heart slowed.

We returned the equipment and walked back to the hotel, stopping at the pool.

"No salt here," he said as he jumped in. There were many women lying around the pool in bikinis. I decided that it must be proper in Mombasa to let men see your thighs. I took off my kitamba and folded it, watching to see if I drew attention. Nothing happened. Phillip was swimming laps across the pool, so I joined him.

"This water does not sting my eyes, but it has an odd smell," I said.

"That's chlorine," Phillip said. He saw the confusion on my face. "Like Javel for swimming pools."

Joyce always washed the fresh vegetables in Javel to keep us from getting diarrhea. "So they put that in the water so that we don't get sick from swimming?"

"Exactly," Phillip said, enticing me to swim across the pool.

I was learning too many things at once. It was giving me a headache, even though I was happier than I had ever been in my life. After swimming, we stretched out on the deck chairs and absorbed the welcome sunshine. A waiter came with fruit juice and coconut milk. I turned to Phillip. "Is this expensive? Should I have some?"

"It's already paid for," he said.

"It is? How does the resort know what I'm going to drink?" I asked. It seemed like an innocent question.

"Kitzi, you are so comical." He chuckled.

"Are you laughing at me, Phillip Schoenberg?" I scolded.

"I am only laughing at the way you make me feel," he confessed.

"Oh, then it's all right to laugh at me, is it?"

When we returned to our room, Phillip locked the door behind us. I felt a sense of panic. I went to the water closet—or bathroom, as Phillip called it—and took another shower. I needed time to think. *What is happening? Do I love Phillip? Does he love me? I have never felt this way about a man before.* I thought about obnoxious Reuben. Caleb the book salesman was friendly, but our relationship was not going past tea and biscuits. I liked Mokoli but could not trespass the territory of his fat girlfriend. But Phillip was different.

Soap bubbles tickled my breasts. The shower stream was soothing as I rinsed off and spent a long time drying. I squeezed the water out of the tiny pieces of cloth called a bikini and hung them on the towel rack. I wrapped my kitamba around me, tied it at my shoulder, took a deep breath, and opened the door.

The Proposal

I OPENED THE DOOR TO see Phillip naked and blurted, "Are you going to rape me in this beautiful place?"

Phillip held two boxes in his hand and said, "No, silly." He got down on one knee and held out the boxes. "I'm going to ask you to marry me."

I took the longer box, trying to avoid staring at him. "Why are you called white? You're mostly pink."

"Will you marry a pink man?" he asked.

The box was wrapped with ribbon, which I struggled to untie. "Now that I am a university graduate, I am worth ten cows."

I had no idea why I had said such a thing. When I untied the stubborn ribbon and opened the larger box, tears welled in my eyes. I took the necklace from the box and counted nine diamonds along its length. They sparkled through my tears.

He stood up, took the necklace from me, and clasped it around my neck. He held out the smaller box. "Here, open this one. It's more important."

The small box contained two rings. He put the diamond ring on my finger. "There. Are ten diamonds equivalent to ten cows?"

He touched each of the nine around my neck, counting

them in Ekegusii, and then touched the tenth diamond on my hand to his lips.

I said nothing. I twisted my hand to allow the oblique light from the picture window to sparkle through my diamond ring. At one angle the light refracted into a rainbow.

"Will you marry me?" he repeated, holding the wedding band to my finger.

I pulled back and touched each of the stones, counting them again. Emotion congested my chest. I tried to respond, but my voice was only a mutter.

"Naigotire. I am satisfied to marry you."

It was embarrassing to see a naked man laugh. I had seen naked men before when my girlfriends and I snuck down to the river to watch the men bathe, but to hold Phillip's flanks and feel his muscles convulse was a new sensation. My embarrassment turned to joy.

He untied my kitamba. It dropped to the floor. "I may be pink, but you sure are black." He caressed my breasts, spinning his finger around my nipples. "They look just like Oreo cookies."

"What are Oreo cookies?" I asked.

"I'll show you when we get to Boston." His hands finished exploring my breasts and then wandered over my flanks, belly, and buttocks. Then he hugged me. I was paralyzed and stunned to feel his arousal. I pushed him away.

"You are touching me like you want to have sexual intercourse with me. When are we to be married?" I demanded.

He turned to pull his briefcase out of the closet. I giggled to see his buttocks wiggle. I ran my fingers along the tan line at his waist. It seemed odd not to be able to feel the transition. He shuffled through the papers and pulled out a certificate.

"Remember the papers I had you sign for your application to graduate school?"

"Yes," I replied, curious as to the reason he asked.

"Did you read them all very carefully?"

"I think so."

"One was an application for a marriage license." I scanned the paper, recognizing my signature. "If you are willing, I have made arrangements for us to be married tomorrow."

I read the certificate line by line. I was stalling. "It's legal. It even has the stamp of the Kenyan Government on top."

I flipped the paper over. "You have been very sneaky and clandestine … but I accept your proposal."

"The minister will be here at ten o'clock in the morning. This is our honeymoon," he shouted, twirling around the room.

"Is he a Christian minister? Joyce wants me to have a Christian wedding."

"He's Lutheran," Phillip said. "Just like me."

I was giddy. I danced and jumped around the room, no longer conscious that I was naked. His eyes followed my every move.

"Will we be legally married tomorrow?" I asked.

"Yes," he said.

I stopped and stared into his eyes. "Will I be a woman then?"

I could tell that the question befuddled him. He twisted his face. "You will be my wife then."

Phillip's body delighted my eyes. I traced my fingers across his abdominal muscles and down his thighs. His magical response recurred. I kissed him, compressing my breasts into his chest. "You like the feel of Oreo cookies?" I asked in a breathless voice.

"Yes," he said, barely able to catch his breath.

"We should wait until tomorrow, after we are legally married, but my body seems primed to copulate with you."

My mind was racing. "So, let's have sexual intercourse," I shouted and pushed him on the bed.

"You and your vocabulary, Kwamboka."

Wedding

My WEDDING DAY STARTED WITH a trip to the spa. Although Phillip and I were naked on a table, the masseurs were discreet with their towels. Besides, they were all women. I was more concerned about them seeing my husband-to-be as we were rubbed and oiled and even had hot rocks placed down our spine. I dressed in the nicest dress Joyce had made me. Phillip offered to buy me a new dress at the shop at the resort, but I said, "No, I prefer to wear the dress Joyce made for me since she is not here to celebrate with us."

The wedding was on the beach under a canopy. I recognized the words from the weddings I had attended at Joyce's AIM church. Jesus promised to protect our marriage. Phillip and I vowed to love each other forever, even if we got sick. I played our vows over and over in my mind as the minister prayed for us, ending with, "In Jesus Christ's name, amen."

At noon we joined other couples who had been married at the resort. The manager came to congratulate all of us. "I am so pleased that you have honored Serena Beach Hotel and Spa by choosing to marry here," he said. With a bow and a smile, he ushered us into the seafood buffet.

"Do you really mean those words you promised in our ceremony?" I asked Phillip as we sat down with our plates of food. "Or is this just a ritual?"

"Yes," Phillip said. "I promise with all my heart."

"Even if I get sick and don't give you any children?" I asked.

"Even then," he answered.

"Even when I get old and scraggly?" I continued with my barrage of questions.

"Yes, even then," he patiently answered.

"What if my thighs get flabby?" I continued.

"Kwamboka, I promise to love you forever."

I dipped a piece of crab into the sauce. It was so spicy that I grabbed my mouth, but it was good. I had never eaten at a buffet before and couldn't believe that I could just take anything I wanted. I looked around to see if anyone was keeping track of what I ate.

"Will I be your only wife?" I asked. "You won't need another one?"

"Yes—I mean, no. I will not need another one."

I had not eaten lobster before. The taste was exotic, and the fried fish was different from the fish we caught in the river back home. "And you are promising today to love me till one of us dies?"

"No matter what happens." Phillip sipped his champagne. I tasted mine, but after a couple of sips, I felt dizzy and decided to leave it. Besides, the bubbles made me sneeze.

"Until one of us drops dead?" I took a bite of the pasta. In Nairobi we ate hot pasta with tomato sauce, but this pasta was cold with a creamy cheese sauce and shrimp.

"Yes, till then." He took my left hand and twisted the wedding band around on my finger. "I promise."

He kissed my hand. "Did you know that everything I own now belongs to you?"

I swallowed and wiped my fingers and mouth with the serviette. "Oh, what do I own now?"

"Me." He held up his champagne glass. I toasted his glass

with mine and took another small sip. "Congratulations, Mrs. Kwamboka Schoenberg."

"Besides you, what do I own?"

"You wouldn't believe it if I told you."

It was two weeks of wonders. We sailed, rode a camel, went deep-sea fishing, and snorkeled, not to mention ate at countless buffets and drank many glasses of mango juice at the pool every day. Phillip got sunburned, so I had to lather him with sunscreen. He said that he was jealous of my black skin.

One day we took the free resort shuttle to Mombasa. It took over an hour to get there. As we drove under the tusks at the entrance to the city, Phillip said that almost a million people lived here. On the streets I saw lots of tourists, so I thought there were more than a million. When I saw poor people begging at the market, I felt guilty that I had eaten so well at the breakfast buffet. Then some young girls dressed in fancy clothes caught my eye. "Prostitutes, transactional sex workers," Phillip explained.

Many of the people seemed to be Moslem, and I recognized the mosques from what I had seen in books. I was wearing another dress Joyce had made for me with my kitamba wrapped around my waist. When I saw the Moslem women, I wrapped my kitamba to cover my head. That met with several nods of approval.

The shops were filled with carvings, baskets, and handcrafts. Phillip told me that I could buy anything I wanted, but I was too overwhelmed to decide. I didn't buy anything, but it was fun shopping.

We ate lunch at the Zanzibar Café and listened to Taarab music while we ate. I was thankful to not have to choose at a buffet. Phillip ordered for me. I was too distracted by the musicians to even look at the menu.

In the afternoon, we toured Fort Jesus, built by the Portuguese in 1593. It had nothing to do with the Jesus Joyce read about in the Bible. We had a good walk, and our guide taught us some history of Kenya that I had never read in the history books in school.

When we returned to the Serena Beach Hotel and Spa, there was still time to walk on the beach. The tide was out, and we searched for curious creatures in the tide pools.

"Kwamboka, look at this." I hurried to see what treasure he had found. In one of the coral tide pools were little fish of all different colors swimming around.

"How lovely," I said. I was wearing my bikini, but now that I was married, I felt more comfortable. If this was how my husband wanted me dressed, then it was all I needed to wear. I had not even brought my kitamba. Several times I caught him looking at my thighs, but there weren't any other men walking the tide pools. Besides, he was allowed that privilege now.

We squatted to look at the fish.

"I love you, Kitzi," he said. His tone was so sweet.

"Now that we are married, Phillip, please do not use my made-up name. That is a girl's nickname. I am now a woman and your wife. I like being Mrs. Schoenberg, but my husband should always call me Kwamboka."

He stood up and put his hand across his chest. "Now that we are married, I promise to always call you Kwamboka." His antics were so funny.

By the end of the two weeks, we had done more things than I had ever dreamed of doing in my whole life. I had eaten things I didn't know one could eat. I lost count of how many times we had sexual intercourse. I didn't understand why it was so humorous, but Phillip laughed every time I whispered in his ear, "I enjoy copulating with you."

Thursday evening at supper we made plans for me to go to Boston. Phillip already had a ticket to return to the United States when we got back from our honeymoon. He would arrange for me to join him when he got settled.

"We need to get you a passport with your married name. We should go to the US embassy," he chattered as I ate my crab meat. "We'll go to Barclay's and get you a credit card. Then you can charge your ticket and join me in Boston."

He grabbed my hand. "You can use the credit card to buy anything you want. You are a wealthy woman now."

"I am?" My eyes glistened.

All good things on earth eventually come to an end. It had been a great honeymoon, but now we had things to do. I had much to explain to Joyce. I felt a cramp in my belly as I packed my bag. I ran to the bathroom and found that my menses had started.

"Did you have a good time?" Phillip asked as we drove under the Serena Beach Resort and Spa sign.

I leaned back in the seat and stretched. "I thought I was in heaven. I am filled with joy and lots of your sperm."

His face flushed, and he laughed. "Kwamboka, I never know what is going to come out of your mouth."

We turned onto the main road. I saw the kilometer sign for Nairobi. We would be back in Nairobi in eight hours.

"You will have to try again," I said.

"Try what again?" Phillip asked.

"Filling me with sperm. My menses started today. You did

not make a baby yet, Phillip, but I am filled with the joy of our honeymoon." As darkness filled the sky, I wondered whether the joy would last.

HIV-AIDS

"I HAVE SOME ERRANDS TO run," Phillip said as he dropped me off in front of Joyce's tailor shop. "Meet me at the Thorn Tree Café at about six o'clock. We'll have something to eat before I head to the airport."

"All right," I said as I jumped out of the rental car. "Don't be late."

We had just been to Barclay's. I had a shiny new credit card. Phillip let me try it in the ATM. I pressed the button to view my balance when he wasn't looking. I owned millions of shillings.

I bounced into the shop. "I had a great time, Joyce."

With a critical gaze, she glanced up from her sorted receipts. I put my left hand on top of her papers. The diamond sparkled in the sunlight coming through the shop window. "I'm a married woman now."

"So you did have sex with him," Joyce snarled in dismay.

"Not till we were married." I almost told the truth. "It's legal. I have the papers. I am only sorry that you couldn't come to the wedding."

Silence.

"I know you don't approve of Phillip, but I love him. And he proposed, so I married him." I withdrew my hand.

"Is he taking you to Boston?" she asked in a hushed tone.

"His plane leaves tonight at ten o'clock. I need to get some

115

papers from the embassy, a visa, before I can join him. He is going to find us a nice apartment in Boston. Maybe you can even come and visit us there. Would you like that? Phillip says that it isn't far away if you take an airplane."

"Do you honestly believe that, Kitzi?" she screeched.

I knew that I was being scolded. "Yes I do, Joyce." She was no longer my mother. I was a married woman now.

She closed the shop, and I followed her home, trying to explain our plans. She listened but just grunted her responses.

When we got home, I changed clothes, put my necklace and wedding rings in my leather pouch, and stashed my things in the corner out of the way.

"Why aren't you wearing your rings?" Joyce said. "Are you ashamed of him already?"

"No." I put my hands on my hips. I felt a twinge of menstrual cramps. "I'm meeting him at the Thorn Tree Café and then seeing him off at the airport. I don't want to wear jewelry in downtown Nairobi. You know it isn't safe. You're the one who told me that."

He was late. When he did arrive with suitcases in tow, he looked ashen. He sat across from me at the circular table and bit his knuckles.

"I might as well be blunt. This is no time to be dishonest." He heaved a sigh. "My HIV test is positive, Kwamboka."

He caressed my hand as the tears flowed down his face. "I just found out. I went to the clinic before we went to Mombasa to have them screen for tropical diseases. They drew a HIV test. I have AIDS. I am so sorry. We should have used condoms. I'm sorry. I am so sorry."

He wept like a lost child. "I've destroyed the life of the

one person I love the most in the whole world." He started to tremble.

"How did you get HIV?" I was numb. I didn't even know what to ask, but the question came out.

"You changed me, Kwamboka. I have not had sex with anyone since the first day I met you in your anthropology class."

He rubbed the sweat off his forehead with his serviette. "But before I met you, I was doing research in the Serengeti."

His neck muscles convulsed as he swallowed. "I had sex with any village girl who would not tell her father." He added with a sardonic laugh, "Condoms are hard to find in the bush."

He beat his head with his fist. "Why was I so stupid?"

He focused on his wristwatch. "Oh, shit, I've got to get to the airport."

He waved shillings at the waiter. He had not drunk any of his tea. "Here," he said, handing me a card with his address and a hundred-dollar bill. "Get tested. That should be enough money to start antiretroviral drugs if you're positive. Write me."

He turned and said in a tender voice through his tears, "If you want to annul our marriage, go ahead. I deserve it." He kissed me as tears dripped onto his shirt. Then he grabbed his luggage and ran to the hotel van.

I didn't know what to do. The waiter picked up the shillings. "May I finish my tea?" I asked.

"Of course, madam. Would you care for anything else?"

"No, thank you." I felt nauseated.

I stared out at the street as Phillip climbed into the New Stanley Hotel van. *Phillip had HIV-AIDS, and I had sex with him the whole two weeks—unprotected, wet, gooey sex. And just before I menstruated. Isn't that the most dangerous time? I must be infected.*

Where should I go? Where should I get tested? I ran my

fingers over the hundred-dollar bill and Phillip's office card. I tried to read the address, but my eyes would not focus. The words meant nothing.

I bowed my head and recalled my father wasting away, eating and then vomiting. I remembered the uncontrolled diarrhea just before he died and the coarse rattle of his breathing. That was what was going to happen to Phillip … and then to me.

I stood up and looked around the café. My legs felt like they would collapse. Others were waiting for the table. My special good-bye to the man I loved was ruined. We were both dying. I tried to cry, but my eyes were dry. Phillip must have felt horrible, maybe worse than I felt. He had killed me.

I looked at the card and forced my eyes to see the numbers dancing at the bottom. Would I ever get to call that number? Would I ever see him again? Should I just throw the card away? But I was married to him. The voice of the minister echoed in my head: "till death."

What was Joyce going to say? I stuffed the card and the money in my pocket as I left the café. Where should I go? Joyce was going to be angry and say that she told me this would happen. She didn't want me to go to Mombasa in the first place. She told me not to go, but I was stubborn. Would she kick me out of the house? I supposed I was an orphan again. I didn't belong anywhere.

I walked with elegance to disguise my grief. Kisii girls do not show their anguish. Once on the street, I just couldn't decide where to go. The doorman at the New Stanley Hotel smiled at me. "Have a good evening, madam."

Which way? Right or left? Did it matter? I turned left. The streets looked dirty and congested. Behind me the thorn tree, from which the café got its name, no longer held messages from my beloved. My romantic feelings for the little round tables, the tree growing in the middle of the restaurant, and the message board were dissipated. My future was gone. I should have let Uncle Osiemo kill me. *Maybe I should walk back to Kisii and let him. He could beat me with his stick and let the mob burn me in a ditch.*

My feet throbbed as I walked, not knowing where. Was the virus circulating in my blood already, poisoning my cells? How long would it take to kill me? The sweet stench of rotting fruit discarded along the road mixed with the smell of urine and feces made me realize that I didn't know where I was.

Kidnapped

TWO MEN IN POLICE UNIFORMS approached. I let them pass. I thought about asking them for directions, but before I could turn and open my mouth, they grabbed me from behind. Their grip was painful and crude. "We've been watching you, whore. Don't you know that prostitution is illegal in Kenya?"

I tried to wrench free, but one pulled out a gun and pointed it at my forehead. "I'm not a prostitute. I'm a student at Nairobi University," I pled.

"We'll see about that," the one with the gun said.

I tried to scream, but one of them shoved a rag in my mouth to gag me while the other blindfolded me and pushed me headfirst into the backseat of a car. One sat on each side of me.

"Now be a good little whore and sit still," he said. "Then this gun won't blow off your face.

"Step on it," he yelled to the driver and we sped around a corner.

I could tell from the lessening sounds of traffic that we were driving outside the city. It was almost an hour before we stopped. They pushed me out of the car and pulled off the blindfold as the driver sped away. I strained to catch a glimpse of the driver, but I couldn't.

The sight of a building with rusted fixtures and trash blowing across cracked clay suggested that we had arrived at an abandoned warehouse. They twisted my arms to force me through a rusted steel door. One light illuminated a myriad of ceiling pipes and vents. The ceiling was falling down in places, and except for the door we entered, the inside doors to empty rooms were falling off their hinges.

"You're not policemen," I shouted when they removed the gag. "Did my uncle send you to kill me?"

But there was no reason to yell. No one else could hear me, and neither of the two answered me. They jerked me inside a building and threw me onto the cement floor. Rats scattered.

"We have a bright one this time, Faraji."

He laughed as he bound a rope around my hands, swung it over a low pipe, and then yanked my arms up over my head. I could just barely stand on my tiptoes.

"And pretty too, Chuki," said the one holding the gun. A table in the middle of the room had two chairs. Obviously, I would not be sitting much tonight. Faraji set the gun on the table.

"Don't kick, now, or we'll have to tie you tighter." Chuki tied my ankles to a trashed wheel rim. At least now I had something to stand on.

"You may scream now as much as you want. But no one can hear you."

Faraji laughed. "Come on, let's hear you scream. It gets us all excited."

I remained silent. He tickled my chin. "Just a little scream."

I refused. Kisii girls are taught from the time we are young not to respond to physical threats, much less verbal harassment. These two did not understand Kisii girls.

"Now, whore, let's see what you got," said Chuki as he dug in my pockets. "No ID. Faraji, imagine that. Nothing we have to be careful to destroy. What's your name, sweets?"

He set the items on the table to examine. Holding up the hundred-dollar bill to the light, he said, "We hit a gold mine,

Faraji. Look at this. It's the best we have ever done. You must be one of those high-class whores."

"Our little bonus," said Faraji.

"Madame Mimi always says that we can keep anything we find on them, right?"

His grin was breaking his face. "Yes, anything we find."

He pocketed the money and looked at Phillip's card. "She fucked an anthropology professor."

He threw the card in the waste can beside the table. "Are you ready to see what kind of a whore we've got, Faraji?"

"Yeah, let's take off her clothes." He seemed very eager.

I wanted to scream, but that would only make things worse. Death seemed sweeter than humiliation as Faraji unbuttoned my blouse and cut my bra. Chuki bounced my breasts in his hands.

"Nice and firm," he said. "She hasn't had any babies yet to make them all droopy. Let's pull down her pants." He clapped his hands in anticipation.

Faraji pulled my pants down to my ankles and then my panties. "Beautiful, no stretch marks." He ran his fingers over my belly and down my thighs, inspecting for flaws.

"Can I do her right now?" said Chuki. "This is the prettiest one we've ever kidnapped."

He grabbed my flank, twisted me around, and squeezed my buttocks. "Nice tone."

"No," Faraji said. "You're too rough. Your prick is too big."

They howled at their joke. Faraji became serious. "You bruised the last one so badly that Madame Mimi cut the price. No, this one will fetch us more schillings than all the others put together, plus this hundred-dollar bonus."

"Come on, let me just fuck her once. I'll be gentle," he coaxed.

"No," Faraji said, slapping Chuki's head. "What don't you understand about finances?"

Chuki sat down on one of the chairs, rubbed the welt on

his face, and then pulled down his pants. "Looking at her won't lower her price."

"Stop it," said Faraji as he pulled up my pants, pulled my blouse together, and buttoned the middle button.

"Now what did you do that for?" pleaded Chuki. "Can't I at least look at the merchandise? Come on, just another little peek. I wasn't done."

"Shut up, Chuki."

I felt like a criminal waiting on death row. Now I was going to be sold to Madame Mimi, whoever she was. I set my jaw and stared at my kidnappers. They would not get the satisfaction of a response from a Kisii girl. The rope burned around my wrists, and my arm muscles cramped. It had been a very long, bad day. I was sure all this was planned by my uncle. Right now, I hated my uncle.

Sold

"I HAVE TO PEE," I managed to squeeze out in a little voice.

"Pee your pants. See if I care," said Chuki.

"If I do, my thighs will get all red and raw. You'll lose money on me," I said.

Faraji looked up from the newspaper that he was reading, "She's right. What's wrong with you? Take her to the water closet, Chuki."

Chuki seemed reluctant, even disappointed. I suppose once they sold me, he would have to pay for sex, and he preferred to get it free. He untied my legs from the wheel frame and then my hands, pulled the rope off the pipe, and yanked me over to the table. I feigned falling and knocked over the trash can. I grabbed Phillip's card from the floor before Chuki yanked me to my feet.

"You clumsy whore, we don't want you all bruised up. Stay on your feet," he barked.

The water closet was a six-by-six-foot concrete room that must have been a storage closet when the building was a factory. A hole had been chipped through the concrete floor to make a crude toilet. He threw me inside and slammed the door. The ammonia of old feces and urine burned my eyes as I looked down the hole.

"I'm listening for you to piss. You better hurry or I'm coming in to watch you."

Chuki sweetened his voice. "I'd be glad to help you get started."

I squatted over the hole to urinate, making sure he could hear the urine trickling down the concrete hole. I didn't have to go, but I was intent on putting Phillip's card in a secure place inside my panties.

"What's taking so long?" Chuki yelled.

"I have to defecate too," I yelled back.

He started laughing. "Faraji, she takes a shit and calls it defa … something. She's really high class. That means big money for us."

"Now you're getting the picture, Chuki. Why does it take you so long to understand these things? Once we get paid you will have more than enough money to fuck any whore in Nairobi."

When I finished, they tied me to another pipe so that I could slump against the wall. I couldn't sleep, but at least my muscles stopped having spasms. Faraji and Chuki took turns holding the gun. When they fell asleep, I tried to free myself but couldn't. My mind fluctuated between the horrible events of the day and thoughts of how I might escape.

"Time to go," Faraji announced as dawn crept through the smudged windows.

I was blindfolded again. My wrists were retied behind my back, and I was thrown behind the seat of a clunker pickup truck. Scattered tools and greasy rags were my bed.

We drove mostly downhill. I listened for clues as we slowed down to drive through several towns and kept a mental log of the distance. About midday, the truck slowed to a stop.

"There's no one around. We'll stop here," said Faraji, who was driving. "I've got to take a piss."

They extracted me from behind the seat. It felt good to stand up. By the position of the sun on my face, I was sure were heading east. I took a deep breath, analyzing the smell of the air. It seemed familiar.

"All right, girl who has no name, this is your only chance to piss," said Chuki.

Faraji sounded intellectual. "Take advantage of this opportunity, miss."

I could tell by the grip that Chuki was the one holding the rope to my hands. He dragged me off the road and pulled down my pants. "Squat," he said.

I squatted and immediately was pricked in my buttocks by a thorn bush. I jumped in surprise.

"Oh, that was a good one," Chuki said with a boisterous laugh. He led me as I waddled forward, my pants tight around my ankles.

"Go ahead, no surprises this time." He sounded serious. "Piss to your heart's content. I promise to watch."

This time I squatted with great hesitation, anticipating another thorn bush. Feeling nothing but air, I urinated.

"Are you enjoying watching me urinate, Chuki?" I asked.

"Oh yes," he said.

"Then I thank you for the blindfold."

It was evening before we stopped again. The anticipation in their voices suggested that they expected a lot of money for my sale. When they pulled me out from behind the seat, I recognized the smell of fish and salt water. We were near the ocean.

Chuki yanked me forward into a building. I tripped on the threshold, but Faraji grabbed me. The building smelled like wet concrete, but there was also a sweet, nauseating smell of cheap perfume.

Jerked into a room, I heard a door slam shut. The still, humid air was rank with the stench of foul body odor and stale semen.

"Untie her," commanded a woman's voice, "and take off that stupid blindfold."

The woman was an imposing figure, obese yet muscular. Her black hair was straight with grease. I did not recognize her tribe. She seemed impatient. "Well, let's see the merchandise."

A massive, muscular man blocked the doorway through which I had just come. The woman, who was clearly in charge, seemed to recognize the direction of my attention.

"This is my security guard, Mwalimu. He is here to keep you safe."

"Take off your clothes," Faraji said, "so Madame can tell us what you're worth."

I pretended to be modest. After what I had been through, there was no point. I just wanted to hide Phillip's card. I turned away and slipped it into my vagina.

"Hurry up," said Chuki, "or I'll help you."

Was he anxious to see me naked or to see how much cash I would put in his pocket? I wasn't sure from the tone of his voice.

I stood naked, posturing like I had seen the man in Leonardo da Vinci's drawing. I closed my eyes and tried to relax.

"So what do you think, Madame Mimi?" Chuki asked. "Perfect, isn't she?"

"You boys did well, very well," Madame Mimi said, running her calloused hand along the form of my breast and down my flank. She squeezed my thighs, and her fingers wandered over my groin. She spread my labia, but she didn't find Phillip's card.

"No sores or cuts. So Chuki kept his fat dick out of this one?"

"Yes, Madame," said Faraji.

"Not for lack of interest," said Chuki, rubbing his pants.

"Shut up, Chuki," snapped Faraji.

"She talks funny," said Chuki, "uses big words like urinate and defa … something."

Madame Mimi gave me a kitamba. I recognized the coastal pattern. I had seen such patterns in the shops on our honeymoon. I wrapped up, even though everyone in the room had seen me naked. She grabbed my clothes off the floor before I could touch them and gave them to Faraji.

"Burn these. They might be incriminating. Mwalimu, take her to her room."

Mwalimu grabbed my arm. His grip was forceful but in an odd way gentle. Besides, there was no reason to resist now. We paused, as there were further negotiations.

"There is a little matter to settle first," said Faraji. "We took good care of her. I held Chuki off, so we expect our usual fee … and maybe a little bonus."

Madam Mimi pulled a small purse from between her huge breasts and gave Faraji a wad of money. "The bonus is for keeping Chuki's paws off her. I don't like bruises."

They bowed. "Thank you. You're so gracious."

I overheard Madame Mimi thank them as "regular suppliers," but I hoped to never see them again. If I ever had the chance, I would kill them, Chuki first. Maybe if he had raped me I could have at least infected him with HIV.

Mwalimu showed me my room. It was a concrete box without a window. A curtain hung in the doorway, but there was no door. A single lightbulb hung from the ceiling, and a suspended dowel was the closet. There was one chair in the corner. A sheet of plywood balanced on cinder blocks with a thin mattress was my bed. There was no other furniture.

He shoved me onto the bed. Madame Mimi's massive body presently filled the doorway.

"I have rules here." She paused, staring at me. "I'm sorry, I missed your name."

She hadn't asked my name. I clenched my jaw in silence and glared back at her eyes, which protruded through her fat, greasy cheeks.

"It doesn't matter," she said, apparently tired of the silence. She held her finger to her temple. "We'll call you 'Chui.' You remind me of a leopard or a black panther. 'Chui' is easy for our customers to remember."

She shifted her mass. "You're expected to entertain our clients from four o'clock until the last man is served."

She wrinkled her nose. "We don't serve lesbians here—well, sometimes some Indian or Pakistani women."

She shifted. *Her feet must be sore*, I thought. "After the last customer is served, the time is yours. But I recommend that you get some sleep. We serve our meal at eleven o'clock."

I noted the singular noun.

"If you're not at the table, you go hungry. You can eat anything in the evening that your client buys for you. Have tea anytime you want. I expect you to be clean. We have a shower, and you have till four o'clock to spruce up. I have a variety of perfumes available."

She grabbed a stick that had been leaning on the other side of the doorway. "I am very kind, and I will not beat you. It's bad for business. The customers complain about bruises. But if you misbehave, I keep all your profits. If you behave, you get 10 percent. Do you understand?"

"What can I do with the money?" I asked.

"Oh, you can talk. Great, I thought you might be mute."

She tapped her stick on the floor. "A jewelry merchant comes every Monday, our slow day. You can buy at a discount."

"Can I buy my freedom?"

"When you're ugly you're free," she said, laughing so hard

129

her massive breasts bounced. "I can't afford to feed someone none of the men want. But if you try to disfigure yourself, I will beat you till you wish you were dead. I pay dearly for my girls' looks, and I paid an extra bonus for you."

"What if I get pregnant?" I asked.

"We take care of that. But I hand out pills every mealtime to prevent it. That's bad for business too."

She waved her corpulent hand at me. "Enough questions. You missed dinner today, but many of our customers like their girls on the thin side anyway—especially the tourists."

She turned to leave the room and then hit her stick on the wall. "Get some rest. A bell will ring, and then you are required to be in the common room, straight down this hall."

She looked at the gaudy watch hanging around her neck. "In one hour, I'll introduce you to the other girls."

Mwalimu never took his eyes off me until he left through the curtain. As Madame was talking, he flexed his biceps in a nervous twitching motion. His head was shaved, and he seemed to have no sense of humor.

I looked down the hall. I noticed the reception room and the door Chuki had pushed me through. Mwalimu paused to chain the door. The hall had several doorways covered with distinctively colored curtains. I assumed they were other girls' rooms. At the far end was a doorway. *That must lead to the common room*, I conjectured.

I ducked behind the curtain as Mwalimu passed. I collapsed on the bed like a corpse. The sheets reeked of stale perfume. I was a prisoner. My mind played back what I had heard as we passed through the towns. Based on when we slowed for traffic, the distance traveled, and the angle of the sun, I concluded that I must be back in Mombasa, probably in the Back Bay area, the part of town we avoided on our honeymoon.

Am I expected to perform for customers tonight? I wondered. It turned my stomach to think of filthy men sticking their penises into my vagina. But more horrible, would Phillip reject me if I escaped?

I took Phillip's card out of its hiding place. Where could I put it? Would I always be in this room? Hiding it under the mattress would be too obvious. I scanned the room. It was of painted concrete, with no cracks and no windows. But a frame held the curtain rod over the doorway. I moved the chair without a sound so that I could reach the frame. I looked down the hall. No one was there. I stood on the chair and slipped Phillip's card behind the mahogany rod holder. Then I flopped back on the bed.

The sooner the AIDS virus killed me the better, I decided. Phillip had AIDS too. He would die in Boston, and I would die here where he married me. *Before I die,* I thought, *should I give some pathetic men pleasure? Maybe I could infect the bastards, and they could die with me.* Then I thought of my father. I pictured him having sex with a prostitute while on his overnight trucking trips to Nairobi. Did his prostitute intend to kill him? Did she expect to kill Mother and me too? Did my mother have AIDS when she died?

Searching for answers made my head hurt. I turned over, hid my face in the mattress, and wept. It stunk. I had seen the best of Mombasa, and now I would see the worst. Maybe I could escape. Then Phillip and I could die together.

The bell rang. It was four o'clock. I sat on the edge of my bed. It was time to meet the other "transactional sex workers," as Phillip would say.

Employed

"I want you all to meet Chui," Madame Mimi said.

"She looks like a black leopard," said a buxom girl sitting at the other end of an elongated dining table.

"Don't interrupt, Ruth." Madame threatened with her stick. "She has decided to join us."

I didn't decide any such thing, but I thought it wise to remain silent. Madame Mimi seemed jovial. The security man, Mwalimu, stood with his arms folded across his chest at the exit—or the customer entrance, depending on your orientation.

"Welcome, Chui," all the girls except Ruth chorused.

"We have many clients scheduled tonight, so look sharp, ladies."

At that command, we all lined up as Madame Mimi administered birth control pills. The other girls were dressed in either seductive European-style clothes or traditional garb that left their breasts and bellies partially exposed. They had all different body types.

"Zipporah, you still haven't taken your shower. You have to be clean for our clients. Chui has had a long journey today. You show her the shower. You both need to get cleaned up," demanded Madame.

"Yes, Madame Mimi. I overslept." She smiled. "I was busy last night and made lots of money, didn't I?"

"You made Mimi proud."

Zipporah clapped her hands. "Follow me, Chui."

We shared a single shower head, but Zipporah was so petite that it didn't matter. She had a childlike face, even though she claimed to be nineteen years old. "How did you end up here, Zipporah?"

"My father brought me here because we ran out of food. His crops failed three years in a row."

She rubbed bar soap into her hair. The bubbles cascaded down her thin chest. Her breasts were two small nubs, the only adipose on her frame. "Madame Mimi gave my father money to buy food, but it was too late. My baby brother died."

She scrubbed her cheeks with the bar soap. "But my parents are still alive. My father comes every week, and I give him all my money so they can live. My mother is pregnant again, so maybe I will have a brother after all."

As she showered, I stood to the side and scrubbed. She stepped out of the shower, and I stepped in to rinse. She looked at me. "You are very pretty, Chui. The men will like you. Maybe they will pay just to look at you. You can make lots of money for your father."

"My father is dead," I said.

"Oh, I'm so sorry." She trembled like a frightened gazelle. Her tight skin broke out in goose flesh. "Can you send your money to your mother?"

I rinsed off my face and started to dry myself with the fragment of a towel I found on the rack.

"She's dead too," I said.

"Then you can buy jewelry. Madame Mimi has the jeweler come right to our house," she said with a childlike lilt. She dressed and ran out the door to join the others.

It took a while to get to know the girls in my "family," as Madame called us. Ruth was Kikuyu and wanted everyone to know. Her large breasts afforded her a faithful clientele. She was the same height as I but must have weighed twice as much. Her churlish, domineering attitude did not endear her to the other girls, but some of the men loved it.

Esther was normal in height and weight. She was the oldest "girl." Her face was marred with acne, but some of the older men preferred her. Beaten by her husband and left for dead along the road, she treated Madame as a savior.

Kerebe was the only other girl who did not use an anglicized name. She was the product of a British soldier's indiscretion with a teenage girl who had been out late to fetch water for her family. Because her mother had been raped, she hated British tourists and refused to service them. "I'd rather die," she often said. Madame accommodated her after several Brits refused to pay. She had flawless caramel skin, and her figure was proportioned like a model's. The gossip among the girls was that she was the one Faraji and Chuki sold in bruised condition.

Agnes was an albino with pink eyes and white hair. She constantly applied lotion and sunblock to her delicate skin. She was never without sunglasses during the daytime. Promptly at six o'clock, she perched them on top of her head. Agnes was a card shark. She knew every card game any client suggested. She almost always won, even when she played with Madame, who also had quite a reputation at cards. "You need to let the clients win sometimes," Madame would tell her.

"When they're good enough to beat me I will let them," Agnes said.

Several other girls had formed cliques. They were difficult to get to know. They kept changing their names, and I was not even sure how to address them. Several were quite light skinned, although not as light as Kerebe. One girl always dressed in red and claimed to be Maasai, but I doubted it. The few Maasai words I knew she didn't recognize. I thought she dressed as Maasai to attract the tourists.

After the first client each night, my room smelled like hot semen. The smell that had been so erotic between me and Phillip nauseated me now, but it didn't matter. I was a cow waiting for slaughter. It was just a question of when and how. Would I be gutted like the cows at the festival with some sexually transmitted disease ripping through my pelvis? Or would I slowly bleed out like the Maasai who drained blood from their cow's neck veins? Was the AIDS virus Phillip had given me draining the life from my marrow?

I soon learned how to get my customers to have a good firm, painful erection as quickly as possible. "It's better for productivity," Madame said. That way I got a break between clients.

When Madame Mimi complained that I worked too fast, I just waved the shillings in front of her face. "What's the problem? Did the other girls make this much money tonight?" It kept her from threatening me.

But for me the money was worthless. The world of transactional sex was slimy, and I hated it. When the jewelry merchant came, I bought as much as I could with what I had saved up. Maybe I could use it in trade if I tried to escape. But now my whole life, my education, and my friends back at the university all seemed futile.

I devised a new system. I kept a basin of soapy water in my room and washed my clients' genitals. "Why are you doing that?" a young man asked as I lay him on my bed and held up his penis to soap his groin.

"It gets you more excited than you have ever been. You want that, don't you?"

"Oh yes, I want that. I want that." he responded. Like the others, he was naïve and comical. As long as they thought the cleansing was part of the arousal, they agreed to it, even the most aggressive clients. But I really didn't want their putrid, sweaty penises up my vagina, even if I was dying of HIV-AIDS.

"Wash me more. Wash me all over." In the sweltering heat of the night I washed off the fetid sweat from the young man's armpits, belly, and chest. "The other girls never got me this excited." He gave Madame a nice tip when I was done. She gave me half the tip and 10 percent of the fee he paid.

The washing ritual soon gained me a reputation for really knowing how to get a man excited. But Madame was skeptical. One morning before our eleven o'clock meal, she confronted me in front of the other girls.

"What are you doing this washing thing for? It wastes time that you could be serving more clients." She crossed her arms in a stance that was stern and uncompromising. "Besides, it's a waste of water. From now on I insist that you buy the soap with your tips. I'm not paying for it anymore."

"Did I serve fewer clients than Ruth?" I saw Ruth shift her generous buttocks at being singled out.

"You served just as many, but I'm not authorizing this practice."

"I'm just trying to improve repeat business." I remembered the phrase from my business administration class. I put my hands on my hips in a defiant stance. "If I get clients to return, it's better for you."

I could see shillings jangling in her mind. "Repeat business is good, I suppose," she muttered. "But I'm still charging you for the soap."

Later that day as I was showering with Zipporah, who was by then my permanent shower partner, Ruth barged in.

"You can clean up later, Little Mosquito." She grabbed Zipporah by the arm and heaved her out of the shower. Zipporah stumbled and fell into the towel rack.

Then Ruth grabbed me and shoved me against the concrete with her corpulent body, flattening me against the wall. "Don't you ever embarrass me again, do you hear me? I work as hard as anybody around here."

I was covered with soap and slipped from her grasp. I twisted away, but she grabbed my throat and threw me up against the shower controls. The faucet handle sent spasms down my back as she grabbed my hair and yanked me upright. I could barely get the words out. "I'm sorry, Ruth. I know you work hard. I didn't mean to embarrass you. I apologize."

She flattened me into the corner again and tried to strike me with her fist. But she hit the cement wall, and I slipped between her legs. Wrapped in a towel, Zipporah returned with Madame Mimi.

"Stop," Madame yelled and grabbed Ruth.

I cowered on the shower floor.

"We're not doing nothing," said Ruth. "I'm just teaching this freak some humility."

Madame grabbed Ruth's bleeding fist and examined the abrasion across her knuckles.

"See what this stinking leopard did to me, Madame?" Her anger turned to a manipulative whimper.

"Have Mwalimu put a dressing on it till it stops bleeding. I don't want any client complaints tonight." Ruth gave me a stinging glance as she daubed her abrasion with my towel and left to find Mwalimu.

Madame grabbed my hair, twisting my neck and holding my face to hers. "Next time you injure one of the other girls, you'll be confined to your room without a shower, Chui. When your body starts to stink, no man will want you, water ritual or not. Is that understood?"

She threw me back against the shower controls. The sharp pain dropped me to my knees.

I hung my head in submission; my hands made a futile attempt to cover my body. I was more concerned with harm from her stick than my nakedness. "I understand."

137

The rough cement abraded my knees as I tried to get up, "I am sorry. I did not mean to offend Ruth. Please forgive me. I hope Ruth's hand heals quickly."

"Get dried off and get out of here." I scrambled at Madame's command.

She pushed Zipporah into the shower, yanking off her towel. "Get cleaned up. Why are you always the last one to take your shower?" Zipporah covered her face in shame but said nothing.

In a strange way, Madame Mimi took good care of us. It was in her financial interest to have as many healthy girls as possible for the constant stream of clients. She provided birth control because pregnancy interrupted our work and, of course, her income. I surmised the pills were donated from some humanitarian NGO because they came in a package labeled "not to be sold." She fed us one meal every day, porridge and vegetables, but on Sunday we got meat. She let us snack on whatever clients brought for treats, and sometimes that constituted an evening feast. She had strict rules of discipline and maintained a reputation for cleanliness and service.

If you got sick, you were supposed to tell Madame immediately, and she would have Mwalimu take you to the doctor. One day, I was really sick.

Clinic Visit

ONE MONDAY MORNING, I FELT horrible with sweats, chills, and fever. When I opened my eyes, everything was blurry. I concluded that I was dying of HIV-AIDS. This wasn't the way my father had died, but maybe it was different for girls. My belly burned with pain, and my vagina felt hot. The last clients on Sunday night had caused me extreme pain with intercourse, but we were not allowed to let clients know if sex was painful. It was a rule. We could tell Mwalimu after the client left.

When I didn't show up for mealtime, Zipporah checked on me and brought Madame Mimi to my room. "She is sick, so sick."

Zipporah's high-pitched voice chimed like broken church bells. "Look at the sweat on her head, Madame."

Madame Mimi laid her massive hand on my forehead. "You're burning with fever, Chui."

"She has to go to the doctor, doesn't she?" said Zipporah as she knelt by my bed and stroked my hand.

"Mwalimu," Madame yelled. He appeared in the doorway. "Take Chui to the doctor. I want her well by tomorrow night. I have lots of reservations for her, and we don't want to lose her business."

"Yes, Madame," said Mwalimu. He wrapped my naked

body in my tattered, sweat-stained sheet and carried me out to the van.

"We'll get you fixed up in no time," he said as he laid me on the floor. There even seemed to be some compassion in his voice. Maybe to him I wasn't just a cow to service the steers. He climbed into the driver's seat and turned the van toward town.

The road was rough, full of potholes. In the months since I had arrived, I had been confined to the house. "If you pass your probationary period you will be able to go out with the other girls," Madame Mimi had promised. From the floor, it was hard to tell which way we were going, and I bit my tongue as Mwalimu hit a pothole.

"Sorry, Chui, I didn't see that one."

I heard voices outside as he slowed. *A sharp turn must mean that we are going to the back of a building*, I reasoned. He stopped the van and picked up my fever-wracked frame from the floor. I gave a pathetic laugh as I focused on his arm muscles bulging from his T-shirt. He was so strong, yet gentle.

He took me through a back door and into an exam room. He placed me on a paper-covered table. The room smelled of antiseptic, iodine, and alcohol. The one window, high in the corner, had metal bars over it. The room was newly painted, but water damage had left peeling bubbles on the ceiling. I saw no medical equipment other than a small enameled metal cupboard in the corner.

"I've got a sick one, Doctor Patel," Mwalimu said from outside out the doorway.

Despite the heat, Doctor Patel entered wearing a white coat, a white shirt, and a blue striped tie. Yellow sweat stains under his arms marred his professional image. He was a slight, short man, either Indian or Pakistani. I had seen Indian merchants in Kisii on occasion, and I had a regular

Pakistani client who claimed he ran an appliance store in town.

In my delirium, I focused on the physician's hands. They were small hands with long, delicate fingers and manicured nails. He had a soft touch on my forehead.

"She has bad fever." He spoke English with an accent that sounded more British than mine. Mwalimu stood at attention beside me as the doctor pulled down the sheet and palpated my chest. My heart was pounding against my ribs. Limp from dehydration, my breasts hung to the side.

"She could be septic," the doctor added.

"Is that serious?" Mwalimu asked.

"Could be." He examined my belly. I grimaced despite not wanting to show pain. His hand went deep into my lower abdomen. It was uncomfortable, and I held my breath. With a sudden movement, he let up. I gasped and wanted to scream.

"Peritoneal sign," the doctor smiled at Mwalimu.

"What does that mean?" asked Mwalimu.

"I need to do a pelvic exam." He pulled gloves out of the metal cabinet. The sheet I had been covered with slipped to the floor. No one picked it up, but I felt cooler naked.

The doctor bent my knees and told Mwalimu, "Hold her."

Mwalimu leaned his massive frame across my chest, holding my arms with his forearms and placing his hands on my forehead. The doctor thrust his gloved hand up my vagina. My pelvis exploded in pain as my buttocks lunged for the ceiling.

"Just as I expected," Doctor Patel said.

The pain diminished, and I rested my butt, lowering it back onto the paper. Mwalimu released his grip.

"She has PID, pelvic inflammatory disease. One of your customers must have given her gonorrhea. You should make all the clients wear condoms. It's a public health issue," Doctor Patel said to Mwalimu. He said nothing to me.

"We always do," he said.

"No we don't," I whispered, but I doubt anyone heard me.

"Maybe one of the condoms broke," Mwalimu suggested.

My legs slid down flat on the table. In my delirium, I remembered as a little girl going to market and seeing the goats skinned and gutted, laid out on the table for the meat inspector. If he rejected the meat, the carcass was thrown in the trash heap. The beggars would come during the night and steal the rancid meat. I rolled on my side toward the wall. Would I be discarded?

I heard the doctor take a pad of paper out of his pocket and wrote a prescription. "These pills should cure her. I'll give her a shot now to get her started and some fluids to hydrate her. She should be better in no time." I rolled over just in time to see money exchange hands. My blurry vision prevented me from seeing how many shillings passed between them. I wanted to see what I was worth.

The doctor left the room. The sheet that covered me remained on the floor, but I didn't care that I lay there naked. Was it the fever or the hot, humid Mombasa air? Mwalimu stood beside me but made no attempt to cover me.

A nurse came in the room with a needle and syringe. She jabbed it into my thigh. I didn't flinch. She started an intravenous like I'd had in Kijabe Hospital. She spoke Swahili but not to me. "All right, you can take her as soon as all this fluid is infused. Call me when the bottle is empty, and I will take the needle out." She left the room.

I don't remember much from during the infusion. I heard the traffic outside, an occasional dove singing, and the mumbling of the doctor with other patients. I was too confused to remember much other than the feeling of my rancid-smelling body drenching the paper underneath me with sweat.

When the nurse returned to remove the needle, Mwalimu picked up the sheet and wrapped me up. I felt comforted. "All right, Chui, you're going to get better now. Hang together, kid," he said.

A kid is a goat, so I must be a goat, I thought. *Would the inspector approve of me or discard me in the ditch?*

After we returned to the brothel, Mwalimu sat on the bed beside me to make sure I took the prescribed medicine. He forced me to drink water and juice. Sometime during the night, my fever broke. By Tuesday morning, I was feeling alive again, and my mind was clear. On Tuesday afternoon Madame inspected me.

"Let's see if she's ready to work," she said as she laid me flat, whipped my sheet off, and prodded my belly. She pulled a latex glove out of her pocket and snapped it onto her thick right hand. "Hold her," she said to Mwalimu.

"It's not necessary. I won't move," I said.

"All right then." She shoved her right hand up my vagina and squeezed my uterus between her gloved hand and the hand on my belly. I refused to wince at the discomfort. At least it was not as painful as when the doctor had done it, so I decided that I must be healing. As she mashed her hand inside me, I just stared at her.

As she finished my exam she reported to Mwalimu, "She's ready to work tonight." As the two of them left my room I scrambled out of bed and covered up in my kitamba, grabbing my belly until the cramps let up.

The first client's thrusting was painful, but he interpreted my groans as climax euphoria, so he thrust even harder. The rest of the evening I kept my groans to myself. Most of my clients were focused on their own ejaculation, not me, so they were gentler. I was thankful.

As the infection in my pelvis healed, a strange healing occurred in my soul. The despair left me. Why hadn't I died already? Could I escape? Could I find Phillip? I started complying with Madame's requirement that every client wear a condom. I didn't want to go through the pain of a pelvic infection again. Then I thought, *since I already have HIV and the infected clients pay well if I don't require a condom, I can make some escape money if I don't require a condom. Besides, those clients tip better because I won't discriminate against them.*

A month later my left breast was red, hot, and sore. Pus dripped out of the nipple. Some of the clients liked to bite, but Madame charged fines if they did. "Back to the doctor," Madame said. "You're costing me a gold mine."

This time I was healthy enough to dress and sit in the backseat. Several of the other girls were going for checkups "to stay healthy," as Madame reminded us. The ride to the physician's office was much more pleasant this time, and I got a sense of where in the city our brothel was located.

No other patients were in the waiting room when the eight of us piled in from the van. Ruth and Esther got into examining rooms first. The rest of us waited in the waiting room. This visit must have been a scheduled appointment.

"Chui," the nurse called out.

I stood and followed.

"You look much better than last time I saw you," she said. "What's wrong today?"

"My left breast is sore," I told her.

She laughed and pulled aside the curtain into the examining room. "Strip. The doctor will check your breasts, but he needs to do a pelvic exam to make sure you are healed from last time."

No gown or sheet was provided. The exam table had no covering. I found a piece of newspaper in the trash that had no stains on it and set it on the table. I undressed and folded my clothes, putting them on the wooden chair in the corner. Despite the heat of the day, I shivered as I placed my bare butt on the slip of paper.

Dr. Patel came in and laid me down. He pushed my breasts around. "Tender?" he asked. Tears came to my eyes, but I said nothing. "Left breast inflamed and indurated," he said as he made a note on my chart.

"All right, let's make sure your PID is cured."

I knew the routine. I bent my knees and spread my legs as he put on a glove. As his gloved hand crawled up my vagina, there was no pain. He spread my labia with his fingers and inspected them as he pulled his hand out. "Oh, we got a problem here."

He sat me up and pulled my labia out so that he could show me the ulcer. "How long has this been there?"

"I don't know. It doesn't hurt," I answered.

"Nurse," he yelled. The nurse shot through the curtain.

"Look at this," he said, pushing me back down to show my vagina to the nurse. "That's syphilis. We need to arrange appointments for penicillin shots."

He turned to me and smiled. "The shots should clear up your breast infection, too."

How clever, I thought.

Madame Mimi was furious when she heard the news. She pushed me flat in the bed and spread my legs to examine my ulcer. "That doesn't look nice. Keep the light off. Light only a candle in her room tonight so the clients can't see that," she instructed Mwalimu.

"She was already treated with a shot," he said.

She grabbed my hair and pulled my face to hers. "You're letting the clients be sloppy about wearing condoms. Why do you think I insist they wear them? For your protection, that's why. And this costs me money. I'm taking the cost of these shots and the gasoline to drive you to the doctor out of your pay."

She slapped my groin and yanked my pubic hair. "Will that help you to remember?"

I didn't mind the shots. It meant that Mwalimu gave me a ride to town every morning for fourteen days. He often stopped for supplies, and since he was not allowed to leave me alone, I had to accompany him into the stores. Madame confiscated all my money, "for additional expenses," so I could only pretend to shop.

I lost my composure once when we stopped at a store where Phillip and I had shopped on our honeymoon. I hid my face behind a rack of dresses. I wondered how Phillip was doing. Was he getting treatment for his HIV? Did he finish his research? Did it matter? Would I ever see him again?

After the trips to town to complete my syphilis treatments, Madame asked to see me in her office.

"Chui, I'm impressed with you," she said. "You never complain about anything, even when I am forced to punish you. And you didn't even argue when I docked you for gas for the van. I've decided to trust you to go on the excursions with the rest of the girls. You have completed your probation period."

Now I could go out with the other girls on Mondays. I was delighted. The brothel was closed on Mondays. This provided opportunity for exercise: "Recreation and fitness," Madame called it.

"But there's a problem." Her face became disgruntled.

"What's that?" I asked.

"You got syphilis from a client who was not wearing a condom." She shook her finger at me. "Don't you dare say a condom broke. I've checked your trash. From now on I am counting the condoms in your room. They'd better match the number of clients you've had or you will feel my stick on your bare bottom whether it shows or not. Do we understand each other?"

"Yes, Madame, I understand."

At last I was released for recreation. Mondays were great. Sometimes we played soccer with local boys. They always won; the other girls didn't play too seriously. But more often we went to the beach. Madame provided bikinis. They were a size too small, "for business reasons," she said when Ruth complained.

I didn't mind that my breasts didn't stay in the bikini top, but I brought my kitamba to wrap around my waist. I had been comfortable with Phillip seeing my thighs on our honeymoon, but my cultural self-consciousness returned when I was on the beach with the tourists walking by.

Most of the girls enjoyed the waves and walking in the surf, but I was the only one who knew how to swim. I swam out past the breakers, feeling free. But Mwalimu was always standing on the shore waiting for me. We played volleyball and invited anyone walking the beach to join the game. The people who played with us on Monday afternoon were often our clients on Tuesday night. It was another business strategy.

The first time we went to a beach where Phillip and I had lain in the sun on one of our forays from the resort, I welled up with emotion. I ran into the surf and splashed my face to hide the tears. Mwalimu didn't suspect a thing, but he was standing at the water's edge when I came out.

He was always present. He did protect us. One time thieves snatched Zipporah's purse. A man with a bloodied face returned the purse later with a timid apology. I was never afraid to be out for "recreation and fitness," but I suspected that his main job was to keep us from running away.

Judy, one of the clique girls, was impressed with his massive muscles. She told me, "He can break a neck with his bare hands. I've seen him do it."

"When did that happen?" I asked in a hush.

"One time before you came, a client pointed a gun at me. He wanted me to do something I didn't want to do. I screamed. Mwalimu came into my room and saw the gun. The next thing I knew, my client was dead on the floor."

"Did the police come?" I asked.

"Of course. But when they saw the gun, they reported it as self-defense. No one even went to court."

"What about his family?" I asked.

"Oh, his parents were so embarrassed that he died in a brothel that they didn't say a thing."

I wandered down to the shore. I looked back to make sure I had Mwalimu's approval. I found a nice spot where the sand was warm and each wave tickled my toes. I closed my eyes to rest in the sand.

"Take your top off, Chui," Mwalimu's deep voice commanded. He was standing a few feet up the shore with his arms crossed.

"I don't want to. I'm resting," I said.

"Take your top off or I'll take it off for you. And get rid of the kitamba," he ordered.

The tone of his voice frightened me. I sat up, bared my breasts, and undid my kitamba. Laying my head back, I closed my eyes. The sun felt warm on my bare skin. I felt self-conscious, but I enjoyed the warmth. I curled my toes and touched my feet together, trying to allay my embarrassment. All I was wearing was a tiny triangle of a too-small bikini over my groin.

Why did Mwalimu want me like this? Hadn't he seen me naked enough times? Was I pleasuring him? I opened my eyes. I saw him adjust his sunglasses, but he wasn't looking at me. Two fellows were walking down the beach. I was right in their path. They were two blond young men with European build and clothes who were clearly tourists. They turned and gawked at me.

"Good afternoon, young men. Are you enjoying Kenya?" I said.

"You like what you see?" Mwalimu asked. He handed them each a card from his sport shirt pocket.

When they're out of sight I asked, "Can I wrap up now? I'm cold."

"It is forty degrees centigrade and you're cold? You can wrap up unless I tell you to take it off again," he said. He didn't move a muscle. There were other men walking down the beach.

"Nah, just leave it off." He smiled. "Good advertising."

I sat up and checked to make sure my pubic hair was covered, flipped my top into my shoulder bag, and spread my kitamba over the sand. Then I lay back to enjoy the warmth of the sun. I might as well have been naked, but that might bring the police.

That Tuesday night was busy. I had just finished with a regular, a vegetable merchant whose wife had died, when I heard Mwalimu's booming voice. "You got a double, Chui."

I was sitting on the bed wrapped in my kitamba when the two fellows from the beach were escorted into my room. Both were dressed in shorts and Mombasa T-shirts. Both were young. One wore glasses, and the other either was prematurely bald or had shaved his head. I stood and untied my kitamba. The fellow with the glasses stopped me with a gentle hand, and the three of us sat on the bed together.

"We just wanted to meet you," he said. His accent was American. "My name is Eric."

"It is nice to meet you, Eric. I am called Chui, Swahili for leopard."

"You are the most beautiful Kenyan we have seen on our whole vacation," the other said. "And you have such a nice British accent. My name is Jason."

"Nice to meet you, too, Jason."

"Where did you learn English?" Eric asked.

"My mother was a school teacher, and I've taken classes at Nairobi University."

149

Their eyes brightened. "We've just finished our summer research project at NU ourselves," Jason said.

We discussed classes and mutual professors and laughed about some of the antics they experienced during their summer research. I felt relaxed and stimulated to have such an intellectual conversation.

Eric whispered, "What's a smart girl like you doing in a place like this?"

I glared at the doorway and spelled out "KIDNAPPED" on his palm.

Their faces displayed sudden understanding.

"Time's up, boys," said Madame Mimi as Mwalimu shoved aside the curtain.

Eric and Jason stood and held out a fistful of shillings. "We'll pay double for more time."

Mwalimu crossed his arms over his chest. "Madame Mimi said that your time is up."

They stood up and pushed past Mwalimu. "I didn't even get to service them," I protested.

"Do it faster next time, Chui. You have clients waiting." Madame and her guard left. There was no one waiting. But that was the day I decide to escape, even if I was dying of HIV-AIDS. I wanted to die free. That day I totally changed.

Swimming Lessons

I EXERCISED AS MUCH AS I was allowed. In the mornings I did sit-ups and push-ups while everyone else was asleep. I needed to be fit to escape. I knew it didn't make sense. Dying people shouldn't care about being fit or escaping. But I felt better and decided that I wanted to be as healthy as possible when I died, even though I knew that wasn't logical.

On our Monday adventures, Mwalimu set the schedule. We'd go to resorts for lunch and then shop for clothes. Of course, the expenses were paid with our tip money. Zipporah almost never ate or bought anything since all her money went to her parents.

Mwalimu allowed us the illusion of freedom in town, but he was never far away and often incorporated some of his friends to help supervise us.. Over the course of the next few months we scouted out every beach Mombasa offered. That was where the tourist clients came from. Madame inspected our outfits each Monday morning as we stood at attention in the dining hall. She insisted that what we wore attracted the right kind of attention: that is, slightly immodest. Tourists paid better than locals.

Even though our Monday adventures were for advertising, I still enjoyed them, especially the beach. Kerebe and I got to know each other well since we had both ended up in Madame Mimi's care under similar circumstances. We often spread out our towels next to each other. "I enjoy the water, but I really don't know how to swim," she said.

"Come on, I'll teach you." I grabbed her hand, and we walked into the surf together. I looked back to see that Mwalimu approved. He was standing at the high-water mark in the sand.

"Now, just squat down in the water and get used to the waves. Take a deep breath just before the wave comes." I demonstrated as a wave crested over my head. Kerebe tried it. At first she coughed and sputtered, but with a few tries she got used to the waves. I had her kick while I held her up, and she was quick to learn the crawl and breaststroke.

"This feels great," she yelled, exhilarated.

All afternoon I worked with her so that she lost her fear of the water. "Thanks, Chui. This really is fun. I just wish I were brave like you," she said.

We waded out till the water was up to our waists, jumping up into the surf as a wave towered over us. I stayed close beside her and picked her up as she coughed.

"This is so thrilling," she screamed. We walked back toward shore until the water was at our knees. She turned to face the sea, pulled me to her face, and whispered, "Have you ever thought of escaping?"

I turned my eyes to see if Mwalimu was watching. He was focused on the girls' volleyball match. "Yes," I responded.

"Tell me your plan and I'll tell you mine," she offered.

"All right." Kerebe whispered part of her plan. Actually, I didn't have a plan, but before I could speak we were interrupted.

"It's time for you two to come in closer," Mwalimu called to us.

"Later," I whispered as I took her hand in mine and we sauntered back in compliance with Mwalimu's command.

Madame Mimi seldom went on excursions with us. She complained, "The sun gives me a headache. Besides, I have book work to do." Mwalimu, a van driver, and a local merchant who closed his shop on Mondays were our usual security. I suspected the local merchant, who favored Ruth, and the driver, who favored Karen, received sexual favors in return because I never saw money change hands.

Mwalimu was definitely in charge of our excursions. Several times when our clothes were a little too risqué, money was given to the local policemen. But when drunks tried to manhandle us, they were no match for Mwalimu. We were his source of income, and he protected his investment.

Agnes never came with us. The sun was bad for her albino skin, and Madame allowed her anything she wanted to keep her skin soft. It was well known in Mombasa that if you wanted to have sex with an albino, Madame Mimi's was the place to go. Agnes was famous around Mombasa; ruining her skin would have been bad for business. She was the only one who went out on Monday nights, always escorted, of course. Since her natural hair was yellowish-white, Madame let her dye it any color she wanted. Sometimes it was red, sometimes green or blue—whatever attracted clients. Some of her repeat business came just to see what color she had dyed her hair that week. She even dyed her pubic hair, which was quite an attraction. But she was a picky eater and never gained weight despite her lack of exercise. When she wasn't oiling her skin, she was playing cards.

I didn't want to get syphilis again. Those penicillin injections every day hurt. And now that Madame was counting my used condoms, it was more difficult to make extra tips. I didn't want to infect someone with HIV like some prostitute had done to my father, especially if I liked the client. But if the guy was a slug, I didn't care. Let him get infected. I inspected them carefully during the washing ritual for any ulcers or discharge, but I didn't care if the HIV-positive men wore condoms. They scared the other girls, but they were the means for my escape.

"Oh, nice lady, that feels so good." My short, scrawny client ejaculated, and we were done. He was my last client of the evening, so I wrapped up in my kitamba and stood in the doorway as he got dressed.

"Don't forget the required extra," I said, looking down the hall for unwanted ears. "Madame said you were HIV positive, and I let you have real sex without a condom, so I expect a generous tip."

"Having HIV-AIDS is expensive," he said as he took the required extra shillings out of his pants pocket and handed them to me. "Next week I'll use a condom and cut your price."

"I can't wait," I said with a sarcastic tone but added in a mellow voice, "but it won't be near as much fun." My kitamba slipped off my breast. He reached out to touch me.

"Sorry, time's up." I covered myself.

He swished the curtain aside, and I'm sure that he left with visions of my body dancing in his head. I pulled a condom out from under my mattress, stretched it out, lay in bed, scooped the semen out of my vagina, and filled the condom, squeezing the milky fluid down to the end before discarding it in the trash. Then I rolled over for a much-needed night's sleep.

Strategic Planning

"THANK YOU SO MUCH," ZIPPORAH said as she drew letters in the clay. It hadn't taken me long to realize that she was illiterate. Her family couldn't afford the cost of books and uniforms to send her to school, so she never had the opportunity to attend.

We were sitting on a mat in the "garden," as Madame called it. It was a courtyard with an eight-foot brick fence surrounding it. "The broken glass embedded on the top of the wall is to discourage unwanted guests from entering," Madame had explained. But I was sure it was to prevent us from escaping. There was a gate to the street near Madame's office window which was always locked, except when a vehicle delivered new "orphans." There was also a door that led from the brothel to her office. The only other door was near my room, the one that was padlocked with a chain. We could only enter the garden with permission through Madame Mimi's office.

Nothing grew in the garden except a few weeds, which eked out survival among the stones and clods of dirt. Today we were using a smooth area of red clay as a writing surface for Zipporah to learn her letters.

"I am so excited to learn words." She copied "MBWA," Swahili for "dog," in the clay with a stick.

"I had a pet dog when I was a little girl." She rubbed it out and spelled it again. "Is there a spelling for every word I say?"

"Yes, there is," I replied to my innocent pupil.

"Even for my name?"

"Yes, especially for your name." She reminded me of my inquisitiveness when I was young.

I spelled out "Zipporah" and read it to her so that she would know what sound each letter made. She traced through my lines. I could see that she was trying to memorize not only the lines but also the movement to make them in the dirt.

"It's a beautiful name when it is written, isn't it?" she said.

"Yes, very beautiful," I said.

She twisted around on the mat and tried to duplicate her name without looking. She spelled out the first three letters. "I think that is the most I can remember."

Some of the other girls liked to "play school" and asked me to teach them things. They seemed to mostly enjoy stories. But Zipporah was my most enthusiastic pupil. She was ecstatic about each discovery.

"How is she doing, Chui?" Kerebe asked, having been allowed to join us.

"Pretty well. She has conquered the first three letters of her name," I said.

"That's great. I almost finished secondary school before I …" She stopped in midsentence.

"What are you three doing out here?" Madame Mimi said as she came out of her office.

"I'm teaching Zipporah how to spell," I answered.

"What good is learning for her? It's a waste of time. You two should be getting some rest so you are lively for our guests tonight," she chided.

Zipporah cowered. I stood up. "If she knew how to read and write, the clients would not be able to cheat her. Remember last week when that guy cheated her because she couldn't add the numbers on the shilling notes he gave her?"

"Oh," Madame said. I could tell that she was contemplating the financial benefits. "I guess you're right. But make sure you don't tire her out. She's fragile."

"I promise," I said as Madame left.

Zipporah relaxed. "Madame Mimi says that I can learn letters?"

"Yes, and numbers too," I added.

She stared at the wall as I wrote "CHUI" for her to copy. "Do you know what's beyond that wall?" she asked.

"No," I said, forming the letters of a simple sentence in the clay.

"There is a large field where I used to kick a ball when I was little. It's full of garbage now." I handed her the writing stick to trace through what I had written. "There are some stores on the other side, and then up the hill is the highway. My father let me play in the field when he was selling his produce. But he told me that the highway goes all the way to Nairobi. Have you ever been to Nairobi, Chui?"

"Yes, I studied there," I said, recollecting moments of my student life. *I shouldn't have said that*, I thought.

"They taught you letters and numbers in Nairobi?" she asked.

"And stories too," I said, arousing her curiosity.

"I love your stories. You are the best storyteller," she said.

"I enjoyed your story, Zipporah," said Kerebe, "especially the part about the highway."

Later, just before we were commanded to come in, I asked Zipporah how far it was to the highway. She told me, "Just a quick run up the hill."

Kerebe's Fate

IT WAS A BEAUTIFUL MONDAY with not a cloud to be seen. We were traveling to North Beach. Mwalimu seemed suspicious of Kerebe from the moment we piled in the van. "You're sure bringing a lot of stuff to the beach," he said to her as she climbed over Ruth.

"I brought my lotions and a dress to look nice if I get too much sun," she said while sitting down next to me. She fidgeted, and Mwalimu kept turning the rear-view mirror from his perch in the front passenger's seat to check on her.

At the beach, she spread her towel next to mine. She seemed agitated.

"What's wrong, Kerebe? Are you upset about something?" I asked her.

She shot me an angry look. "I got here the same way you did. You should know." She undressed down to her bikini but kept her bag close by her side.

I contemplated her words and was deep in thought, soaking up sunshine, when she said, "Go for a swim, Chui."

Her tone startled me. It was a command, not a suggestion. "Are you coming with me? I'm glad to give you another swimming lesson."

"Not today," she said. I gave her a quizzical look as I headed for the ocean.

It always drew Mwalimu's attention when I swam out into

the surf. The waves were high today and swarmed over my head. I loved swirling around in the breakers. I stood up as the wave passed to relieve Mwalimu's concern and yelled, "I'm fine."

Beyond him, on the road leading to the parking area, I saw a bus stop. I hadn't realized that the bus from downtown Mombasa stopped here. The sign on the bus said, "Jesus Saves." I laughed and dived into the surf to swim farther out. When I turned to reassure Mwalimu, I saw that the van driver had taken his place on the shore to watch me. Beyond the beach, Kerebe was getting on the bus. Mwalimu was in pursuit. He stopped as the bus pulled away, and he pulled out his cell phone. I gasped.

That night when we returned, rather than have time to ourselves, Madame made us sit in silence around her as she beat her stick on the table. She lectured us about how ungrateful we were, how much she had provided for us, how blessed we were to have her caring for us, and how she was interested in our welfare. "You would all be out on the street begging for food if it weren't for me."

Her harangue ended when two policemen appeared at the door with Kerebe in handcuffs between them. "Nice bracelets you have, Kerebe. They are very becoming on you," Madame Mimi snarled. "I want to thank you, officers, for bringing Kerebe home. We will take good care of her."

I glanced over, expecting them to remove her handcuffs, but instead Mwalimu gave them money in exchange for the key. "You are all confined to your rooms till tomorrow at mealtime," Madame said. "Now get going."

She beat the table with her stick. We moved like stampeding gazelles.

Kerebe's room was two doors down the hall from mine. As I went to the common room for mealtime the next day, I whisked her curtain aside. She was handcuffed to her bed with a gag in her mouth. Mwalimu was climbing off her naked body and pulling up his pants. I rushed to the dining room, avoiding his gaze. When she came to eat, her left hand was cuffed to the table. Her eyes were red and swollen. She said nothing.

That night Madame Mimi was animated with the clients. "We have a half-price special tonight, gentlemen. No condoms necessary." I figured that Kerebe was the special. She would get no tips; all the money would go to Madame.

Long after my last client that night, there were still men lined up in the hall outside her room. Two of them were the policemen who had brought her back.

Kerebe remained behind when we went to the beach for recreation each Monday after that, but the worst was three weeks later when it was time for our regular physician appointments. It wasn't much fun going to Dr. Patel so that his gloved hand could poke and prod our vaginas, but it got us out of the brothel, and he did treat our medical problems. We assembled in the dining room, ready to go. Kerebe sat shackled to the table leg, her head down on the table.

Madame noticed our inquisitive looks. "Kerebe is learning that a health checkup is a privilege. She won't be going today." We boarded the van in silence.

A week later, Kerebe gave her food to Ruth at mealtime and pleaded with Madame, "I am too sick to work tonight. I have cramps and diarrhea. And I was vomiting all night."

"A night off is a privilege, and you have not shown yourself worthy of privileges," Madame said. There was no sympathy in her voice.

Madame took the sorghum porridge away from Ruth and gave it back to Kerebe. "Eat your food."

Madame force-fed her with a wooden spoon, stopping only when she gagged. "You are so ungrateful for what I give you."

When Madame was done, Kerebe leaned over and vomited. Mwalimu unshackled her and dragged her to her room while the cook cleaned up the mess. Nobody said anything. Zipporah couldn't finish her food. I had already eaten but wished I hadn't.

The next Monday night when we returned from playing volleyball, Madame Mimi told us that before we could change out of our bikinis that we had to assemble in Kerebe's room. Our cheerful mood soured as we crowded together in the small concrete box. The scene was horrible.

Covered with a blanket, Kerebe lay limp with her arms extended overhead, cuffed to a hook on the wall. Her pale skin exuded sweat and fever.

"Please, take me to the doctor," she whimpered.

"You have not demonstrated that you can be trusted, Kerebe." Madame Mimi used her stick to whip off the blanket, exposing Kerebe's naked body. Her breasts were flaccid against her visible ribs. Her belly was emaciated. I could see the pulse of her aorta against her sunken belly. Mwalimu forced her legs apart at Madame's command. She moaned. Her inner thighs were encrusted with dried blood. Gray-green pus dripped out from her swollen labia. Diarrhea stained the sheets. Purulent sores had erupted down her thighs. Madame poked her belly with her stick. Kerebe groaned as a green clot plopped out of her vagina. The other girls retched, and some vomited. The smell was overpowering. They were excused, but I was not.

Kerebe was my friend, and I refused to show my revulsion. So Madame made me stay to watch her agonized breathing. She kept looking at me and scrunching her nose. "Like what you see, Chui? Like what you smell? Do you see how lack of thankfulness for all I've done for you can have consequences?"

She prodded Kerebe's dehydrated breasts. Her stick left a puckered imprint. "Call the doctor, Mwalimu. See if he can make a house call," she ordered.

He took out his cell phone and left the room. I was left

standing at Kerebe's bedside. Madame scowled at me, "Have you learned an important lesson here, Chui?" She poked my bare belly with her toxic stick.

"Yes, Madame Mimi, I have learned an important lesson."

"Then you may be excused," she said, giving me a whack across my buttocks with her stick as I left.

The next day the doctor came to pronounce her dead. "Looks like she died of malaria," he said, exchanging glances with Madame Mimi.

"Yes, she had a real high fever," Madame confirmed.

I expected another harangue about the consequences of running away and how wonderful Madame Mimi was to care for us, but nothing was said. I suspected that she had decided the visual lesson was sufficient. But I was not dissuaded. I just needed a better plan.

Escape Plan

"YOU ARE A WONDERFUL GIRL," my last client of the night said as he dressed. "I have never felt so fulfilled as a man." He smiled and cradled my breasts in his calloused hands.

"Time's up," I said, knocking his hands away and wrapping my kitamba around me.

"See you next week, then." He smoothed his stocking cap over his matted hair. "I don't mind the extra tip if I don't have to use condoms. I hate those things. That's not real sex."

He pushed aside the curtain and put his finger to his mouth. "Our secret," he said, handing me the extra shillings.

Hiding the no-condom money from Madame Mimi was a problem. She inspected everything in our rooms when we were in the shower or away for exercise and recreation, but she was not an outdoor person. During the time we were allowed in the garden, I found a loose brick in the wall behind the water closet. I hid my extra tips there. The day I escaped, I would need some money.

I soaked a clean rag in the basin of cold water beside the bed and reclined on my mattress. Putting a cold compress on my groin took away the irritation. I gazed at the ceiling. There were three spiders. They maintained webs in the corners of my room. I tried to keep my room tidy so Madame Mimi wouldn't think she needed to clean it. I didn't want her sweeping away my spiders. They had done their job so far. I had no mosquito bites in the mornings like the other girls complained about, and I had never gotten malaria. Spiders were my friends. The best-fed one I named Ananse. I thought the other two were her children.

"I am getting quite a clientele, Ananse. These men sure like to bare their genitalia. And they are all so much the same." I laughed. "But they like to think they're unique." I got up to refresh my compress.

"This is so wearisome, Ananse. I expected to die of AIDS by now. Why am I still alive? I feel healthy." I lifted the cool compress. "Except my femininity is a bit sore. But that's understandable, isn't it?"

I stood on my bed to scrutinize her expression. "You don't care about my femininity, Ananse, do you? But I respect your opinion."

A fly buzzed over my curtain from the hallway. It flew right into her web. I watched it struggle and then saw the spider paralyze it. I sighed as I explained things to the spider. "Should I trust Engoro, the Kisii god who made everything? But I have trouble believing in him. When I was a little girl, Father always said, 'Trust Engoro,' but then he got AIDS and died. Uncle Osiemo called himself a true and faithful believer, but he claimed that Engoro told him to beat his wives."

I stood on my chair to get a closer look. The fly was being wrapped in silk. "When I die will the life be sucked out of me like you're doing to that fly?" I watched, enchanted by the process.

"Mother was a Christian like Joyce. 'Trust in Jesus,' Mother said when Father died. 'Jesus will take care of us.' But she got burned as a witch. Did Jesus protect her?"

I poked my finger in Ananse's web. "Are you listening to me, my spider friend?" She scooted to the center of her web. "Did Engoro create you, or did Jesus?"

I quit irritating her and lay down on my stinky mattress

wrapped in my kitamba. I missed Joyce. In Kijabe she had told me many stories about Jesus. And the hospital workers had said that Jesus helped them find me in the brush near the Italian chapel. Could Jesus help me? Did Jesus approve of prostitutes—or, as Phillip would say, transactional sex workers? I missed Phillip.

Once when I was discouraged about all I had to do for my university classes, Joyce had read me a story from her Bible about Jesus and a prostitute. "Neither do I condemn you," Jesus had said. I had grabbed the Bible from her and read it for myself. There it was, written in the Holy Bible.

Engoro didn't like prostitutes. I didn't even think Engoro liked women. Besides, to Engoro, I was still a girl. I would never be a woman.

"I love you, Joyce," I said to the darkness as I blew out my candle. But Joyce didn't like my husband. I compressed the throbbing in my groin. Sex with Phillip was so different from sex with my clients. My clients loved only themselves; I was just a tool for their fantasies. Phillip loved me, and I had been married as a Christian woman. The minister said so. "I love you, Phillip."

"He'll take advantage of you." Joyce's words reverberated through my brain. Had he taken advantage of me? He had infected me, but he was devastated. I should have listened to Joyce. Now I was stuck in this brothel waiting to die.

"Just trust Jesus." Joyce's voice rang in my ears. But hadn't Joyce taken advantage of me? She had made nice dresses for me, but wasn't I just a mannequin to promote her business? Did she really care about me? If I escaped, would she take me back? It had been so long.

In the darkness Ananse enjoyed her meal. "Flies don't bother me as much as mosquitoes, my friend. But I suppose flies are juicier, aren't they? Are you on guard up there? I don't want to have any mosquito bites in the morning."

I rolled over in bed. Pastor Joseph had said that Jesus

made spiders. But did Jesus also make mosquitoes? I was confused. "I want no mosquito bites in the morning, Ananse. If Jesus made you, I'll trust Him, but then He must show me a way to escape."

Opportunity

"THERE IS SOMEONE IN MY office to see you," Madame Mimi came to my room to tell me after mealtime the next day.

I assumed this was a special client requiring midday service. I couldn't help my disgust as I mumbled, "This is my time off."

Quickly, I covered my mouth to muffle my complaint and lowered my eyes. "Yes, Madame Mimi." We got privileges taken away or lost our tips if we talked back.

Her gaze was stern, but there was no reprimand in her voice. "He's not a customer. He is a clinical researcher. He pays for you girls to see the doctor every month. He wants to talk to you about your blood tests."

Ah, so this was how Dr. Patel was paid for our regular health checks. He didn't volunteer his services. I rewrapped my kitamba. Madame Mimi seemed impatient, but then, she always was. She grabbed my arm and pushed me ahead of her into her office. Her grip was strong and painful, but I knew it would not leave a mark. She was careful about that.

A tall, middle-aged Caucasian man in military uniform stood behind her desk. Madame Mimi introduced him. "This is Colonel Johnson. He is a physician with the United States Army. He has been doing research on all of you. Remember when you signed the permission forms?"

"Uh huh" came out of my mouth, but it was a reflex to

avoid punishment. I was unaware that any of us had given permission for any research. I stood opposite the desk as directed. Madame Mimi tapped her stick on the door frame. "Now pay attention, Chui."

"Nice to meet you—Chui, is it?" He shook my hand and turned to Madame Mimi. "I would like to conduct this interview in private, if I may."

"Yes, Colonel, whatever you wish." Madame stepped back and closed the door. I assumed she stayed right outside, eavesdropping.

I recognized his American accent. It sounded odd. He offered me a chair to sit in beside the desk. "My real name is Kwanboka Muwami," I whispered.

"What's that?" He handed me a paper and pen to write my name.

If he was here to tell me about my HIV-AIDS results, I wanted him to know my real name. "I do not have my Kenyan ID card with me," I said out loud.

Then I whispered again as I passed the paper back to him, "But that's my real name." My formal speech felt refreshing. "I'm just a 'chui' to my clients. Do you speak Swahili?

"Yes, I know 'leopard' in Swahili," he said.

I sat back in the chair. "Am I dying, Colonel Johnson? Do you have the results of my ELISA and CD4 test? How long do I have to live? I already know that I am infected with HIV and that I have AIDS. You can be honest with me."

"You're so articulate. How much education do you have?" he asked.

I softened my voice to frustrate listening ears outside the office. "I have a degree in sociology. But my husband was infected with HIV, so that is how I became infected. Then I was"—I mouthed the word "kidnapped"—"brought here. I am now being patient, waiting to die."

He tapped on the desk to annoy those listening outside the door and whispered back, "So you are not here by choice?"

I shook my head.

He raised his voice and became formal. "The Unites States Army is very interested in you. Before I tell you what I am here for, can I ask you a few questions?"

"Sure." I spoke in a normal voice.

"Have you had sex with partners who are known to be HIV positive?" he asked.

"Yes, many times," I answered.

"Do they always wear condoms?" he continued.

I shook my head in the negative and answered, "Madame Mimi insists that all clients wear condoms."

He sensed my hesitancy and pushed paper and pen toward me. I wrote, "Since I'm already infected, I charge more for not requiring a condom. They pay cash."

"I understand." He opened his briefcase and stuffed the note with my name inside. He pushed aside a Holy Bible as he pulled out some other papers. He shuffled them and handed them to me. "You do not have AIDS. Your ELISA is negative. I did PCR for HIV, which was also negative, and your CD4 count is normal. Do you understand this?"

I nodded. "PCR amplifies the tiniest bit of viral nucleic acid."

"That's right." He seemed startled as he passed the laboratory test results to me. "You have no virus in your body. You are not infected. You do not have AIDS."

My brow wrinkled, and I pointed to the door. He went to the door and opened it. Madame Mimi was right outside. "For what I am paying for this meeting, I expected privacy. Or would you prefer that I take her to my office in town? She does not have AIDS. The rest of our conversation is none of your business." Madame held up her stick, but I couldn't hear what she said.

"All right, then, get away from the door." He waited until she crossed the room and sat next to Mwalimu. Colonel

Richard Roach

Johnson closed the door and moved his chair next to me. We sat knee to knee.

"How did you know that I had unprotected sex with men known to be HIV positive? Why are you talking to me and not all the girls?" I asked.

He hesitated for a moment. "Kwamboka, I am in charge of US Aid for treatment of HIV-AIDS. The US government sponsors a clinic in town for AIDS patients. I suppose I am not breaking confidentiality to tell you that several of our patients have told me that you are the only one of Madame Mimi's 'orphans' who is willing to have sex with them without a condom. So, since the US Army is authorized to research HIV transmission among transactional sex workers, I was very interested when I got the results of your tests." He pointed to the negative PCR. "I expected you to be positive."

He fumbled with his papers. "Answer me honestly. It is very important to our research. Do you consistently have sexual intercourse with HIV-positive men without shield protection?"

"Yes, almost every day. But I am the only one. That is why I have so many clients compared to the other girls. Madame Mimi is suspicious, but so far I don't think any of my clients have told her." I swallowed hard. "So it is disturbing to me that you should know this."

Fear strained my face. "But how could it be that I am not infected? My husband is positive."

"Your PCR is negative. You do not have HIV-AIDS," he emphasized. "In fact, you show no sign that the virus has provoked any immunologic response. We have been studying a group of women like you. It appears that about 5 percent of the female transactional sex workers we've studied do not have the receptor for the virus on their lymphocytes ..." He looked at me to see if I understood.

"Continue. I understand," I urged him.

"If you do not have the receptor, the virus cannot attach

to your lymphocyte membranes. No attachment means that it is impossible for you to get infected. So prostitutes"—he paused—"I'm sorry."

"That's all right. That's what I am," I responded.

"We have studied transactional sex workers in Nairobi and here in Mombasa who have had extensive"—he cleared his throat—"sexual exposure to HIV. Those without receptors are immune. This genetic variant may lead to a cure for AIDS."

"My father died of AIDS, so he must have had the receptor."

"And your mother?" he asked. I could see the consternation in his face.

"She was murdered a year after my father died. She was not sick at the time," I said.

"I'm sorry." He held his chin and studied the ceiling as he thought through my history. "So despite having sexual intercourse with your infected father, a year after he died, she was still free of any disease? At least clinically, she had no obvious illness? Was she ever tested?"

"Not to my knowledge," I answered.

He picked up his pencil and made some notes. "Studies in Uganda show that virus transfer to a spouse is only about 20 percent per year. So it's possible ..." He set down his pencil. "If you come to Nairobi, I will pay you a thousand schillings to have a bone marrow test to study your blood cells."

I smiled, thinking of the negotiating skills Joyce had taught me and the price I charged clients for not wearing a condom. He recognized the humor of his offer. "I suppose that's inadequate—and how do we get you to Nairobi?"

I raised four fingers.

"You want four thousand shillings? You're expensive, Miss Muwami."

"Are you a Christian, a follower of Jesus, Colonel?" I asked.

"Yes, why do you ask?" he responded, surprised at my question.

"I saw the Holy Bible in your briefcase. I have prayed to Jesus to help me escape." I got up and edged toward the door, opening it a crack. Madame Mimi was still sitting across the room, pouting. Mwalimu stood beside her. I returned to my seat.

"The back door is chained and locked. I can't get out. I could never fight my way through Mwalimu. But if I could escape out the back door and over the wall, I would be glad to come to Nairobi and let you study my lymphocytes."

He tapped his pencil on the desk, picked up my laboratory results, and stuffed them into his briefcase. I assumed we were done. He would think my plan too dangerous.

When he spoke, his voice was cautious. "Next Thursday the Kenyan health department is planning to make a surprise inspection of this 'orphanage.'"

We both smiled at the word.

"I will make sure the inspector insists that the chain on the door be removed. It is a fire hazard, and there are laws against it." He saw my objection and held up his hand. "I know Madame will put it back as soon as they leave, but that will give you a few minutes. Be ready. The highway to Nairobi is just a few blocks north of here. A black car with a US flag on the antenna will be waiting. I could even bring you to the US embassy in Nairobi for your protection."

He latched his briefcase. In a loud voice he said, "You're clean, Chui. You do not have AIDS."

"Thank you, Colonel, for that information. I will continue to be very careful with my clients." I followed him out of the office to the door. He shook hands with Madame Mimi. "I am glad to say that Chui is free of HIV-AIDS. I know you were concerned that she wasn't using condoms properly. Dr. Patel told me that much, so I had her checked."

"We are glad as well. I wouldn't want any of my orphans to suffer." Mwalimu stepped aside and opened the door. Cash changed hands. Madame smiled at her unexpected profit.

Mwalimu looked at me with suspicion. I did not want to answer any questions that might be on his mind, so after thanking the colonel, I bowed my head and said to Madame, "I need to take my shower now, if I may."

She was all charm in front of the colonel. "Yes, certainly."

She turned to her guest. "You see, Colonel, we run a clean house here."

No one was in the shower when I got there, not even Zipporah. Most of the girls took a nap after mealtime, so I was alone. I stripped and danced under the spray. I didn't have AIDS. I couldn't even get it. And next Thursday would change my life.

Madame Mimi's voice boomed as she shoved aside the shower curtain. "So what did you and the colonel discuss?" She waved her stick in my face.

"He told me that I did not have HIV," I responded.

"None of you girls has HIV. Dr. Patel has told me that. What else did you talk about?" She poked her stick into my flank. "What was so secret?"

I turned off the water and faced her. "I have a membrane receptor deficiency on my lymphocytes." I was sure she didn't understand but would be too proud to admit it. So I explained, "I have very weird blood cells."

"That's all?" she snapped.

"That is confidential information." I whimpered for effect. "My blood cell membranes are different from everybody else's. It's a genetic deficiency. I don't want you to share that with the other girls. Please don't tell them. They will make fun of me." I started to cry.

"I promise not to tell." She lowered her stick and turned to leave.

I grabbed my towel. "As he closed his briefcase, he mentioned that the Kenyan health department is making a surprise inspection of the orphanage next Thursday."

She smiled at me. "Thank you, Chui. We will be ready, won't we?"

"Yes, Madame Mimi. I will be ready."

Escape

THE INSPECTOR SHOWED UP WITH thick glasses that reminded me of the owl that lived in the old, dead tree beside our house when I was a child. On moonlit nights, I would sneak out of the house and sit on a rock by the doorway to watch the owl's big eyes looking for mice in the field next to our house. He kept the mice out of our grain. Father said owls were like watchmen. Would this one be watching for me?

The inspector was a slight, distinguished man with graying hair combed straight back. He appeared in his pinstriped, three-piece suit shuffling reams of paper. He was accompanied by two Kenyan police officers in pressed uniforms. They looked like brothers. Both were muscular, with shaved heads and square jaws with scars from adolescent acne. Mwalimu didn't seem to recognize them. *Good*, I thought.

"I'm Inspector Naiguta from the Health and Safety Department. Are you in charge of this facility?" The inspector looked over the top of his glasses and blinked rapidly as he spoke to Madame Mimi. I nearly laughed.

"Yes. We have a very clean place for these orphans, and I take personal responsibility for their health and welfare. They see the physician at the clinic on a routine basis, or more often if needed." She took a deep breath, presenting her large bosom to the inspector at eye level.

Mwalimu had lined us up and told us to dress in our most modest clothes. Madame Mimi insisted that we wear jewelry to demonstrate her excellent care. The inspector turned to Esther.

"Is that true"—he looked at the registry Madame Mimi had handed him and followed the names with his finger—"Esther?"

"Yes," Esther said. "Every three months we go to the doctor. He treats all our troubles."

"Excellent. Do you each have your own room?" He made a check on his clipboard and moved down the row.

"Yes, we are each having our own rooms," said Agnes, "and I go to the doctor more often because of my skin condition." The inspector took off Agnes's sunglasses. He seemed fascinated by her pink eyes. "You see how soft and nice my skin is. Without the doctor, I would be covered with sores."

"I see." He made another check mark.

"Zipporah," he said, noticing the next name on his sheet. "You're quite thin. Do you get enough to eat?"

"My father's crops failed three years in a row." She held up three fingers. "My baby brother died. We were so hungry. But Madame Mimi feeds us every day. My stomach is never complaining at me here. I am very thankful for the good food Madame gives us every day. And we always get meat on Sunday." He put a check mark beside her name and shifted to Ruth.

"Ruth, do you get enough exercise?"

"Monday is recreation day. Madame Mimi sends us places to get exercise, but I get exercise all the time carrying this weight around." She laughed. He did not respond to her joke.

He asked a question of each girl and made a check by her name. I was last on the list. I noticed that he had already put a check by my name. "Are you allowed to bathe every day, Chui?"

"Yes, sir, I do." I tried to see how Madame Mimi was responding. "We take showers every day. It's the rule that we are to be clean." I could see her beaming behind the inspector.

He turned to Madame. "Now I want to see each girl in her room for inspection."

"Girls, to your rooms," Madame said. "Show Inspector Naiguta how neat and clean your rooms are kept."

We had been roused up early this morning by the tap of Madame's stick on our door frames to clean our rooms. As we left the common room, Mwalimu took his post by the front door. He would be too busy guarding the front door to see me escape out the back if the chain was removed.

At the curtained frame to each of our rooms, we stood at attention. Inspector Naiguta put on white gloves and checked for dust in each room. I could hear the other girls answering his questions as he marched down the hall. Madame Mimi's mass filled the hall. She focused her eyes on each one as they answered.

When he came to my room, I had everything in order. Usually I felt a sense of security in my room, but today I was ready to leave. Fear made my heart race. If I got caught, I would be punished. The image of Kerebe's dying body flashed through my mind. I would be chained to the bed to service Mwalimu, and then there will be the discount special: "Half off, boys. No condoms tonight." Or if I were lucky, maybe Madame would sell me to one of the brothels in town where they beat the girls. We had met some of those girls on the beach. Their description of how they were treated made me cringe.

"Very nice," the inspector said of my room, "not a speck of dust." Then he looked up at the ceiling. His white gloved hand stretched toward the spider webs. "What's this?"

Madame Mimi entered to investigate his concern.

"Oh, sir, those are my pet spiders," I said. "Please do not

disturb them. They keep the mosquitoes out of my room. I have not had malaria since I came here because my pet spiders protect me."

I clasped my hands to my chest. "And Madame Mimi is very gracious about letting me keep my pets as long as my room is spotless." I saw her fat cheeks pulsate with concern.

"All right, I'll let that pass." He made some notes on his clipboard and walked out of my room.

"And what is this?" His voice raised an octave higher in surprise. "Why is this door chained and locked?"

"For security purposes," Madame said. Her plump cheeks turned scarlet. I couldn't tell whether it was from anger or embarrassment.

"This is a serious infraction. If there were a fire, the girls in this hall would all die. I will have to report this to the fire marshal."

Madame yelled, "Mwalimu, come here."

As he strode down the hall, the other girls ducked into their rooms. "What's the problem, inspector?"

"This door is chained and locked," he said, documenting the infraction in his notes.

"That is for security, sir," Mwalimu replied.

The inspector folded his arms across his chest. "It is also a fire hazard. Code number 687-342 states that all doors must be able to be opened from the inside. I understand your concern to prevent intrusion from the outside. You need a locking system that keeps it secure, but one that the girls can open in case of emergency." He turned to look up into Madame's eyes. "Take the chain off immediately."

"Yes, inspector," she said. I had never seen her submissive side before. "I will have a new lock system installed as soon as possible. Thank you for graciously bringing this to my attention."

Mwalimu produced the key from around his neck and

undid the lock and chain. He hung the key back around his neck. The chain slipped onto the floor.

"Madame Mimi, let's proceed back to your office to review my inspection." The inspector grinned. "Except for this very small problem with the door, you are in compliance. I am impressed with how clean and neat everything is, and the girls in your charge seem genuinely happy under your care."

He closed his folder and adjusted his glasses. "Now I need to speak to your kitchen staff and review your menus. The health department requires adequate protein in their diet."

He reopened his folder and peered through his thick glasses at his notes. "Yes—Zipporah, I believe, said that you serve meat every Sunday."

"Yes, on Sundays we usually serve chicken or goat with all the trimmings. And thank you, sir, for your kind words about my orphanage. Right this way. I have the kitchen staff on hand to review the menus."

Madame looked back down the hall. "Come, girls—all of you in the dining room."

I wondered what "all the trimmings" was supposed to mean and what would be on the menus other than sorghum porridge. But the door was unchained. I needed five minutes to escape.

Mwalimu tried to walk behind the inspector, but he politely waited for Mwalimu to proceed ahead of him down the hall. "Mwalimu, as head of security, I need to ask you some questions as well. Have you had any intrusions?"

Madame Mimi grasped her bosom. "I want all you girls present to hear the inspector."

Since my room was last, I followed in the wake of the others. When we got to the hallway door, I took one step back and let it close. Slipping silently to the back door, I thought, *This door hasn't been opened since Faraji and Chuki led me through it months ago. What if it is rusted shut? What if I can't*

*open it? What if it makes too much noise? I would be as good
as dead.*

I heard a cry and paused to listen. Zipporah was whining
in the dining room, "Madame Mimi, I think I have diarrhea.
I have to go to the WC bad. Please let me go. I will come right
back."

That was just the distraction I needed. I pushed the door.
It opened with a squeak drowned out by Zipporah's antics.

Run

OUT IN THE GARDEN, I ran behind the WC to grab my money stash. As I loosened the brick, Zipporah appeared. "You'll need help over the wall," she said.

Intent on my escape, I turned to see what she meant. She held her hands folded together. I stepped into them, and she boosted me up the wall using strength that I didn't know she had. I could just grip the top of the wall where the broken bottles were cemented in the concrete. I grabbed a broken Tusker beer bottle that was mostly intact. It cut the top of my hand, but it was enough to let me kick my leg and catch purchase on the edge.

"Don't forget me," Zipporah said, "You have been like a sister to me."

I jumped down the other side. "I won't forget."

I landed in trash piled beside the wall. I looked up. Overhead, clouds off the ocean were racing across the sky. I panicked. Not only had I not taken the money, but I had forgotten Phillip's card. I searched for something to use to climb back. There was nothing.

I didn't want to get caught, and I was sure Zipporah was gone. I focused on the open field in front of me. Everything was unfamiliar. I gauged the position of the sun to make sure I was heading north. Colonel Johnson had said the highway was just a few blocks north of the brothel, but I could not see the road. Dried brush, broken bottles, and lots of trash were piled around. The stench of rotted fruit and dog feces pervaded the air. To the north, the field was bordered by the back sides of market buildings. There was no place to hide. Zipporah had said that there was a field, then a road where her father sold produce, and then, north of that, the highway.

I tied my dress up with my kitamba and ran, ignoring what I stepped on. I heard things crunching under my bare feet, but I was too afraid to check to see if I was bleeding. Thorns scratched my legs and grabbed at the pretty dress I wore for the inspection. I tripped in a hole and fell, shredding my dress. My knee was abraded and bleeding, but there was no time to tend to it. I jumped up and ran faster. When I made it to the back of the buildings, I looked back. No one was following. I slipped between two walls, out of sight, and gasped for breath. There was too much blood on my feet to tell what kind of lacerations I had. It didn't matter.

Edging toward the street, I saw no one. Had my escape been discovered? How did Zipporah know I was going? Would she be punished for helping me? She was so fragile. I jumped from my hiding place and crouched behind an oil barrel. The road in front of the market was dirt. That couldn't be the highway? I thought back to our honeymoon. The highway had been paved from Nairobi to the resort and all the way to Mombasa. I had to find that road. Besides, there was no black car waiting on the dirt road.

Recalling what Zipporah had said, I decided that the paved road must be farther north. I dashed across the dirt road. I heard a voice from the kiosk.

"Is that you, Chui?" It was the vegetable merchant, one of my regulars, who came every Friday night.

I grabbed a corner of my kitamba to cover my face and ducked between two buildings on the other side. I rested only long enough to catch my breath and take a quick check of my feet. The thick calluses I had developed from walking barefoot around the garden seemed to have prevented severe injury.

I coughed a few times at the dust a passing truck threw into the air and then ran between buildings and shacks. I jumped over several low fences and found my way between piles of garbage. I quickened my pace as I heard, "Is that you, Chui?" play over in my mind. Even if he hadn't seen my face, he would have recognized my kitamba. My escape was no longer a secret.

When I found a path going my direction, I scrambled up the hill. I could taste blood in my mouth. I hadn't trained well enough. As I neared the top of the hill, I saw the highway, but a ten-foot chain-link fence blocked my way. Which way should I run? Was there a gate through the fence? Zipporah hadn't said anything about a fence.

I ran left. Was that the direction to Nairobi? Logic escaped me. Nairobi was hundreds of miles away, but left seemed to be the correct way. I crouched to avoid attention, but there were so many things in the way. A small shed made of clay bricks with a tin roof blocked my progress. I noticed a barrel beside the shed, so I ran and jumped up onto the barrel, which gave me enough spring to vault onto the roof of a small shed. I could just reach the top of the fence from the roof. Could I get over it? A roll of barbed wire crowned the top. Its sting stopped me. I looked left and then right. Was there another way?

The black car with the American flag on the antenna was parked just a few yards down the street. Outside the car a United States marine with sunglasses stood at attention, scanning the street in both directions. I was close enough to hear him say, "I don't see her, Colonel. Maybe she didn't make it. That fence is pretty wicked."

I was ready to scream to the marine for help. I felt a surge of adrenalin. But then I saw one of my clients in a kiosk to the right. If I yelled, he would see me. Right now he was focused on selecting vegetables for his customer. *It is now or death,* I told myself. I cringed, gripped the barbed wire, stuck my toes in the top links of the fence, and swung over. My toes caught in the chain links on the other side as the barbed wire ripped my dress and arms. Extricating my skin from the barbs, I jumped down. I felt my ankle give as I hit. A quick glance revealed the merchant was still minding his customer.

Then a strange thing happened. The sun glinted from between the clouds. Everyone in the market was blinded by the sudden brightness. They shaded their eyes, and I sprinted to the car and dived headlong through the open door. Curled up on the floor, I was too breathless to speak.

"Let's go, Sergeant. Here she is," said Colonel Johnson.

The marine slammed the door and climbed into the driver's seat.

"Drive at a normal speed, Sergeant," the colonel told his driver. "We don't want to draw attention."

Emotion spilled out of me. "One of my Friday clients saw me," I cried. Tears dripped down my cheeks, stinging the cuts on my chin. "He saw me run across the dirt road."

I grabbed my face with blood-smeared hands. "They'll come after me. They'll kill me."

"Sit up here and let me check your wounds." Colonel Johnson reached behind the seat and pulled out a white plastic box with a red cross on it.

"I always bring a first-aid kit." His voice soothed my fears until he added, "Although I've never actually opened it before."

I leaned back and closed my eyes. *Am I free?* The seat felt soft and comfortable. I stretched out, palms up, as the colonel disinfected my wounds. The antiseptic stung, but I didn't care.

"Am I safe?" I asked, but no sound came out of my mouth.

"Police roadblock ahead, Colonel," the sergeant said.

"Get down on the floor, Kwamboka," Colonel Johnson commanded. I rolled off the seat onto the floor. It was so good to hear my real name. I would never be Chui, the leopard, again. Colonel Johnson and the sergeant sat in military posture as the vehicle slowed. The sergeant opened the front window.

"Diplomatic business," he said to the police officer. I looked up through the tinted window and saw Mwalimu standing behind the policeman. He was trying to see through the tinted glass. The policeman was a regular client of Ruth's.

"Sorry to disturb you, but we've had a kidnapping reported and are checking every car, sir," said the officer.

Colonel Johnson leaned forward over the front seat. "Are all your girls healthy, Mwalimu? I left money for them with Dr. Patel this morning."

"Oh, Colonel Johnson, it is so good to see you. Yes, sir, everyone is healthy. Thank you so much for asking."

"Do you know these people, Mwalimu?" the officer asked.

"Oh yes, the colonel here pays for our orphans' medical care," Mwalimu replied.

Huddled on the floor, I hardly recognized the pleasant tone of Mwalimu's voice.

"Well then, you can move on, Colonel. Sorry to delay official business." The sergeant saluted, and the policeman saluted back.

As we sped up, Colonel Johnson helped me back onto the seat. I felt a sudden sting in my thigh. "Ouch," I yelled, "what was that?"

He laughed. "That was your tetanus shot."

"Oh, tell me before you shoot me," I said.

"I didn't want you to have the option to refuse," Colonel Johnson said.

I felt the adrenalin surge that had prevented me from experiencing pain dissipate. Now every cut and scrape hurt. My muscles felt weak, and I could barely move my legs as the scenery blurred past the tinted windows. My mind jelled as I wondered what pain awaited me in Nairobi.

Back in Nairobi

DARKNESS FORCED THE CITY LIGHTS to twinkle as we arrived in Nairobi. Colonel Johnson escorted me to a hotel I had never been to near the Nairobi University Hospital. The doorman looked askance as I approached the door in my tattered dress with multiple bandages, but he stepped aside when Colonel Johnson said, "She's with me."

The colonel directed me to one of the large, comfortable couches in the lobby, where I collapsed. My eyes feasted on the exquisite oil paintings of elephants, leopards, giraffes, and Maasai warriors throughout the lobby. I noticed the Internet connection, an accoutrement I could hardly comprehend after living in a brothel the last few months. After running the colonel's credit card, the receptionist gave him a room key with a smile. "Room 412. Checkout is at noon."

Colonel Johnson called me to his side. "You'll be safe here. It is close to the hospital, and I need you to be at the outpatient department by nine o'clock tomorrow morning for a procedure, the bone marrow analysis we talked about. The research on your lymphocytes requires that kind of specimen. It's going to hurt a bit."

He looked at the bandages on my hands, legs, and feet. "But it will be nothing compared to what you've been through."

I looked at the number on the key and rolled it into my hand. Was I dreaming?

The receptionist's voice pulled me back to reality from my fugue state. "The lift is over in that corner, Miss. Your room is on the fourth floor. Turn left when you get off the lift."

I turned to leave, too tired to think and only conscious enough to follow her command.

"Just a minute," Colonel Johnson said, putting a hand on my shoulder. "I don't want you coming to the hospital in your kitamba or that torn dress. You need some clothes."

A store in the lobby displayed tourist offerings. I refused the sweatshirt he first picked out. "You'd look nice in this," he said. It was bright red with a Maasai warrior.

I shook my head. "The Maasai are enemies of the Kisii."

"Oh, you're Kisii?"

"Yes," I said.

"You are a long way from home, aren't you? Is this green one with a giraffe on it better?" he asked.

"I'm willing to wear that," I conceded.

He grabbed a black pleated skirt that had animals marching around the hem and a leather belt. "And is this okay?"

"That's fine." He grabbed underwear and a matching bra with an elephant print without asking me and handed the purchases and his credit card to the retail clerk. "What about toiletries?" I nodded as the clerk added toothbrush, toothpaste, and a bottle of aspirin from the shelf behind the register.

My eyes were flooded with tears as I took my purchases, my gifts, and headed for the lift. "Don't be late," he cautioned me.

"I won't, I promise."

"Send a wake-up call to room 412 at eight o'clock, please," was the last thing I heard him say before the lift shut.

My room was stunning. I locked the door and collapsed

on my knees beside the bed. "Thank you, Jesus. This is like a honeymoon with you, Jesus."

I couldn't stop crying. I stripped off my smelly, torn, bloody dress and threw it in the trash. I washed the kitamba in the sink with hand soap. I removed the dressings from my hands and legs and set them carefully on the counter so that I could reapply them after my shower.

As the hot water poured over my body, I realized that I didn't have to share the shower with anyone, and Madame Mimi was not going to suddenly appear at the doorway. I detached the shower head and sprayed my groin. How refreshing. Tonight I didn't have to have sex with anyone before I went to sleep. I lathered the soap all over my body and started to sing. I felt like I had been resurrected. My cuts stung, but I didn't care.

As I dried myself with the nice, fluffy towel I inspected each of my cuts, especially the ones on the bottom of my feet. All seemed superficial. They would heal. I sat on the bed to contemplate. Would I heal? After months of sex with all those filthy penises, would I recover? Would I ever enjoy sex again? Would I feel the tender touch of Phillip? Or would his touch remind me of the thousands of violations that I hated? Was Phillip even alive? Would he hate me if I told him what I had experienced?

That night as I crawled between the cool, soothing sheets with the air conditioner on full fan, I wiggled my frame on the thick mattress and thought about Joyce. Would she accept me? I had just disappeared. It had been so many months. Had she given up on me? Had she thrown all my things away?

Proper Procedure

I ARRIVED EARLY FOR MY procedure, dressed in my green giraffe T-shirt, black skirt with the animals dancing around the hem, leather belt, and of course my new elephant underwear and bra. Several beggars approached me for money, thinking I was a tourist. They were disappointed when they heard my Swahili reprimand.

At the time I was scheduled for my procedure, I approached the receptionist. "You will have to wait. We have been busy this morning," she said. But when she informed the nurse of my presence, I was immediately escorted to a small room. There I was instructed to undress and put on a hospital gown.

The bone marrow test was painful but quick. It felt like a sharp stab in the back with a knife. I cringed when I saw the needle. It was huge compared to the needles used for penicillin injections and IVs, but it represented freedom. After the humiliation of being a slave and transactional sex worker, this stab in the back was of no consequence.

Returning from the procedure room on a gurney to my room, the nurse said, "You can't leave yet." She rolled me on my side to check my incision.

"No bleeding. Looks good," she reported.

"May I get dressed?" I tried to keep the impatience out of my voice.

"Yes, but let me check with the physician to make sure he

obtained an adequate specimen. We don't want to have you come back if we need a better specimen."

I dressed and waited.

She returned. "He got a good specimen. Are you feeling light-headed at all?"

"No."

She checked my pulse and blood pressure. "Then you're free to go."

She handed me an envelope. "This is for you."

The sealed envelope had the golden eagle insignia of the US Army. I thanked her but waited until she left the room to check the contents. There were four thousand shillings inside. I tucked the envelope under my T-shirt inside my new skirt.

Out on the street I was besieged by beggars. The green giraffe on my T-shirt must have attracted them. At least it did not attract mosquitoes. One of Joyce's dresses would have been more comfortable. I gave a quick exclamation in Swahili, and the beggars scattered.

The boulevard down the center of Nairobi was beautiful, graced with hotels and fine-art shops selling exquisite carvings of animals to the visiting tourists. The smell was not African but a mixture of European women's perfumes and businessmen's cologne. A row of jacaranda trees grew down the boulevard, adding to the scent. It always looked nice.

I walked down the boulevard, rejoicing in my freedom. I caught myself taking deep sighs, breathing in the delicious flavor of escape from the life I had been living. But then I quickened my pace. I wanted to catch Joyce in her shop. Maybe she would let me explain what had happened in a public place. Would she even let me explain? I wasn't sure.

Captured

FARTHER DOWN THE BOULEVARD, IN front of the New Stanley Hotel, a gathering of people under the jacaranda trees caught my eye. I stopped and took a second glance. Martha Gathoni, from my anthropology and economics classes, was standing under the tree only a few yards away. I wanted to ignore her. She had been so unkind to me because I scored well on the economics exam. But she was a classmate from the pleasant years of my life. I was sure her hostility would be long gone.

Then I noticed two uniformed men were with her. They had their backs toward me. A young woman dressed in a short skirt with a halter top, like a prostitute, stood between them. It appeared that she was being arrested. I crept forward to get a better look, curious as to what was happening. When I was on the sidewalk opposite the boulevard where I thought she could hear me, I yelled out. "Martha, I haven't seen you since graduation. *Jambo*, how are you?"

She turned at my greeting. She did not look happy to see me. The two uniformed men turned as well. In an instant I recognized Faraji and Chuki. I screamed, "Martha, stay away from them. Those are the men that kidnapped me."

Then I saw that Faraji had the young woman in the miniskirt handcuffed to his wrist. I was frantic. "Martha, be careful."

Policemen rushed to the scene from every corner. Two

policemen grabbed Chuki. The apparent victim drew a gun from under her skirt and held it to Faraji's head. A Kenyan policeman grabbed me from behind, twisted my arm behind my back, and escorted me to the group gathering under the jacaranda tree. A troop of police officers appeared with clubs to hold the crowd at bay.

Chuki's hands were cuffed behind him. He collapsed as a policeman clubbed him behind the knees. Faraji covered his face with his free hand, still bound to the woman who had held a gun to his head. "Can you identify these two men, miss?" one police officer asked.

"Yes, I can identify them. These are the men who kidnapped me." Then I noticed that Martha's hands were being held behind her back by two policewomen.

One of the policemen removed the handcuff from the pistol-toting young lady and cuffed Faraji's wrists together. The "victim" slipped on a uniform over her halter top.

The scene became clear. The person I had assumed to be a prostitute was an undercover policewoman. She started laughing at me as my police escort released his grip on my arm. "You almost ruined our sting operation, young lady."

"Martha, what's happening?" I asked.

The sting operative asked me, "You know this woman too?"

"Yes, from Nairobi University. She was in my economics and anthropology classes."

A flood of memories accosted my brain. Martha must have written the note accusing me of cheating on the exam. She had teased me for being a rural girl who "knew nothing." My graduation accolades must have angered her. Was she involved in my kidnapping? Then I remembered that I had never seen the driver. I was blindfolded, and the driver never spoke. *Was Martha the driver?*

"Can you identify her as the one who arranged your kidnapping?" one of the policemen behind me asked.

"No." I hesitated. "I only saw Faraji and Chuki when I was

kidnapped. I was blindfolded and never saw the driver of the vehicle. Were you the driver, Martha?"

She spat at me and tried to kick me. The policewomen kicked her behind the knees and dropped her to the ground.

Chuki was bleating like a sheep. "How did you get away?" he said, wrestling with the officer who held him. "How did you escape? Madame Mimi said you would never escape."

"Shut up, Chuki, you've said too much already," Martha said.

The apparent victim in the miniskirt, now clearly a policewoman kicked Martha in the stomach. She crumpled face first to the ground and vomited. "That's for kicking me," the female officer said, grinding her pistol barrel into Martha's temple.

A police van arrived, and the three had their legs chained. They were pulled to their feet and pushed into the back by armed officers without concern for their comfort. The policewoman in the miniskirt directed the entire scene. When all the perpetrators were locked away and the police had dissipated the crowd, the boulevard was as quiet as if nothing had happened.

The policewoman turned to me. "We need to talk. Let's have tea."

She buttoned up her uniform over the halter top and directed me to the Thorn Tree Café. Without asking me what I wanted, she ordered tea and pastries for both of us. "Official business; put it on the department tab," she told the waiter.

"Right away, Officer Kiriamiti."

She held out the aluminum chair for me beside the famous thorn bush tree. "They know me around here." She smiled.

"I'm pleased to meet you, Officer Kiriamiti." I felt stunned as I sat down.

"Oh, please, just call me Johdi. We've been trying to capture this gang for some time. Let's hear your side of the story. You are?"

I sat in shock. I kept grabbing my throat, trying to swallow so that I could speak. Johdi Kiriamiti put her hand on mine, seeming so gentle compared to how I had seen her behave during the sting operation..

The waiter brought the cups, a large pot of tea, and pretty little decorated pastries. "My favorites," she said as he set the table. She took out a notebook from her purse. "Now, go ahead."

My voice returned as I took a sip of tea. "My name is Kwamboka Muwami."

I set down my cup and added a spoonful of sugar and some hot milk. "Thank you for the tea … Johdi."

I stared at her. Behind the gaudy makeup, I recognized her. "Your name is Kisii like mine. I recognize you. You're the Kisii girl who ran in the African games and won first prize. You were in all the newspapers. You're famous in Kisii land."

She smiled and switched to Ekegusii. It was so pleasant to hear my native tongue after so long. "Yes, that's me." She grinned. "Now I'm a policewoman because I can run faster than the criminals." Her smile turned serious. "Thank you for remembering my famous run," she said. "Now, down to business. Do you have your Kenyan ID card?"

"Not on me. It's at my foster mother's home." I hoped that was true. "I can bring it to the police station tomorrow. I've been at the hospital all morning getting blood tests and didn't bring it with me."

"I'm surprised you didn't need it to get your blood drawn, but whatever. I will need to see your identification, but tomorrow is fine. Are you willing to testify in court against these three?"

"Oh, yes," I said between sips of tea and nibbles of my pastry. "I'll tell you the whole story."

I started from the beginning, and tears filled my eyes as I related the humiliating events of my capture and sale. I left nothing out except my grief at watching my husband leave for the airport. I was garrulous at times while speaking my native language. She stopped me several times to catch up on her notes and focus on the facts she needed.

"Your story is vital to this case. Our sting today will only put them behind bars for attempting to kidnap me." She laughed and added, "And assaulting an officer. Your testimony will put them away forever."

She gulped the last of her tea. It must have been cold because she summoned the waiter for a refill. She put her notebook back in her purse as he brought a fresh pot. "So how did you get away? I noticed the scratches on your legs, arms, and hands."

"You are very observant, Johdi Kiriamiti."

"I'm paid to be. Now, how did you escape?"

As I told the story of my life as a forced transactional sex worker and my escape, she became intrigued and pulled out her notebook again. "That's not our jurisdiction," she said, "but we might be able to pass this information to the proper authorities in Mombasa." She thanked me and nodded at the waiter.

I stood in front of her. "But if you pass it on to the police in Mombasa, nothing will happen. Several of the policemen are paid off by the brothel. It will require higher authority than the local police."

"I suppose," she said as she edged her way to the street. She held my hand. "You are one brave woman, Kwamboka—and tenacious. I don't know if I would have survived what you went through." She gave me a hug with an Ekegusii farewell.

"Now you're even more my hero," I told her as she walked away. I had to admit that she did look like a prostitute. But then I wondered how I had looked on the streets of Mombasa or on North Beach, topless. I headed for the bus stop.

Homecoming

THE BUS TRAVERSED UNIVERSITY STREET. I got off and walked to the tailor shop. It was closed and locked. I looked toward downtown. The sun was setting between the buildings. Brilliant reds and oranges refracted through the dust from the game park. I walked down the street and turned into the alley as the sun dropped below the horizon. I stood in front of Joyce's door like a statue. I used the code: two hard knocks, a soft one, and four more. There was no response. Where could she have gone? I panicked. I still had plenty of money from Colonel Johnson, but a hotel might require identification. As it got darker, I perceived a faint flicker of light under the doorway. She was home. She would never leave a lamp burning if she wasn't home. I knocked the code again.

Still there was no answer. "Joyce, are you there? It's me, Kitzi. Have you forgotten our code?"

The light under the doorway went out. "Joyce, I know you're there. Please let me in. It's Kitzi. It's me, Joyce. It's really me. It's Kitzi."

A faint voice came through the door. "My daughter Kitzi is dead. Don't fool me."

"I'm not fooling you. I am not dead. Remember when you rescued me at Kijabe Hospital?"

"Kitzi, if that's you, leave me alone. You're dead to me. Go back to your husband or I'll call the police."

"Joyce," I stammered, "I'm back. I did not run away to my husband. I was kidnapped. I escaped."

I kneeled in front of the door. Tears streamed down my face. "Joyce, I am not dead. You're the only person in the whole world who loves me just the way I am. Please open the door." I could not stop crying.

Click, click.

"What are doing out there?" she said.

Click, click, click.

"If you want me dead, Joyce, I'm piling up rocks for you to throw at me. I have a nice pile gathered here. Stone me. I deserve it. If I had listened to you, none of this would have happened. Come and stone me to death, just like in the story you read to me from your Bible. But if I remember correctly, Jesus did not throw stones at the woman."

Click, click, click.

"I belong to Jesus now. He kept me alive all these months. I would have died without Jesus. Would he throw stones at me, Joyce? Would Jesus refuse to open the door to me? Isn't that a Bible verse you read to me? Seek and ye shall find. Knock and the door shall be opened."

Click, click.

"I have the stones all piled up ready for you, Joyce. They are in a nice pile. Come and throw them at me. I will kneel down to make it easy for you."

I collapsed in the dirt.

She unlatched the door. "Why are you saying these things?"

"I am ready to die, but I belong to Jesus. When you stone me, I will go to heaven and be with Jesus. He saved me. A Christian man rescued me so I could come home." I bowed my forehead to the red, dusty clay in the yard.

She opened the door. "Get in here right now," Joyce

commanded. "What are you doing out there in the dark all by yourself?"

She grabbed my hand and jerked me up. She kicked over the rock pile. "Something bad could happen to you."

"It already happened," I said, bursting into tears. She hugged me. Once inside, she locked and bolted the door. I collapsed on the sofa sobbing, overwhelmed to be home.

"I'll make tea," she said as she put the kettle on to boil. "Have you had supper yet? You look so scrawny. Haven't you been eating well?"

"No, I was at the hospital all morning and then ..."

"Let me make you something." She scurried about the kitchen cooking gruel. I feasted my eyes on the place I had called home for four years. The couch and chair were in the same place. None of the knickknacks on the shelf had moved. Despite the luxury of the hotel room, this was beautiful. A pile in the corner caught my eye. In the many months since I had be kidnapped, Joyce had made an altar of folded dresses and my other belongings stacked together with my leather pouch on top.

I grabbed the pouch and dumped it out on the coffee table. The necklace from my honeymoon and my wedding rings tinkled as they sprawled across the surface. I put on the necklace to calm my turmoil as the diamonds sparkled across my chest, catching the light from the kerosene lamp. I put on my wedding rings. They were a bit loose. I must have lost weight while living as a prostitute. I counted the sparkling jewels: nine on the necklace and the tenth on my finger. I was worth ten cows again.

"I saved all that stuff for you, my dear. I prayed every day that you would come home." She set two bowls of gruel on the table and smiled. "But when you didn't come home I got angry."

She covered her eyes, sniffled, and wiped the tears away. "But today Jesus brought you home and answered my prayers, even though I am ashamed to admit that I gave up praying for you."

She lifted me off the couch and hugged me so hard I couldn't breathe. "Thank you, Jesus, for bringing my lost daughter home."

We sat at the table, and she folded her hands in mine. "Thank you, dear Jesus, for this food that we can eat together. Bless you, Jesus. Forgive your weak servant for her lack of faith. Take away my sin of anger. Amen."

Tears flooded both our eyes as we sipped tea and spooned the flavorless gruel into our mouths. "I never thought I would see you again," she said. "I cried myself to sleep so many nights that I became angry."

"Thank you for your prayers." I put my hand on hers.

"I was so angry. But one night my blessed Jesus told me, 'I won't let Kitzi come home until you give up this anger.' I am so ashamed, Kitzi. In church last Sunday I asked Jesus to forgive me for my anger. I gave it up to Him. Oh, my Blessed Redeemer has had compassion on my soul and let you come home."

After we ate, Joyce kept busy washing dishes. She was avoiding looking at me. I stood behind her and kissed her neck. She burst into tears. "Now leave me alone, or I will never get these dishes washed."

Back on the couch, the contents of my pouch drew my attention. Familiar treasures flooded me with emotion. I pocketed my Kenyan ID card. "I have to bring this to the police station tomorrow, Joyce."

She stopped, wiped her hands on a towel, and turned to face me. "Why is that? And why are you wearing that ridiculous outfit? And why are you covered with bandages?"

"Oh, you noticed."

"Don't make me cry again," Joyce said as tears welled up in her eyes.

"I'm sorry. I will explain, if you want to know."

"Tell me," Joyce insisted.

She pulled the kitchen chair across from me, and I began. "Today I was on my way here from the hospital and saw the men who kidnapped me. I yelled, and the police captured them. I'm sure it will be in tomorrow's paper."

She grabbed my hands. "They caught the men who kidnapped you?"

"Do you want to hear the story? It is a very bad, evil story."

"Tell me some of it," she said, "but not the parts that will hurt my soul. And why were you in the hospital? You haven't told me that part yet."

"Remember, I went to meet Phillip at the restaurant to say good-bye. His flight was leaving Nairobi that night."

"I told you to leave him alone," Joyce reminded me.

"Joyce ..."

"I'm sorry." She raised her hands. "Oh, forgive me, Jesus."

"Yes, maybe I should have listened to you." I twisted the engagement and wedding rings around my finger. "But I love Phillip. And we are married." *If only I could convince her*, I thought.

"Tell me more. I'm sorry I interrupted," said Joyce, ready to hear more of the story.

"I was very sad because he was leaving that day. You remember?" She nodded and put a hand over her mouth. I decided not to tell her any more about our parting. "I was wandering the streets downtown, walking off my sadness, when these two men in uniforms just like policemen grabbed me."

I explained how Faraji and Chuki pretended to be policemen and how they tied me up. "They sold me as a slave in Mombasa. That's where I've been all these months. I have been working as a slave to a fat woman. I couldn't get away. There was a chain on the door."

"You were a prostitute, weren't you?"

I had chosen my words with care, but Joyce was not naïve to criminal activity in Kenya.

"Yes." I hung my head.

"I am not able to hear any more about this." She got up from her chair and walked down the hallway. "You do not have to tell me the rest. I am glad you have returned from the faraway country. Let's leave it like that."

Was she angry? I tried to stall her. "Thank you for not throwing these things away, Joyce. They mean so much to me." She kept walking.

"Mother Joyce, did I offend you?" I followed her to her room but stopped in the doorway. For all the time I lived with her, I had never been in her room.

She looked for something in her room and then handed me a letter. "This letter came to the shop. It's for you. It came while I was angry with you, and I meant to burn it. But I prayed to Jesus, and he stopped me. Now I am glad in my heart that I didn't burn it."

I took the letter to the table and opened it by the oil lamp. It was still sealed.

"What does it mean?" She put a tender hand on my shoulder. "I was afraid of it. It came from the United States of America."

As I opened the letter, the embossed insignia of Boston College flickered in the lamplight. I unfolded it in anticipation. Phillip's card fell onto the table. Joyce grabbed it and read Phillip's name. "I knew I should have burned this," she said.

I snatched the card away.

"I am just teasing, Kitzi."

"Well, you are not very good at it." I spread the letter on the table. "This letter means that you should be very proud of me."

Dear Kwamboka Muwami,

We are pleased to accept you to the doctorate program in the

School of Public Health here at Boston College. We anticipate your matriculation in September 2010.

I couldn't read the rest; my vision blurred with tears of joy. I grabbed Joyce and danced with her around the room. "Your prodigal daughter is going to be a doctor." I yelled and screamed.

She stopped. "You are going to leave me again, aren't you? That is why I did not want you to have that letter."

"Joyce, be happy for me. I will come back to you ... as a doctor."

She held me to her breast and cried. After a deep breath she whispered in my ear, "I don't want you to leave for the United States of America, Boston, but the grasshoppers have stolen many months from you. I know the rest of your story is evil, but now Jesus is going to give you a time of gladness. I should not stop you from what Jesus has for you."

I bowed as an obedient daughter, and she kissed my forehead. "You are in Jesus's hands. That evil fat woman doesn't own you, I don't own you, and Phillip doesn't own you, but Jesus does. You must do what He says. I will go to church and ask Jesus to forgive me again."

Her blessing thrilled me. Months of despair dissipated like smoke, but now I had many things to do. I tried to picture Boston in my mind. *It must be a big city. What does the University of Boston look like?* My mind failed me.

After Joyce went to bed, I lit a candle and scattered the rest of the things from my pouch on the coffee table. My student ID had expired. I picked up the Barclay's credit card that Phillip had given me and checked the expiration date: February 2013. It was still active. Could I use it?

My treasured secondary school test scores and acceptance letter to the Nairobi University were treasures no longer, but they held memories of my trek across the Maasai Mara from Kisii land. Two opened letters were still in their envelopes. I knew what they were but checked them anyway. One was my TOEFL test score. I had done well but had expected to, since I had spoken English with my mother since I was a child. The other was my GRE score: 1538. I had no context for what the score meant, but Phillip had said that I could go to any graduate school in the United States that I chose. Now I had an acceptance letter from Boston College to start in September.

The last paper, yellowed with age, was the title deed to my father's property in Kisii land. I wadded it up to throw away, but it was the last vestige of my parents. Spreading it flat again, I folded it up and stuffed it in the bottom of the leather pouch. Would I ever return to Kisii land? It was a long way from Boston.

I danced in the candle light and held up the dresses Joyce had made me. I took off the tourist garb and put on one of the dresses. The fit was very loose. I wondered how they would look in Boston. Phillip had told me that it got cold there sometimes. But after what I had endured, I was sure I could resist any cold.

Preparation

COLONEL JOHNSON HAD GIVEN ME the address of his office. As I entered, I noticed all kinds of spears and shields on his walls. They were all Maasai, but his secretary was a pleasant Kikuyu woman. "Come right in. The colonel is expecting you."

I walked into his office. The whole room smelled of a musky aftershave. It had dark paneling but bright lighting. Around the walls were pictures of a woman with two children on a beach I recognized.

"Those were taken at one of the beaches in Mombasa," he said. "I took my wife and children with me a couple of times. But they live here in Nairobi."

He offered me a chair across from his massive desk. On the corner was a large picture of the same woman, his wife. I noticed she wore a necklace with a cross. "Is your wife a Christian too, Colonel Johnson?"

"Yes, absolutely."

I sank into the soft leather chair. It felt so comfortable. I had never sat in such a chair before. And the room was such a pleasant temperature; the air conditioner cooled the sweat on my brow from my brisk walk in the Nairobi heat.

"The test results from your bone marrow are very exciting," Colonel Johnson began, looking at me from across his oak desk. I assumed it had been imported from the United States of America. We did not have such wood in Kenya. I ran my hand over the soft grain.

He must have noted my distraction. He started again, "The test results confirm what I suspected from your blood tests in Mombasa. You do not have the receptor for HIV, the AIDS virus."

"I'm so glad." My hands covered my face to keep my emotions at bay. Too much was happening all at once.

He handed me a tissue. "I read in yesterday's paper that you were involved in catching the gang that was kidnapping women for the sex trade. That must have been very upsetting for you."

I sniffled to regain my composure. "Yes, I identified them on the street during a sting operation. One of my classmates from Nairobi University was the mastermind. Now I have to testify in court when their trial comes up."

"I'm sure that will be painful." I felt his compassion as he touched my hand.

"Is there any more I can do for you with your AIDS research?" I asked, trying to change the subject. I blew my nose in the tissue.

He leaned back in his leather chair and gazed up at the ceiling. "Not here in Kenya. I wish I could take you to the NIH laboratory, where they are doing research on lymphocyte receptors."

"Is that near Boston College?"

He turned to me. "Why do you ask?"

"I've been accepted to the Boston College PhD program in public health this September, and I was wondering if you could help me get my visa to the United States of America. I don't know how to do that." I looked down at my feet, embarrassed. "I have to return for the trial, but the police said that I can leave the country for education until the trial date."

He jumped out of his chair. "Kwamboka, is this real?"

I showed him the letter.

"This is your I-20, and they promise you a stipend," he said.

"I didn't understand that part. Does that mean they will pay me money to go to school? I don't have to pay tuition?"

"That's what it means." He folded the letter and handed it back to me. He picked up his telephone and dialed. "US consulate? This is Colonel Johnson, US Army. I need to speak to Ambassador Ranneberger right away, please."

Some of the conversation I didn't understand, but he was so excited that he leaped out of his chair. He nearly pulled the telephone off his desk as he paced around the office. I grabbed it as it slid to the edge. He mouthed a thank-you. When he hung up he grabbed me up out of the chair. "A car will be here in twenty minutes. It will take you to the US embassy to complete your visa application. The ambassador promised to fast-track it."

He held my hands in his. "How soon can you be ready to leave?"

I considered Joyce's feelings. She would need time to adjust to me going so far away to a strange land. I opened my acceptance letter to see when I was supposed to start. "Before September."

He looked at his calendar. "I'll be back in the States in September. I'll introduce you to some of the people at the National Institute of Health. I believe Massachusetts General Hospital in Boston is doing some of that research. It will be perfect."

I was overwhelmed with his enthusiasm. I stood there like a mannequin, not knowing what to do next. He checked his watch. "Hurry downstairs. Your car will be here soon," he said.

Everything happened so fast. The car was waiting. I sped through the noon-time traffic in a black air-conditioned limousine driven by a chauffeur. When I arrived, the people at the embassy greeted me with a warm welcome and shoved a myriad of papers at me and a pen. I sat at a desk to fill out all the papers. Then there was a long wait even for a Kenyan. I went to the receptionist and asked, "Should I come back later?" Her name tag read, "Julie Hanson."

"No, just have a seat. Kwamboka Muwami, is it? We are very busy today, but Ambassador Ranneberger will see you soon."

"You say Kenyan names very well," I complimented her.

"Lots of practice," she said and returned her focus to the work on her desk.

It seemed strange to hear my given name. I sat down and thought about answering to "Chui" for so long and to "Kitzi" whenever Joyce or her friends spoke to me. I liked the sound of "Kwamboka Muwami," but how would "Kwamboka Schoenberg" sound? When Julie called me back to the desk, I had been waiting so long that her voice startled me.

"Ambassador Ranneberger will see you now, Miss Muwami." I flashed my wedding ring at her to show that I was married, but she looked away when she escorted me to the ambassador's office.

"It is a pleasure to meet you, Kwamboka Muwami." He stumbled over my name. "Colonel Johnson said that you are very important to his research. We have contacted Nairobi University and verified your matriculation, and we have contacted Boston College to verify your acceptance to their graduate program. Sorry it took so long, but they are eight hours earlier than us. It took a while to talk to someone from their office."

"I understand."

"However, I did not understand what you have been doing since you graduated," he stated.

"Did Colonel Johnson explain to you how he rescued me?" I asked him.

"Rescued you?" A confused expression crossed Ambassador Ranneberger's face.

"Yes. I was kidnapped, and … well, he helped me escape from where they were retaining me. He can verify what happened if that is necessary. It is too painful for me to talk about." I hoped he would not insist on hearing the details.

"Oh, yes, I read something in the paper about a kidnapping scam." He read through some of the papers I had filled out. "And I have a copy of your I-20. How do you plan to support yourself? Are your parents wealthy enough to provide for you in the United States?"

I hung my head as the memories overwhelmed me. "My parents are deceased."

"Oh, yes, I see that here. I'm sorry. So how do you intend to support yourself?" he inquired.

"I've been promised a stipend while I am in the PhD program."

"I see," he said, distracted by the pile of papers that he was perusing.

"And my husband, Phillip Schoenberg, will support me," I added proudly.

"You're married to a US citizen?" he asked, raising his eyebrows.

"Yes, in Mombasa almost a year ago." I passed my marriage license onto his desk.

"I'll have my secretary copy this and give it back to you." He collated it with my other papers and closed the folder.

"It is highly unusual to fast-track an education request. You should have applied months ago."

Did he not understand what I was doing months ago?

"I will speak with Colonel Johnson, and we will have to confirm your support, your marriage license, and the stipend at Boston College. This will take some time, so why don't you check back in a week?" he advised me.

I got up out of the chair and edged back toward the door. "I appreciate your kind consideration."

"Your English is excellent, Kwamboka …" He looked at the marriage license again. "Schoenberg. We'll verify things, and then your visa should be available." He smiled as he shook my hand. "Don't worry. We will have you in Boston by September."

"Thank you so very much. It is a great honor to meet you." I grabbed his hand with both of mine, in a Kisii sign of respect, and bowed.

"You're entirely welcome."

He ushered me out of his office and closed the door. I sat paralyzed in front of the secretary's desk. The morning's events had left my legs weak.

"Miss Muwami—I'm sorry, Mrs. Schoenberg—your car is waiting." Julie smiled. "I didn't realize you were married until I copied your marriage license. Here's the original."

"Oh, thank you, Julie Hanson. Are you married?"

"No," she said, holding out her left hand to show an engagement ring, "but here's hoping. He's back in the United States. I hope he is being faithful."

"I am sure a man would be faithful to such a nice person as you, Julie Hanson." It made me wonder about Phillip Schoenberg. Should I write him or call him? Calling would be so difficult, and I wasn't sure how to do it. I decided to write to his university address and tell him that I was coming.

Waiting

"YOU MIGHT AS WELL GET to work until your visa comes," Joyce said when I finished telling her about the day's events. I wasn't thinking about working at the shop; I was thinking about supper.

I had bought fresh goat meat at the butcher shop. Joyce cooked it in a spicy sauce with greens. The whole house smelled delicious by the time we sat around the oil lamp to devour our feast. I ate ravenously and much too fast. Joyce was still nibbling meat off her bones when I sat back, too full to move, and patted my full belly. I smiled at the bones piled on my plate. *Too much happiness all at once*, I thought.

Joyce interrupted my thoughts. "You can greet the customers, and it will give me more time to sew." Her eyes sparkled. I was sure she was happy about the required delays I had described. "And with all your education, you can help me balance the books and go to the bank and ..."

"You have been like a mother to me. I owe you that." But I resented how happy she was about my visa difficulties. The arguments of the past came to mind. I recalled her insistence that I come home before dark, her conviction it was unnecessary for a woman to have an education, and her suspicion about Phillip's motives for marrying me. Maybe she was right. Maybe I didn't need more education. I had a roof over my head; I was no longer a sex-slave. I should learn

211

to be content helping with her business or maybe getting a job at a local bank. But I had made a Christian vow to my husband.

The next day I jumped up from my couch bed and decided to be thankful. We worked together all day, and Joyce demonstrated her appreciation with pleasant conversation. That evening when we left the shop, Reuben appeared and walked with us as we headed home. "How are you, my dear nephew?" Joyce asked.

"I am doing well," he responded.

"How is my brother doing?" Joyce asked.

"Father is off to Maasai country to pick up more sculptures from his suppliers and baskets and bracelets that the women make. They are selling well, so he is searching for more suppliers."

"So you and your father are becoming rich?" Joyce asked.

"No, we are not rich, but we have meat to eat," he said.

I recognized the colloquial expression that meant that their business was thriving, but they didn't want anyone to be jealous. I said nothing. I felt uncomfortable around him, especially based on the way he looked at me when Joyce turned her head.

"You are looking very beautiful today, Kitzi," he said.

"Thanks," I said politely.

"That dress fits your body very nicely," he asserted, attempting to elicit more conversation.

I didn't respond. We walked in silence. I didn't want Reuben to hear anything I shared with Joyce.

When we got to the house, he didn't leave. He just stood at the corner of the doorway scuffing the dirt with his feet as Joyce unlocked the door. "I'll start supper. It looks like you two have things to talk about," she said, hurrying toward the kitchen.

Rueben's stare appeared lecherous. I asked, "Do you have

ten cows?" I really wanted him to leave. He took my hand and led me outside.

"I heard that you've been a sex worker. What's your fee?" He whipped out a wad of shillings and pressed them to my breasts. "Is this enough?"

"I was kidnapped, Reuben. What I did, I did to stay alive. That part of my life is over." I pushed his money into his face. "And that isn't even close to what I was usually paid. Besides, I am married."

I made a fist with my left hand and pushed it into his face. "See the wedding rings?"

"You are?" he snapped with a stunned expression on his face.

"Yes, to a wonderful man," I announced.

"Did he pay ten cows?" Rueben sounded sarcastic.

"No," I said and watched as his eyes became inquisitive. Then I added, "He paid ten diamonds."

He stuffed his shillings back in his pocket. "Does he know that you're a whore?" he snarled. Then he spun around and disappeared down the alley.

Several weeks later, I was sitting at the counter working on the books. Some of the numbers didn't add up. Did a customer pay more in advance than Joyce had written down, did someone given her a tip, or did I add wrong? I couldn't quite figure out why we had more money than was written down under receivables. The bell above the door rang. I was lost in my numbers and answered without looking up, "Can I help you?"

"Kwamboka Muwami."

I was startled when I heard my name. At first I didn't recognize the customer. The bright afternoon light shimmered through the window, making the customer a mere silhouette. "Can I help you?" I repeated.

"Aren't you Kwamboka Muwami—or rather, Mrs. Schoenberg? I messed that up again."

"Yes." My eyes adjusted to the glare.

"Are you the woman who is applying for a fast-track visa to study at Boston College?" she asked.

"Yes. That's me," I answered, suspicious as to how she knew my name.

"Your visa arrived," she blurted out in excitement.

I ran out from behind the counter and recognized her. "Julie Hanson." She gave me a hug. "Do I have a visa? Can I go to graduate school in the United States of America?"

She laughed at my exuberance. "Yes, I've been waiting for you to come back to the embassy. Most people waiting hound us every day."

"That is excellent. Did you come here to tell me?"

"No, I came to get a dress. The word at the embassy is that this is the best place to come." She laughed at my antics. "Can I get a fitting today?"

"Joyce," I yelled. "We have a customer for a fitting." Joyce peeked through the curtain to see the two of us dancing around the shop.

"What's going on here?" she said. She sounded indignant.

"Joyce." I stopped to take a deep breath. "This is Julie Hanson. She is here for a dress fitting."

Joyce pulled her tape measure out of her apron pocket, "Nice to meet you, Julie Hanson." She turned to me, annoyed. "That does not explain why you are dancing with the customer."

"She is the secretary to the US ambassador. She just told me that my visa is approved. I can go to graduate school." I could see that Joyce was battling with her emotions. I quelled my enthusiasm and gave her a hug. "Joyce, my mother who loves me, who has taken care of me all through my years in the university, I will return—I promise—as a doctor."

We got to the business of fitting Julie for a dress. Joyce took the measurements, and I wrote them down as she

:

dictated. I was amused that Julie was not a good negotiator and accepted the first price Joyce offered.

I gave Joyce a disgusted look. She turned to Julie and said, "Since you are the ambassador's secretary and you have been so kind to my daughter, I will give you a discount." She calculated and gave her a new price.

Julie clapped her hands. "That's great. Oh, thank you."

I mouthed to Joyce, "That's better."

That night Joyce and I walked home hand in hand. There was a mist in the air that intensified all the smells of the city: coffee, tea, paradise flowers. "I am pleased that you did not take advantage of Julie Hanson."

"I was shocked when she agreed to the first price. I was expecting ..."

"I know, but I don't think United States women understand negotiations." Then I noticed that she was crying. "What's wrong, Joyce?"

I let go of her hand to skirt a mud puddle. On the other side she hugged me.

"I never had any children who survived. They all died as babies. I am a disgrace to my family, but you have taken away my disgrace. Most of my friends at the market think that you are my real daughter, but they can't understand why you keep running away. I am proud of you, but I can't bear to lose you again."

"I am not running away. You prayed for me when I was kidnapped without hearing from me. This time will be different. You will hear from me every week. I will write letters to you so that you will know I am healthy. You can show the letters to your friends at the market."

We stopped to turn into our alley. "I can see you now, Joyce. 'Look ladies, I got another letter from my daughter. She is becoming a doctor in the United States of America.' That is what you will say, isn't it?"

She managed a painful grimace, covered her mouth with her hands, and nodded affirmation.

"Please, Joyce, I need your blessing."

That night as I lay on the couch, I couldn't sleep. I couldn't picture Boston in my mind. I wondered if there would be big buildings. Would the classes be difficult? Would I have trouble with the exams? Where would I live? But most of all, I wondered if I would find my husband. I had written several letters to him, to his office in Boston College, but had received no response.

Leaving Kenya

I STOOD FOR A LONG time outside the travel agent's office looking at the pictures of airplanes in the window. My heart raced as I convinced myself to enter. *I don't belong here. Rural Kisii girls don't go to travel agents*, I thought. The bright fluorescent lights startled me. A young, chocolate-skinned agent with straight black hair wearing a blue dress suit was adjusting a poster of a lighted bridge over a grand river. She greeted me with a cheerful "welcome" and ushered me to a seat at her desk. I stammered as I explained that I needed to go to Boston in the United States of America.

"KLM is less expensive than British Airways, but both are expensive on short notice. You don't mind going through Amsterdam instead of London?" I shook my head, but she didn't seem to notice as she focused on her computer. In the silence my eyes wandered over the huge travel posters advertising the bright colors of Italy, Belgium, France, and England.

"The best ticket I can get you will be $2,017.67 in US dollars. Will that be cash"—she chuckled at what she must have thought was a joke—"check, or credit card?"

I was stunned. Where would I get that much money? I had never seen that much money in my whole life. I tried to calculate the cost in Kenyan shillings and couldn't do it. The numbers were too big. My mind was boggled. I fished through my leather pouch to stall as I panicked. I would have to tell her that I would come back later. Then in the bottom of my pouch, I caught the glint of the plastic credit card Phillip gave me. "Credit card, if I may, madam."

She took the card, and I held my breath. My pulse was banging in my head. Would the card accept the charge?

She scanned it through a small machine, waited a few minutes, and smiled. "Sign here." She seemed so matter-of-fact. I concluded that she had been through this many times before.

"No problem?" I asked, uncertain as to what had just happened.

"Did you expect a problem?" She winkled her brow at me.

"No, it's just that ..." I didn't know how to finish my sentence.

She ignored me and turned to her printer, took out two cards, and leaned over the desk. "So here's your ticket from Nairobi to Schiphol, Amsterdam. There is a bit of a layover, but the airport has a casino, hotel, restaurants, and even a museum. Then here is your ticket for Amsterdam to Boston. I picked window seats, just like you asked. Oh and here's an itinerary." She smiled. "Anything else I can do for you? Do you need a hotel or car when you get there?"

"No, my husband will pick me up," I answered.

"Alright, Kwamboka Schoenberg," she said as she returned my passport to me. "Have a nice trip."

I walked out of travel agency in euphoria. It seemed like the flowers in the boulevard had an even more intense smell, and the light glinting off the buildings was brighter. I stopped in the middle of the block to feel the tickets and make sure they were real. I looked at the word "Schiphol" and tried to pronounce it like the agent had. *Very odd word*, I thought.

A bus drove by, and the diesel exhaust spun me back to reality. I consulted my list. My next appointment was with the police department to find out when I would be required to testify at the trial. Would it interfere with my plans?

"It will probably take a year, maybe two. We are in no hurry for those creeps," Johdi Kiriamiti told me when I finally was received into her office. "Go to school. Keep in touch with a current address. We will give you plenty of notice. There was no bond posted, so they aren't going anywhere." She smiled. "You're our prime witness to put these rascals away … forever."

I thought of Martha and her gang sitting in prison awaiting trial, but I could not feel too sorry for them. I still did not understand Martha's hatred. Her gang was just in it for the money, but why would Martha, who had a college education and belonged to the dominant tribe in Kenya, do such a thing?

Johdi twirled a pen over the papers on her desk. "The judge said that you can leave the country as long as you return when summoned."

Back home, the night before my departure, I spread my papers out under the oil lamp. "See, I'll be safe, Joyce. Look where I will be." I handed her all the color brochures describing the campus at Boston College. They had sent information, including pictures, of the campus, the cafeteria, and even the dormitories.

"Will they feed you? You're so scrawny. I worry about you eating strange food in the United States. I can send some porridge with you. You would just have to cook it. Will there be a place for you to cook your food?"

I hugged her as we danced around the room. "No porridge, please. My suitcase is full of all the nice dresses you've made for me. And I am sure they have porridge in the United States."

"Will there be a place to raise a goat so you can get milk every day? I want to make sure you get some milk every day. Your glow is just now coming back." I loved how Joyce showed maternal concern.

"I don't think they let you raise goats in Boston. But they have milk in the store." I tried to allay her fears.

"But that costs lots of money. It's not like here in Nairobi, where goat milk is inexpensive." She shook her finger at me. "And remember to negotiate the prices. Those United States women might take advantage of you."

I grabbed her hands in mine. "I will make sure they don't."

She collapsed on the sofa beside me. "I don't think you should go."

"I'm going. We have talked and talked about this."

"Oh, all right. But if you forget to write letters to me, I will …"

"I won't forget." I hugged her to my shoulder, but I had a gnawing apprehension. Phillip had not answered my letters. Had he died of HIV-AIDS? What would I do if he didn't meet me at the airport? The United States of America was a big place, bigger than Kenya.

Boston 2010
Finding a Husband

As I WAITED IN THE airport to board my plane to the United States of America, I thought about the miracle I had just experienced. The woman at the desk had asked for my passport. I was so proud of it and the visa that I had awaited for such a long time. She took my bag and weighed it, checked her computer, and gave me my boarding pass. There was nothing to it. *Amazing.*

I found the gate, but they were not ready to have us board. Out the window, the airplane seemed so gigantic that I wondered how it could get off the ground. Was this really happening to me?

Too nervous to sit still, I decided that now that I was going to the United States of America, I should drink coffee. I walked down the hall searching for a place to buy some and discovered the Nairobi Java House departure lounge near gate 14. It smelled good just to be at the lounge. I hoped that coffee tasted as good as it smelled. I knew from geography class that Kenya grew great coffee, but I had never tried it.

"One cup of coffee, please," I said to the young woman behind the cash register.

"How do you want that?" she asked.

"In a cup, please," I responded.

She laughed. "I mean, do you want milk, cream, sugar … or do you want mocha?"

"Just coffee … with cream and sugar. Is that how most people drink it?"

My face felt hot. "This is my first cup of coffee ever, but I am going to Boston in the United States of America, and they drink a lot of coffee there, so I thought I should try it."

She laughed at me but made my coffee. I handed her some shillings. "Oh, sorry, we do not take shillings here at the airport gate. Do you have US dollars or British pounds?"

I panicked and pushed the coffee back. "No." Then I remembered Phillip's credit card. "But I have this."

She swiped the card and handed it back. "No problem." She pushed the coffee toward me with a smile. "Enjoy."

Coffee took some getting used to. My first impression was that it tasted like burnt rubber, but after a few sips, I started to appreciate the nutty flavor. I added one of the packets of sugar and used the cream pitcher at the small kiosk to the side of the counter. Then I decided that coffee was best with cream and sugar—lots of them. I wandered back to my departure gate sipping my coffee.

Just as I arrived, the announcement to board came over the loudspeaker. "KLM, Nairobi to Amsterdam, boarding at gate 36."

I expected to be scared, but I wasn't. I looked at my ticket and tried to memorize my seat number. When they called out my number, I got in line. The nice lady scanned my ticket and smiled. "Welcome aboard." I thought that was nice, but she was saying it to all the passengers.

Even though this was my first time in an airplane, the takeoff seemed smooth. I loved the feeling of acceleration. When I looked out the window, I had to laugh. The lights of Nairobi were like fallen stars on the ground. I cinched my seat belt tighter. In the morning, I would be in Amsterdam, a place I had studied in geography but had never dreamed of seeing. I wondered if they spoke proper English there. It had been a very long, emotional day. I thought of the sadness of seeing Joyce cry and the joy of boarding this big plane. *And the coffee was good*, I thought as I fell asleep.

The flight attendant disturbed my sleep with a meal tray. "Joyce already fed me," I responded, thinking, *It must be after midnight. Why would I eat now?*

"Beef or fish?" She seemed in a hurry.

"Beef." She set down a hot tray. I opened it and tried bits of everything, but I was either too full or too tired to eat. The beef did have a tasty sauce. The man next to me in the aisle seat ate everything.

"I'm going to sleep now. When that nice lady comes, she can have my tray," I told him.

"I not speak English," he said. I repeated the same thing in Swahili, but I was not sure he understood that either. He reminded me of the man who had given me water in the Rift Valley. Maybe he was Japanese. I turned toward the window and went to sleep.

I was awakened with a lemon-scented washcloth. The attendant gave me a small tray with fruit, sweet-tasting bread, and a little cup of coffee.

"Cream and sugar, please?" I asked. She gave me some little packets. The coffee was not as good as at the Java House by gate 14, but it did wake me up. The pastries were too sweet, but I nibbled on some of them. The fruit was good, and it was already all sliced up. I didn't need to peel anything.

She returned to collect everything just before we landed. I tightened my seat belt as the plane shuttered and made a frightening sound. The man behind me said to his wife, "Landing gear's down." The landing was anticlimactic. My nose was glued to the window watching the ground get closer. With a subtle jerk we were on the ground. Some passengers cheered.

We arrived at six o'clock in the morning. It was foggy. I

entered the airport unsure of what to do. It smelled like a jumble of different perfumes, flowers, and coffee. My flight to Boston wasn't until two o'clock in the afternoon. I searched for the gate, but when I found it there was no one there. There wasn't even a flight on the board. The small breakfast on the plane had not been very filling. As I wandered around, my stomach started gnawing at me. I was still hungry. I went looking for a place to eat.

Schiphol Airport is heaven to a poor girl from rural, western Kenya. I wandered among the concessions for hours, amazed by what was available. I checked out the wooden shoes and the store with tulip bulbs. I wandered into the Rembrandt museum. I had heard about him in my art class in secondary school. Now I was standing in front of his pictures. My legs felt weak, as if I were about to faint.

I couldn't believe how many kinds of cheese were available, and there was chocolate in all kinds of attractive packages. That made my hunger worse. The pastries in the coffee shop looked delicious and tempting. The credit card worked again, and the people at the kiosks spoke English. I ordered the third cup of coffee of my life, explaining that I needed cream and sugar. Then I sat by the window looking out over the airport and took small bites of a croissant smeared with orange marmalade, which I had never eaten before, as I watched the planes appear and disappear in the gentle fog.

"Where are you from?" asked the young Dutch clerk at the counter when he finished serving everyone. He wiped up spilled coffee from an elderly Indian man who had a tremor.

"Kenya," I said.

"I have always wanted to go to Kenya to see the animals. I didn't know that there were such beautiful women there too," he said.

I flashed my wedding ring in front of him. "And some of them aren't married yet," I said.

"Sorry, I was just teasing," he said, returning to his counter.

It did not sound like teasing to me; it sounded like something my clients would have said. But as I looked at his face, he seemed kind. "Have you ever been to Boston?" I asked as he returned. "That is where I am going to meet my husband. He is a professor at Boston College."

"No, can't say that I have. But I've been to New York City."

We spent an hour talking about New York City. He told me about the museums and restaurants. It sounded like a magical place. "I hope Boston is near New York City, so I can go there and see everything you're telling me about."

"I'm sure it is. Is your husband meeting you?" he asked.

"Yes, I sent him several letters, so I hope to see him as soon as I get off the airplane." I was still concerned that I had not heard from Phillip.

"He can't go through security. He'll probably meet you outside baggage claim, after you go through immigration," the clerk informed me.

"Oh, thank you for telling me," I said.

After eating, I went back to the Rembrandt museum to see the drawings again. All the women in the drawings were so corpulent. I wondered whether all Dutch women were so well fed.

Next to the Rembrandt museum was a casino. I did not understand gambling. I knew the men in my village gambled, but that was with cards and dice in the dirt behind the petrol station. This was a bright, shiny palace. I didn't go in.

I bought some chocolate to surprise Phillip and drooled over the cheeses. By the time I had explored the whole airport, it was past noon. The food in the cafeteria looked delicious. I noticed Italian pasta and decided to try it. I was a little nervous when the cashier told me how much it cost. Food was very expensive in Amsterdam, but the credit card didn't seem to care.

The sauce was mild and the pasta was flavorful. I had a Coke with it, another thing I had seen in Kisii kiosks but my mother had never let me buy. It had good flavor, and I liked the way it made my tongue tingle.

After lunch I checked the boarding gate. They weren't boarding yet, but there was a notice on the electronic board that announced the flight. I decided to wander around some more. One kiosk had Italian purses for sale. They were a fancy version of my leather pouch. The prices confused me, but I decided to get one. It looked so well made, and it had all kinds of secret compartments. The credit card accepted that too.

I wandered through the airport. There were so many passageways, and each had interesting stores and restaurants. I was overwhelmed and thought that it would be a great place to stay for a couple days. Paying attention to the giant clock in the hallway, I decided to wander back to my gate. I sat down just to think about everything I had seen. Taking a deep breath, I could smell the flowers, the leather from the shops, the sweet smell of pastries and, of course, the rich, nutty smell of coffee that I was learning to like. I dozed in the seat.

I awoke to an announcement that it was time to board. A lot more people were at the gate than when I had fallen asleep. "You have to be interviewed by the security person from the United States," a tall blonde woman in a blue uniform informed me. I stood and lined up with the other passengers. The security man asked me all kinds of questions about why I wanted to go the United States of America. I must have answered correctly because he let me pass.

The flight to Boston was uneventful. I felt so sophisticated, knowing what was going to happen on the flight and what to expect from the nice attendants that brought me things. I quickly learned how to work the monitor to watch movies. Some were quite silly, but other movies scared me. I turned the monitor off.

When I got off the plane in Boston, I was so disoriented

that I felt like I had landed on the moon. And the time didn't make sense. I had spent eight hours in the airplane, but the clock said it was only two hours since we left. How confusing.

I had to go through security again. I tried to explain that I was married to a United States of America professor, but the woman in uniform was more interested in my passport and the computer information when she scanned it. I stood still. *Are they not going to let me in? What will I do then?*

"Welcome to the United States," she finally said and let me pass.

Now I was in this strange place where I would be living and going to school to be a doctor. I was so excited. I followed the signs to the baggage claim area and picked up my one suitcase. Phillip was not there to pick me up. I waited until after six o'clock, thinking maybe he had to work late, but no one came.

Wandering around, I saw the sign for the subway. The information woman told me that it would take me right to downtown Boston. Maybe Phillip was waiting there. After getting some United States dollars out of the ATM with my credit card, I took the subway into the city. I was glad Phillip had written down the PIN for me and that I hadn't thrown it away, not knowing what it was. I got off at the Long Wharf station because it sounded like a nice place.

I popped up out of the ground in a glass box. Outside I walked around the corner, drawn by the smell of the sea. It reminded me of our honeymoon. Ships bigger than I had ever imagined were docked along the wharf. There was a clock on a tower nearby. It showed seven thirty. I looked for Phillip, but there was no one I recognized. I felt lost and tired. The buildings were huge, and there were so many of them. How would I ever find Boston College?

It was too late to find it that night, I decided. I needed a place to stay. I turned around looking at all the massive architecture. Right behind me was a hotel that read, "Marriott

Long Wharf." It looked nice, so I decided to stay there and search for Phillip in the morning.

The reception was up a long escalator, and the lobby was huge. "Do you have a room for one very weary married woman? I just flew here from Kenya," I asked the clerk at reception.

"Do you have a reservation?" she asked.

"No. I did not expect to be staying here, but my ride did not show up," I explained.

She was focused on her computer. "There is a convention in town this week, so we are pretty full. All the rooms are booked. Oh, the wedding suite is available." She laughed. "But you wouldn't want that, would you?"

"I am too tired to not accept."

She flicked her eyebrows. "All right then." She asked for my credit card and swiped it. She gave me a plastic card and explained how to open the door to my room.

A bellhop appeared and helped me carry my suitcase to my room. He walked in and explained how to adjust the air conditioner, showed me the closets, and showed me how to work the shower and television. I thanked him and gave him some of the money from the ATM. He seemed very happy, so I thought I must have given him enough.

The room was huge and smelled of perfume. I looked out the window toward the bay. How beautiful. The sun was setting over the city, but there were still glints of sun bouncing off the waves in the bay. As I scanned the magical panorama, I decided that tomorrow I must find my husband. One thought nagged me: Was he still alive?

Boston College

THE RECEPTIONIST THE NEXT MORNING was not the person I checked in with but a very handsome gentleman in a formal suit. He was most gracious explaining to me how to take the bus to get to Boston College. He even gave me a small map to use. I followed his directions, but it took a long time to get to Boston College. When the bus stopped the driver said, "End of the line, everyone off."

I asked, "Is this Boston College?"

"Yep, every building up that hill is part of the campus."

The campus was huge, but there was a map, so I found the Anthropology building and asked the secretary for Phillip's office. She seemed most kind. "His office is down the hall. Last door on the right," she said, looking at her wristwatch. "You should still catch him. He's cleaning out his desk. Oh, and here's his mail."

The secretary gave me a bundle of mail secured with a large rubber band. Two letters with elephant stamps stuck out the end. The letters I sent had not even been opened.

"Why is he cleaning his desk?" I asked. But her telephone rang, and she didn't answer. I walked down the hall and tapped on the door just below the sign "Phillip Schoenberg, PhD" emblazoned in black and gold letters on frosted glass. The door was ajar.

"Anyone home?" I asked.

The door pushed open when I tapped. A gaunt man stood at the desk, packing a box. "Kitzi. What are you doing here?"

He fell backward into his chair. The content of his box scattered across the floor as he dropped it.

"Aren't we married anymore? You called me Kitzi. You are supposed to call me Kwamboka," I said.

He hyperventilated in his chair. His emaciated hands reached out to me. "You still want to be married to me?"

Anguish seemed to cross his face, or was it pain? I wasn't sure. "You are so beautiful, Kwamboka. I still love you. I'm just in shock. I didn't know you were coming."

I undid the rubber band and spilled the mail across his desk. "Here are two letters I sent you that would tell you I was coming and to meet me at the airport. How long has it been since you opened your mail?"

I sorted out the letters from Kenya. "If you read these letters, they will tell you that your wife is coming."

A weak grimace was his response to my chastisement. "I don't know what to say."

My eyes searched his office. Bare nails betrayed the pictures, diplomas, and calendars that had once hung on the wall. The computer and keyboard were the only items on the desk. The screen was blank. I kneeled to pick up the things that fell out of the box. Phillip clutched the unopened letters. "Where are you going?" I asked.

Sweat beaded on his sallow forehead. He offered me a seat beside his desk. I put the retrieved items back in the box and set it on his trembling knees. I'm taking a sabbatical," he said as he caught his breath. He reached out from his chair to offer me a one-handed hug.

He closed his eyes, biting the lips that remained silent. When he opened his eyes, he stared at me, twisting his neck in the process. There was a prominent lump in his neck.

"You deserve better." He palpated the lump. "I have cancer, a lymphoma. It's caused from HIV-AIDS."

Tears welled up in his eyes; his breathing was shallow and labored. "I've caused you so much trouble. I thought I killed you, Kitzi—I'm sorry, Kwamboka."

He swallowed. It seemed painful. The lump in his neck was immobile. His forehead scrunched. "Did I give you the virus? I'll never forgive myself."

I shook my head. "No, you didn't."

He started to cry. "Kwamboka, I'm so glad. I have fought the nightmares of you going through what I've been through." He sobbed and grabbed a tissue from the paraphernalia in his box. "You look so healthy and beautiful."

I slipped into East African English. "Don't you be saying that. I'm tired of people saying I'm beautiful."

He seemed stunned by my venomous response.

"You know your wife, she beautiful, but I don't want no person I love to say it." I moved my chair closer and put my hands on his knees. The muscles were gone. The athletic quadriceps that I had admired on the beach had melted away.

I switched to proper English. "Why are you so sick? Don't the doctors in the United States have medicine for your cancer? This is such a magical country. I thought you had everything here."

He grabbed my hands. I noticed his rough and dry skin; the nails were cracked. Atrophy of the muscles in his hands had left his fingers spindly.

"I had a lot of bad side effects from the AIDS medicine. I had to go off the drugs. And now I have a lymphoma. I'm going to the hospital. They gave me my last dose of chemotherapy last week." He hung his head. "But it didn't work."

A tight grimace crawled across his face, "But what about you? You look ..." He stopped, afraid of my reprimand. "I'm so glad to see you, Kwamboka. But why are you here?"

"I am here to find you."

My response was so quick that he tried to laugh. "You are

231

balm for a fainting soul. But other than finding me, what brought you to Boston?"

"I am enrolled in the doctorate program in the public health department here at Boston College."

"That's great. You are so intelligent; you deserve that opportunity," he said.

"You interrupted me," I snapped.

He put his hand over his mouth like a child speaking out of turn.

"The second reason is that the NIH, that is the National Institute of Health ..."

"Yes, I know what the NIH is." He held up his hands. "Sorry, I interrupted again."

"The NIH is interested in doing research on my blood cells." I smiled because now I knew that he was afraid to speak. "I have magnificent blood cells that cannot receive the AIDS virus. I do not have the receptor. Colonel Johnson, a physician from the US Army, discovered me in Kenya." I paused and waited for him to understand the implications of my explanation.

He shook his head. "I don't understand all that, but I am flabbergasted to see you again."

"I like that word, 'flabbergasted.' It's a wonderful word," I said.

"Now you interrupted me." He put his hand on mine. "It's all right. I'm trying to tease you. It's just that I never thought this day would come. But what you're saying doesn't make sense. I never heard of such a thing, and I've read everything I can about HIV."

"Are you trying to make your wife angry? You do not know everything about HIV." I wanted to explain more, but he was too sick.

He glanced at his watch. "Oh, I got to go. I have an appointment at the hospital."

"To die?" I asked.

He did not answer. He struggled to pick himself up out of his chair, so I took the box out of his lap and helped him. He grabbed my two unopened letters out of my hands. I saw a third letter with a Kenyan stamp. It had Phillip's address and even his telephone number at the bottom but was addressed to "Chui." "Ah, this letter is for me."

He looked at the address. "You're the leopard?" he translated the Swahili.

"It is a story that I will tell you, but later." I dumped the rest of the mail into his box but shoved the letter addressed to me into my Italian purse. "Now your wife is taking you to the hospital." He paused to lock his door.

"I think it is odd to lock the door since the office is empty."

"Security doesn't want to lose the computers," he explained.

"Oh, I have much to learn about Boston College."

I carried the box and followed him out to his car. Clutching the two letters, he stopped several times to catch his breath. He needed to rest even before putting the key in the ignition. "They offered me a bone marrow transplant. My mother was checked as a donor, but somehow she is incompatible. My father died of a heart attack six months ago. I guess they have no one in their registry that is compatible either."

I leaned over and kissed him. "I'm so sorry. I wanted to meet my father-in-law to show him my respect." He started the car and turned off the radio. "I can't work. I get too tired, and this chemo is worthless."

He backed out of the lot and headed toward Massachusetts General Hospital. "Yes, Kwamboka, my dear wife, I'm going to the hospital to die."

"I do not want you to die. I just found you, and we have much to discuss. Besides, the minister married us in sickness and in health. You are sick but not dead yet, so we are still married."

Bone Marrow

I SAT IN PHILLIP'S HOSPITAL room watching him breathe. The room smelled of disinfectant and disease. The nurse made me wear a paper gown and put a mask over my face. Since he had no infection-fighting cells, the nurse explained to me, he was in "protective isolation." Two horrid IVs ran life-giving fluid into his body. One was in his shoulder. I was glad they did not put a needle in my shoulder at Kijabe Hospital.

I wondered if the nurse had told him not to move because he hadn't moved since I arrived. He didn't respond to me except to groan. So I sat in silence and watched his chest rise with each inhalation.

Bored, I pulled out the Kenyan letter addressed to Chui and opened it.

Dear Chui,

> *The nurse is helping me write this letter since I have not learned this many words to write. Madame found me in the WC with diarrhea so she did not suspect that I helped you. The chain went back on the door. I started coughing after you left and was assigned to your room. That's when I found Phillip Schoenberg's card behind the curtain holder. I hope you get this letter. Madame says that I am too weak to work*

and sent me to the hospital. I have TB but am considered a charity case so the nurses are helping me. My medicine is free because Kenya pays for TB medicine. The doctor is a different one from Dr. Patel, but he is also from India.

Your friend,
Zip

PS: I found the money you left for me behind the brick. Thank you for showing me where it was before you jumped over the wall. It is keeping my mother alive, but my father died.

Poor Zipporah. I decide to contact Colonel Johnson and find a way to send money for her care. So, my forgotten shillings weren't rotting in the wall. Zipporah's mother needed them a lot more than I did.

The nurse came into the room. "They are ready to draw your blood in the laboratory, Mrs. Schoenberg."

"Thank you. Can you show me how to get there? I am lost in this big hospital."

"Sure, of course," she said and gave me directions.

It was quite a walk, and of course, I had to wait when I arrived. There was more activity here than there was in Nairobi during rush hour.

"You're Phillip Schoenberg's wife?" the laboratory technician asked as she inserted the needle to draw my blood. She was a round-faced, corpulent woman who was almost as black as I was.

"Yes, I am his wife. We have been married for over a year." I thought about how little time we had spent together.

"I love your British accent. I'm sorry, but I was a bit shocked when I called you from the waiting room. I guess

I was expecting a Caucasian woman. Are you African?" she said.

"Yes. Your accent is American, but you look like you are from West Africa," I replied.

She laughed. "I guess my ancestors came from Liberia about two hundred years ago."

"What tribe are you from?" I asked.

"I have no idea," she responded.

"I am Kisii, from western Kenya, but I think it is wonderful that in the United States of America it does not matter what tribe you are from."

"Were you married in Kenya?" she asked.

"Yes, our magnificent wedding was on the beach in Mombasa," I said, reminiscing about our honeymoon.

She pulled out the needle out of my arm when she had enough blood. It stung. I started to laugh. "You were making me talk to you so I would not notice how much blood you were taking. You are very clever."

"Not completely true," she said, giggling, "but close. Anyway, I hope you're compatible. Your husband is such a nice person. I have drawn his blood many times. His mother was a match for a transplant, but something happened. I guess she didn't want to go through the procedure." She put a cotton ball on my arm and taped across it. "We should know by tomorrow morning."

Phillip was more alert the next morning, but he started to vomit when the physician came into the room. Dr. Levine looked at me. "Is this," he stammered at Phillip, "your ..."

"My wife, Kwamboka. You may call her Kitzi. Everybody does," he said. Then he whispered, "Except me."

"We have good news—Kitzi, is it? You are a perfect match.

We will do the bone marrow transplant tomorrow. You understand that we will wipe out your marrow, Phillip, and give you hers. If we are successful, you will only have her blood. There is about a 15 percent mortality risk during the time that your white cells are gone and hers are regenerating."

"I'm dying this way, Dr. Levine, so what difference does it make?" Phillip held his basin to his mouth but only had dry heaves. "I just can't tolerate the chemo for the lymphoma, and I didn't do well with the AIDS drugs either."

"That's true. This is really your only option for survival. Hopefully you will tolerate the transplant drugs. They will only be temporary. If you accept the transplant successfully and do not develop graft-versus-host disease, you may not need any drugs. With such a perfect match, I am very hopeful. Well, I'm not speaking about the antiretroviral drugs." He shook Phillip's hand and then mine. "Nice to meet you, Kitzi. Do you have any questions about the procedure to harvest your marrow?"

"No. I've had a bone marrow test before, and I understand that it isn't too different," I replied.

"Oh, why did you have a bone marrow test?" He stopped and stared at me.

"The US Army is studying my lymphocytes. I have a receptor deficiency." I searched the doctor's eyes, hoping he understood, because I didn't want to explain anything more right now. I hadn't told Phillip about being kidnapped, and I wanted to share it with him in private.

"Well, the lab has done all the testing. I don't suppose a receptor deficiency has any effect on the likelihood for transplant success or they would have told me." He closed the chart and walked out.

"Phillip, is it time for me to explain some things to you?" I was ready to confess to him everything that had happened to me.

He vomited again, and I emptied the basin in the toilet and washed it out in the sink.

"I need that basin back. Quick." I rushed back with it, but he only had dry heaves. "Just be here for me," he gasped. "That's all I need right now."

Transplanted

THE FIRST NIGHT I STAYED at Phillip's apartment—now ours—there was a terrible storm. Clouds darkened the sky, and the lightning and thunder shocked me. We do not get much lightning and thunder in Kenya. I spent part of the night at the bay window of Phillip's brownstone apartment watching the sky, finally collapsing to sleep on the unmade bed as the storm passed.

The bone marrow procedure was nothing for me the next morning. I teased the doctor, while he was sticking the needle in my back, that we had sharper needles in Kenya, but he did not laugh at my joke. In no time I was done and returned to Phillip's room. He was gone for the transplant. I waited.

When the transport person, a handsome young black fellow, brought Phillip to his room, I was informed that he had to remain in protective isolation. To enter his room, I was required to wear a paper gown, gloves, hood, and mask. As I suited up and grasped his hand, I told him that I loved him. His response was garbled. I presumed that he must still be sedated. I wasn't sure he even recognized me, so I left to go home.

He had left the place in a shambles, so that next week after the transplant I spent cleaning. I found the coin-operated washing machine and dryer in the lower level. A nice lady from another apartment showed me how it worked. Then it was a matter of picking things up and discarding the refuse. Once the bin outside was filled with weeks of neglected garbage, the apartment felt quaint and pleasant. I bought some eucalyptus leaves from the local florist, which made it smell like home.

In the *Boston Globe* that I found in our mailbox each day, there were articles about the heavy rainfall and the construction on the new subterranean freeway, the Big Dig. I found it all fascinating. I did read some articles about politics, but I didn't understand them. I did not let my eyes read the articles about murders and rapes. I intended to be a well-informed Bostonian.

I registered for graduate school and was warmly welcomed by the professors. They gave me a tour and showed me my office. I had to share it with three other grad students, but I had never had my own office before. I just hoped Phillip would be out of the hospital by the time I started classes.

About a week later I walked into his hospital room to find him alert and talkative, sounding like himself again. The lump in his neck was gone, but he still looked pale. The paper gown crinkled as I sat in the chair beside the bed, waiting for the doctor to visit.

"Your donor cells are responding well," said the doctor on rounds. "Your white count"—he looked at me—"or Kitzi's white count, however you want to look at it, is rebounding so well that I can discontinue the isolation." Excited, I ripped off my mask and paper gown.

He laughed at me. "Just give the nurses time to recognize the order, Kitzi. I haven't written it yet." He turned to Phillip. "You should have enough cells to fight infection now."

The color was coming back into Phillip's face. His cheeks were flushed when he smiled at the physician. "Thank you, doctor, for your report. I feel a lot better."

"Don't thank me; thank your donor here. She saved your

life." He turned to leave, but just then the infectious disease resident came rushing into the room.

"I can't believe it," he said to the transplant physician. "He has no detectable HIV. The PCR is negative."

"Oh, I can believe it," I said. The room fell silent, and all eyes turned to me. I giggled at their attention. "That is why the US Army was studying my lymphocytes. I have no receptors for HIV, so there are no cells for the virus to infect. Call Colonel Johnson, the United States Army physician at NIH. He will explain it to you."

"You mean I am cured of AIDS?" Phillip asked, turning first to me and then to the infectious disease specialist.

"Whoa, I didn't say that," the resident said. "Maybe, but I can't believe it. We need to do more testing."

Phillip jumped out of bed and kissed me. "You're the best woman that ever happened to me."

"Excuse us," the physicians said as they left the room. "We'll have more information tomorrow. You two clearly have a lot to talk about." They closed the door behind them.

Many joyful hugs and kisses followed. We caressed on the sofa by the window. His hand slipped inside my Boston Red Sox sweatshirt. "You aren't wearing a bra."

"Do I have to wear a bra in Boston? I don't like them," I complained.

"Not for me." He giggled, cradling my breasts in his hand. It made me giggle too.

"I see that you realize that you are a man again," I said, enjoying his fondling.

"With a hot African woman's blood pumping through my body." He kissed me while his hands explored my belly.

As much as I was enjoying the attention, I pushed him away. He looked puzzled. I went to the door and to make sure it was shut. There was no lock, so I pulled the curtain across the doorway and sat on the opposite side of the couch.

"It is time for a very important discussion. Kwamboka

241

must explain some things to you before your man member gets too excited. Do you remember the day you left me in Nairobi?"

"How could I forget? I cried for three days."

"Do you remember that you gave me the choice to annul our marriage?"

"Yes," he answered and nodded. A concerned look crossed his face. "What is this about, Kwamboka?"

"I chose to remain married to you. I remembered the vows the Christian Lutheran minister made us say: 'In sickness and in health, till death do you part.' Neither of us is dead today."

He took a deep breath. "Right. I'm feeling very alive today."

I watched his eyes widen. "But now I will give you the same choice." I avoided his touch when he reached for me. "I will tell you what happened, and then you can choose whether you still want to be my husband."

In slow, calculated words he asked, "Does this have something to do with how you found out that you are missing a receptor for HIV?"

"Yes."

Moment of Truth

AT THE END OF THE story, I was exhausted and sweaty. Phillip had remained silent until I was done. "So you see, I was kidnapped, raped, had sexually transmitted diseases, and copulated with more men than I can count. I have been a contractual sex worker for many months. I have only kept back some awful things that you do not need to know, but I will tell them to you if you insist."

I stood up, took off my wedding rings, undid my necklace, and put them in his hand. "Now, Phillip Schoenberg, you must choose. Do you still want to be married to someone who has been a prostitute? Would you ever want to have sexual intercourse with a wife who has had so many men stick their penises inside of her that she lost count? If you choose not to be my husband, I will understand. I can live in student housing, and you never have to see Kwamboka ever again."

Phillip's touch was gentle. He stood beside me, put the necklace back around my neck, and then held my hand.

"With this necklace I paid the bride price for you." He touched each diamond and counted them in Ekegusii. "This ring is the tenth diamond for your bride price." He put the engagement ring on my finger and then the wedding ring. "And with this ring I married you. Now, I renew my vow to be your faithful husband, Kwamboka. You are more honorable than me."

"Than I," I corrected him.

"Yes, than I. Understood verb, nominative case, right?" We hugged, cried, kissed, and caressed. I had waited so long to be enveloped in his love. I felt like a woman.

The door burst open. We jumped apart. An older woman pushed aside the drape.

"Phillip, there are some charges on your Barclay's Visa that are fraudulent," she said. "I protested the charges, but they have to hear it from you or they won't remove them."

She seemed very intent on the papers in her hand. "Leather goods and food items in Amsterdam, $340 for the Marriott Long Wharf, and over two thousand dollars for a plane ticket." She looked up. "And even coffee at the Nairobi Java House. This is audacious and ridiculous."

She looked up from her fistful of papers. "What's this black thing doing in your hospital room?" she sneered, pointing at me. She was thin with dyed black hair, gray roots showing, and dressed in a prim, laced blue blouse, gray suit, and skirt. Crocheted gloves completed her ensemble.

"'Who' is the proper pronoun when referring to a person," I said, extending my hand, "and I assure you that I am a person, not a thing."

"Kwamboka Muwami Schoenberg is my bone marrow donor and my wife," Phillip said. "She saved my life."

He tried to give the intruder a hug, but she pulled away. "You may call her Kitzi."

"Kwamboka, this is my mother, Irene," he announced, seeming embarrassed by her behavior.

She refused my hand as I greeted her. "It is a pleasure to meet you, Irene."

She clung to her pocketbook and the Barclay's Visa bill. "She sure is black … and tall … and thin. Your wife, you say?"

"Yes, Mother, we're legally married. Kitzi is your daughter-in-law."

"I'm sorry to be rude, Kitty. I didn't know Phillip was married," she snipped.

"Kitzi," I corrected her, but I knew she would always call me Kitty.

"You know he's got HIV, don't you? He's dying. He was a naughty boy and got the virus from a prostitute."

She turned to her son. "Damn you, Phillip. My only son has to screw whores."

"Yes, I know my husband *had* AIDS that he got from a Kenyan woman," I answered.

"Had?" She looked at me. "What do you mean?"

"Sit down, Mother. It's a long story." Phillip embraced me.

My mother-in-law pulled up a chair, still waving the Visa bill. "We have to do something about this right away, Phillip."

"The charges are legitimate, Mother. I'll explain." I sat on the couch. Phillip sat next to me. His touch was thrilling since there were now no secrets between us.

"After we were married, Mother, my wife was kidnapped. That is why she didn't come to Boston as I expected." He patted my hand and placed it on his thigh. "But she escaped with the help of the US Army."

Irene appeared incredulous. "The US Army rescued you? I didn't know we had an army in Kenya."

"Yes, Colonel Johnson arranged for my release," I added.

"When she came to join me here in Boston, she incurred those charges on the credit card I gave her." Irene folded the credit card bill and thrust it into her purse. "She was a perfect match for my bone marrow transplant. And ..."

"You do look a lot better, son. I expected to find you in intensive care." She tilted her chin and turned away from him.

"I'm out of ICU. But I haven't told you the best part yet, Mother."

"What, that you're cured of AIDS?" She laughed. "Even if you are, you don't deserve it."

"Yes, Kwamboka …"

She furrowed her forehead at the name.

"Kitzi," he started over, "does not have the receptor for HIV. So when they transplanted her blood cells, the virus had no place to go. It died. I no longer have AIDS."

"Really?" Her mouth fell open. She held her chest with both gloved hands.

Irene's silence gave me the opportunity to kiss Phillip.

"But she's so black," she said with disdain in her voice that I could not ignore.

"It's her *white* blood cells that saved me, Mother, not her *black* skin," Phillip said.

"And my husband is mostly pink. Don't you think we go well together?" I said, trying to sound sarcastic.

The Town House Move

A WEEK LATER, PHILLIP WAS discharged from the hospital on almost no medication. Irene insisted that we live with her until he was stronger. I was apprehensive about moving from Phillip's apartment, where I had been quite comfortable, to Irene's town house. I was not sure she and I would get along. She had stopped calling me "the black thing," but I was still "Kitty." I still left most of my things in the apartment, since it was close to Boston College. I told Phillip I needed a quiet place to study. I thought I might need to escape from Irene too.

The town house was delightful. It sat on a tree-lined street on what I learned was "Nob Hill." I thought Phillip said "Snob Hill" at first, but he corrected me. There were four bedrooms, although two had been converted to offices. I was shocked by the grandeur: three bathrooms with showers and tubs and another small bathroom off the kitchen. An incredible walk-out deck allowed a view across a wooded park. The house was bright and cheery. Everything was in its place. Irene was an immaculate housekeeper. Phillip warned me not to leave anything out and told Irene that our bedroom and bathroom were off-limits to her. Phillip was fastidious, but I was thankful that he was also more casual.

We moved to the town house on the day he was discharged from the hospital and the day my classes started. I was

Richard Roach

excited about the opportunity to work with the professors. They were quite curious about my background and made me feel welcomed. There was a lot of reading to do, but Phillip told me that I could buy the books I needed to read. I didn't have to stay at the library to read my assignments.

I decided that Phillip and I must be very rich. It was difficult for me to convert dollars to shillings, but when I figured out the conversion, I started to realize what I had spent at the hotel and for the Italian purse. I was embarrassed, but Phillip said that the purse looked nice and that if he had opened the letters I sent, the hotel would not have been necessary. "It was my fault," he said.

Irene was certainly rich. She had gotten most of her money from her late husband's business, but Phillip said that his father had a huge insurance policy. "She'll be able to live off that the rest of her life, not to mention all the money from selling Dad's business."

When I ask him to convert to shillings the value of the town house, I gasped, "I don't think they have that many shillings in all of Kenya." I knew it was a stupid thing to say as soon as I said it.

One afternoon I was in the living room studying for an exam. I had several books opened around me at the table. I heard Irene tell Phillip, "Tell Kitty that ..." I didn't hear the rest of the conversation, but I felt like a piece of unwanted furniture.

"I'm going out for a walk," I told the two of them. "I will pick up my books when I come back." I checked Irene's face to see if she would glare at me. She was focused on Phillip.

Phillip told me that the area around the town house was maintained by a gardener. When I came around the corner, he was pruning a bush. He was very dark skinned, wearing a khaki uniform, and holding pruning shears to the bushes.

"How are you today?" he said without looking at me.

When he turned, he stopped what he was doing and asked, "Do you belong here, Miss?"

"I'm Phillip Schoenberg's wife, Kitzi," I said extending my hand.

"Oh, excuse me. I didn't know he was married." He stood up and stared at me. "I'm Joshua. I would shake your hand, but my gloves are dirty."

"We've been married over a year now." His accent sounded odd to my ear. It did not sound like the Boston accent I was used to. He continued to stare, holding a twig in one hand and shears in the other. So I asked, "Why are you staring at me?"

He shook his head. "I am so sorry, missy—I mean, Mrs. Schoenberg."

"Please call me Kitzi."

"The way Mrs. Schoenberg, your mother-in-law, treats us black folks, I'm just surprised that she let her son marry you." He dropped the twig he was trimming into a bucket. "And the other reason is that you are a sight for sore eyes." Now he was smiling so widely I could see all his teeth.

I squatted down near the bush he was trimming and saw a spider. I jostled its web. "Do they have lots of spiders here in Boston?"

"You're not afraid of spiders? Now you're shocking me again. Ladies are afraid of spiders. Where are you from, sister? May I call you 'sister?'" he asked.

"Yes, you may. I'm from Kenya. Phillip and I were married in Mombasa."

He looked confused, so I continued to explain, "It's on the Indian Ocean, in East Africa. Anyway, I hate mosquitoes. They cause malaria and kill people. Jesus made the spiders to eat them. That's why I like spiders." I stood up. "Are you a Christian? Joshua is a Bible name."

"Praise God I am, sister."

I put my hand on his bare arm. "I am so glad to meet

you, Joshua. Please pray for me. I am trying to love my mother-in-law."

"That's a hard job you have there, sister. I be praying for you fervently, Kitzi."

Joshua and I talked about the plants. He explained why he had certain flowers in each bed in the garden and how each one bloomed at different times so there were always flowers in his gardens. "God made so many beauties, didn't he?" he said.

"You're not talking about me, are you?"

"I'm trying not to, Kitzi, but God made you exceptionally beautiful," he said.

"Like a flower in His garden, right?"

Joshua nodded his head. "But I won't be saying any more to embarrass myself. I just think Phillip is one God-blessed white man."

"He's mostly pink under his clothes," I volunteered.

He laughed. "I'd better get back to trimming this hedge. You are something else, sister. And I be praying for you. You can count on me."

As I walked back into the house I heard. "Those black things are so stupid." I grabbed my books from the table and headed for the bedroom.

Phillip yelled, "Mother!" And that ended the conversation. I couldn't wait to move back to the apartment. Phillip was much stronger, so that night, as we cuddled in bed, we picked a weekend to move.

It was late October. I was enjoying the bright yellow, orange, and red leaves fluttering from the trees outside the kitchen window. It was Thursday. I needed to have *Where There Is No Doctor* by David Werner read by Monday. It was required reading for one of my classes.

Irene was puttering around preparing to make dinner.

"Phillip is looking good," she said. "I am thankful that you were willing to donate your marrow."

"That's what wives are for, to be helpmates," I mumbled, trying to maintain my focus on what I was reading.

"He should be able to go back to teaching Monday," Irene speculated.

"Yes, we're planning on moving back to his apartment this weekend," I said, barely audible.

She came to my side and started rubbing my arm. I put my book down. "The black doesn't come off, does it?" she asked.

"No."

She smiled like a sheep caught out of its pen. "It's just that … Well, I've seen black people at the market before, and I even have a black gardener."

"Joshua," I interrupted.

"Oh, is that his name? I hired him through an agency." She sat at the table across from me. "It's just that I've never really known any black people—you know, had them as friends and talked to them. And now …" She pursed her lips. "I'm related to one."

She picked up my hand off the table and stroked my fingers. "I'm afraid that I have been very spiteful to you, but your kindness has won me over. You are good for my son. You not only saved his life, but I can see that he treats you like none of the other women he has ever dated. I can understand why he married you. You are so kind."

"In my culture it is necessary for a young bride to be respectful of her mother-in-law no matter how she treats her," I said.

"I am very thankful for your culture teaching you that." The teakettle whistled, and she got up and made a cup of tea for both of us. She served me and then sat down again. "I hated you when we met that day at the hospital. I swore at you, and that other time I called you a …"

Tears formed in her eyes as she set down her teacup. "Kitty, can you ever forgive me?"

She jumped up, grabbed a tissue, wiped her eyes, and blew her nose. When she sat down again, she grabbed her chest and took a deep breath.

"Are you all right, Mother Irene?" I asked.

She shook her head. "Oh, I'm just fine. It's just that never in my whole life have I ever asked anyone to forgive me." Between sobs she added, "You know, I've never been wrong before."

"Mother Irene." I took her hand in mine. "Kwamboka forgives you."

Emotion burst from her as we hugged. She was convulsing on my shoulder when Phillip barreled into the kitchen.

"Got the groceries," he said.

I held up my hand to stop him. When Irene regained her composure, I wiped her eyes with a tissue. "Your mother has decided that she likes me."

"Actually," Irene said between bursts of blowing her nose, "I love you, Kwab … Ah, I'll never get your name right."

She started crying again. "May I call you Kitty? I know that's not your name, but …"

"As my mother-in-law you have the privilege in my culture to call me whatever you choose."

"I love you, Kitty, and I love your culture that gives me such nice prerogatives. Let's get dinner ready. You want to help me?" She put her arm around me and turned to her son. "Don't you ever be unkind to this wife of yours or I will beat you."

"Yes, Mother," Phillip said.

"Now, Kitty, let's fix dinner. That is, of course, if my son remembered to get what I told him. He usually forgets the list at home and then doesn't get the right things."

"I remembered the list and checked off things as I got them."

"Don't get defensive with me, son. I'm just telling the facts." She unpacked the bags as Phillip gave me a kiss. Her back was turned, so he was uninhibited in his caress. She turned on the burner and started browning the sausage.

"I'm making Phillip's favorite spaghetti tonight. If you would like, Kitty, I'll show you how to make the sauce just the way he likes it."

She turned to get our approval. "You two should go in the bedroom if you're going to do that." She folded up the paper bag. "What's this? Oreo cookies weren't on the list."

Phillip picked the cookies out of her hand. "That's a little something Kwamboka wanted to try. She's never eaten an Oreo cookie before. I told her about them on our honeymoon."

"Well, fine, but don't eat them till after dinner, I don't want you to ruin your appetite when I'm making your favorite meal," Irene scolded.

"I would like to help you, Mother Irene. I want to learn how to make this Italian food."

"That's great. Here, I'll show you the secret to this sauce." Phillip absconded with the Oreos to the bedroom.

That night I shaved my armpits with Phillip's razor. I had noticed that women in Boston did that, and I was trying to be a real Boston woman. Then I let the stream of the shower soothe me and tingle across my back. I loved showers. Stepping out I rubbed my entire body with coconut oil. The smell reminded me of home. I felt soft and smooth all over. As I returned to the bedroom in my terrycloth robe, Phillip passed me and went in the bathroom to take his medication and wash up as he did every evening.

He hardly noticed me as he passed, but I was determined to change that. He would notice Kwamboka tonight. I undressed. Rolling the sheets and blanket to the foot of the bed, I stretched out naked in the middle. I took one of the Oreos and separated it. The frosting stuck to one side, and I ate the cookie without the frosting. It tasted good, but I knew what to do. Phillip was feeling better, and the last couple nights he had even seemed amorous.

I took another and divided it, brushed the crumbs off my chest, licked the frosting, and then stuck the two halves with frosting on my breasts, squishing the cream onto my hardening nipples. He came from the bathroom wrapped in his towel and stared. His eyes wandered over my body. He dropped his towel.

"This is why you bought the Oreos, isn't it? Or did I misunderstand?"

He reached for one of the cookies teetering on my breast.

"No, no, not with your hands." He pulled back. "You told me on the night before we were married that my nipples reminded you of Oreos. I didn't even know what they were then."

He slid next to me on the bed and nibbled the cookies off my breasts, licking the sticky frosting from my nipples. I ululated softly as I stoked his penis.

"It's your blood making me erect," he proclaimed with a mischievous smile.

"Phillip, my dear, you have starved long enough." I spread my legs. "Welcome to the feast. But penetrate me slowly so I get adequate clitoral stimulation, like a husband and not like a client."

"You've been reading too many books, Kwamboka."

"Magazines, Phillip, magazines …" I purred like a leopard.

Cured

PHILLIP HAD A DOCTOR'S APPOINTMENT with his transplant doctor and asked me to come with him. It just happened to be a day that I had no classes, but I had planned to work on researching journal articles for my thesis.

It was only a short subway ride to the physician's office and it was a beautiful day, so I decided to go with him. On the way I noticed that Phillip was walking briskly as he had in Nairobi. I smiled. "You have made great progress, Phillip. You are walking as fast as Kwamboka."

"It's been a long road."

We arrived at the office and waited. I picked up a *Cosmopolitan* to read some of the articles. Phillip just kept looking at the clock on the wall.

When the nurse invited us into the exam room, I took my *Cosmopolitan* magazine with me to finish the article. We sat in silence waiting for Doctor Levin.

He came in with a bounce in his step. Scanning the electronic chart on his mobile computer he said, "It's been a year since the transplant, Phillip, and reviewing your lab tests here, I see no sign of rejection or graft-versus-host disease. Oh, by the way, I ordered the tests the infectious disease consultant requested on your blood as well, including an HIV PCR. Our lab reports it as undetectable. There was a case like this reported in the *New England Journal* in 2009

255

from Germany. All I can say is—" Dr. Levin looked up from the electronic medical record and smiled at me. "You picked the right donor."

"And the right wife," Phillip said, giving me a hug.

"I did call Colonel Johnson, Kitzi. He confirmed what you explained to me. You knew more about HIV receptors than I did." He laughed and turned to Phillip. "You don't need any drugs now. You never developed any signs of rejection, so how are you functioning at work?"

"I'm teaching all my classes and even getting some research done," Phillip reported.

He asked a number of questions to see if Phillip was having any obscure side effects. Then he cleared his throat and looked at Phillip. "Any erectile dysfunction?"

Phillip blushed. "At times."

"I have to work hard to get him properly aroused," I explained, "but he erects well eventually, and then he ejaculates ..."

"Too much information." Dr. Levin held up his hand, "I see you two are working that out." He closed the electronic medical record on the screen. "I would say that you have had a pretty smooth course. I would like to see you in six months. At eighteen months, if you still are PCR negative, ID would like to publish your case. You will be the second HIV-AIDS cure in the medical literature."

"Where in Africa are you from, Mrs. Schoenberg?" the doctor asked.

"Kisii land." I could tell he didn't understand. "That's western Kenya, right near Lake Victoria."

"Oh, I worked at Eldoret when I was a medical student," he said.

"That's not far from Kisii land. So you know Kenya?" I replied.

"I loved working there. The people were so friendly." He stood to shake our hands. "You two are the nicest couple. I always look forward to seeing you. I can tell that you are very much in love."

"We've had to work at it," I said as he opened the door. He shook his head and disappeared down the hall. Phillip gave me a hug. He was chuckling, but I didn't understand why. We left the clinic and headed toward the T station.

As we descended into the subway to catch the green line back to our apartment, Phillip said, "Are you sure you aren't a witch?"

I stopped. "Phillip, what provoked that?"

"Calm down. I'm just impressed with how you charmed the doctor today and, before that, my mother. You have a better relationship with her than I do. I just wondered whether you put a spell on her." He laughed.

I frowned. "I am not a witch. And my mother was not one either, even if they burned her for being one."

I swatted at him, and he backed away. "All right, that was culturally insensitive. I was just trying to compliment you."

"Why would you say that to me? I told you what my uncle did."

"May I start over as if I never said that?" he said.

I put my hands on my hips. "This had better be good, Phillip Andrew Schoenberg."

"My mother—" he started.

"Yes, that is a safe start," I interrupted.

"—whom I have known all my life as a bigoted, self-righteous, neurotic woman, adores you." I breathed more slowly. "When I was a child she would warn me not to play with the colored children at school. Now the two of you chatter about everything. She even calls every night and doesn't want to talk to me. She wants to talk to you. She takes you out every Saturday for the two of you to get your hair done, and then she takes you out for lunch. If she took me out for lunch, which she has never done, she would make me pay for it. How did you do that? How did you change her attitude?"

"She is a mother to me. Now that she has apologized to me, we are learning to love each other. In some ways, she reminds me of my mother. The fact that she has pasty-pink skin like you makes no difference to me."

He started down the steps, and I grabbed his coat.

"Listen to me, Phillip. When we are having sexual intercourse, I am not thinking that your little man-member is pink and my thighs are black." Phillip looked around to see if anyone was paying attention to our conversation. I grabbed his chin and made him face me. "Are you listening to me?"

He was silent, so I continued, "I am thinking that I love you because you are my husband who cares about me, and I love my mother-in-law because she is the mother of my favorite man in the world."

He kissed me first on the cheeks and then on my lips. I thought he was trying to get me to stop talking. "I'm sorry," he said. "May I be forgiven?"

The escalator wasn't working. I led him down the stairs. "You're forgiven because I love you, but don't call me a witch ever again."

"I didn't actually …"

I turned and glared at him.

"I won't. I promise. Come, we don't want to miss the green line," he said as he took my hand into his.

Thinking about Home

THE DAY I FINISHED MY coursework, the PhD review board asked to meet with me regarding my doctorate dissertation proposal. We met in the conference room in the anthropology building. It was formidable. Five professors were sitting on one side of the long table, and one chair had been placed on the other side. The room was dark, with the reflected afternoon sun just peeking in through the windows. I sat and pulled out my dissertation, but I knew it by heart.

"My project involves IQ testing children when they first start school and then retesting them a year later. I would correlate the results with their age of matriculation, since many children in Kenya start elementary school late, when their parents no longer needed them to herd cattle. I hypothesize that children starting school at age six would not show an IQ change, whereas children starting school at ages eight to twelve years would show a dramatic change in IQ because of the acculturation school provides."

I paused as the four gray-haired men and one woman leafed through copies of my dissertation.

"The board is intrigued," the chairman said. "This is a radical project, Mrs. Schoenberg, but for a long time we have been hoping for a project with more international appeal. This project fits with some goals we did not expect to achieve. Where will you get funding?"

"I've applied for a grant from the Bill and Melinda Gates Foundation and have already received a positive response to my proposal," I replied.

"Excellent."

"Dr. Phillip Schoenberg—"

"Your husband," the chairman interrupted.

"Yes. The IRB thought an anthropologist should assist in the process. That would fulfill the cross-cultural considerations. The foundation approved that aspect of the study as well, even though he is my husband."

The chairman smiled. "We anticipate the results with great expectations." He looked to the rest of the committee, who all agreed.

That evening as we climbed the steps at our brownstone apartment building, Phillip seemed surprised when I explained the review board committee's decision. "I'm so glad your doctorate thesis proposal received such an enthusiastic response. I expected to be up all night helping you make changes to your thesis."

I grabbed the mail out of the box and sorted it as we headed upstairs to our apartment. One letter looked official, and I stopped in the middle of the stairway to open it. I flashed the envelope to Phillip so he could see the official Kenyan seal. He looked concerned.

"I am being summoned to return to Kenya to testify in court on that kidnapping case. I have to be there in four weeks." I calculated in my head. "That will be the beginning of summer vacation. Do you want to come with me?" I turned the letter over to him.

He read it. "Sure, I'm not teaching any summer session classes. Besides, I need a break."

"I would like to spend some time with Joyce so she remembers that I love her. I've been supporting Zipporah and her mother in Mombasa with some of my stipend money, and I would like to go to Kijabe Hospital and pay my bill."

Phillip kissed me. "Maybe we could go to Mombasa for a second honeymoon?" he said, rubbing his hand down the small of my back.

"That would be great. While we're there we can search for Zipporah and check on her TB treatment," I added.

He hugged me. "Besides, I wouldn't want you to go alone. Someone might kidnap you." We both laughed.

"But I do have a proposal for you." He hugged me to his side as we walked up the steps to our apartment. He unlocked the door, whisked me in his arms, and carried me across the threshold. "I didn't get to do that before."

I rushed into the apartment. Phillip had flowers on the table and eucalyptus sprigs among them. It smelled great. "When did you do that?"

"I had them delivered between classes."

I smelled the flowers and then rushed into the bedroom. "I want to hear your proposal, but tell me in a minute."

An understanding glance passed between us as he closed the door. Once in the bedroom I shed my clothes. Even though we had been married for almost three years, we hadn't really gotten to know each other until we moved to this apartment. We were still discovering each other's idiosyncrasies. He was neurotic about rolling the toothpaste tube and positioning the toilet paper on the roll in the bathroom.

But he said that the most shocking of my idiosyncrasies was the first night after we moved in, I came home from class, took off my clothes, and wrapped in my kitamba.

"Kisii girls get tired of all these clothes," I told him.

"It's just that you're almost naked," he said.

"You're my husband. You've seen me naked before." He explained that his mother always insisted that he be properly dressed outside his bedroom. I understood and had complied while we were living with her. But this was our own home.

"I am properly dressed," I said, smiling, "for a Kisii girl."

But, being a proper wife, I asked permission of my

husband after that. I just looked at him, and he knew what I wanted. If he nodded, I knew that I could wear my kitamba.

"Now, what about that proposal?" I asked, cuddling up next to him. He had stripped to his underwear and the silk bathrobe I had gotten him for Christmas. I had taught him well.

"I've been thinking," he said.

I twirled his chest hairs around my finger as he talked. "You have always wanted to build a private school. Your research involves testing children as they enter school." He pushed my kitamba aside to caress my breasts. "What about building a school in your home village? You could be the director, I could continue my anthropologic research, and you would get the data for your doctoral thesis. And ... we would be providing an education for your community."

"What about my uncle?" I lay my head in his lap as he continued.

"Correct me if I'm wrong, but if I give him a bride price for you and he accepts it, wouldn't your father's land become mine? And yours, of course." He kissed my forehead. We curled up together in silence as I thought it out.

Running my hand through my hair I said, "I already have a deed to the land. It's just that in Kisii territory, they don't always follow Kenyan law. But if he accepted the bride price—"

I shifted to resting on my elbow, watching the brilliant red of the setting sun out the window across our living room. I refocused on the proposal. Resting again on his lap, I smoothed the hair across his temples. "Then it would be our land both by Kenyan law and Ekegusii law." I ran my fingers across his moist lips.

I sat up. "But he would never agree to that. He would rather see me dead."

"Calm down," Phillip said making soft circles down my flanks with his finger. I closed my eyes, enjoying the delicacy of the moment. Then he gave my buttocks a tight squeeze. "He might agree if it was in his financial interest."

"What would you propose to make it in his interest?" I untied my kitamba. I was feeling hot and sweaty, although I was sure the temperature in the room hadn't changed.

"What if I gave him ten cows? That would be the going price for a college=educated woman." His fingers resumed their wandering over my thighs.

"What about the tea factory? Could we buy it from him?" I explored his groin and found him responding.

I jumped up. "Are you intending coital intimacy, Phillip? Otherwise, I'm hungry, I didn't have any lunch."

"Your vocabulary, Kwamboka."

Return to Kenya

UPON RETURNING TO KENYA WE stayed at the New Stanley Hotel where Phillip had stayed when he was in Nairobi. I was too nervous to walk, so we took a taxi to the courthouse every day of the trial. On the last day we had planned to have a nice dinner together since I had found it hard to eat anything during the trial. "Convicted or not, it will be over," Phillip said.

That evening we dressed in our finest clothes and were seated at a quiet table. Phillip had ordered bird of paradise flowers for our table. I collapsed in my chair.

"I'm glad that's done. That cross-examination was grueling. I felt like a criminal, not the victim," I said as I took a sip of champagne and wiggled in my seat. It felt good to be back in Nairobi. I glanced across the restaurant as the waiter brought our appetizers.

"I thought you handled yourself with a great deal of poise, Kwamboka. Your vivid description and precise answers made it pretty difficult to dispute."

He took a sip of my champagne, and it fizzed onto his face. He wiped it off with a serviette. "It's just that some of the things you described, I really didn't want to know. I almost had to leave. Do you think the government will go after the brothel owner for buying you?"

"I don't know, but I sure am ready for that second

honeymoon you promised. I'm hoping we can find Zipporah. I know enough people in town."

Phillip flushed. "I'm sure you do. Just don't tell me how you know them when we're there. But a couple days of sand and sun sounds fun."

"Can we stay at that same resort? I need a break after this trial." I took a deep breath. "Then we can try to find Zipporah. She wrote that she and her mother live on a little plot of land outside of town. You'll just have to hug me if I burst into tears."

"Agreed," Phillip said. Then he looked back at the door to the restaurant. The maître d', dressed in his bright red uniform, was searching for our guest. "Do you think she'll show?"

"Oh, yes. I arranged the taxi. She will be here."

Joyce appeared at the door clutching her purse. The maître d' offered her a gloved hand and escorted her to our table.

"This restaurant is very nice, Phillip," Joyce said as she sat down. "I am sure it is way overpriced."

The waiter filled her glass with juice, and she took a sip. "Very good. Mango juice is my favorite. You knew that, didn't you, Kitzi?" She examined the stitches of the serviette. "I like these little round tables and the white linen tablecloth, and the waiters are so handsome. I didn't know they had such places in Nairobi. I suppose this is mostly for tourists. I have never been to a brunch before."

She set down her glass and straightened her silverware. "Kitzi says that I am to treat you like a son-in-law, so, thank you for inviting me."

It seemed the phrase was painful for her to say.

"I have to admit that I am deciding to like you. I said some pretty mean things about you when you first started being interested in my Kitzi. But I know that am not following Jesus to keep those angry, bad thoughts in my heart." She

265

sighed. "Especially when you have been so kind to me. Can you forgive me?"

Phillip took Joyce's hand and answered in Swahili, "You're forgiven, mother of Kitzi."

Joyce laughed. "I didn't know you were so skilled in Swahili."

"I ordered eggs benedict for you, Joyce," I said, switching to English. "I hope you don't mind."

"What are eggs benedict? Are they from a benedict bird? I've never heard of that."

"No, Mother Joyce, they are called that because of the special sauce."

"I've never had sauce on my eggs. I usually eat them ..."

"I know, but here they put sauce on the eggs," I said.

The waiter brought our orders and filled my champagne glass.

Joyce put her hand over hers. "Just water, please. I'm a Christian woman." She glared at my glass. Phillip ordered wine.

"I'm a Christian woman too, Joyce. Phillip and I go to the Lutheran church in Boston every Sunday. But Boston Lutherans are allowed to drink alcohol."

"But you are not in Boston now, Kitzi."

Phillip interrupted. "I propose a toast to the end of the court case."

I sipped my champagne, Phillip his wine, and Joyce her water. Phillip continued, "I can't imagine what it was like for you when Kwamboka disappeared."

"Horrible, just horrible," Joyce said, taking a bite of her eggs. "Oh, this is good. Benedict eggs? Is this a Catholic sauce? I am not Catholic, you know."

"Eggs benedict, Joyce. It has nothing to do with being Catholic."

"Kwamboka thought that you would like the sauce," said Phillip.

"Oh, I do." Joyce reached across the table and grabbed my

hand. "I still can't twist my tongue around your Kisii name. Phillip says it very well, but you will always be Kitzi to me."

"I don't mind being Kitzi to you. But I insist on my husband using my proper name." I took a bite of pastry. "His mother can't even say Kitzi. She calls me Kitty."

Joyce laughed.

"At least I am not Chui the leopard anymore."

Phillip winced. "Please don't remind me of your testimony."

"I heard those kidnappers were convicted. Do you feel better now?" asked Joyce as she patted my hand.

"I lost many months of my life as a slave, but I'm glad they were convicted. What surprised me was that Martha was the ringleader. I knew she didn't like me, but I didn't think she would arrange my kidnapping. In fact, I thought my uncle had arranged it when it happened."

Joyce turned to Phillip. "I was angry when Kitzi didn't come home. I thought she ran off to America with you."

Phillip said, "I wanted her to, but she needed a visa first."

"Oh, I hadn't thought of that. Well, anyway, she was the chief promoter of my business," Joyce covered her face. "I sort of abused her."

She straightened her serviette on her lap. "But now I have quite a business providing the embassy ladies with dresses, so I have enough to buy meat."

"We have another reason that we wanted to talk to you, Joyce." I set down my fork. "This is radical, so listen carefully."

"This sauce is good. I've never had sauce on my eggs before," she repeated and then looked up. "All right, I'm listening."

The waiter filled her teacup. She jumped in surprise. "I'm sorry, I'm just nervous. I've never been in a place like this."

"Phillip and I have talked to Ratemo Michieka."

"He was the vice chancellor under Kenyatta. He is a big man in Kenya. How did you get to talk to him?" asked Joyce.

"Phillip and I would like to start a private school, and

since Mr. Michieka is Kisii, we thought he would like to be involved. He has agreed to be chairman of our board of directors. But we need a lawyer to incorporate the foundation and do a lot of other things. Your part would be to make the school uniforms. Could you do that? Beautiful Mountain Education Foundation would pay you for them. It would keep you in business for months, and every year there would be new students who would need uniforms."

"I would make the uniforms?" She set down her fork. I could see numbers buzzing through her head. "How many boys would need uniforms?"

"I know you don't think girls need an education, but we would need uniforms for girls too. We would probably need a hundred and fifty to start out."

Her eyes widened as she looked back and forth at Phillip and me. "You are not making a joke of me, are you?"

"No. But we are going to Kijabe Hospital for a visit. I would like Phillip to meet Pastor Joseph. And then we will go to Mombasa for a few days. There is someone I need to find there. Then we need to return to Boston. Phillip has classes he has agreed to teach, and I need to take a few doctoral classes. In the spring, probably May, we'll return to Kenya. We can't start construction until we have a clear title to the land. I hope to open the school a year later."

"I will make one uniform for a girl and one for a boy. When you return from Mombasa, I will have them ready. But when you need all of them, I will have to hire someone to get them finished."

"Agreed. Thank you, Mother Joyce," I said and kissed her hand. "And yes, I will continue to send the weekly letters."

"Thanks, Mother," said Phillip. The word paralyzed her. Benedict sauce dribbled down her chin. Phillip wiped it from her face with his serviette.

Kijabe Hospital

DRIVING TO KIJABE HOSPITAL FROM Nairobi took a long time, but it was a lot faster than taking the bus that stopped all the time to let people in and out. I still remembered where to turn off the highway to the hospital entrance. I smiled when I saw the sign for "Casualty," remembering how naïve I had been when I first read the word from my bed. I recognized the smell of disinfectant as we entered. We were directed to the business office by one of the patients leaving to go home.

"We would like to talk to Pastor Joseph," I told the woman at the business office desk. "Is he still the chaplain here at Kijabe Hospital?"

"Yes, he is. Can I tell him what this is regarding?" she asked.

"I have a bill to pay."

"I can check to see how much you owe," she said. "What's your name?" She turned to her secretary. "Paul, go see if you can find Pastor Joseph."

"It would be under Kwamboka Muwami." I spelled it for her.

Phillip and I waited as she scanned through her computer registry. Her face was intense as she studied the screen. "Is this an old bill? I'm not finding it. Muwami, is it? Could you spell it again for me?"

I spelled my family name for her.

"Sorry, I am not finding it. How many months back was this bill?" she asked, searching her records.

"Spring 2002."

She laughed so hard she had to grab her desk. "Honey, that was eight or nine years ago." Just then Pastor Joseph appeared.

I bowed my head to him. "Pastor Joseph, do you remember me?"

He looked at me. There was no sign of recognition.

"I am the girl who was walking to Nairobi. The nurses found me collapsed by the Italian chapel."

"Kwamboka." he said with a startled look, "Forgive me for not recognizing you, but you were a scrawny, dehydrated, sick child then. Now you are a mature woman." He was suddenly serious. "You aren't sick are you?"

"Oh, no, I am very healthy. Thank you for asking."

"Bless you, child. You had those tremendous test scores on your secondary exam," he recalled.

"Yes, I have completed my studies at Nairobi University and am working on my doctorate at Boston College in the United States of America."

"I knew you would do well," said Pastor Joseph. "Praise the Lord."

"This is my husband, Phillip. He's an anthropologist, specializing in Kisii culture."

Joseph extended his hand. "You have one very intelligent wife, young man. I hope you treat her with great respect."

"I do, pastor. She is amazing," answered Phillip.

"So if you are well, Kwamboka, what brings you to Kijabe?"

The billing director was still smirking. "She wants to pay her bill from 2002."

Pastor Joseph shook his head.

I stopped him and explained, "Jesus has saved me from so many things since I was here. I am so blessed, but I feel guilty that I never paid Kijabe Hospital for saving my life. Do you know what my bill would be?" I asked.

He gave me a hug and turned to Phillip. "You are a very blessed man, Phillip." He turned back to me. "Kwamboka, that bill has been paid long ago."

"Then may I make a donation to the hospital?" I asked. "I want to do something to repay the hospital for taking care of me."

Pastor Joseph turned to the billing director and then turned back to me. "That would be most generous but not necessary."

Phillip handed him a check. Pastor Joseph looked at it and sat down. He passed the check to the billing director, whose eyes just stared. "I will make you a receipt," she finally said.

"I am struck dumb," said Joseph, "just like Zachariah, the father of John the Baptist."

I kneeled in front of him since he was so short. "I owe this hospital my life, Pastor Joseph. This is a mere pittance."

He laughed. "You shocked me before with your vocabulary, and now you have done it again. God bless you richly, Kwamboka."

"Can you give my dear husband a tour? Is Dr. Charles still here?"

"I sure can give you a tour. This will be the best-paid tour ever. And yes, Dr. Charles is now chief of staff here at Kijabe. He will certainly be glad to see you." He headed out the door as Phillip and I followed.

"The main hospital is here. We have a special building for children with cerebral palsy and orthopedic problems." He turned to Phillip. "At the end of the tour I will show you the very bed where your wife stayed."

"Then you probably need new beds," I said.

He put his arm around Phillip. "Did she ever tell you that

she complained about her IV the whole time she was here? Let me tell you, she was a challenge."

I wasn't too sure I wanted Phillip to hear this part, but I thought that I might as well get used to the specters of my past. Mombasa would be worse.

Search

"Zipporah, where are you?" I yelled, ducking my head into a mud hut. We had traveled over bumpy rural roads to the place that I was told she had returned to live with her mother. The whole village was nothing but shattered hovels.

"Are you sure this is the place?" Phillip asked. "This whole village looks abandoned." He kicked a termite hill growing in the doorway.

"I'm pretty sure. That man's Swahili wasn't too good. I wish I knew his tribal language. But I agree it doesn't look like anyone's lived here for a while." We stood and searched the surrounding area. We had searched other hovels, but they were all abandoned.

"What should we do?" Phillip asked.

"Let's drive back toward Mombasa. If we see someone along the road, I'll ask again." We climbed into the Land Rover. The road was full of ruts, and we could barely drive fifteen miles per hour without bouncing our heads on the ceiling. The sun was beating down, and the dust swirled behind the Land Rover from lack of rain.

"When you get away from the tourist area, this country is pretty desolate, isn't it?" Phillip said as a rut twisted the steering wheel out of his grasp.

"What the tourist sees is a veneer on rotten wood," I said as we reached the main road and Phillip shifted into second gear. On the way back to Mombasa, we stopped and asked people along the road if they had seen Zipporah or if they knew what had happened to her. I got the impression that some knew but weren't telling.

"Look at that beautiful fruit," said Phillip, stopping at a roadside stand. "Let's get some mangos to eat in our room at the resort."

"Wait," I said, but he didn't hear me. I slipped out of my side of the vehicle and stayed in the background. I didn't want the owner to see me.

A woman in colorful clothes weighed out mangos for Phillip. The owner looked up and was startled when he saw me. "Chui?"

Phillip dropped one of the mangos and stooped to pick it up. I remained stoic, flashing my wedding band. My flesh tingled. I wanted to send Phillip away, but he had already guessed the situation. I managed to get the words out. "Mr. Okayo, I am looking for Zipporah."

"The little mosquito," he whispered, avoiding the saleswoman, "flew back to the swamp."

"Thank you, Mr. Okayo." I turned to Phillip. "Let's go."

"These are beautiful mangos," he said as he counted out shillings.

"The best," the saleswoman smiled, apparently delighted that he did not negotiate the price.

"He was one of your clients, wasn't he?" Phillip said as we climbed back in the vehicle.

"Zipporah has gone back to the brothel," I said without answering. We both took a deep breath.

"I don't want to see where they kept you," he said.

"But I can't go back alone," I said, pleading.

"Will we have to buy her?" asked Phillip.

"Madame Mimi is quite a negotiator, especially if her bodyguard is there." I felt defeated. "Wait. We went to the chapel service on the beach this morning. This is Sunday. Tomorrow they will go to the beach to play volleyball."

Phillip wasn't following my train of thought. "How will that help us?"

"I have an idea. Let's go back to the resort. I have some telephone calls to make and some shopping to do," I said.

Back at the resort, I headed straight for the dress shop.

"Can I help you?" asked the saleswoman. She was short and petite, wearing a flamboyant dress that stopped at midthigh.

"I like your dress," I said trying to make my tone believable. "Do you have one like it for a tall person like me?"

"Sure, right over here." A line of dresses in garish colors sporting flowers on a purple background hung in a row. I picked one that was my size and asked to try it on.

"What are you doing?" Phillip asked. "You never wear dresses like that."

"Wait and see," I said as I slipped into the changing room. The dress was ridiculous, with loud colors, and for a tall Kisii girl it wasn't long enough. I put my clothes back on.

"I'll take it," I told the salesgirl. "And add in that big straw hat and those crazy sunglasses." I pointed to the display.

Phillip had a look of astonishment across his face. "You never wear stuff like this."

"Do you think this will make me look like a tourist?"

"Yes, definitely, but why?"

"Now I need to make a telephone call." I walked out of the dress shop and left Phillip to pay for my purchases. He raced to meet me at our room.

"What are you doing?" he asked. I waved him away.

Being a gentleman, he opened the door for me. I grabbed the telephone and dialed. "Hello, Jambo, I would like to talk to Officer Johdi Kiriamiti, please."

While I was on hold I started to explain my idea to Phillip.

Then I heard her answer on the other end of the line. "This is Kwamboka Muwami Schoenberg," I said and switched to Ekegusii. "Johdi, I need your help."

Volleyball on the Beach

FROM THE SECURITY OF OUR rented Land Rover, which we had parked in the lot designed for the beach crowd, I spotted Zipporah. I handed the binoculars to Phillip. He stuffed the last of his croissant into his mouth and took a look. The last flakes fell on his pants, and he brushed them off as he searched the beach.

"The petite one sprawled out under the palm tree is Zipporah," I told him.

He sat upright, focused the binoculars, and whistled. "They're not wearing much. The ones playing volleyball have some good-looking bodies."

I poked him in the ribs.

"Ouch. Except the heavy one."

"That's Ruth. Stay away from her. She's dangerous," I warned him.

"Oh, I see Zipporah now. Is she wearing anything?" he said, stunned.

"Probably just a string bikini," I replied.

"She looks like a child," Phillip said in disbelief.

"She's lived through more trauma than most old people." I adjusted my wide-brimmed straw hat and put on my glitzy sunglasses. The dress I had bought at the resort had animals parading around the print. My beach bag completed my ensemble as a well-fashioned tourist. "Do you still remember how to proposition a whore, Phillip? I mean, a transactional sex worker."

"I gave that up, Kwamboka." He seemed annoyed with my question but kept his eyes peeled through the binoculars.

"Recall your skills," I demanded. "This time they might save a woman's life."

We walked behind the row of palm trees to get as close as we could without being seen. "Now go flirt with Zipporah. Mwalimu will come over and give you a card for the brothel. When he returns to the volleyball game, tell Zipporah your name. That letter she wrote was addressed to you. She should remember. Then tell her to follow you up the beach. When she does, Mwalimu will confront you. That's when I take over."

Phillip scanned past the group playing volleyball. "Mwalimu is the big guy?"

"He's killed men with his bare hands," I said.

"Thanks, Kwamboka, that's reassuring," Phillip said sarcastically under his breath.

I leaned over and gave him a kiss. "I love you, Phillip. Without you I would be on the beach with them today and having sex all night with the locals tomorrow."

"What a grotesque thought." He added, "Please don't elaborate."

"We have to give Zipporah a better life. She helped me escape." I turned to him. "Ready?"

"Charming as always." I coached him as if we were running a race.

We parted ways so Mwalimu wouldn't see us together. I sat under an umbrella set up on the beach by the local bar. A vendor came to take my order for a drink. Phillip positioned himself near the volleyball game. He appeared to be enchanting the girls. I doubt he was faking that part, especially when they invited him to play and he joined the game. He stood and stared when breasts popped out of their tops. *Had I sent my lamb among wolves?*

After one athletic save, he waved that he was tired and sat down next to Zipporah. Mwalimu didn't seem to mind. They were just talking. Zipporah glanced across the beach at me, but Mwalimu was watching. I didn't dare respond.

It didn't take long for Mwalimu to approach Phillip and to offer him a card for a discount on Tuesday night. Phillip played along and smiled as he fingered the card. *You don't have to look so happy*, I thought. Everything was happening as planned, but now came the part I couldn't orchestrate. Would Zipporah be willing to come?

Camel venders crossed the beach offering rides. Phillip offered to pay for Zipporah to go for a camel ride. That was creative. But Mwalimu intervened and shooed the camel jockey away, so it was back to the original plan.

Phillip offered something, I think to buy her a drink. He tried to get her to follow, but Mwalimu shook his head. I picked up my empty glass, and we met at the bar.

"She's willing to come, but she's afraid," said Phillip. He had his back turned to me. "That Mwalimu guy is even bigger close up. Are you sure you can handle him?"

"Just watch for an opportunity and bring her toward the Land Rover when you get a chance," I said. "And keep an eye on Mwalimu."

"This won't get us both killed, will it?" Phillip asked.

"I hope not."

I loitered at the bar until he was back in the volleyball game. Zipporah seemed delighted with her drink. I took up my position under the umbrella. Something had to happen.

Phillip made it happen. I knew that he had played volleyball for Boston College as an undergraduate. When he had the opportunity, he spiked the ball right into Ruth's face. Her nose gushed with blood, and she screamed. The other girls surround her, and Mwalimu attended to her.

"Oh, I'm so sorry," Phillip said as he faded back, grabbed Zipporah, and ran toward the Land Rover.

I took the cue, grabbed my stuff, and ran behind the row of palm trees to meet them. When we were out of sight of the beach, I embraced Zipporah.

"I'm so glad to see you." My eyes filled with tears.

"Chui, I love you. Thank you for the money you sent." She hung her head. "But my mother died."

"I'm so sorry, Zipporah."

A smack to the head dropped Phillip to the ground. Zipporah screamed and cowered beside him. A painful grasp on my arm whipped me around. I was facing a giant.

"What do you think you're doing?" Mwalimu said as he dug his fingers into my arm.

I tossed my hat and removed my sunglasses.

"Chui." His grip weakened.

"I'm taking Zipporah away." I enunciated each word in Swahili.

"I can't let you do that," he said.

"You will want to before the day is over," I asserted.

"You're bluffing," he scoffed.

"Did you figure out how I escaped?" I said.

"Not exactly," he said, "but I have a pretty good idea."

"Then maybe you shouldn't say that I'm bluffing." I pulled the Nairobi newspaper out of my beach bag and thrust it into his chest. "Faraji and Chuki were just convicted for kidnapping me and are spending the rest of their lives in a Kenyan prison. Now, you were nice to me when I was under your care. If you let me have Zipporah, I will testify on your behalf."

He dropped my arm to scan the front page of the newspaper. The picture of Faraji and Chuki being led away with arm and ankle shackles was graphic. The lighting was perfect for catching the anguished looks on their faces.

"Madame Mimi will …"

"Trust me, Mwalimu, after today she won't matter."

Phillip picked himself off the ground, still dazed. "I'm sorry my husband had to hurt Ruth. It was the only way," I said.

"He's your husband?" asked a sober Mwalimu.

"Yes, we were married before you and I met. You prostituted a married woman, the wife of a US citizen. How many years in prison do you think that deserves?"

There was a synchronous click behind him as bullets were chambered. Mwalimu turned to face four Kenyan soldiers with automatic weapons. "What's this?" he said.

"Just a little insurance so that you would do the right thing. You know why I couldn't trust the local police."

He dropped the newspaper and held up his hands in surrender. I picked it up and tucked it in his belt. "The article is quite good for the interested reader—and I'm sure you're interested."

Phillip opened the door for Zipporah, who climbed into the backseat.

"You'd better go back and check on Ruth. You know how nasty she gets over every little thing. She's probably having a fit over that nosebleed my husband gave her," I said, observing the evolving scene on the beach. "It looks like your van driver and that merchant *volunteer* both have their hands full."

The soldiers lowered their guns as Mwalimu backed toward the beach, lowering his arms.

"Take them back to the brothel, Mwalimu. A welcoming party has been arranged," I ordered.

Zipporah

A DAY LATER, WE WERE sitting at the Serena Beach Hotel and Spa under the canopy over the open-air restaurant. The smell of the ocean and the local flora wafted through the air. The waves splashing on the beach provided background music. Phillip had ordered the buffet for all three of us.

"I think that went well. At least, it seems so after a good night's sleep," I said adding cream and sugar to my cup of coffee.

"Except for the lump on the back of my head," Phillip said.

"I'm sorry about that. It wasn't part of the plan."

Zipporah finally came and sat down. She had been wandering around the restaurant checking the serving tables, looking out at the ocean a few yards away, and skipping and jumping among the tables. "Oh, Chui, this is a magical place. They have so many kinds of food I have never seen before. I didn't know there was so much food in the whole world. Can I really eat anything I want?"

"Yes. It's called a buffet. You may have anything you want to eat. And you may even go back if you're still hungry."

"I have a very tiny stomach, Chui." She got up from the table and murmured, "I must be in heaven." She took her plate over to the table that was loaded with fruit.

Phillip looked up from the Mombasa newspaper. "They're charging Madame Mimi with promoting prostitution and jailing all the girls. According to this reporter, Mwalimu is plea bargaining to be a witness at the hearing."

"Johdi promised that if they get enough evidence from the other girls, Zipporah and I won't have to testify and the girls that provide information will be released. That way we'll just keep Zipporah out of the whole thing." We watched her trying to decide what to put on her plate. She seemed overwhelmed with choices.

"Did you enjoy sleeping with two prostitutes last night, Phillip?" I teased.

"She sure has no sense of modesty, does she?" he said.

"It's been trained out of her, I suppose."

Phillip swallowed and then cleared his throat, "You're the only woman I need, Kwamboka, but I'm glad she slept on your side of the bed. I've made a commitment before God and witnesses, you know."

"And your mother."

"Yes, and my mother. And I intend to be faithful." He got up and gave me a hug and kiss.

I stood and gave him a hug. "I love you very much, Phillip."

"I love you too, Kwamboka. But I'm very hungry after yesterday's ordeal. Let's go to the buffet. I think Zipporah needs help. She still has nothing on her plate."

The few days we spent at Serena Beach Hotel and Spa were healthy for all of us. The lump on Phillip's head healed. I had become more relaxed since our plan succeeded, but thinking about what could have happened gave me nightmares. Zipporah continued to be in ecstasy, like a child discovering a new world. She smelled all the flowers, tasted small bites of everything at the buffet, and even rode the camel with me. Phillip tried to teach her to swim, but she was too frightened.

Wading in the shallows was enough for her. She thought the pool was "an ocean in a hole in the ground," and she walked around it but was afraid to jump in. With much persuasion she was willing to dangle her feet in the shallow end.

We went shopping in town to one of the dress shops we used to visit with Mwalimu. Zipporah pulled me aside. "Phillip hasn't had sex with me yet, but he gave me this money, Chui."

She showed me the shillings she had crumpled in her hand. "Should I save it, or may I spend it? Will I be punished if I spend it? Can I get more later?"

"Phillip and I have plenty of money. You can spend it, and then we will give you more. You won't be punished."

"Oh." She shook her head. "I don't understand all this, Chui, but it sure is wonderful." She went to the counter and bought a straw hat.

When we all felt relaxed, it was time to return to Nairobi. Zipporah was so inquisitive on the drive, having never seen any of Kenya outside Mombasa, that I thought she would never stop asking questions. As we approached the city that evening, her eyes widened as she scanned the lights of the city. Alone in the backseat of the Land Rover, she kept jumping from side to side.

"This is Nairobi?" Zipporah asked. "Oh, Chui, I can't believe it. Look at all the lights. It is so big. Does it go forever?"

I kept silent. It was impossible to answer her questions.

After turning in the rental Land Rover, we took a taxi to the New Stanley Hotel. Phillip checked in, and Zipporah and I wandered around the lobby. "We would like a room with two double beds," Phillip said to the receptionist and winked at me. When we entered the room, Zipporah ran in and bounced on the bed.

"Why don't you take a long, hot shower," I said, escorting her into the bathroom.

"This is bigger than my room back at … We don't want to talk about that, do we?"

"Let's not. You have a new life now." I showed her how the shower worked, as it was quite different from the simple one in Mombasa.

When she was done, she danced out of the bathroom naked swinging her towel over her head. "Wow, what a wonderful shower."

Phillip ran into the bathroom and locked the door. I laughed at his antics.

"Am I going to be Phillip's second wife, Chui?" she whispered. "He is such a nice man, but this is many nights now, and he has not had sex with me yet. Doesn't he like me?"

I couldn't help smiling as I hugged her. "He likes you, Zipporah. It is just that his God only lets him have one wife."

"Oh, that's too bad. I've always dreamed of having a husband. I think it would be wonderful to only have to please one man, not a whole group of men every night."

"Maybe I can find a husband for you," I offered.

"I would like that very much. Would I be allowed to have children, or would I have to keep taking those pills?"

"You would be allowed to have children," I said.

She jumped up and down on the bed. "That would be heaven, Chui. I am too happy."

When she was dressed in the new clothes she bought with the money Phillip gave her, I knocked on the bathroom door. "You can come out now, Phillip. We're ready to go down and eat."

We headed downstairs to the restaurant. "Now this time you have to choose what you want to eat and they will bring it to you."

We waited for a table. A bus of tourists had filled the hotel restaurant.

Phillip soon joined us. "Table for four," he said.

"I feel just like a queen," Zipporah said as she turned to

Phillip. "Chui told me that I am not your second wife because your God only allows you to have one. I am sorry. I would be glad to be your second wife if it were allowed. I would work very hard to please you and do everything Chui told me to do."

"Thank you, Zipporah. You are very beautiful, but I am sure Kwamboka and I can find you a nice husband," Phillip responded.

I looked toward the maître d'. Joyce was on time.

"Joyce, I want you to meet Zipporah. She is the young woman I told you about who had TB, and I paid for her medical care. Now her mother has died, so she has no family."

"Glad to meet you, Zipporah," said Joyce.

"Oh, I am glad to meet you too. Chui said that you agreed to let me live with you until I find a husband. Phillip's God does not allow …"

I stilled her with my hand. "Joyce, I am Chui to her."

"I was wondering where that came from," Joyce said, leering at me.

"Chui was teaching me to read words and numbers when I helped her escape," Zipporah added.

The waiter came to take our order. We all placed our orders, except Zipporah. She whispered in my ear, "Chui, I haven't learned to read all these words yet."

"Would you like chicken?" I asked.

"Oh yes, that would be great," she replied.

I pointed at the phrase on the menu and whispered, "This one says chicken. Just tell the waiter you want that one."

"I'll have this chicken one," she said out loud.

"Right away, madam."

She giggled in her chair. "What's so funny?" I asked.

"He called me madame. He doesn't know that I don't look anything like Madame Mimi."

"No, you don't." I laughed with her.

"Private joke," I told Phillip and Joyce.

The conversation was light. Zipporah asked questions about everything, even details such as using separate glasses for water and juice. If she wasn't asking me something, she was asking Phillip.

"Thank you for being willing to take Zipporah to live with you, Joyce. She has agreed to be your housekeeper both at home and in the shop. As soon as we get things arranged to go to Kisii, we will take her with us."

"I will work very hard, and Chui will tell you that I never complain," said Zipporah. "I don't know how."

"I brought examples of the uniforms." Joyce took the samples out of her bag and laid them on the table.

"These are perfect, Joyce—just what we need."

"You made these?" Zipporah asked. "Can I learn to sew like this?"

"I will teach you," said Joyce.

"That would be wonderful. I am a very good student. I listen carefully and do what I am told. Don't I, Chui?" Zipporah said.

"Yes, you are a good student," I replied.

"When are you going to Boston?" Joyce asked as Zipporah examined the seams of the uniforms. "I hate it when you leave, but you have been faithful about sending letters every week. The women at the market now ask to see your letters every time I see them."

"I told you that would happen. I can just see you at the market." I laughed. 'To answer your question, our flight leaves late tomorrow night. We will bring Zipporah over to your house and make sure she is all settled before we leave."

Joyce looked sad.

"But when all the arrangements are made for Beautiful Mountain Education Corporation, we'll be back. And I will keep sending you letters."

"Do I get letters too, Chui?"

"Yes, I will send you letters too."

She turned to Joyce. "Would you read the letters to me? I don't know all the words yet that Chui writes."

Joyce laughed. "We will read our letters together."

Zipporah jumped out of her chair and hugged Joyce, who looked quite surprised. She said, "I will be your best housekeeper ever."

Zipporah picked up the uniform in Joyce's bag. "I think this would fit me. I am tiny, you know. They called me the mosquito. Isn't that funny?" She turned to me. "When school starts, may I be a student too? There are too many things I do not know yet, Chui."

"You can be a student too," I promised.

Our food was served, and Zipporah was quiet as she ate her chicken, picking tiny pieces off the bones. Joyce, Phillip, and I were able to discuss the plans for our school uninterrupted. When we were done with dessert, Phillip went to the desk to call for a taxi to bring Joyce home.

"I will start making uniforms. How many do you want?"

"Just make a dozen each for boys and girls to start out with," I said as I gave a wad of shillings to her. "That should be enough to get you started."

"More than enough," she said, counting the money with a smile. Her smile turned stern. "Now, don't forget about me when you're in Boston."

"I will never forget about you, Joyce." I looked up. "Oh, your taxi is here."

I hugged her. I didn't think she would let me go. Tears were in her eyes. "I'll never forget you, Joyce," I said again. She let go of me and ran for the door.

"Is Boston magical like Nairobi?" Zipporah asked.

"Even more so," I responded.

"I would like to learn about Boston too," she said.

Preparation

BACK IN BOSTON, PHILLIP AND I returned to our routine. I worked on my thesis, and as a TA I taught several anthropology classes. Phillip had his usual classes to teach as well. In the evenings we prepared for the next step. Sitting on the floor in our living room one cold February evening curled up beside our gas fireplace, we had papers scattered out in front of us.

I sighed. "We need to legally establish Beautiful Mountain Education Corporation and then buy the land and then build a school and then hire teachers and then ..." I felt exhausted considering all the details. I took a deep breath and sipped some red wine from my Lismore glass. "How can we do all this?"

"It will have to be a Kenyan corporation," Phillip said. "I've spent some time on the Internet researching the requirements of Kenyan law. We'll need a Kenyan lawyer."

"I don't want to pay a lot of money in bribes," I said, resting my chin in my hands. "When we build, we need an honest contractor. And I would like them to hire local help as much as possible. Kisii need the jobs."

"And we need some honest people on the board of directors to finalize the incorporation." Phillip droned on about all the requirements he had read about from his research. I felt discouraged, overwhelmed, and unable to concentrate. I stood and went to the window. Snow was swirling in small snow devils out on the sidewalk. A halo of snow accentuated the street lights. Our windows must not have been well insulated, as ice crystals were forming leafy patterns on the window panes. I shivered. *How different from my Kenyan home.* Then, I felt his warm touch on my shoulder as he kissed me.

"I just don't know how to do all this," I said as tears came to my eyes.

He caressed me. "Do you still have that property deed?"

"Yes. It's in the top drawer of my dresser, under my panties. Why?"

"Let me look at it." I went to the bedroom and retrieved my leather satchel. It looked so worn and rough compared to my Italian purse. I smelled it. I could still smell the smoke from my burning house. The leather scent reminded me of the Kisii cows that were so important to our village. I pulled out the worn, yellowed deed and presented it to Phillip.

Phillip scanned it. "We have a Kenyan marriage license, and if I offered a couple of cows to your uncle, would that be enough to claim your property?"

I smiled and hugged him. "But I am a college-educated girl, so as you so informed me when you proposed, I'm worth at least ten cows."

"That can be arranged. We'll offer your uncle a bride price he can't refuse and then present the deed."

"He will need encouragement, maybe with loaded weapons."

Phillip jumped and grabbed the broom from the closet. "What is it?" I asked.

"There is a spider in the corner of the ceiling."

"Stop," I screamed and grabbed the broom away from him. Standing on a chair to see better, I focused on the spider. "Don't hurt her. She's beautiful, and she eats mosquitoes Any of God's creatures that eat mosquitoes are my friends."

"There are no mosquitoes in Boston in the winter, and we don't have malaria here either," Phillip said.

"But there are flies, their nasty relatives. Besides, it doesn't matter; I won't have you killing my friends."

I gave him the broom. "Now put this away."

He grabbed the broom. "A brave woman like you, who is not afraid of spiders, should not fear Uncle Osiemo either."

I got down from the chair and sat on it. I smiled at Phillip. "Not if I have enough friends to help me."

After we finished teaching our classes, we stored our possessions, found students to rent our town house while we were gone, and packed to spend an extended time in Kenya. Explaining our plans to Irene didn't go so well. Irene protested, "I have my son back. Why are you taking him away?"

I explained that once we were established we would invite her to join us, all expenses paid. I saw her concerned look melt as the possibility of traveling to Kenya suddenly sparked her interest. "Will I be able to see giraffes and lions?"

"Yes, Mother, and warthogs and gazelles," I added.

"Then I think you should go and get everything ready for me. I will be Irene, the world traveler. Just imagine—" She paused for a moment. "What the girls will say at the garden club. I will be the talk of Bean Town."

That ended the argument.

Back in Kenya

WE RETURNED TO THE NEW Stanley Hotel. We were welcomed at reception, since Phillip had stayed there so often. Bouquets of flowers and a large bowl of fruit were in our room as we entered. But I felt too jet-lagged to enjoy them until the next morning.

After a good night's sleep, we wandered down to the hotel dining room for breakfast, feeling too tired to explore other options. The waiter offered us menus and gave me a copy of the Nairobi newspaper. Flipping through the paper, too groggy to concentrate, I couldn't read anything. Then I noticed an advertisement. A smiling Mokoli in the picture announced the opening of his law office. "Phillip, I think I just found a lawyer to help us." I showed him the advertisement in my excitement. Then I paused. "But, but ..."

"What's the problem?" he asked. I explained the incident in the library. Phillip just laughed. "He is probably married to her by now and she has a dozen children. Don't worry so much."

Phillip called and made an appointment.

The very next day, we walked into his office. It smelled of tea. Pictures of coastal scenes filled the walls of the reception area. An elderly woman in a flamboyant dress, obviously Achonyi, greeted me.

"Jambo," she said. Then she turned to Phillip. She didn't

seem quite sure what to say to this white-skinned man who had walked in with me. Phillip introduced us. She checked her apparent disapproval and opened her appointment book. "Yes, Phillip Schoenberg, you are right on time." Then she offered us a cup of tea while we waited.

She left her desk to inform Mokoli that we had arrived. When he walked through his office door he recognized me. "Kitzi, this is surely a pleasure. I didn't know it was you. Mr. and Mrs. Phillip Schoenberg is hardly a clue."

He laughed, shook Phillip's hand, and then held my hand as he looked into my eyes. He turned to Phillip. "You have a most beautiful wife, you know. I was quite infatuated with her at the university."

"Her beauty saved my life," said Phillip. I knew he was referring to my beautiful lymphocytes.

Mokoli didn't respond to that remark but turned and welcomed us into his office asking what we had in mind. I scanned his walls, which were covered with pictures of his children and a portrait of a young woman I didn't recognize. He paused in his discussion with Phillip when he noticed my attention to the picture. "I didn't marry that girl you met in the library. She was too controlling," he said with a coy smile. "I made a much better choice."

He turned to Phillip. "Good thing you married Kwamboka before I got the chance."

We all sat down as Phillip explained our mission. Mokoli took notes. "It will take some time and a lot of paperwork to set up the corporation. You will need some other Kenyans on your board of directors. Any ideas?"

"Not yet," said Phillip.

I squeezed his hand. "I know some people that I am sure would be interested," I said.

Mokoli made some notes of and then looked up. "I will draw up some papers and meet you next week to go over them. Can you have the other people you think are interested being on the board of directors meet then?"

"Thorn Bush Café, next Tuesday?" I suggested, and he agreed.

"Great, I have some business at the bank near there that morning anyway. Nice place for lunch."

The three of us reviewed the details we had to work out. When we left we were confident that Beautiful Mountain Education Corporation would soon be a reality.

I rolled the ice cream around in my mouth as Mokoli and Phillip discussed details he had outlined on a legal pad for the Beautiful Mountain Education Corporation. Distracted by the tourists roaming the boulevard, I felt content and closed my eyes to listen to the sounds of Nairobi's traffic and to enjoy the smell of the bougainvillea trees in full bloom.

I startled alert when Phillip gasped. Two armed police officers had their hands on his shoulders.

"Mr. Phillip Schoenberg, I presume." They spoke in deep bass voices.

Phillip broke into a sweat. He looked pale, and I thought he might faint. Everyone in the restaurant turned. Even Mokoli looked startled. I laughed.

"Let me introduce my friends—actually, my cousins," I said. "Morani and Sokoro are Uncle Osiemo's stepsons."

They pulled up chairs around the table and sat down. I signaled the waitress and ordered coffee and pastries for them.

Morani spoke first. "I understand that you need some firepower to make this corporation work." He patted his holstered gun. "Our father, or stepfather, is a bit of a rascal. He is going to need encouragement to make this happen."

"And some important people like us need to be on the board of directors of your corporation," said Sokoro with a grin that demonstrated his well-kept teeth.

I could see the color returning to Phillip's face. Mokoro stood to shake their hands and complete the introductions.

Morani said, "We were just kids when our father was killed in a brawl at the local bar. He had been an elder in the village and was trying to break up a fight when it happened. Our mother, Nychoke, married Osiemo about a year later, after the proper period of mourning. That gave us a father and Osiemo a lot of status. Our stepfather was now a big man in the village."

Sokoro added, "Our mother is quite a strong woman and made sure that we got a good education and kept us away from his influence. Besides, Osiemo became distracted by a cute high school girl and got her pregnant." Both brothers laughed as Sokoro continued, "Her father made Osiemo marry her, demanding two cows."

"He did the honorable thing," said Morani. "I'll give him that."

Sokoro said, "Then for his third wife he married this poor man's daughter, Abigail. He always told us that he liked her because she was so good in bed. She told him how big he was, if you know what I mean." He smiled with a twinkle in his eye.

Morani laughed. "He got her pregnant pretty quick, but the kid is a runt."

I turned to Phillip. "That was about the time he tried to marry my mother, who would have been his fourth wife. Morani and Sokoro, you were away at school then, as I recall."

"Yes we were, but we heard about it," said Morani. He turned to look me in the eye and took a deep sigh. "Sorry about your mother. We knew he had arranged to have her killed, but there was nothing we could do about it then."

He turned to Mokoli. "So we want to be in this corporation.

295

Our mother is elderly and quite ill, and we were planning on going back to Kisii land anyway. We want to make sure Osiemo doesn't sell away our inheritance."

Mokoli took over the meeting and described what each needed to do as officers in the corporation. Papers were signed. An hour later he looked at his wristwatch. "Sorry to go, but I have another appointment. Phillip, everything will be in order when you are ready to head to Kisii land." He shook hands around the table.

"Thank you all for coming," he said as he left.

The waitress came to the table and asked if we needed anything more. "We could use some more coffee," Moroni said.

"Have you heard the latest gossip, Kwamboka?" said Sokoro.

"What now?" I asked.

Sokoro whispered, "Wise father Osiemo married a very beautiful young woman. The elders say she is the most beautiful woman the ancestors have ever sent to our village. Her name is Panya." The three of us snickered.

"What's so funny?" Phillip said, looking confused.

"It means 'mouse,'" I said.

"That's not her real name, of course, but it fits," Sokoro said. "She cost him a lot of cows, and ..."

"Father Osiemo has been having a little *dysfunction*." Morani emphasized the last word. "So the little mouse has been quite active at night, finding other beds to sleep in when she fatigues poor father Osiemo. She's pregnant now, but obviously not by Father."

Phillip shook his head with the scandal and said, "Back to the plan. We will send Mokoli ahead to buy the land adjacent to the land Kwamboka rightfully owns. Then the truck should arrive with ten cows, the proper bride price for a college-educated wife. If and when he accepts ..."

"Oh, he will," said Sokoro.

"Then we will fly in, and I will present the land deed for the rest of the property."

"You know," said Morani, "that's when the trouble will start."

Flying Home

"THE FIELD IS CLEARED. IT'S safe to land," Mokoli texted me over my cell phone. I motioned to Phillip and pointed down.

"Ready to land," Phillip said into the microphone to the pilot.

Helicopters sure are noisy. I had to strain to hear anything, even with our headphones in place. It was my first time in a helicopter, and I felt that the whole thing was unstable. I gripped my seat till my hands cramped from fatigue. When the pilot turned the contraption to circle the field, I thought I was going to fall out. I grabbed my seat harness and gasped.

With my last bit of bravery, I glimpsed my uncle standing at the edge of the field with his ten cows staked to the ground around him. Mokoli was waving. The pilot brought us down for a soft landing. Red, rich Kisii dust filled the air. I stayed in the helicopter taking deep breaths and coughing from the exhaust and dust.

Phillip climbed out with a briefcase. From my vantage point I could see everything. Curious to see my uncle's reaction, I watched as Mokoli proceeded with introductions. I couldn't hear anything until the helicopter engine shut down. Then the quiet was intense, and the air cleared.

I listened to Mokoli make introductions. "This is Phillip Schoenberg, Kwamboka's husband and the president of Beautiful Mountain Education Corporation."

A crowd of men who had sighted the helicopter gathered around. Most were admiring the cattle, some the helicopter. "I've never seen a helicopter," one old man said as he ran his withered hand over the shiny surface. I didn't know his name, but I recognized him as one of my uncle's drinking buddies.

"Nice to see you again, Osiemo," said Phillip.

Uncle Osiemo acted confused. "Have we met?"

"We met when I was doing my PhD research here some years ago," Phillip said in an attempt to jog his memory.

"Oh, yes, you were the boy who wanted to talk to all the pregnant girls," Uncle Osiemo recalled.

Phillip laughed. "I suppose that's your interpretation of my research." He set his briefcase on a portable table Mokoli had just unfolded. Osiemo seemed to be paying more attention to the shillings stacked to the side than to what Phillip was saying.

"First I need to show you our marriage license. I understand that you have accepted Kwamboka's bride price." He pointed at the ten cows staked around the perimeter. "This is to document that we are legally married by Kenyan law."

"Yes, yes," Osiemo said, "I accept." He laughed. "Ten cows are quite generous for my scrawny niece."

He turned to the gathered audience and spoke in Ekegusii. "She's not even a woman, you know." Several of the men laughed; none of the women did.

"Therefore," Mokoli said to the assembled crowd in Swahili, "by Kenyan and Ekegusii law, the land of Kwamboka's father now belongs to Phillip Schoenberg."

"That's my land." Osiemo turned and swung his stick at Mokoli.

It was time for me to climb out of the helicopter. There was a gasp from the crowd. From my leather pouch I produced the title deed to my father's land. I handed it to Mokoli so that he could show it to the assembled elders. Two Kenyan police officers, Sokoro and Morani, climbed out of the helicopter and stood beside me. Their tall, muscular physiques impressed the crowd, especially when they put their hands on their holstered weapons.

"I assume you know Nychoke's sons, Morani and Sokoro," Mokoli said.

"Nychoke's my wife. I raised these two boys to be men." He snarled at them. "After all I did for you, you come to betray me?"

"So then," Mokoli continued, "the only negotiation we have yet to consider is how much rent your tea factory owes Kwamboka Schoenberg for using her land. By Kenyan law she has owned it since the death of her mother. Representing Kenya, I have permission from the judge to negotiate a settlement for illegal expropriation of her land to build a plantation and factory."

Osiemo shook his stick at his stepsons. "What do you two get out of this theft?"

Mokoli continued, "These gentlemen are on the board of directors of Beautiful Mountain Education Corporation. I also represent them in the negotiation of their mother's land, but that is a different matter for another time. I understand that she is not feeling well."

He shifted a set of papers aside. "We can start the negotiation with the owners' asking rent of eight million Kenyan shillings per year."

Osiemo beat the ground with his stick. He said in Ekegusii, "I should have killed you when I had the chance, Kwamboka. Do you not fear my stick anymore?"

"So before these police officers you admit that you tried to kill me?" I said in Ekegusii. "But I am not prosecuting you for that. It will be my little gift."

Smiling, I stepped forward, snatched his walking stick, and threw it toward his cattle. "Nor will I prosecute you for beating me with that stick. Did you forget that your stepsons speak Ekegusii? They have just heard your confession. Do you want to confess to arranging my mother's murder while you are at it?"

Mokoli intervened. "There is another possibility, Osiemo," he said. My uncle looked shaken. "The owners are willing to buy the factory you've built on their land."

I saw him admire the shillings glittering in the sunlight as Phillip opened his briefcase. There was a long, palpable silence. The gathered crowd was watching for a response.

It was time for one more lesson. I turned to the crowd. The clan elders, necessary witnesses to the legal transactions, formed a circle around us. Women came in from the fields; men emptied the kiosks. At the ring of the school bell, curious children gathered.

I asked for a box to stand on so that I might address the crowd. As I waited I searched the gathered elders for one specific person. When I saw him, I climbed on the box two men had brought and began.

"Mr. Osebe," I said in Ekegusii, "you are a leader of our clan and an Abaragori, discerner of witchcraft. Examine me now. Am I a witch?"

The crowd backed away until the old, gnarled man stood alone. "Do you require a payment? My uncle will gladly pay whatever you require, just as he did for my mother. Just look at his beautiful cows. Now come and discern before all these witnesses: Am I a witch?"

He glanced around at the crowd and limped to the makeshift podium with a small bag that he snatched from the leather pouch over his shoulder. I stepped off the box and held out my hands. I knew the procedure. He poured the bones into my hands, grasped them in his, and then shook them.

His voice cracked with age and intensity. "Pour the bones out on this rock."

I did as he commanded. He knelt on his bow-legged knees

301

to examine the configuration on the rock. With great effort he stood, looked at the assembled crowd, and said, "She is not a witch."

The village people cheered. I saw him turn to scan the herd of cows. He was probably considering which one he would ask for payment.

"And for the future?" I asked, redirecting his attention and staring into his wrinkled face. "What of the future?"

"And," he yelled to the crowd, "she will never be a witch. She is not capable of being a witch."

Drums started to beat. The men fell to the outer ring as the women gathered around me, dancing in concentric circles. They were singing the welcome song that they sang to new brides. I started dancing in their midst, so glad to be home.

Reconciliation

MONTHS LATER, I STOOD IN the doorway of Uncle Osiemo's hospital room with my head down in respect. The nurse gave him a pill. "This is for your pain," she said and left.

The three clan elders continued their conversation. I was not supposed to be listening. "Panya ran off with that truck driver from Nairobi, but her father is willing to give you three cows for her divorce."

"I gave him six." Uncle Osiemo twisted in bed and grabbed his belly.

"I think you should take the three cows and call it good," said the oldest. "She claims that you did not make her pregnant, so her father is saying that you did not fulfill your responsibilities of the marriage."

"She's pregnant now, isn't she?" It was hard for me, outside the doorway, to tell whether he was angry or in pain.

"She said at the clan investigation that she had to go out and get pregnant because you could not serve her properly."

"I was sick." His scream was pitiful. He turned and faced the elders. It seemed that he was resigned to the facts, as the wrinkles in his face softened. "Oh, it doesn't matter. I'm too sick to fight about it."

The three elders stood. The oldest spoke. "We are sorry for your illness. You have made many good decisions for our clan, and we honor you for that."

"All right, I accept three cows. But Panya's progeny do not get any of my inheritance."

"Sounds reasonable," the three said in unison.

I backed up and bowed as they left the room.

"Kwamboka, the love of my brother's life, do not be afraid to come in," my uncle said. The room smelled like urine and baby poop. Abigail crawled out from under the bed, where she has been sleeping on a piece of cardboard. Her toddler screamed as he gained his footing beside the bed. He was wearing a pair of dirty shorts. A bare newborn suckled at Abigail's withered breast. She appeared emaciated as she sat on the chair and switched nipples. She wore only a kitamba wrapped around her waist.

"I would have been nicer to you sooner if I had known you would make me so rich," Uncle Osiemo grunted.

"I would not have chosen to make you rich, Uncle," I replied.

He chuckled and grabbed his bloated belly. "I've been a good uncle for you. If I had not chased you away that day …"

"And tried to kill me," I added.

"Yes, that too. But now you are a fine, educated, wealthy woman. That would never have happened if I didn't force you to leave Kisii land. I made you independent, and you returned to me with more money than I have ever had in my whole life." He coughed, and I gave him a hospital tissue.

"Another thing," he said. "My son Joshua wants to marry that mosquito you brought from the coast. What's her name again?"

"Zipporah," I said.

"She has no parents? She is a true orphan?" Uncle Osiemo asked.

"Right."

"Good. Then there is no bride price to pay, and that study-crazy runt of a son of mine, Joshua, is off my back. Maybe I can get some work out of his mother after all," Uncle Osiemo said. He sighed, and even the wrinkles in his weather-worn face relaxed.

"Is there anything else you wanted to discuss with me?" I asked.

"Yes, one important thing. I have decided that since you have been so gracious to me, I will divide my inheritance among my three wives and you," he announced.

"Yes, I overheard that you are divorcing Panya. But I really don't need anything," I said.

"Oh, you deserve it more than anyone." He grimaced in pain.

"Since I am found in your favor—" I hesitated. "I know a proper Kisii girl should not ask, but did the doctor find out why you were vomiting blood at Aunt Nychoke's funeral?"

He glanced at Abigail, who cowered in the bedside chair, soothing the sparse reddish hair of her sick baby. "The doctor put this black hose down my throat that he could see through and looked in my stomach. He said that he expected to see sores from all the aspirin I eat for my sore knee, but instead he found cancer. But I don't believe him."

He tried to push himself up in bed. The muscles in his arms flexed but were too weak to change his position. Abigail set the baby in the chair and helped him sit up.

"I think some sorcerer paid the doctor to say that. I just need to make a big enough sacrifice and I'll be fine."

He shifted to his side and leaned on his elbow. "How is your school and house coming?"

The equipment and trucks with supplies came today. They should be laying the foundation tomorrow. We have a contractor noted for his honesty, and we're hiring local Kisii to do the work. It should be finished by the end of August. I want to open the school in September."

He smiled but then drifted off to sleep as the pain medicine infiltrated his brain.

"How's your baby, Abigail?" I asked.

"I'm sure he will be fine when the diarrhea stops. The herb doctor gave me some medicine."

"Why don't you bring him to the clinic here at the hospital?" I suggested.

"I might if he doesn't get better soon."

"How is your oldest son? The child you had when I left?"

"Oh, he died of malaria. But this boy is strong," she said as she grabbed her toddler's arm. "Aren't you, boy?"

He diverted his gaze to the floor.

"I had so many miscarriages that I expected him to die too."

I stood in the corner staring at my uncle. His grunting respirations betrayed his pain even when he was sedated with medication.

"I suppose I should make something for my husband to eat when he wakes up," she said, picking a pot from under the bed. "They have a kitchen here where they let the families cook."

She gathered her baby to her breast, covering the child in her kitamba, and grabbed the toddler with one hand and the cooking pot with the other. The brood shuffled out the door.

As I followed them down the hall I asked, "If you would like some meat for him, come over to the hotel. I'll make sure you have some healthy food. Or I could go with you to market and buy whatever you need."

"Oh, you don't have to do that. If Engoro chooses for him to live, he will."

"Take the baby to the doctor at the clinic. I'll pay for any medicine."

"Thank you, Kwamboka."

Home

I COULDN'T BELIEVE IT. THE school had been completed on time, and now it was December. Since I had been declared not a witch, parents all over Kisii land sent their children to the school. Parents were impressed with the school uniforms that they did not have to pay for. Hiring teachers was a problem. Many from my graduating class at Nairobi University wanted to stay in the city, not wander out west to Kisii, but I found good ones in time for the first classes even though I had to teach some of the classes myself. For a moment, I sat at my desk and watched the ceiling fan.

"Hey, Chui," Zipporah said, running into my office. She stopped, closed her eyes, and scrunched her face. "I know, I am supposed to address you as Dr. Director Kwamboka Muwami Mrs. Schoenberg. Did I get that all right? You sure have a lot of names to remember."

I couldn't stop laughing. "When it is just the two of us, you may call me Chui."

"Oh, thank you. It was hurting my head to remember all your names." She plopped down in the chair in front of my desk. I have two things to talk about. First, Joshua, your uncle's second wife's oldest son, proposed to marry me. He said that if I only worship Jesus God that I can be his wife. He said that Jesus God doesn't allow him to have more than one wife. So I will be his first and only wife. Isn't that great?"

"I'm so happy for you, Zipporah."

She jumped out of the chair and danced around the room. "I will worship Jesus God forever. I only have to make one man happy. And I don't have to take pills. He said he would let me get pregnant. Oh, I am so happy."

Then she sat down. Her mood changed. "The other thing is that I caught Janis breaking curfew again. She and her boyfriend were out by the basketball court. I caught them around midnight."

"What were they doing?"

"That boy still had his pants on, but Janis was doing …" She paused.

"What?"

"You know what we used to do to get our clients to do it faster?"

I took a deep sigh. "I'm sorry to hear that. I talked to her once already."

Zipporah stood and went to the door. "I scheduled an appointment for her to see you in twenty minutes." She smiled. "Chui, do you like the big words I'm using, like 'scheduled' and 'appointment?'"

"I do. And thanks, Zipporah. Congratulations on your engagement." She did a quick dance as she left the office.

An hour later I was focused on Janis. She refused to understand the seriousness of her actions. She acted out with such defiance.

The security guard knocked and interrupted, "Kwamboka, the airplane just buzzed the school."

"Thanks, Ibraham. Get the truck ready. I will be there in a moment." I turned back to my student sitting in front of my desk. "Janis, you are a very intelligent young woman. I want you to study hard and be able to realize your potential. Staying out past curfew is breaking the rules."

"I was just talking to my boyfriend out on the basketball court. We didn't do nothing." She sneered at me.

"You didn't do anything," I corrected her.

She squirmed in her seat. "Besides, why do I have to do what Zipporah says?"

"She is only conveying the school rules that I set up. And they were designed for your protection and benefit. You know that."

Janis swore at me. "Did you know that she was a prostitute, a cheap whore, before she came here?"

I had had enough of her defiant attitude. "Did you know that her brothers died of starvation? Did you know that she was sold into slavery because neither her father nor her mother had enough education to get a job? Did you know that her father died in the field trying to raise a little food for his family? Did you know her mother died because she had no money to go to the doctor? Is that what you want for your life?"

Janis hung her head. "You're reprimanding me just like my father does."

"As school director, I take very seriously the trust your parents have placed in me. If your boyfriend really loves you, he will want you to do well in school. If he marries you, your education might save his life someday."

I took Janis's delicate hands in mine. "You are an intelligent young woman. I know from your test scores. I am only asking that you use the gifts God has given you."

"I will try, Mrs. Schoenberg. Can I study with my boyfriend?"

"I am making a rule just for you, Janis, to keep you safe. You may only be with your boyfriend in the library for the next three months."

"That's not fair, Mrs. Schoenberg. How can we talk?"

"You can write notes to each other. I'm even willing to correct the grammar, if you want to turn the notes in to me for extra credit. If you abide by this rule for three months, I will let you meet your boyfriend outside the library, in public, until six each evening."

"Yes, Director Schoenberg." She stood with her head bowed.

I looked at her, hoping she was convinced. This was the third time she had broken curfew. Her parents were concerned. Her father realized how intelligent his daughter was, and unlike many of my students' parents, he encouraged her to get an education. I didn't want her pregnant. Her parents would remove her from the school and force her to marry.

"All right, Janis, you may be excused. I expect an A on your geography test tomorrow. Your boyfriend was quite good in geography last year. He should be able to help you."

"Thank you for not kicking me out of school. I guess I expected you to. I will try much harder on my studies. I will tell my boyfriend that if he really loves me, he will help me get high scores on my tests."

She turned to go but hesitated at the door. "I'm sorry for what I said about Zipporah. I was angry. She is a very kind matron in our dormitory, and I know she cares about us."

"Thank you, Janis. I will tell Zipporah how you feel about her."

I walked out with her and watched as she headed for the library. I locked the door behind me and stopped at the school office to notify my secretary that I was leaving. "Lucy, could you ask Beatrice to run the staff meeting? I have to meet one of our supporters at the airport."

"Not a problem," she said and smiled. "The visiting supporter wouldn't happen to be your mother-in-law?"

I sighed. The secret was out.

"Don't worry, Director Schoenberg," she added. "We're ready for her."

"Lucy, we were classmates at the university. You may call me Kwamboka."

"I will try to remember that, Director Schoenberg."

I laughed at her teasing and ran outside to find Phillip. He was waiting in the pickup truck. Ibraham and several of our school workmen had piled into the back.

"Do you think her room is acceptable?" I asked as I slid in the seat beside Phillip.

"Before my mother met you, I would have said no," said Phillip. "But she is so impressed with what the school is doing. And since she donated the money for the library building, she has a vested interest. The room will be fine."

"The books I ordered from Caleb are supposed to be on the plane as well. I am so excited." I beamed.

"Who is Caleb?"

"A young, handsome man I've known since student days. I even dated him for a while before I met you."

Phillip turned and stared at me.

"Nothing happened, jealous one." I giggled and tousled his hair. "He owns the biggest textbook store in Nairobi now. That's where I used to meet him. He would take me out for tea and biscuits. Besides, he gives me a nice discount. And he was willing to pick up Irene at the airport and get her onto the private plane."

Phillip put his hand on my thigh. I pushed his hand off. "Keep both hands on the steering wheel. There are lots of ruts in this road."

Phillip grabbed the steering wheel to miss a pothole. "I'm sure Mother appreciated having someone bring her to the airport this morning. I wondered how you arranged that and who it was, but don't mention to Mother that he was your old boyfriend. She thinks you are the perfect angel. Not to mention ..." The truck hit a rut, stopping all conversation.

We bounced across the ruts and turned onto the gravel road leading to the airstrip. It wasn't really an airport; there were no buildings on the property. Phillip had bought the field from a farmer and then hired a local construction crew to grade it smooth so that we could get supplies by bush plane. Two days ago the school workmen had spent a day knocking down the termite hills and scraping away unnecessary foliage. A windsock hung on a flagpole in the corner for the pilot.

As we turned onto the gravel, I looked through the cattle fence to see that the plane had already landed. As the pilot was securing it, Irene grabbed her hat so it wouldn't blow away. The pilot then set her three suitcases in the grated red clay beside the plane.

Phillip stopped the truck beside the plane, and a whiff of red dust settled on the boxes of books the pilot was starting to remove from the hold. The workmen jumped out of the back of the truck, finished unloading the cargo, and put the boxes in the back of the truck. Phillip thanked the pilot and paid him.

I gave Irene warm hugs as Ibraham took charge of her suitcases.

"There sure are sure a lot of Africans here," she said as she watched our workers arrange the shipment boxes. Ibraham smiled at her.

She smiled back. "That was a stupid thing to say, wasn't it?"

"It's all right, Madam, Phillip's mother," said Ibraham. "This being your first time here in Africa, you are forgiven." He extended his hand. "I'm Ibraham."

"I'm Irene." She said with a smile. Then she turned toward me and gasped.

"What is it, Irene?" She pointed behind me. I turned to see a young Maasai man leaning on his ebony-handled spear at the edge of the runway.

I left my mother-in-law in Phillip's care and ran toward

312

the tall grass where he was standing. He didn't move. As I approached, he spoke Swahili. "I do not have to throw stones at you this time to see that you are alive."

His grin showed all his teeth. He loped toward me and put his hand on my shoulder. "You are a big director now, a big woman in Kisii land. I see that you have built a school. It is too late for me, but my son is here."

With a hand signal, a young boy ran out from the brush and nestled his head under my hand.

"I want learn things," he said in English.

I turned to his father and extended my arm to his. We clasped in a Maasai greeting. "Friend, your son is welcome in our school."

"I see you keep your promises," he said.

"You saved my life, but I got diarrhea from that water," I said.

He laughed. "Kisii stomach is not strong like Maasai stomach. My goats didn't get sick."

"I can laugh now, but I was plenty sick." I looked at the group huddled around the truck and then back to the warrior. "Do you want to ride to the administrative office in the truck?"

"No, we know where the big director's office is. We will run there and register. Thank you for accepting my son. He does not like to herd goats. He would rather read books." He took his son's hand and disappeared into the brush.

"What was that all about?" asked Phillip when I returned to the activities at the truck. He wrinkled his brow. "Not another boyfriend, I hope?"

"No, silly husband I adore. He wants to register his son in the school."

"This is a long way from Mombasa." He looked to the east.

I poked Phillip in mock anger.

"I wasn't implying a client relationship," Phillip protested as he got behind the wheel. I opened the door for Irene.

"Where did that savage come from?" She was trembling in the seat beside me.

"He is man who saved my life once, not a savage, Irene. He is Maasai. That's why he carries a spear."

"Oh," she said and grabbed her hat when we hit a bump.

"How was your trip from Boston?" I asked.

"Very nice," she said. "And the hotel I stayed in last night had such a comfortable bed, just like home."

"So you approve of the New Stanley Hotel?" I inquired.

"Oh yes. The hotel shuttle was at the airport right after I claimed my luggage. I tipped the driver with US dollars. I hope that was all right? And then this morning a handsome young man came in his car to bring me to the private airport. You know him, don't you? He had all those boxes of books to send on the plane. The pilot weighed each one. He even weighed me. But I think his scale was off. He said that I only weighed sixty-five pounds."

"That was probably sixty-five kilograms, Mother," Phillip proposed.

"Oh. Well, anyway, I was glad to get out of Nairobi. What a hectic place."

"The flight here went well?" I asked.

"The pilot, Joshua, let me be the copilot. What a lot of dials to look at. Then he let me see the herds of animals and the crater. The view of Mount Kenya and Kilimanjaro was extraordinary."

"I'm so glad you enjoyed your first view of Africa," I said, relishing her appreciation for my country.

She whispered in my ear, "But you know, Kitty, of all the Africans I've seen since I got here, you're the prettiest." She turned to look out the back window of the truck. "But that Ibraham is sure handsome."

"He is the head of maintenance and quite a skillful man," I said. "He can fix almost anything."

The truck lurched when we slid into a rut. Irene gasped.

"Phillip, pay attention to your driving. My suitcases are in the back, and so are all those nice men who helped me."

By the time we reached the house, we were shaken and dusty. Ibraham set her suitcases inside the door before Irene was out of the truck. She rushed to his side. "Are you married, Ibraham? I'm a widow, you know." She stood gazing at him.

"Yes, madam, I am married with four lovely children," he answered.

"Oh, that's too bad. I mean, it's good. Congratulations," she said.

"He is going to tell his wife some great stories tonight," I whispered to Phillip.

Then I turned to Irene. "This is our home. I hope you're comfortable here." I realized that I was interrupting her flirtation.

"This is ranch style; I was expecting something more colonial," she blurted out.

"This is modern Kenyan architecture, Irene. We built it when we moved here." I took her hand, and we paraded along the veranda to the open door. She turned to wave to Ibraham. "I've arranged a light lunch and then this afternoon a tour of the school, ending with a special visit to the library."

"Can't I see the library now?" she asked.

"Be patient, Mother," Phillip said. "Nothing happens fast in Africa. You will get to see everything."

The table was set; the air conditioner was blowing, flickering the curtains as we sat down. Abigail had arranged the table with a cut flower in a vase at each place. The tablecloth had embroidered flowers to match. She served carrot soup. "I hope you hungry, Ms. Irene. I make wonderful things for you." She returned to the kitchen to get the next course.

Irene wrinkled her nose. "You have servants? How quaint, how colonial."

"We are wealthy, Mother," said Phillip. "In this country

you share your wealth by hiring people. It is considered selfish not to."

Irene wrinkled her forehead. "She looks like she is the same age as you, Kitty."

"She is my aunt and needed a job," I said.

Abigail served the main course. It was her version of goat stew, but I was not going to tell Irene that it was goat. Abigail stood at attention, waiting for Irene to take her first taste.

Irene took a sip. "This is really good. Beef tastes different here in Africa."

Abigail started to correct her, but I held up my hand to stop her. Phillip bit his tongue and winced in pain.

Irene scolded Phillip, "I've told you since you were a child not to eat so fast, Phillip. Now mind your manners."

"You see, Irene, the meat we use is from animals that are free-range," I said.

"So your meat is organic?"

"Exactly," I replied.

"No wonder it tastes so good," she said, finishing her soup.

"I not speak English good. Thank you for liking my food," said Abigail.

"You're so young for being Kitty's aunt," Irene said, looking bewildered.

"My husband, he die. My children very hungry. Phillip, he teach me cook. Now children very happy with full belly." She returned to the kitchen to prepare dessert.

"You taught her to cook?" Irene asked her son.

"I used your recipes, Mother. Are you surprised?"

"I'm flabbergasted. How is it that she is so young and yet your aunt? And her husband died. That would be your uncle?"

"She was my uncle's third wife. She was sixteen when he married her. I was seventeen at the time. My uncle was in his forties," I explained.

Irene gasped and then grabbed her son's hand. "I'm not in Boston anymore, am I, Phillip?"

"No, Mother," he replied.

"Everything is so different. I should have traveled more when I was younger," she said.

After lunch we took a rest, which required an explanation, since Irene was anxious to see the library. An hour later we started the tour, and she was enthralled. It was almost five o'clock in the afternoon before we reached the library. Hot tea and biscuits were set out. The library staff, in uniforms Joyce had made, stood at attention.

"Thank you, Ms. Irene," they sang in unison, "for our beautiful library."

A drum started beating, and the staff danced in traditional Kisii style. Irene started dancing with them. When they were done with their program, each of the library staff members offered personal thanks, and then students paraded by in appreciation. The older students shook her hand, but the younger ones bowed their heads.

"They want you to touch their heads, Irene," I explained.

Uncomfortable touching their heads, she hesitated but did so. Irene was cautious at first, but by the time she had greeted them all, she was acting like their grandmother.

"The library is just like I imagined. It's so beautiful. What is that acid smell?" she said, almost breathless.

"That's the way poured concrete smells. Termites won't eat it; the material lasts forever. The smell will soon be replaced by the smell of books and students. Don't worry."

Out of the corner of my eye I saw our workmen carrying the boxes of books that had come on the plane. The library staff opened them as if they were Christmas presents.

"I guess Caleb found all the books I ordered," I told Phillip.

That evening before dinner, Irene took a shower in tepid water. "I need to buy you a better hot water heater," she said as she came out of her bedroom refreshed but chilly.

"Let me show you our hot water heater," I said and directed her out to the side of the house. "See, it is a tank with a woodstove underneath. Our workman builds a fire after he fills it with rainwater from that tank. Abigail got carried away washing the dishes from lunch. She gets excited about hot water. You can have a hot shower in the morning. The worker will be here at five o'clock to start the fire. By the time you're up, there will be plenty of hot water."

Under the glow of our yard light, Irene inspected the water tank. She opened the door to the small stove underneath and sneezed at a whiff of smoke. "Clever design."

By the time we returned to the living room, Joyce had arrived, and I introduced her to Irene.

"This is my Nairobi mother, Joyce. She rescued me and took care of me all through my university years. She is a professional seamstress who has sort of retired from her business now, but she makes all the uniforms for the students. She also made the uniforms for the library staff, and …"

Abigail appeared, starched and bright. "And she made my uniform. Dinner is ready."

Joyce and Irene sat down next to each other, although Phillip had planned for them to sit opposite. There was instant attraction as they chatted. "You have a wonderful daughter, Joyce. Did you know she saved my son's life?" They were so engaged in their conversation that Phillip and I felt as if we were eavesdropping.

Abigail served roasted chicken trimmed with dressing from leftover bread from our local bakery. I told her not to tell Irene where she had obtained the dressing ingredients. Abigail's assortment of roasted vegetables was picturesque and not overcooked.

"This is delicious, Abigail," Irene said as she followed her into the kitchen. I ran after her to translate and to make sure Abigail understood Irene's extended monologue.

Abigail responded in Ekegusii, "Your mother-in-law is very kind to me, and I appreciate her coming to tell me how much she appreciates the meal. But I am embarrassed to have her in the kitchen."

I translated, "She thanks you very much, Irene, but she wants you to sit at the table and enjoy the good things she has made for you."

When Abigail brought in a huge bowl of tropical fruit, Irene was delighted. "I could never get fruit like this at Faneuil Hall Market. And even if they had it, the prices would be too high." She took a bite. "And it wouldn't taste this good. What is this?"

"Guava, pineapple, papaya, and I think she threw in a little coconut," I answered.

When we finished eating, we relaxed out on the veranda. The Milky Way was only minimally obscured by the lights around the school yard, and it presented an inspiring display.

"I have one more surprise for you two," I announced. Joyce and Irene stopped chatting.

"Phillip and I wish to announce"—I gave him a hug—"that I'm pregnant. You are both to be grandmothers."

"Will the child be black?" asked Irene.

"Or white?" asked Joyce.

"Probably a pinkish brown, like delicate cream in strong Kenyan coffee," I replied.